Praise for the novels of Hazel Beck

Small Town, Big Magic

"The magical world of St Cyprian is one readers will never want to leave. *Small Town, Big Magic* is an absolute triumph of a debut… Hazel Beck has created the perfect blend of magic, humor, world-ending peril, friendship and romance, brewed into a spellbinding combination that readers will adore, and that will have them desperate for the next book!"

–*New York Times* bestselling author Maisey Yates

"Emerson Wilde is a smart, funny protagonist whose unshakeable belief in herself will charm the reader from the very first page of *Small Town, Big Magic*. A diverse coven of witches, an enchanted history, and a dangerous adversary all add up to an absolute delight of a magical tale."

–Louisa Morgan, author of *The Age of Witches*

"A fresh, fun, zany spin on paranormal romance, *Small Town, Big Magic* casts a big spell. Take one girlboss witch, add a magical journey of healing and self-discovery, and sprinkle in a dash of romance, and you've got an enchanting read perfect for fans of *The Ex Hex* and *Payback's a Witch*."

–Ashley Winstead, author of *Fool Me Once*

"[A] spellbinding magic-infused rom-com… Beck delivers a wonderfully realized heroine with a voice so clear readers will feel like one of her friends. This is sure to be a hit with any fan of paranormal romance."

–*Publishers Weekly*

Big Little Spells

"Beck's second entry in the 'Witchlore' series brings back a charming cast of characters and offers a heart-rending story of personal strength, growth, and fated love."

–*Library Journal*

Also by Hazel Beck

Small Town, Big Magic
Big Little Spells

To learn more about Hazel Beck, visit www.hazel-beck.com.

TRULY MADLY MAGICALLY

HAZEL BECK

GRAYDON
HOUSE

GRAYDON
HOUSE®

Recycling programs
for this product may
not exist in your area.

ISBN-13: 978-1-525-80473-1

Truly Madly Magically

Graydon House
22 Adelaide St. West, 41st Floor
Toronto, Ontario M5H 4E3, Canada
www.GraydonHouseBooks.com

Printed in U.S.A.

If you have a mother, are a mother or play those roles in your chosen families, this book is for you.

1

WHEN I OPEN MY EYES, I KNOW IMMEDIATELY
that I'm not dreaming.

The woman sitting at the end of my bed is *here*. She's spirit
rather than flesh and blood, but it's her. Not fully herself, but
so much *her* it hurts.

Zelda Rivers is the aunt of my best friend, the mother of
my ex-boyfriend, and she was one of the few adults who never
made me feel bad about the fact I'm only a half witch. Zelda was
confirmation that my mom was right that not *all* the witches
out there were going to look down their noses at the mixed-
blood half *human* and *sniff*. Dramatically. The way so many did
here in St. Cyprian, Missouri, the charming little river town
that's also the hidden-in-plain-sight witch capital of the world.

But I know exactly why Zelda is here tonight, a couple of
months after she died in June.

"Ellowyn, you have to tell him."

I think about pulling the covers over my head and pretending she's a dream. But she sets me straight. Three loud bangs

shake the whole room and what feels like my entire apartment, my tea shop below, and most of Main Street.

Zelda was always excellent with the nonverbal communication.

"Ellowyn Sabrina Good, you have to tell him."

My hated middle name, courtesy of my human father who thought it was "cute," does the trick.

I look at Zelda, or the fuzzy vision of who she was when she had a body. She was with us on Litha back in June, her spirit having not made the crossing yet as she'd only died that very morning of the summer solstice, but I haven't seen her since. Ghosts need time to figure out how to be dead, after all.

Time's up tonight, apparently. She sits there, her eyes the same gray and gold—and worse, she reminds me of the *him* she's talking about.

"Now," she tells me, in that firm mom voice of hers. It makes me remember the time she caught me and Zander a little too naked in the storage room at Nix, the bar that the Rivers family have run as long as anyone can remember. It's almost a fond memory now, when I let so few of my high school memories of *him* be fond.

"Tell him," Zelda orders me, though her voice is waning along with her image.

I'm a Summoner, and the past is my thing. And I've learned in my many run-ins with the spirits of the past that newly deceased spirits are still learning. How to project, to connect. It takes a significant amount of energy—and I don't know how spirits gather their energy in the great beyond, but Zelda's is currently running out.

Her form is getting paler. I can see my window behind her. Through her.

"You can't wait, Ellowyn. It's imperative you don't wait." Then she slips away once again.

Leaving me wide-awake, feeling guilty and wishing it didn't *hurt*.

Some would say the connection I have with the past is a gift, and I try to think of it that way. I really do. But sometimes, being alive in a sea of the dead and gone, lost and forgotten, feels as isolating as being the only half witch in your generation.

Imperative, she said, that I tell Zander what's going on—but that's an odd way to put it. He'll figure it out eventually. Do I really need to *tell* him?

Yes. Zelda's voice, or my conscience, is firm then.

I sigh. Because I know she's right, no matter how little I like it. Hence the guilt. I have to tell him. Hiding it is getting harder by the day. An extended glamour takes a certain amount of energy, and that's just to glow things up. *Hiding* things is even harder to sustain for any length of time.

I haven't told Zander. I haven't told *anyone*, not even my very best friends—who also happen to be my coven, the River-wood. I think Jacob North might have his suspicions, but that's the problem with being friends with one of the most power-ful Healers in the world. You can't claim hangovers and food poisoning all the time—I'm half human, so I can *claim* that I might suffer from such all-too-human ailments sometimes—without a Healer wanting to help.

He's never *acted* like he knew. He's never *said* anything to me about my little secret that would have stopped being a se-cret to him the moment he touched me. A brush of a hand, a jostle, anything.

Hell, he probably knew before I did.

I moan and groan and kick my bed a few times, and then I roll over and poke the screen of my phone. Harder than nec-essary. The time reads 2:45 a.m., flashing a bright light in my dark room, like one more *imperative* I could do without.

He'll be up. It doesn't matter that he's been working the ferry nearly all day, every day, because his dad is still only barely func-tioning after losing Zelda. Zander still works his shift at the bar and doesn't stumble home until around three in the morning.

Things I wish I didn't know, but I do, like his every move is etched into my bones.

If I get up, I can beat him there. Then again, I could also send a note. Or Ruth, my owl familiar, to do the dirty work. People always want to kill the messenger.

How kind of you to volunteer me, Ruth says in my head, where only I can hear her, filled with owlish sarcasm.

I throw the covers off and get myself ready with a glamour. Not *for* Zander. But for myself. I consider it battle armor.

I look at Ruth, perched on my windowsill. "You can stay here."

But the drama, my familiar says wryly in my head, her eyes gleaming as she performatively ruffles her feathers. *How could I miss that?*

I wrinkle my nose at her, but I also know she's not going to let me out of her sight. It's got very little to do with the *drama* and much more to do with *war*.

The war that the Joywood, witchkind's ruling coven, promised us was coming on the night they intended to kill us in full view of the whole town and claim it was *justice*.

Absolutely nothing noteworthy or overtly terrifying has happened since that June night. We stood up to the Joywood and somehow lived—but the dread gets worse by the day.

None of us are safe.

I shake off the sense of impending doom and picture Zander's place, his little house on stilts across the river. He can look out over the water and see our hometown, a gathering place since not long after the Salem Witch Trials for witches, spirits, and more than one enchanted statue that might once have been a magical creature.

I want to cry, but I never cry. Instead, I push it away, and focus on what needs doing. Call me whatever you like—I can promise you, I've heard worse—but I will *always* suck it up and do the thing. Eventually.

Tonight the glamour takes a lot more muttered spells than usual to hide my little *bump* from the outside world, and when I'm done, I don't look as bright and energetic as I wish I did.

I guess that's fair enough in the middle of the night.

Though I'm seeing an ex, so obviously I'd rather gleam.

Instead, I strap my trusty athame to my hip. I tell myself, piously, that vanity has no place here on this night of great virtue and overdue truth-telling.

It's not that I lied. I can't tell a lie to save my life. I literally, physically, can't form the words to lie. It's a curse.

An actual, very real curse, courtesy of my well-meaning mother.

But omission hides a host of sins, and magic helps.

I step out the little door onto the second-story balcony that runs along outside my apartment. Half of why I picked this building for my tea shop when I inherited my grandfather's little nest egg was this balcony. I can look down St. Cyprian's pretty Main Street in the middle of the night and lose myself in the way the quiet streetlamps glow, the graceful trees stand like sentries down by the river, and the Missouri starlight dapples over the bricks. Magical bricks. Protective bricks.

Because this is the one place all witches and magical beings are supposed to be safe—even half witches keeping all-too-unmagical secrets.

I breathe in the night air. Summer is hanging on even though we're in September, but autumn is there too. The soft scent of gently letting go underneath that stubborn Midwest humidity that doesn't want to lift. I close my eyes and let the magic take over.

Then I fly.

Up above the buildings and into the stars. The night pulses around me, bright with starshine magic. I hover for a moment, high above the river, and follow the gleaming line of it with my gaze to the place where three separate rivers—only two to human eyes—merge and mingle and meld. The reasons the witches chose this place to settle after the ravages of Salem.

Power. Magic.

Wild as the stars, thick as the night, and almost lost to the dark.

I helped save that confluence. Me, a piddling half witch with a questionable ability to control her magic, the past, the spirits, or any of the things a Summoner is supposed to do with ease. Still, I fought. I always fight and I always will. To help my friends. To save my family.

But that word hits harder tonight.

Because as soon as I share my secret, *family* means more than my mother, the slightly notorious Tanith Good of the more-than-slightly-notorious old Good family of witches going back centuries. Currently tucked away in her historic house with her partner, Mina Rodriguez.

Does she suspect the little secret I've been carrying around since Beltane? I'm not sure. Tanith is not the kind of woman to keep quiet, especially if that's the wiser course of action.

But it's hard for me to believe that the mother who knows me so well doesn't have *some* inclination that there's something *different* going on.

I run my hands over my little bump. Then I fly away from my view of the confluence. Ruth soars lazily beside me, down along the Mississippi toward Zander's place. The stilts it sits up on are a nod to the capricious nature of the rivers and the determination of river town residents. Floods are in our bones, even when we're fighting against them. Maybe especially then.

The lights in his windows are on, and I see him moving around inside. He's probably exhausted, and I wouldn't be surprised if he was a little drunk. God knows he hasn't been eating right or taking care of himself since Zelda died.

Out here in the dark, I allow myself to feel the intense sympathy I never let him see.

The only good news about Zander's grieving this summer is that he hasn't been partaking in his usual string of human one-night stands. Don't ask me how I know that or, better yet, why I track it so I can stick my fingers in *that* unhealable wound.

I land on the rickety porch, also on stilts. I can hear the sound of birds huffing about up above. No doubt Ruth greeting Zander's eagle familiar, Storm. I don't know what familiars get up to with each other, or even how they communicate, but I know Ruth and Storm have never had any of the animosity toward one another that I felt they should.

Traitor, I think pointedly at Ruth, but she ignores me.

So I take a deep breath. I knock, hard, before I think twice.

There's a beat as I stand there on the porch. Then Zander hauls opens the door. Maybe someday the *punch* of him won't wind me, or so I like to tell myself—but tonight it does, the way it always has, since we were young and stupid. Even though his dark, wavy hair is disheveled and a touch too long, his moody gray eyes are shadowed, and the beard that I know hides a moon-shaped birthmark just under the right corner of his lips is getting a little wild these days. He *reeks* of alcohol, which I know could be the bar or his choices lately.

I think it's probably both.

He looks behind me as if expecting the rest of our friends, clearly not believing I'd come here on my own. And I wouldn't. Not for any other reason. Not on a random night in September, anyway.

"Can I come in?" I sound weird and formal, but it's the best I can do.

"Uh. Sure."

He moves out of the way, and I step inside.

Zander's never been known for being particularly neat or tidy. He's a typical *guy*, but this is a new low even for him. Paper plates litter every surface. Empty beer cans, stacks of mail, dirty clothes everywhere with random socks scattered across the floor, T-shirts tossed over the backs of furniture, and a half-empty bottle of whiskey on the counter in the small galley kitchen. Next to a whole lot of empties. The air is scented with the sharpness of hard alcohol and the heavy staleness that comes with grief and depression.

He'd refuse to admit to feeling either of those things if I asked.

I don't ask.

I've spent a decade hardening my heart to this man, but the past few months have made my previous attempts at ironclad resistance wear thin. I feel for him. I worry about him. I want to comfort him.

I have allowed myself almost none of these indulgences. There's a reason our historic deal remains in place. We're weak when it comes to each other. That's always been true.

But we're also fucking toxic.

Our friends think we're bad *now*, with our bickering and general harshness toward one another. They have *no* idea how we've grown and matured.

The fact we can even share space these days is a testament to that. And how much we love Emerson Wilde, I suppose, because watching out for her after the Joywood wiped her magical memories at our high school graduation ceremony forced those of us who love her to grow up. Fast.

Emerson's sister and my best friend, Rebekah, had to choose exile to survive, but the rest of us stayed for Emerson. Zander. Me. Georgie, her best friend, always right by her side. Jacob, too, but with enough emotional distance to stave off what I think must have been inevitable—given that they're engaged now.

Maybe I hate the Joywood for that as much as anything else.

Which is why, along with the fact I love my friends, I'm part of this whole coven thing in the first place. Made up of castouts, grumpy Healers, former spell-dim witches, the most feared once-immortal witch of all time, and Zander. We've decided we want a chance to ascend—to become the ruling coven ourselves. A decision that has earned us all targets on our backs. Not to mention the enmity of the most powerful witches alive or dead, and ample opportunity to fight off their dirty, too-dark magic

In the meantime, Zander and I are going to be parents.

Another fast-forward leap into serious adulthood that I can't say I'm at all comfortable with, but here we are.

I know I should start laying the groundwork on that. *So, remember Beltane this year? After I got sick but Jacob healed me right up?* I can't bring myself to go back there. The past might be my thing, but *my* past is a shitstorm.

What I can deal with is this pigsty, so that's what I do. I magic the trash away and the clothes into one pile in the corner instead of many piles strewn about. With a lift of my hand, the bottle of Jack hovers off the counter and upends, dumping its contents down the sink.

Zander watches all this and scowls at me. I conjure up a little concoction, and because his place is *disgusting*, I even magic up a mug from my own apartment. Everything lands with a thump in front of him on the counter where he's planted his palms.

"Sober up," I say to him, because I'm a gentle, comforting soul in all things.

Also to see if I *can* say it. That I can tells us both that it's the truth. He isn't entirely sober, though given the clarity of the way he's glaring at me, I wouldn't call him *drunk* either.

He does that growling thing too well. "You know, this is low. Even for you."

We tend to start off angry with each other ever since our epic Beltane prom (the witch version of that very human high school dance) breakup ten years ago. It's our default. It's what works. It's what keeps our bleeding hearts firmly tucked away behind their little walls.

Healthy walls. *Necessary* walls.

Boundaries, you might say. Or armor against idiocy.

So the *tone* of the comment isn't unexpected, but I don't really understand what he's getting at. "What is?"

"I don't need *pity* sex, Ellowyn."

The *audacity*.

"I am *not* offering *any* kind of sex," I reply, my voice going up an octave in shock.

And if I was, it sure as hell wouldn't be looking like *this*. I'd at least have on some sexy underwear. But I feel about as sexy as an overinflated balloon, even *with* the glamour.

"Then why are you here?" Zander glares the way storms rage, with those thunderstorm-gray eyes of his, and I've never been immune. I'm not now either, and not only because I'm currently a hormone factory. "Somehow I doubt you've discovered your tender, empathetic side at three in the morning."

Given the momentary insanity of my sympathetic thoughts toward him earlier, this *incenses* me. Any notion that I should soften the blow I'm about to deliver deserts me. Hard.

"I'm *pregnant*, you asshole."

And there it is. The thing I've been striving to keep a secret for the past few months, a secret no more. While Emerson talks of ascension, while we've all been trying to figure out what to do about Zander and his grief along with our own, while the creeping dread of the Joywood's unlikely quiet seeps into our bones like poison.

I am pregnant.

Hecate help me.

2

HE CLEARS HIS THROAT. "WHAT?"

I could repeat it, but that feels like a kindness, and kindness hurts. "You heard me."

"But we haven't. Not since..."

"You can count. Congratulations."

I don't tell him that I haven't been with anyone else since then. He doesn't need to know that. We've always been very good at letting each other know *all* the other people we've slept with. It's possible we've even slept around *at* each other, enjoying witchkind's disinterest in what I've heard called *consensus morality*.

It's never had much to do with morality. Not for us.

It's that there's nothing out there that's better than what we do to each other. The sex isn't good. It isn't even great. It's *world-altering*.

I spent many years dedicated to the sole mission of proving that wrong, and failed.

Repeatedly.

All that aside—and I like to keep it as far aside as I can get it—it doesn't matter how old we are or how mature we try to become. It doesn't matter how many old wounds we've healed or how many worlds we saved right here in St. Cyprian in the last year.

We are *bad* for each other. Even when it feels way too good. Maybe especially then.

I used to lay all the blame for that on him. But as the mature adult, successful local businesswoman, and grown-ass woman that I am, I can say now that some of it was, indeed, my fault.

Though I am less to blame than him.

His dark gray gaze moves over my body, a late-summer storm, and I *could* drop my glamour to prove myself. But I don't. I want him to believe me without evidence.

I'm protecting myself and our baby, that's all.

Because protection is the name of the game. If I hadn't learned that when my father's disastrous double life came to light, causing my mother to accidentally curse me, I certainly learned it when Zander decided that our senior year Beltane prom was the time to break up with me when we had promised each other we were going to be together. Forever.

"I don't understand." Zander sounds grim, but also confused, and I know he's working through all the same things I did when I finally understood what my weird symptoms meant. Having cycled through all other options first. Twice. "All those years we…?"

I know he doesn't mean the years in high school we were so hot and heavy that it's a wonder we didn't burn the whole town down. He means that secret we keep from *everyone*, and have for a decade.

Zander and I don't spend time alone. Because we don't get along—to put it mildly. We don't like to breathe the same air, and no one who knows us has any doubts on this score. We make sure of it.

This is true every day of the year—*except* on Beltane.

Because those first few weeks after Beltane prom our senior

year, our breakup was terrible, but we still couldn't seem to keep our hands off each other. All wildfire and terrible storms day in and day out until we were both half-sick with it. Screaming at each other in high school hallways, parking lots, the middle of Main Street. Sobbing on the floor. Punching fists through walls. *Nothing* worked. Nothing settled us down. We could *hate* each other, and we often did, and still want our hands all over each other.

No matter what damage it did to both of us.

Hate is its own protection.

But it exacts its own price.

Back then, we made a compromise. Total abstinence from our destructive, all-consuming hunger throughout the year, with one cheat day. One very, very long cheat night. On Beltane we eat each other alive and don't talk about it when the sun comes up. On the days I can't think for wanting to punch him *and* fuck him, well, I know I can hold off until Beltane, when I can do both.

And do.

Back in the beginning, I figured it'd work so well we'd only need one Beltane, maybe two, to be cured. I was sure there had to be *someone* else out there who knew their way around an orgasm so I could move on at last.

These days I suspect we'll never be cured.

But he's right that we've had ten years of secret Beltane nights with no consequences. Until this one. The great thing about being a witch, even just half a witch, is the ability to use magic as birth control. Go figure, mine finally let me down.

"I don't know how or why I'm pregnant. I just know that I *am*."

He holds up a hand, and his gaze changes. Darkens, somehow. "May to June. To July. August. September." He ticks off the months with his fingers. "Four months. You haven't told me for *four* months." He squints at me, still not entirely sober because he hasn't taken even a sip of my cure for him. But that sudden, intense focus I see on his face is definitely him trying to break through my glamour. Also I can feel it.

His magic has a flavor a lot like his scent. Woodsmoke, whiskey, and the pull of the rivers all around us.

I know he'd probably break right through the glamour if he was full-on sober, but I don't want that. So I do what it takes to protect myself. Not with magic, but with my other tools.

"You try breaking that news to someone, Zander. Oh wait, you're a man, so of course you'll never have to. You could have children littered all over witchdom for all you know."

He has the *nerve* to roll his eyes. "Why tell me now, then?"

That gives me pause, which is less fun than poking at him. I'm all for hurting Zander in the ways *I* can hurt him, but I don't want to use Zelda as a weapon. That feels like stooping too low, even for us.

But I can't lie. And the evasions I can use to twist around my curse don't work on him. Or anyone who knows me well enough to know what my pointed evasions mean.

"Why now?" he repeats, with that same focus, more sober by the second.

I don't know if he suspects something or if he just knows I'm hesitating because it's going to hurt. The problem is that we know each other too well. We know where all the wounds and scars are, because we're the ones who hurt each other first and worst. Like too many things in my life, it's as much a blessing as it is a curse, and right now it sucks.

"Who else knows?" he asks, changing tactics.

I brace myself against that *voice*, serious and dark and low. "No one drawing breath on Hecate's madly spinning earth." Not a lie. Spirits can't breathe. "I was always going to tell you first." I said it so it has to be true, but I know I have to tell him about Zelda. Because it's the right thing to do. And I like to be salty, I won't deny it, but not about this. "Your mother came to see me tonight."

Zander sucks in a breath, like I've reached out and stabbed him with my athame instead of staying right by the closed front door with an entire room between us.

"Nice." His gruff voice hurts to hear. His storm cloud gaze hurts to hold. "She say hi?"

He doesn't wait for my answer. He goes for his cabinet, where we both know he stocks the alcohol he actually bothers to put away. To throw more oblivion on the problem like he's been doing all summer.

I've spent the past months he's just counted out in denial, but when I can't hold on to that, I've practiced what I would say. How I would behave. It hasn't gone to plan—shocker—but there is one thing I have always known I'd tell him. "You don't have to be involved."

His hand drops from the cabinet door. He skewers me with a look that is somehow both outrageously hurt and volcanic. It's the worst I've ever seen from him, and that's saying something. "Fuck you, Ellowyn."

I don't want to analyze why that simple statement, said almost quietly, sends a wave of panic through me rather than the typical tsunami of fury. "We know how bad we are at getting along. You think we should raise a kid together?"

I'd love to say this is why I've put off telling him. That I didn't want an argument.

But I love an argument.

The real reason is that it hurts. It all *hurts*. Like I'm eighteen and he's breaking up with me at Beltane prom all over again. Not before or after, like a normal person who is also a stupid boy. Actually *at* the prom.

Not because he thought I'd been flirting with Tony Alward in potions class (I wasn't) or I thought he'd been staring a little too hard at Michelle Holland's miniskirt while she pretended not to understand spellcasting (he definitely was). No, Zander was being *noble*. He wanted to *set me free*.

So I used that freedom to destroy us both in the way I knew he would hate the most.

Even ten years later, I keep waiting to look back and think, *Remember how* huge *that felt? What babies we were.*

It was never *baby stuff*, though, even when we were.

I'm still waiting for that freedom.

"I have a right to be in my kid's life," he says in that deadly quiet way that makes my stomach twist into a million knots, because *quiet* Zander is a dangerous thing. It's the real him. The Guardian he always has been under all the smiles and jokes and masks.

I wish I didn't know that.

"We're already in each other's lives with the coven and Emerson's ascension bullshit," he continues, like I'm so stupid I can't possibly understand the things happening to both of us, all our friends, and—no big deal—the entire world thanks to the Joywood. "Our child is going to be there since *you* are. I'm just supposed to pretend he or she isn't *mine?*"

I am so not ready to think about what's growing inside of me as a *child*. One that will be real. And here. And have to come *out of me*. Zander's right. We can't cut each other out. Even without the extenuating coven and ascension issues, we've never been any good at that.

"You know what?" I say to him—because a great defense is *always* an asshole offense. "I'm not going to get into this with you. I told you. That's all I came to do." I turn toward the door, *horrified* that tears are stinging the backs of my eyes. It's the hormones, I assure myself. Even witches aren't immune when growing *life* inside their own bodies. "When you decide to be civil, we can—"

"*Civil?* You've got some fucking nerve."

I do. Oh, *I do.* Just to show him, I fling out some magic that has every cabinet fly open. With another wave of a hand, I slam every liquor bottle in the house—and there are a lot—on the counter next to him. "Drink yourself to death. See if I care."

Then I whirl away and open the door. A few sparks fly as he hurls out his brooding, angry magic to stop mine, slamming the door shut again. I throw mine back and the door wobbles, caught between both of us trying to impose our will on the other. Trying to *win*.

Welcome to *us*.

I dig in, exulting in the fight the way I always do with him, because I don't have to worry if he can handle what unpredictable thing I might or might not do—I know he can take it.

The door blows open on a huge gust of magic, and I stumble back. My butt hits the floor, not hard, but not like I hit a feather pillow either.

I certainly didn't *expect* to win a power battle with him. I might be angry, I might *wish* I had stronger powers, but at the end of the day, I am only half witch. Even when I can muster something powerful, the control is shaky at best.

Zander is a full witch from a hereditarily powerful witch family. He *should* win, but it still pisses me off, and I start to tell him so—

But a shadow from outside rushes toward me, and I get it then, but it's too late—

This shadow is the source of the blast of magic that knocked me down. Zander must sense it a second or two before me, because a rush of his magic encases me before I can even throw my hands up in defense.

Ruth dive-bombs from wherever she was hiding. Storm screeches out a battle cry.

Suddenly we're in a real fight.

I scramble back to my feet. I can move, but I feel Zander's magic wrapping me in a kind of armor, which makes it impossible to use my own magic unless I can somehow break through his spell.

Something, it pains me to admit, I've never been any good at.

Zander manages to wrestle the shadow back out the door while keeping me inside. He's acting like we haven't fought side by side all damn year, stopping floods, facing down the Joywood, saving our friends and ourselves and everyone—well, almost everyone—we love.

Once again he's making it clear that I'm the very odd one out in a friend group full of not just witches, but *special* witches. Chosen witches.

And me, the half-witch disappointment he *set free* ten years ago.

"Ellowyn," he growls, his voice rough and magic igniting his dark gaze. "Stay put."

I don't listen. Not thinking beyond my temper, I follow him right outside, even though I can't *do* anything in this stupid magic bubble Zander stuck me in. Outside it's dark—much darker than it should be on such a clear night. The stars and the moon were out when I flew over, and it hasn't been that long.

I don't have a lot of time to worry about that, because the shadow is waiting *right there*.

It rushes at me once more, but again Zander's magic meets it before I can do a damn thing. Sparks fly where magic battles magic, gritty and mean. The shadow surrounds him, like it's trying to suck him in, but he fights it back. Again and again, and I can't get his walls of protection off me to lend a hand.

So I do what I can, since he's neutered what I can do here. I call out to our friends. Our coven, the Riverwood. We all promised—if there's a call, no matter what or why, we all come.

The way we promised ten years ago when it was Emerson we were trying to keep safe from all the things she couldn't remember.

It doesn't take long tonight. The past few months have been

too quiet. We know the Joywood are working against us in the lead-up to the ascension rituals that will begin soon and then end at Samhain when witchkind will pick its ruling coven. We've been waiting for *something*.

Maybe not a shadow. Maybe not tonight. But we've all been on edge.

Everyone appears on Zander's porch at once. No one waits to dive in.

It's too dark and I can't see everything, but I can *feel* the bursts of magic. The deep, dark wrongness of something wanting to hurt us all and doing its best to make it so. It's not the hideous, supposedly mythical adlets Emerson fought off back in March. It's not the Joywood themselves we all had to fight in June. It's just a shadow.

Yet something about the dark, slimy way it glistens, darker than the dark itself, reminds me of something—

Before I can put my finger on it, the protective bubble around me drops. The first thing I feel is the cold, when it's still warm—or it was, earlier.

I know Zander didn't let me go because he suddenly trusted me to fight. He dropped the walls because he doesn't have the magic to maintain it *and* fight.

I don't like that notion at all, so I wade in.

Because I might want to pound on Zander right now—and really all the time—but I'm not about to let anyone else have the pleasure.

With all seven of us fighting, the tide turns. First that nasty, sickening shadow looms large, but slowly, surely we surround it. I finally figure out what this weird black thing that isn't fully formed reminds me of.

Back in the spring, when we first fought the Joywood. There was all that *black*.

The black that was in the rivers when they nearly drowned the town and most of Missouri. The black that Jacob described as being *inside* Zelda, the cause of the sickness that took her from us. It's all the same, and I have no doubt the Joywood are behind it.

Litha proved that, not that *we* needed it proved. *We* already knew.

Tonight, though, I find myself wondering how much of this black is *in them*. If they're made of it too.

This horrible black magic with no end.

It doesn't matter right now because we're still fighting. The seven of us fall into place, hemming the shadow in on all sides with the magical ring we make. We chant as we move, making it smaller—

"We call on the moon, the confluence, our connection," we intone, while the magic we make as the Riverwood coven blazes hot and bright, shooting deep into the center of that oily dark. *"Give us your might. Strengthen our fight."*

Something screams—

"Indict the dark that threatens the light," we all shout in unison.

It's the shadow itself, or something deep within the shadow, and it seems to recoil. It wraps in and around itself like a collapsing dark star, consuming itself from within.

There's a sickening tearing sound, like rending flesh—

Then it shoots up and flies away from everyone—

Except it veers toward me at the last second.

Right at me.

Right at the baby, as if it knows.

I fling up a protection spell, but it claws through it. A brutal slice, and then there's a searing pain across my abdomen—

Then it's gone. Like it was never there.

3

"WHAT WAS *THAT*?" REBEKAH DEMANDS IM-
mediately, sounding particularly outraged as she stares at the
place where the shadow disappeared.

This is partially because my best friend is also our coven's
Diviner, and she takes it personally when surprised by things
she feels she should have foretold.

Nicholas Frost, her outrageously powerful boyfriend—if
that's what you call a formerly immortal witch—shakes his
head as he stands beside her. He's bleeding from the corner of
his lip a little, but that's the only indication that he sacrificed
his immortality for Rebekah back in June.

When Zander can't even let me fight my own battles ten
years later.

"A problem, but one we handled," Frost says in his usual
resonant voice. "For tonight." He's never one to get carried
away with the optimism, which is maybe what happens when
you have centuries under your belt.

"How cheerful," Rebekah replies, but there's laughter in her
voice, and the way she looks at him is all heat and joy.

I glance over at Zander. He's holding his arm at a very *wrong* angle, gritting his teeth against what must be some considerable pain. I don't like any part of that, and I'm about to reach out to him, no matter how telling that would be right now—

Rebekah takes me by the arm. "You're hurt. You're..." She trails off.

In a very *significant* way.

Significant enough that everyone looks away from the sky and the shadows, to me.

Standing here in all this moonlight with no glamour, because I lost it somewhere along the fight. A four-month pregnancy isn't a *huge* baby bump or anything, but I've been hiding it. While seeing these people every day. So they notice the difference between my glamoured stomach and my actual, pregnant stomach.

They *all* notice.

I can't focus on that disaster because I'm also looking down, and I see the angry claw mark across my tiny swell of belly. Once I do, I *feel* it. For a moment, my brain goes entirely blank, then fills with nothing but terror. I almost pass out. All I can hear is Zander talking about *our child*.

Our child. A little person *we* made, but the shadow—

Then Jacob is next to me. He murmurs some Healer words as his magic seeps into me, but I'm not really listening. I'm looking at the angry claw mark and hearing nothing but a kind of low buzz in my ears. Panic and a million other things.

Things I don't want to name.

Slowly, the marks stop bleeding and start stitching back together. Jacob's work is swift and good. He heals me, and not for the first time this year. Not even the first time this long, hot summer.

"Is *everything* okay?" I whisper at him.

Jacob holds my scared gaze and gives my arm a reassuring squeeze, wordlessly telling me the baby is fine. I begin to breathe normally again, which is when I realize I...wasn't.

The terror inside of me slowly recedes. Only then do I remember Zander's arm. I turn around to find him, to make sure he's okay too—

Jacob's already moving over to him, and though Zander's injuries are different, our Healer repeats the same process.

He calls on his magic so Zander's broken arm starts to straighten. The gash on his cheek and the deeper one across his eyebrow begin to fill in. There's a long scratch across his neck that looks ugly, and I have to force myself to keep still, to keep from doing something incredibly stupid and revealing, like running to his side.

Or like...having his baby? Ruth asks dryly.

I've never liked owls, I tell her in my head. The only place I can lie at will, and do.

She hoots from her perch on Zander's roof. While Jacob works on his arm, Zander's gaze finds mine. We clash there in the moonlight, intense and obvious.

Revealing in its own way, at least to me.

I look around at my other friends then, though I feel off balance. They all look a little bruised and bloody, but we're all on our own two feet. Zander took the brunt of the attack. *Because he brought it on himself,* I remind myself. If he let me help, he wouldn't be so beat up.

Jacob looks at Emerson, our Confluence Warrior, coven leader, chamber of commerce president, and soon-to-be most powerful witch in the world, if we can convince witchdom to choose her—and us—in the coming ascension at Samhain. Jacob gives her a nod, making it clear Zander's okay, though I'm sure he talks to her privately too. That's their fiancé stuff.

Emerson nods back, like the general she is.

Her nose is bleeding, and her hair is in a crazy tangle. There's that *gleam* in her eye. The Confluence Warrior gleam that might

terrify a person if they found themselves lacking the confidence
Emerson Wilde has in herself and her friends.

"We'll go discuss this while we recover at Wilde House,"
Emerson says in her decisive way. "On the bricks, where it's
safer."

Not *safe* like we were raised to believe, not anymore. The lore
tells us that the bricks that make St. Cyprian's historic cobble-
stoned streets were enchanted as they were put in place, a standing vow to all magical beings that no harm could come to them
here. But we're not dealing with magic that follows the rules
these days. So far, this year, there's been black magic and blood
barters and all sorts of twisted histories hidden underneath the
surface of the rules we thought we knew—and the long-trusted
people who govern us.

The bricks are safer, anyway. They offer more protection than
a rickety river porch. My worry over what that vile thing did to
Zander is for a different time. When I'm alone and haven't just
accidentally announced my pregnancy to all of our best friends.

When I can let myself feel the things I prefer to pretend I
have no access to in the light of day. Or even by the light of
the moon, if there are other people around.

Jacob and Frost help Zander, and Emerson links arms with
me. I would tell anyone who asks that I'm not tactile, but my
friends get a pass. And her gaze doesn't linger on my stomach,
thankfully. She's focused on action. On getting us all to her
family's grand old house on one end of Main Street where generations of Wildes have fought off all kinds of threats in their
day. I feel almost teary—again—because it feels like a reprieve.
And I need it.

I'm sure she knows. She always does.

"I imagine your mother felt the fight too," she says quietly, so
only I can hear her. "I can hold her off at the pass if you want to…"
she flicks a glance down at my now-healed stomach "…wait."

I shake my head. No more secrets. "No, she should know."

We all fly back to Wilde House, where Emerson and Rebekah grew up, though lately they both spend more time with their significant others than in the big Victorian that commands its part of town. It has stood here for almost the entire sweep of St. Cyprian history, as elegant and elaborate as houses out this way get. Its turret, where Georgie currently resides, sparkles bright beneath the September moon.

We all land together in the living room that has become Ascension Central, but has always been a meeting space since long before we needed to be a coven and officially fight the Joywood. Even back when Emerson didn't remember all we are or even who she really is.

We met here. We ate. We planned. We helped Em run her festivals and plot her course through the local politics that were thorny and difficult even for someone who didn't know there were witches involved.

Zander and I went whole meetings, now and again, without sniping at each other—much too busy supporting Emerson in her role as the youngest chamber of commerce president in St. Cyprian history.

Because sometimes love is as complicated and as simple as just showing up.

Georgie hands Emerson a flowy bandanna to blot at her nose. Rebekah is holding an ice pack on Frost's cheek, and it's clearly not because he can't do it himself. No one announces that Jacob's pushed his Healer magic to the limit, but there's a communal agreement that there's no point in him healing such tiny injuries that will mend before morning.

Not when there could be a whole war before then that he'll need to be ready for.

"Should she rest?" Rebekah asks Jacob, referring to me.

"She's up for a quick…recap," Jacob says, looking over at Emerson. Again, not at me. "Nothing too involved."

"*She* is right here." But Emerson is looking at Zander when she stands up for me. "So. What happened?"

She doesn't get out a notebook, but we all know that somewhere nearby or out at Jacob's farm, a pen is floating above a notebook and fully prepared to take down every detail in written form. She'll pore over it later. Obsess over every detail. Try to figure out *everything* so we aren't caught unaware again.

It isn't only the Warrior in Emerson that won't ever give up. It's just who she is.

I love her ferocious optimism, even if I can't share it.

Zander looks across the room at me. He's pale—and clearly sober. He's holding his right arm gingerly, and some of the cuts on his face are still visible as faint pink streaks, but he's healing more by the moment. I can see that he is.

There's no reason for me to think I need to go and touch him to make sure.

"Ellowyn and I were having an overdue discussion." Zander turns back to Emerson as he speaks. Something's shifted since Litha, I think. There's a quiet acknowledgment of the change in our coven situation. Because covens have hierarchies. Emerson isn't just a friend, sister, or cousin anymore. She's our leader. "She went to leave, and that shadow thing flew in. So I fought it."

He fought it. Because of course. Zander the Guardian wouldn't dare let *me* do the honors or even help. Disappointing half witches can't be trusted with simple tasks like fighting off evil.

"Yes," I agree, making no attempt to sound anything but mad. Because I am. Because maybe that's more easily accessible than all the other, messier things I also feel. "*He* fought it because he put an unwanted safety spell over me. But I watched. It was the same dark shadow you all saw. No real shape. Just... power, I guess. Dark, ugly power. With claws."

Zander nods. "Dark, yeah, but different." I can't let myself nod along. Casual agreement is a slippery slope to our particular brand of toxicity. "It definitely wanted to take a chunk out of me."

Me, he says, so matter-of-factly. As if it didn't slash a shadowy claw across *me* too.

Typical. "And when Zander was in over his head, I called you guys."

I can see he wants to argue that he was never in over his head or anywhere near it, but I said it. So we all know it's true. I accept his glare as tribute.

Emerson ignores our silent battle of one-upmanship. She's frowning. Thinking. "You don't have any clue what prompted it?"

Both Zander and I shake our heads. I can't imagine the Joywood or anyone else cares that I got myself knocked up. The timing doesn't make any sense.

"What were you guys talking about?" Georgie asks, and the thing about Georgie is that I've known her my entire life. She grew up next door to Wilde House. I still can't tell if she's as dreamy and otherworldly as she seems, her face always in a book—or, lately, talking about seemingly very boring things with her high school teacher boyfriend, Sage. Who...seems nice. Enough.

For a moment, the entire room is silent, like maybe none of us can tell if Georgie is really asking that question either.

I point at my expanding middle. "Hi. Hello."

"So it *is* Zander's," Georgie says, almost wonderingly.

"Obviously it's mine."

His *what the fuck, Georgie*, lingers in the air as if he yelled it. Though he didn't. And I hear an odd creak from the front hall, like the old staircase with the creepy newel post is reacting too.

Georgie only smiles. I can *feel* everyone's eyes on me, and I can practically hear the questions they're very purposefully not voicing. *How? When? Where? Why?*

"Did something happen at the bar tonight? Anything out of

the ordinary that might have caused or hinted at an attack?"
Emerson asks Zander, as if oblivious to all of these things going
on around her when we all know she's not. "Maybe a strange
ferry passenger earlier?" She turns to me. "A customer at your
shop that felt off?"

My customers at Tea & No Sympathy are there for artisan
tea blends, my trademark scowl, and no sympathy, as adver-
tised. They're all a little off, but I don't say that.

"No," I say instead, as Zander shakes his head. And I'm mad
at him, so I continue. "Maybe something happened while you
were busy drowning your sorrows. Hard to see an evil brewing when you're face down in the gin."

Not that I *care* that his grief takes the shape of self-sabotage.

Zander and I get locked in one of those staring battles that
only end in Pyrrhic victories, if any, and only after too much
history passes between us, silently. Bruisingly.

Years ago we forbade ourselves from taking part in any silent, witch-type talking inside each other's heads—not when it
was only the two of us. Taking private conversations like that
off the menu was supposed to make this better.

It didn't. It doesn't.

"We've been waiting for the Joywood to make a move,"
Rebekah is saying, because they all have practice ignoring us.
Even the one who was away for a decade.

"Yes, but the fact they've waited makes me wonder why *now*,
why tonight. We still have over a month to Samhain, and hoops
to jump through yet."

She's talking about the ascension rituals.

Everyone in witchdom knows that ascension means we get
to choose our ruling coven. No one seems to know the details about how that choice gets made. The Joywood have held
their position for so long that no one can recall how they won
it in the first place. We originally figured we'd let Frost fill us

in, because he's lived so long and—rumor has it—was once a member of a ruling coven himself.

But it turns out that losing his immortality when he saved Rebekah means he's lost access to parts of his vast knowledge too. He and Georgie and Rebekah spend hours every day trying to work through the gaps, but it's hard to chase down things you can't remember that you ought to know. What we do understand is that we have to appear before the town council—in a shocking coincidence that shocks no one, said council is also the Joywood—to announce our intentions, complete with certain spells, and the presentation of sponsors. This must take place during the celebration of Mabon, the witch festival that celebrates the autumn equinox.

There's a human festival too—the Apple Extravaganza that Emerson launched a few years ago, which manages to merge the usually still-hot Missouri summer weather with a little fall goodness that gets people on Main Street and into all the shops and restaurants and U-pick apple orchards across the river. Despite impending war and/or ascension, she's maintained her typical schedule with her usual summer activities that keep this place humming and full of tourists, human as well as witch.

"Why haven't they showed themselves?" Georgie asks into the brooding quiet, shaking her head. "We know they're after us. They're the ones who called it a *war*. Why bother with *shadows*?"

"Even they can't get away with bald-faced murder?" Jacob offers, with more hope than certainty, and we all laugh. A little.

Because they're the Joywood. They can get away with anything. If we're right about them, they already have.

"If they really wanted to murder any of you, or all of you, you would have been dead long ago," Frost intones. Because the guy might not be immortal anymore, but he hasn't changed. He is the first, best Praeceptor, the foundation of the witchlore itself, as we were all taught in school. He is also absurdly hot, all aristocratic angles and too-blue eyes, if much more mortal than he used to be.

"Nicholas, you are a constant comfort," Rebekah says, making a face at him, but it's a fond sort of face. I support her need to date an age gap beyond comprehension. I just wish the unconditional support flowed to me too. I can feel it doesn't.

Then again, she's only known that I'm pregnant—meaning, importantly, that I've been sleeping with Zander and not telling her about it—for about thirty minutes. That's not a lot of processing time, I can admit. I decide to forgive her.

A little.

Emerson sighs. "You and Zander need rest, Wynnie." She takes my hand and gives it a squeeze, and once again, I allow the touching and the nickname pretty much only Emerson gets away with. "So does Jacob." The look she gives her fiancé is less coven leader and more worried soon-to-be-wife. "Tomorrow is our usual ascension meeting anyway. Let's all take what's left of tonight to gather our recollections. Leave no detail out, big or small, of what you felt, saw, thought, or even imagined at Zander's. Tomorrow we'll see if we can't determine the *why* we're missing here."

No one verbally agrees, but no one mounts an opposition, so Emerson keeps talking. "I think everyone should stay put here at Wilde House for the time being. Until we really understand what happened tonight. No going it alone. No sleeping off the bricks. That wasn't the hardest fight we've ever had, not even close, but that doesn't mean we can be careless."

Frost does that thing where he *becomes an immensity* as you look at him. An immortal party trick, I would have said—but apparently it's just him. "Surely when you say *here at Wilde House*, you mean Ellowyn," he says in his I Am the Greatest and Most Powerful Witch of All Time voice.

Emerson is unmoved. "Wilde House is the most protected option we have."

Frost blinks. "I have wards on my house that are older than your entire ancestral line."

"You're up off the bricks. Jacob and Zander are across the river, also off the bricks." Emerson shrugs. "I think that at the very least, we all need to stay on the bricks right now. It might not be as protected as we once believed, but it's harder here. Let's make it hard on them. At least until we figure out what's going on."

I have the terrible feeling she means, *until we beat the Joywood.* "My apartment is on the bricks," I point out, because I would love nothing more than to go home to my sweet little apartment above my shop. My bed. *My* space. Alone and protected against all these *feelings* jumbling around the room.

I prefer to indulge in *feelings* exactly once a year, then otherwise pretend I'm immune.

"But alone. So no," Emerson says, not gently. More General Wilde-y, and a few months back, I would have argued. But we're the Riverwood now, so I bite my tongue. "Wilde House is the best option until we know what this is. *Why* this is. And how to protect ourselves against it, particularly if the Joywood aren't showing themselves. Besides, there's plenty of room."

I wait for someone to argue with Emerson, but no one does. I decide that *I* will—but tomorrow. When I have a little more energy. When I don't feel exhaustion creeping over me like a weighted blanket.

When I can close my eyes and not see that shadow flying at me. Or feel that terrible clawing over my belly. Or, somehow just as terrible, watch Zander taking those cruel blows from the same shadow.

"Good. It's agreed. So, we'll all get some rest and—"

"Is *no one* going to address the elephant in the room?" Rebekah finally turns and meets my gaze full-on. Then she points at my stomach, *theatrically*, and she's always been the most dramatic of us when she feels like it. "What. The. *Hell.*"

"Cosign," Georgie murmurs. Not airily.

But that's not a question I'm going to have to answer just yet, because we *all* hear the front door slam open.

Hard enough to make the old house groan.

4

"ELLOWYN SABRINA GOOD!" MY MOTHER shouts before appearing at the entrance to the living room. She's in her cheerful sunflower pajamas. Half her silvery-blond hair is up in a band, the other half hanging at her shoulders.

She might have called out my full, hated name, but she's not looking at me. She's glaring daggers. I mean actual, real daggers, though they hover there in front of her eyes instead of shooting toward their target.

That being Zander, as ever. She points at him, with a finger that seems just as sharp as the blades floating in midair.

"You're lucky I gave up curses," she throws at him, and there are even more edges in her words.

I'm not a saint. I enjoy it. Even if I shouldn't, because of all the things Zander has done wrong—and there are so many— the thing she's mad about tonight isn't one of them.

There's something in his expression that pricks at me now though. I might not understand it entirely, but I see grief there.

A terrible kind of *Sure, throw some daggers at me* grief. With a little too much of *It'd be better than all this*.

And as much as I hate to admit it, much as I'd love to rip it out, shred it into a million pieces and send it to the depths of the underworld, I have a heart. I can try not to have any empathy for this man, but it's not going to work. At least not right now.

So I put my arm around my mother and don't wait for her permission. Or his. I just...protect him.

I zoom Mom and me up to the second floor and the room I stay in whenever I spend the night here. So it's only me and her.

And the little baby bump between us.

Tanith Good is a force to be reckoned with. She always has been, with a temper, a sharp tongue, and a healthy sense of revenge not always tempered with the greatest control.

Apple, meet tree.

She didn't *mean* to curse me. That was aimed at my deserving father. I don't think it was just that my dad cheated that upended her tenuous grip on control, though I know that hurt her pride as much as anything else. It was that he'd gone and *married* a human without telling us. He was expecting a *child* with a human dental hygienist, of all things. And this double life only came out as he was leaving us for the human world, witches be damned.

"I could banish him," my mother is muttering, pacing the room. I lower myself on the bed because I am *beat* and I can't pretend otherwise, the way I would with anyone else. "It's not the same as a curse. Just a simple spell to imprison him in a cave forever."

She's talking about Zander, not Dad, though I can maybe be forgiven for thinking this is a summoned memory from my childhood. "Mom."

"I've had ten years to come up with the perfect plan, Ellowyn. Why not enact it now that he's done *this* to you?"

To me. Oh, if only I could lay the blame of this entire pregnancy on him.

"Maybe you've forgotten now that getting pregnant isn't a risk for you," I say dryly, given that her long-term partner, Mina, is a woman. "Neither one of us did this alone."

She huffs out a breath, but she also stops her pacing. She looks at me for a long moment, then crosses to take a seat next to me on the bed. Carefully, sweetly, she lays a hand over my stomach.

I don't know if I want to cry. Or laugh. Or maybe…sing. It's only that after months of toil and glamours, I feel *right*. The power of a mother, I think.

And I'm going to be one.

I swallow hard.

Mom makes a crooning sort of sound I don't think I've heard in twenty-five years, but I recognize it immediately. On a cellular level. Everything in me…lets go a little as I relax into the sound and the heat of her hand on my belly.

"What happened tonight?" she asks.

I breathe past the prickling feeling at the backs of my eyes. "We're not sure. I'll go out on a limb and guess the Joywood are at the root of it, one way or another."

She scowls at this. But one thing Tanith Good has never said to her only child, even when I wish she would, is that I shouldn't be part of this. If the Joywood wants a fight, Tanith thinks we should all be front and center. She believes I have every right to be part of this coven. That I'm capable.

That they should have arranged the whole thing around my talent, in fact, and she'll fight anyone who says different.

She has.

Tonight what she does is rub a hand over that soft swell, and I know she's accepted that this is a danger I'll have to vanquish. With my coven. Without her.

I can feel how proud she is, beneath the fury and the fear. I don't know how you go from holding a baby's entire life inside your body to letting them go off and fight battles they can't possibly win.

My throat feels too tight to ask.

"Why were you hiding this?" She means, *from me*.

"I had to tell him first. I couldn't." My breath threatens to hitch, and I try to tell her that it's because Zelda died and there's all this ascension stuff going on, but those words won't come out of my mouth. Because they are a lie. But it's my mom, so it's the truth I speak. "It hurt too much."

Tanith runs a hand over my hair. She doesn't ask me why Zander, or how. She doesn't press for all the details my friends will want. She sits next to me in a comforting silence that reminds me that no matter what, no matter how scared I get or how little I know what the hell I'm doing when it comes to pregnancies and babies...my mom has been there. She's done this already, and well. She will be here every step of the way.

All I can think is that Zander doesn't have that anymore.

"It's not the worst thing that could happen," my mother points out. Almost carefully, when she's normally more of a bull in search of a china shop to level. Maybe she senses that I'm a lot more fragile than china tonight. "I suppose you know that if you're already this far along."

I pull away a little and squint over at her. "I thought you wanted to curse him?"

"Oh." She waves that away. "I want to hurt anyone who hurts my baby. I always will. But if I step back…"

She takes my face in her hands now. Her eyes are violet— one of those things I always wished she'd passed on to me but didn't. Because *those* are witch eyes.

My eyes are a deeply unremarkable blue.

"Zander is a Guardian," Mom is saying, intently. "It's in his blood to…guard, protect, and so forth. I'm not saying he's perfect," she hurries to say when I glare at her. "No one is. I'm not saying he's all good or all Guardians are, because we know Festus Proctor is a useless, pompous fool."

Festus Proctor is the Joywood's Guardian, and he is all that and more.

"Mom," I begin.

She's not done. "I know you two have hurt each other over the years, Ellowyn, but he isn't a total dick, and this isn't a midlife crisis. There are worse fathers out there."

She doesn't say *like yours*. She doesn't need to. Bill Wallace is always our personal touchstone for useless men.

But I'm not ready to think of Zander as a *father*.

"I'm more concerned about the fact some shadow creature took a chunk out of you," my mother is saying now, that daggery glint back in her eyes.

"It took a bigger chunk out of Zander."

"Yeah, but you're my chunk. He could stand a few less chunks." She wrinkles her nose at that. "I shouldn't say that. Zelda was a good friend."

It's Zelda, and my mother, and this whole shitty evening that has me pulling away and pushing off the bed. To stand up even though I'm exhausted. Because it's all too *much*. "I should quit the coven."

I don't even get into the ascension situation. Because, spoiler alert: I think we're going to lose.

"Why?" my mother asks from her seat on the bed, but like she's merely curious. Not like she's taking me seriously. A lot like when I made proclamations in junior high, now that I think about it.

"I've got other stuff to worry about now." I try not to relive that angry claw mark across my stomach. I don't say the other part. The part my mother will argue with.

Which is this, and it's inescapable now that we're *the River-wood*: I don't belong. I never did. I can't let my friends down, but if I back out because of pregnancy—which is *part* of my concern or I wouldn't have been able to say it to my mother— they can't argue with that, can they?

Pathetic, Ruth whispers in my head from where she flies or perches somewhere outside.

I'm thinking of making an owl stew, I tell her, because I can. And because I won't.

"I can't go around fighting off dark shadows," I tell my mother. "I've got more to lose now."

"And more to protect." My mother stands and takes me by the shoulders. She looks at me, in that way I think is looking *into* me.

"A pregnant witch isn't fragile, Ellowyn," she tells me. Fiercely. "The life inside of her might be, but she isn't. She is powerful. Fearsome. Not fear*ful*."

I don't tell my mother what I'm thinking. She never responds well to it.

I'm not a witch. I'm only half. Bits and pieces but never the whole.

"Even powerful witches need sleep. I'll stay with you tonight and—"

I would love nothing more than to let my mother baby me, but how can I? I had four months to wallow. Now the secret is out. It's time to suck it up.

"Go on home to Mina," I tell her. "I've got to deal with ascension meetings and all that tomorrow. I don't need a babysitter. I've got Emerson."

She laughs and squeezes me tight. "Let them take care of you. Or I will force my way into this house, turn them all into summer sausages, and do it myself."

"Not summer sausages," I say, making myself smile. "They're so greasy."

She hugs me again. "I hated being pregnant," she whispers, but like hating it is a *fond* memory. "But I loved, and love, every minute of being your mother. Even the hard parts. You will too." She strokes my hair and holds me against her like I'm two instead of twenty-eight, and I wish I was. "Underneath all those walls, you have *everything* you need to be a good one."

Only then I realize how badly I needed to hear that.

"Go home, Mom." I say it with a smile, with all the love in my heart.

She smiles, and Tanith Good doesn't leave anything to chance. Not these days. She leans over to kiss my cheek, whispering words of encouragement that are also a spell. "Yes, my darling child, I will go home and you will stay. And you will be well."

5

WHEN I WAKE UP, SUNLIGHT IS STREAMING
through the windows. I've slept pretty hard, which hasn't been
the case for a while. I've been blaming the pregnancy, and it's
certainly contributed, but there's also been the issue of my intense guilt at keeping the pregnancy secret.

Now everything is out in the open.

And Rebekah is sitting at the foot of my bed.

I push myself into a sitting position, and she hands me a mug
of tea without saying a word. Once I've taken a few sips, I give
her a nod. *Ready.*

"What. The. Hell." She bites the words out even more pointedly than she did last night.

I nod again, accepting the pointedness. I've earned it. "I'm only
telling this story once, so you might as well call the crew in."

Rebekah blinks, and Georgie and Emerson immediately appear, like they were just waiting for the okay.

I'm *not* going to cry.

"Yes, I'm pregnant," I say, blunt and to the point. Always

the best way forward. "Yes, Zander's the father. No, we're not together, and we have no plans to change that, praise the fire goddess. And no, I didn't tell anyone until last night, which is when I finally told him."

I can't bring myself to mention Zelda right now. That feels... raw. Private.

"You guys...had sex?" Georgie says, hesitating over the last word, which makes me wonder if she's ever had sex herself. The fact that she currently has a boyfriend suggests yes, but Georgie has always been tighter with Emerson than me or Rebekah. She could live whole lives I know nothing about. Not that I've ever heard of Historians doing anything but burying themselves in books. "Like...recently?"

I gaze back at her. "Are you expecting me to say that, actually, we conjured a demon baby out of the confluence?"

"Not funny," Emerson says with a curve of her mouth from where she's leaning against the wall, and maybe she's right. Demon babies, once a reliable source of gags around these parts where demons are little more than a punch line, feel a little too possible these days. Just like everything else this long, strange year.

But I'm here to give them facts, not feelings. "Yes. We had sex. On Beltane."

Emerson frowns at me. "You were sick! We took you back to Wilde House. Jacob told you to rest."

She looks at Rebekah, as if for confirmation, but Rebekah only stretches. A little too smugly, wordlessly reminding us all that Beltane was the night she and Frost first got together. "I came later," she says, intimate things like a current of laughter in her voice. "You were better."

"I was sick at prom." As I had been off and on last spring, which is the reason it took me so long to accept that there was something else going on. Well. *One* of the reasons. I take a sip of my tea. "Then Jacob helped me feel better. So later..."

It's ingrained in me to keep this to myself, but what does it matter now? Next Beltane is going to be different, what with a *baby*. It's not a dirty secret anymore because it's over.

Everything has changed.

I can't possibly mourn the end of my dirtiest secret...except I think I do.

"Zander and I have an arrangement," I say, and then sit back, because there. I answered them.

The four of us stare at each other. The sunlight seems to fill the room. I start to think, idly, about work things. Like my new herbal concoctions that I'm planning to bring out for autumn, positively bursting with fall vibes, harvest charm—and magic.

"Are you going to *explain* this arrangement?" Rebekah asks, shaking her head at me, when the silence drags out.

I clear my throat. "Beltane has been a sort of get-out-of-jail-free card for us. If we want to get a little naked, on Beltane and only on Beltane, we do."

Again, a too-long silence. It's clear I'm not the only one who wishes I didn't use the word *naked* at this hour.

"Any Beltane? Not just this last one?" Georgie asks, looking like she's trying to find a way to access the rationale behind this. Bless her.

Emerson looks as if she has images in her head she would rather not. Rebekah just looks speculative.

"Yes. Any Beltane we like." All the Beltanes since we broke up, actually, but who's counting?

Emerson considers me. "Then you wake up the next morning and get right back to hating each other for the other three hundred and sixty-four days out of the year?"

"Just because people have sex doesn't mean they don't hate each other." I have to say it like that. *People.* Because I don't hate Zander, even when I want to.

"It's called hate sex, Em," Rebekah says in that languid way she has, designed to needle her older sister as only she can. "You should try it."

Emerson rolls her eyes.

I can tell my friends don't understand. I expected that from Emerson and Georgie, because they've always been more private and possibly *choosy* when it comes to sex. Assuming Georgie even has sex. But I expected something from Rebekah. She went out and lived an entire non–St. Cyprian life for ten years. She used to send me hilarious morning-after texts, with details.

"I don't know why you didn't tell me," she finally says.

I could feel guilty about that, but why bother with guilt when I can be mad instead? "We both had our secrets, I guess."

She laughs. "I'm not sure my psychotic teenage attempt to raze the town of St. Cyprian with the literal flames of my fury is the same as you banging your ex, my *cousin*, on the downlow, Ellowyn."

What I would like to burn to ash here and now is this conversation and the fact that I have to have it. What I would like to *say* is that it was nothing, but I don't bother to try. I know those words won't come.

"Four months," Emerson says. "And you haven't told *anyone*? Please tell me you got the necessary checkups, though?"

I can see a rant brewing on her face, likely about women's health care and access thereto.

"I went to a doctor." Then, as she frowns, I clarify. "A human doctor."

The expressions on my friends' faces are really something then. Like they're disappointed in me.

The surge of indignation feels cleansing. "I *am* partly human. So is this baby."

"Barely," Rebekah says as she pushes herself off the bed.

"You and the baby are also partly witch," Georgie says, reaching out and giving my arm a squeeze.

"*Mostly* witch," Rebekah throws at me. "You are both *mostly* witch, no matter what mean kids said while being mean, the way kids are, a million years ago."

"It wasn't only kids, Rebekah," I tell her, and it feels a lot like ripping off a scab, the pleasure and pain of being able to say it out loud. Not only because it's true, but because it makes Rebekah the unshameable look slightly abashed.

Georgie squeezes my arm again, but this time it feels reproving. "No matter how *much* witch, you *are* a witch and so is your baby, and that means you should see a Healer as well."

I've been telling myself Jacob would sense if something was wrong, but that isn't the same as having a full workup, I guess. "Our Healer said everything was fine last night."

"That was about the attack, not the *pregnancy*," Emerson says with great authority. "We need to make sure everything is okay. That you're eating right and taking the right supplements."

"Emerson." I stare at her. "I am literally an herbalist. I make medicines and sell them as teas to witches and humans alike. When it comes to supplements, I am covered."

"We need books," Emerson says to Georgie, ignoring me. "We need to plan and prepare."

Georgie nods, waves her hand, and a stack of books appears on my bedside table, towering so high that it would topple over if another stack didn't appear beside it. As if *books* will solve this problem.

"I'll see a Healer," I say, and manage to make it sound as if I've been planning an appointment since conception. "Obviously. Not Jacob though."

Emerson frowns at me. "Jacob is the best Healer—"

"I know how good he is," I say, laughing. "I've known him since we were kids, Em. How are we going to sit around talking about what toppings to put on our next pizza order from Redbrick after he's all up in my *womb*?"

Everyone flinches at the phrase *up in my womb*, as I hoped they would. A girl's got to make her fun somewhere.

"We'll make an appointment with Jacob's mother or one of his sisters," Emerson says after a moment.

It's a concession, but what I focus on is the *we*. That this isn't a *me* thing any longer. It isn't even just a me and Zander thing.

This is how Emerson would be about it even if her magic memory was still wiped and there was no unwinnable ascension looming. She'd have action items and books on her nightstand. She and Georgie would research the best baby items, Rebekah would insist on going to every appointment with me, and they'd probably fight over who gets be my birth partner or whatever else I might need. It's just who they are.

My family, whether I like it or not, no blood required. Taking care of me and my baby because of love.

Not coven duty.

I could tell them what I told my mom last night—that I should bow out of all of this since I'm only ever going to hold them back—but I don't want to see *their* looks of disappointment.

"I'm hungry," I announce. Because I am and also because I know it will spur Emerson into action.

It does. She marches for the door. "We'll have our ascension meeting over breakfast. Then we'll get you an appointment with the best Healer around who isn't Jacob." She looks at her watch. "I'm glad it's Monday and our shops aren't open today, because we're going to need to work out a schedule. No one should be alone until we get to the bottom of this attack. And counter it."

She's already out the door and halfway down the hall, mostly talking to herself as Georgie follows. Rebekah doesn't move. She gives me a *look*.

"Did you want an apology?" I ask. Defensively.

"Do you want to give me one?" Rebekah returns with an arched brow.

I do, but that feels a lot like a slippery slope, and there are too many of those around these days. I say nothing.

She shrugs in that languid way of hers that I know is calculated to be annoying.

It works.

"Then that's that, I guess." She doesn't seem particularly mad as she leaves my room. She's not pissed at me the way she seemed last night. We're not *fighting*.

But there's a rift all the same, and I don't know how to mend it. Or maybe I don't *want* to mend it because that would require acknowledging my feelings. *Feeling* my feelings.

I'll pass.

Before I follow everyone downstairs, I throw on a glamour, but not to mask the pregnancy. That ship has well and truly sailed. Just enough so I'm dressed nicely—by that I mean layers of black—and looking well-rested whether I feel it or not.

With the gleam I wish I'd been sporting last night and my knife on my hip.

I regret it immediately when I walk out into the hall and see Zander—or, you know. Maybe I don't regret it at all.

His expression, already kind of stern, goes entirely grim at the sight of me, but he doesn't slow down or change course. He's clearly on a mission. To see me, I have to assume, since when he crashes here he usually does it on the couch in the study downstairs that is *supposed* to stand untouched unless his uncle is here to use it.

"We need to talk," he tells me as he draws close.

It's annoying that *he* clearly didn't bother with any sort of glamour, because he never does. He looks grumpy and moody, rumpled and *good*.

"Yeah, but ascension meetings and Emerson's timetables." I wave a hand toward the stairs as if these things are set in stone, impossible to rearrange.

They're Emerson's plans, so that's not *entirely* untrue.

I go to move around him, but he stops me. Just by stepping in front of me. I skewer him with a look, tempted to spark some magic at him that might throw him down the length of the hallway, but that would be rude.

And would result in feelings I am *avoiding*.

"Ellowyn," he says. Quietly. *Shit.* "You have to deal with me at some point."

"I…" A million excuses dance on my tongue, but I know I can't get any of them out of my mouth.

If I could curse the damn curse, I would.

"After," I mutter, focusing on a point near his eyebrow.

Because I can't deal with real Zander. Not yet. Not today. Not with Rebekah not-exactly-mad at me and the plans Emerson wants to make for the coming ascension that *she* thinks we'll win and a baby everyone now knows is coming. I feel as if all my edges have gone soft, and I hate it.

Edge-free Ellowyn is nobody I want to meet. Much less *be*. That's got disaster and disappointment written all over it.

"Zander," I say, and I hate that there's even the faintest bit of *pleading* in my voice. I try to make it firmer. I'm so busy doing that, I accidentally look him full in the eyes, all thunder and hard rain and too many other things I don't want to see. "We can talk after breakfast. I'm hungry."

That's true. I said it. I also make a vague sort of gesture toward my belly, as if the baby is demanding I feed it immediately or risk…something. Which is not true.

Given my unsolicited and unwanted relationship with the truth, I usually take it as a win when I get away with stretching it.

Today I just feel like a jerk, because Zander steps out of my way immediately, looking alarmed and concerned and *cute* and… I can't start thinking of him as *cute*. That's a surefire way to sand off all my trademark edges entirely, and I can't let it happen.

I feel a little too shaken—and maybe a little ashamed of myself—as we head downstairs. Maybe that's why it feels like the unsettling dragon-shaped newel post at the foot of the stairs is glaring at me as I pass it.

I know the dragon has a name. Azrael. That doesn't make me feel any better about his gleaming onyx eyes. I murmur a protection spell as we make our way into the big, cozy kitchen.

Emerson and Jacob and Georgie are whipping up a huge breakfast spread, clearly trying to outdo each other as they magic their favorite dishes into place until it looks like the table might collapse under the weight of all those sweet carbs and bacon. Rebekah and Frost are sharing a chair and a coffee mug, clearly having one of their private, silent discussions that I assume must be about the things they get up to in bed, which, mercifully, she no longer shares with me. He looks entertained, something he really only does when he's around her. She just looks…happy, even with everything we have to face.

I tell myself happiness is for other people, and Rebekah certainly deserves hers. Some of us don't get that gift, and that's okay. Here we are, showing up anyway, because that's what matters in the end. What you *do*, not how you feel while you're doing it.

We gather around the table. Rebekah takes her own seat and starts passing the plates around. Emerson starts us off by asking Zander to recount what happened from the moment he got home until the moment we got to Wilde House last night.

Zander's explanation matches mine almost exactly, except I add a few digs into the whole protective bubble situation and what I think of his bullshit, and with every word I feel more like myself and less like that…soft thing upstairs.

I decide I might make it through this pregnancy after all.

Zander stabs a sausage link with his fork. "It's the Joywood. It has to be."

"It doesn't *have* to be," Frost says mildly. "There's no shortage of evil."

That puts a decided pall on the conversation, but not for

long, because Emerson won't be deterred. "The most reasonable conclusion is that it is Joywood and ascension-related," she
says. Decisively, as always, and the thing about Emerson is that
she's usually right. "So we'll continue with that theory until
we can figure out what and why, or learn something new that
changes the conclusion. We need to be careful. I want to keep
everyone close. We'll stay here as long as we have to, and no
one goes anywhere alone."

That doesn't go over well.

"I have a ferry and a bar to run," Zander says gruffly. "Dad
wants to pitch in, but he's not up to it all the time, and I'm not
going to push him on that. We've got Finn helping, but he's
still new."

I think of Zelda sitting on my bed last night. Of the look
on her face. My throat feels so tight that I don't dare try to eat
anything else, in case I choke.

"Rebekah can work anywhere," Emerson says, very calmly,
nodding at her sister, who nods back. "Frost has no job other
than to research with Georgie."

"Some," Frost says repressively, "consider that sort of research the only job."

"Yes, Nicholas," Rebekah murmurs, and pats his arm.
"You're very important."

"Jacob goes all over the place to heal witches in need, but he
can also transport them here if necessary." Emerson exchanges
a look with Jacob, who smiles, a fond look in his eyes that feels
too intimate to share with a whole tableful of friends and family. It also indicates they've already worked this out. Emerson
turns to me. "The bookstore and the tea shop are closed today,
so Ellowyn and I are available to make sure no one with outside responsibilities is alone."

"It didn't attack when Zander was alone," Rebekah points
out. "What's moving in pairs going to do?"

"Help," Emerson says as if she predicted that question. She

probably did. "Ellowyn said it herself. Zander noticed the shadow a second or two before she did, and that second or two made all the difference."

"Because I put a safety spell on you," Zander mutters to me.

I wish I had a ready comeback for that, but I've had a night's sleep, and I have to admit that it's true. He protected me. And because he did, I had the presence of mind to reach out for our friends so we could all fight off the attack. Together.

Maybe I don't want to wander around St. Cyprian in pairs, but it seems obvious that it's the safer option, and we have to be safe. For the baby if nothing else.

No one said I had to like it. I feel like that's a parenting lesson right there.

"The next order of business is almost as pressing. We're running out of time to find our sponsors," Emerson says, and everyone groans a little and shifts in their seats.

Because everything in the witching world can't be fun magic and flying. There are always rules and steps and hoops to jump through. That's what spells *are*. That's what has to happen if we want to continue to keep our existence hidden from humans, who have a tendency to revert to torches in the night and unpleasant witch hunts.

The steps in this case are murky, but the first step to having an actual ascension—instead of the sort we usually have, which involves the Joywood having a party on Samhain and no one remembering when we last chose them—is clear. It was us announcing our decision to go against them in the first place. We did that at Litha.

Despite all the crap the Joywood threw at us to stop us.

Authentic ascension proceedings are shrouded in mystery, given that Frost isn't the only one who can't seem to remember how they're supposed to go. He told the entire town that's because the Joywood seized power and have no intention of relinquishing it. That they're making a bid for the kind of immortality he once had, that even the youngest witch learns early on only happens when you're more bad witch than good.

But they still have control, and they're ridiculously good at convincing people we're liars.

Regardless, we have started the ascension proceedings. According to Georgie and Frost's research, the next step is to produce sponsors. The sponsors must be a magical witch couple—both descended from a founding family—who are prepared to vouch for the new coven. The Joywood, as the sitting ruling coven, are presumed to have already produced sponsors at some point in the past that no Summoner I know can pull up.

Calling it dodgy is an understatement.

The sponsoring couple is required to stand up at the Mabon town hall meeting and give a sort of vocal letter of recommendation. This recommendation needs to act as proof to the wider community that said coven is worthy of taking part in any ascension proceedings.

"Our father continues to flat-out refuse," Emerson mutters, clearly irritated she can't solve the problem that is Desmond Wilde. "He and Mom are deliberately not engaging with the discussion every time they come home from one of their diplomatic trips."

"Which you'll notice they've done exactly once since Litha," Rebekah says. "When Mom memorably told Dad to shut up."

She and Emerson share a smile at that happy recollection, but then Emerson moves on. "Georgie?"

Georgie shakes her head. "Every time I try to broach the subject, I get a lecture about danger and shame and the usual Historian thing. *Pendells don't stick their necks out. A Pendell is for history, the present is for others.* Blah blah blah."

"I don't see why these sponsors have to be a married couple," I say, mostly thinking out loud. It's a strange, antiquated, *irritating* rule. Because if we only needed *one* person, Emerson and Rebekah's mother would do it, but it doesn't count without

Desmond agreeing to sponsor us as well. Zander's father would do it, regardless of how he's doing, but can't without Zelda. My mother would obviously be first in line, but she and Mina have never married, Tanith being a little wedding-shy after my dad. Healers not directly involved have to remain exempt from any hint of politics, which leaves Jacob's parents out. It leaves us searching farther afield and failing. "The whole thing is archaic."

"The Joywood are that," Frost agrees, sounding very nearly merry. For him. "They quite enjoy being so. It certainly makes it harder for you, doesn't it?"

"*Us*," Rebekah reminds him gently.

"You got any bright ideas?" Zander asks. Demands.

Frost has saved us. He's fought with us. He *is* one of us, but there is still some…distrust from some quarters of the coven. The male quarters, mostly.

Because you have to engage in some shady shit to be immortal in the first place.

He studies me, and when he inclines his head, I go a little cold. "There are no rules about the sponsors being *living*."

Since the dead are my territory, I have a bad idea where this is heading.

"*Ghost* sponsors?" Emerson cries as though we have solved all the world's problems here and now. I'm surprised she doesn't fist pump with glee, given her historic love of a good fist pump. "Why didn't you suggest that before?"

"It's not a foolproof plan," Frost replies. "For a great many reasons. But if *we*—" and I catch his sideways glance at Rebekah, who looks proud "—can pull it off with the right spirits who can fulfill the duties required of them, the Joywood can't legitimately mount an argument. Not in front of people they need on their side come ascension time."

Georgie looks the way she always looks when the prospect of piles of books and long days lost in libraries is dangled before her. Delighted. "All we need to do is look through history, find some targets, and then summon them."

Summon two ghosts to act as sponsors for us. "Who are we going to bring in to do that?" I ask, knowing full well this question will be met with disappointment. In me.

Better now than when I fail to summon a damn thing. Or when I summon *everything* all at once. Or, like last spring, when I'm rendered nearly catatonic by the *pain* of it all. I have power, Hecate knows. I passed my pubertatum. I've done my share of a lot of magic.

Control is the issue.

In all things.

Obviously.

"Why do you think you can't?" Rebekah asks, her eyes narrow as she studies me. "Because of the pregnancy?"

I want to say yes. I can't. *Damn it.* "Did you know men see fewer colors than women, on average?"

No one is amused or deterred by my favorite evasion tactic.

Emerson is shaking her head at me in a manner that will very likely lead to motivational posters all over my borrowed bedroom the next time I go upstairs. Worse than that, motivational *chats*, starting now. "There have been some bumps in the road, but you've been part of every ritual, every fight. When are you going to trust that you can do this?"

How about never? But how can I say that in the face of Emerson's boundless optimism and endless belief in her friends?

Everyone is looking at me for an answer, so I make a noncommittal sort of noise, meet no one's gaze, and ride it out.

It takes a moment, but Emerson moves on. "So Georgie will do some genealogy legwork. Look into the founding families and a couple who might fit the bill. We've got plenty of options if we include the dead. All sorts of ancestors if we only use ours." She starts counting off the family names. "Wilde. Rivers. Pendell. Frost—"

"I outlived my bloodline," he says. "I am the only Frost left."

"Thank the gods," I mutter, earning me a low laugh from Zander.

I pretend I don't hear him. Just like I pretend it doesn't make me...warm.

"North, but they're all Healers. Have there ever been Norths who were a different designation?"

Jacob shakes his head. "Not since we came to America, to my knowledge, but I can ask around to make sure."

If you think it sounds like the deck is stacked against us, you'd be right. Yet no one else seems to be as worried about that as I am.

"We can also look at the ancestors of various Joywood members," Rebekah offers. When she gets a few looks for that suggestion, including from me, she crosses her arms. "Just because they're evil doesn't mean they came from evil. People aren't all one thing."

There's a pause.

"Oh, and the Goods!" Georgie adds.

I smirk. "Come on. No one views Goods as founding anything." We might have been here from the beginning, but mostly we were here causing trouble.

"Your family was one of the original families," Emerson insists. "That's just a fact."

"Mercy Good was the scarlet letter who tagged along with that convoy from the Massachusetts Bay Colony," I remind them. "The Good name has managed to be a harbinger for all sorts of scandal ever since she decided that while the settlers here were laying down protective bricks, she'd be better off opening a bordello."

Something my friends should remember from school. Not from classes, but from the way that history was tossed in my face by the likes of Skip Simon, Carol Simon's son who was once the mayor and now…went away, I think vaguely. That kid was always such a weasel.

"It doesn't matter." Emerson says that with finality, as if she can make centuries of a bad reputation disappear with a wave of her hand, like the breakfast dishes. "A Good was with the original group that settled St. Cyprian. So, they count. The sponsorship rules that we've found and that Frost remembers only say it has to be a married couple made up of descendants of *any* two of the founding members of St. Cyprian. *Any* descendants from that group count. We just need to find married ones who might be on our side, then summon them here. Easy."

"Twice," Zander says. Everyone looks over at him in confusion.

Except me. Because I know what he means.

Maybe that's my real curse.

"Twice?" Emerson echoes.

"We'll have to summon them twice," Zander says, too quietly for my taste. He does not look at me while he says it. "Once to explain and get them to consent, and then once again to stand in front of the town hall so they can give their sponsorship speech."

I don't want to do it. But I don't want *him* questioning whether or not I can.

"So we'll do it twice, then," I say as if I have the same confidence in me everyone else pretends they do. "You've just got to find the ghosts first."

And I can't lie, but I know how to keep my mouth shut. So that's what I do, instead of saying what I'm thinking:

I hope like hell you don't.

6

THERE'S MUCH EXCITED TALKING ABOUT FAM-
ily histories and available ghosts at one end of the table. The Emerson and Georgie end, with Frost offering dry commentary on
their different ancestors. That he met. In person.

Zander mutters something about ferry schedules and heads
outside, rolling his eyes when Emerson reminds him to stay in
the yard.

"Yeah, yeah, yeah," he growls, then lets the kitchen door slam
behind him.

Rebekah sits across from me, not even pretending to pay attention to her boyfriend's tales of ye olde forebears and the many
tankards of ale he hoisted with them all, when not battling
them around this or that ritual fire. She is too busy eyeing me.

"Just say what you want to say," I tell her, in as measured a
tone as I can manage.

"You were afraid," she says, very deliberately, her dark eyes
on mine. "You were afraid to tell me. Do you want me to tell
you why?"

"I absolutely do not."

She folds her arms. "Because you know what I'll say."

Rebekah has always been a Diviner, even when the Joywood claimed she had no power. And back in our senior year, between Beltane when Zander broke up with me and Litha when everything changed and we lost Emerson and Rebekah for ten years—in one way or another—she had a vision.

I don't like to talk about it.

"The future is never set in stone," I say now, the way I always do. "You know that as well as anyone."

She doesn't deny that. And I refuse to engage with that vision of hers when it's been haunting me for a decade already. *Destiny dances like flames*, she'd told me. *Though you will call it a lie.*

Thanks, Rebekah, I'd said, heartbroken and furious and still clinging to every word she said like she could lead me through the dark woods of it all. *I can't lie. So there's that.*

Love is the only lie you tell, but it will claim you in the end, she said. *It already has.*

We stare at each other across the kitchen table in the same house where she told me these words, upstairs in her old bedroom with her stained glass window letting the moonlight in but turning it red and green and gold.

Where I made her promise to never, ever speak of it again.

"You're afraid," Rebekah says again, softly, and it sounds like prophecy.

Come outside.

Ruth's voice in my head is a reprieve, and I am not too proud to take it.

Especially when Georgie, who's conjured up her usual pile of books, starts talking about some Rivers connected to a Good, of all things, and I am *delighted* to remove myself.

"Ruth is calling me," I say, and Rebekah sighs, but she knows I'm not lying. My curse for the win.

I have to keep myself from *running* to get out of there.

Out in the backyard that rolls down to the whispering river, it's bright and sunny. It's thick and hot enough in September to make anyone daydream about a good blizzard, but it will be cold soon enough. The gardens are already looking a little tired, more than ready to settle into their fall slumber.

Ruth and Storm sit together on a branch of one of the tall, ancient cottonwood trees that is littered with Georgie's crystals and ribbons. It's Zander my gaze goes to, like we're magnetized. He's standing in the shade of the old tree, frowning down toward the water.

I have the childish urge to turn and walk back inside, but I don't.

That feels like a victory.

Thanks for the warning, I snipe at Ruth.

She turns her head all the way around to give me a pitying look, then turns it back toward the river, disdain in every feather.

Owl assholery is something to behold.

I don't say anything. I magic one of the soft chairs from the patio to a sunny spot and settle myself into it. Rebekah's cat familiar, Smudge, appears and hops up into my lap, and I stroke her soft black fur. A few moments later, Emerson's dog familiar, Cassie, pads outside and curls up next to Zander's feet.

Protection. Sent from people who care about us.

I point that out to Ruth. *Should you ever feel like doing your actual job.*

The way she hoots at me is the owl version of a middle finger. I almost smile.

"I spent a lot of time last night thinking," Zander says finally.

I focus on the cat in my lap, the sun in my face, the sound of the river in my ears. "Do you want me to applaud?"

"Listen. I'm not telling you what to do. I know how *that* goes, and this is too important to reverse psychology you."

I laugh. "Do you think reverse psychology works on me?"

He turns and looks at me, and everything in me…shivers. I know that look. I know it too well. It's Zander in total control, and I normally only see it when we're both naked. "I know it does, Ellowyn. You were all ready to give one of your *my magic isn't reliable* speeches back there in the kitchen—until I even *hinted* that two Summonings might be too hard for you."

I try to tell him I wasn't set to do anything of the kind, but of course I was. So I can't say the words. You'd think that by now I'd be a beacon of truth and never even *try* to lie, since I can't. But I've never done a single thing the easy way, and I don't start now. "It must be so fun to be a man and know everything. What I'm thinking. What I'm feeling. What I was *about* to say even though I didn't."

This is usually the point where he rolls his eyes and storms away. Or where he throws a barb my way and smirks, depending on his mood.

He doesn't do either today, and that shiver works through me again.

Especially when he faces me, crosses his arms over his chest, and says, "Okay, say you weren't."

I blink. *That* response is a throwback to old-school Zander. Literal old-school, high school Zander. Back when we challenged each other. Stood up *to* each other and *for* each other. Back when we didn't let each other get away with our dumb shit.

Because we loved each other and expected to love each other forever.

His storm cloud eyes are trained on mine, the bastard. "Say, 'I, Ellowyn Good, was in no way, shape, or form going to remind everyone who knows and loves me and is part of my coven that I can't do the magic even the Joywood know I can do.'"

I'm too bullheaded for my own good, because I try.

Twice.

And fail, also twice.

Then, because I *can't* say it and because I'm a little too

tempted to punch him, and we know where punching leads, I flip him off instead. "Fuck off, Zander."

He shakes his head. "That's what I thought."

I consider breaking our rule and getting into his head to tell him what I really feel, but he would view that as another victory. I can already hear it. *Is that you coming in hot so you can lie to both of us, Ellowyn? Keep that shit to yourself.*

He lets me sit there awhile, fuming.

"This changes things," he says, in that low, quiet, *too real* way that makes me...hurt. Even though I don't know which *this* he means, specifically. The attack. Ascension.

The baby.

Maybe I don't want to know.

He keeps that brooding gaze on me like if he glances away for even a second, I might disappear, which is fair. I might. "Like Litha ten years ago. Or the moment my mother died. Now this child's existence... Nothing can be the same. Nothing *is* the same. This changes *everything*."

I *hate* the way he says *my mother died*, like every word is a wound. Like there's blood pouring from him with every syllable.

I hate it because there's no fixing it. No one can bandage him up or heal this for him. Some losses are disfiguring, and some grief never fades. Whatever I might like to tell myself about what I do or don't feel for this man, if I could take this pain from him, I would.

"We've got to get our shit together, Ellowyn," he says, like he's laying down the law. Like he's *corralling* me and my apparently untamed, un-together shit.

"*We?*" I scoff at him. "My shit is—"

Just fine, just fine, just fucking fine.

I try so hard to get those words out that I nearly give myself an aneurysm.

His gray eyes gleam with a hard sort of triumph that I tell myself is in no way hot.

"The bottom line, the thing you have to understand above and beyond everything else, is this," he tells me, still not shifting that gaze from mine. "You're not cutting me out. This is my kid too. I'm in it. All of it, from here on out. That means we have to fix our shit."

Like our shit is fixable. "Some breaks are irreparable."

He doesn't even blink, and I've always been pure trash for steely-eyed Zander. "That's bullshit. We've spent the past ten years up in each other's business in an effort to keep Emerson safe. This last year has amped that up, and we've done what we've had to do for the people we love. If we can do that without ripping pieces off each other, we can figure out how to parent the kid we made too. Hear me on this, Ellowyn. We *will* figure it out."

I wish I had his certainty.

"My parents loved each other," he continues, and there's an emotion he's trying so desperately to hide, but I *feel* it. Raw and aching like it's my own, right there in my own chest. "Sure, I saw them fight sometimes, but nothing like what you saw your parents do there at the end. Don't forget that I was around when your dad left. I watched what that kind of nastiness does to a kid."

Not just to any kid. To *me*.

I want to tell him I'm perfectly fine, but I don't bother to try.

"That's not going to be our kid," he tells me, his voice as intense as the way he's looking at me. I want to protest, but I can't, because I'm too busy fighting back a sudden case of allergies from the late summer weather. It has to be allergies, because otherwise it's me trying not to cry. He nods, like he knows that too. "If we have to cast some kind of get-along spell. If we have to wipe our own goddamned memories. We're done being enemies, Ellowyn, whatever it takes. We're parents now."

That word, *parents*, lands on me, bright and hard.

I hate when he lectures me. Because he only does it when he's right and I can't argue. What I *can* do is evade.

I tip my chin up. "The way I see it, we can keep being enemies—as Hecate intended—for about five more months."

"No." He doesn't even stop to consider that. He certainly doesn't laugh. That's party Zander. This is real Zander, and he's always made me a little breathless. I hate it. He looks away then, scowling out toward the river, but if that's my chance to run, I don't take it. "We might not have proof, but I *know* the Joywood had something to do with my mom dying the way she did. They will pay for that. I'll make sure of it."

He turns back to me. "We get along starting now. For our kid, first and foremost. And to fuck the Joywood, because I have to figure they get off on any of us being at odds, and whatever the opposite of that is, I'm all about it."

This time, the things that crowd my mouth are things I *could* say, but don't.

I won't.

Because it would be opening doors we closed for very good reasons.

So I go a different route entirely. I know how he'll react to what I'm about to say, but I can't seem to stop myself. "Everyone's excited about this ghost sponsor thing, but you know as well as I do what happens when I start summoning." I swallow, trying to look very flippant about it. Unbothered, like I don't care that I can't control my magic.

He gazes down at me, and only stubborn pride keeps me from looking away. There's something in his expression, something I haven't seen in a while. A kind of honesty we stopped having with each other. Because it was that or hurt ourselves on it.

"When I say I know you can do it, Ellowyn, it isn't for fun." His voice is hard in a different way now. "It isn't to be nice. That's not exactly our MO, is it? And it sure as hell isn't because you're pregnant with my kid. Protection spells and sending you to Antarctica, far away from this mess, sound a lot better than that. It's because you're a part of this puzzle. Only we can put it together. We wouldn't have gotten this far if it wasn't meant for us."

We. Us. There's been a lot of that. When I wish I could just be a *me.*

Something else I don't dare to try to say out loud, but this time because I'm not sure if I can or not. Maybe I'm afraid I don't *want* to know if I can.

Zander is still looking at me in the same way, like he sees the real me, buried down deep, that only he ever has. "You can do it. And you will. Just like you've been doing since Ostara. Maybe it won't be perfect, but who's expecting that after everything the Joywood has done to us? You're the only one who holds yourself to the impossible standard of perfection."

These are words we don't say. This is…a genuine pep talk from Zander Rivers. Something he would have said to me in high school when I fucked something up because my magic couldn't hold. Not excusing me, not telling me not to worry, but calling me higher. Telling me I had no limits except the ones I put on myself.

I don't want to remember that. I don't want to think back to the time that when we weren't bad for each other, we were pretty good. It doesn't do me any good to remember that.

Of course, telling yourself not to remember something is a surefire way to have nothing but that thing in your head. Then all the other Zander things follow, to the point my face gets a little hot.

There's a little flicker of a moment where I think his mind might be heading down the same path, but he looks away and squints at the river. "I have to get to my shift at the ferry."

I clear my throat. Virtuously, like my thoughts were nothing but pristine. "You're not supposed to go alone."

He doesn't actually laugh, but there's the suggestion of it, thick like the humidity between us. "You offering to be my safety partner, El?"

I am not. Obviously I am not. But it's Monday, so Tea &
No Sympathy is closed, like Emerson pointed out earlier. And
he says it like a challenge—but this time, one I can handle because it doesn't get tangled on my tongue. "Sure. Why not?
You want us to be buddies now, right?"

He laughs, and it's not the bitter one I've grown so accus-
tomed to. It's like an old Zander laugh. Fun. Light.

He immediately sobers, like he noticed the difference too.

"This is better, you know," I tell him. It hurts to say it, but
it hurts worse to keep it to myself.

His expression is wary. "What is?"

"You with your fighting spirit back." He was honest with me
about important things, and this is important too. "You've been
drowning, and that's okay. I figure it's part of it all. I haven't
lost my mother, and I know my dad is still alive so it's not the
same—"

"No. It isn't."

"It's grief." I don't back down at the harsh tone in his voice.
"It's losing the life you once had and thought you would have
for a long time. The foundation you depended on. I think you
have to let yourself drown a little before you swim back to the
surface, because grief never really goes away. But she's here in
spirit. I saw her myself. Her spirit will get stronger as time goes
by, and she'll visit more. She'll meet our baby. I'm not saying it's
the same. I know it's not fair, but she's here for us, Zander, even
if we can't see her."

He looks away, but if he can be the bigger person, so can I.
"There's this article about how grief is a five-year cycle."

He scowls at me, but it's not with that quiet, concentrated
anger that messes with me internally. Just general irritation.
It's almost comforting. "Are you going to pretend you read an
article?"

"Did I say that?" I know I didn't.

"We both know you watched a video somewhere."

Which makes me laugh because he's right. Maybe, just maybe, we *can* do this. This *be parents* thing without ripping each other to shreds.

Maybe, just maybe, we can do this impossible thing *for* this kid, *our* kid, because we know how important that is.

Maybe Zander and I can finally grow up and make it work— maybe not in the way we imagined when we were teenagers, but in a mature, adult fashion that will give the child we made exactly what she or he needs.

For a moment, looking at Zander, and all the familiars around us, and the mighty river in the distance, I believe we can. I believe we actually can.

You know, if we live past ascension.

7

WALKING WITH ZANDER DOWN TO THE FERRY
is a little too much like stepping back in time. You'd think a
Summoner would be all about it, but hard pass. There's nothing
worse than going back to a *happy* place in time that you know
you'll never get to live again.

I could be optimism personified—I could be Emerson Wilde
herself—and I'd know there's no going back to the simplicity of
being fifteen, stupid, and stupid in love with an equally stupid boy.

Emphasis on the stupid.

Walking side by side on Main Street is like walking on broken glass barefoot for me. Because no matter how I try to block
them out, old scenes play out all around me.

Walking down to the bookstore with my mother, not more
than ten years old. Mom bumping into Zelda, who has little
Zander with her. He's the boy who teases me on the playground,
so I stick my tongue out at him from behind my mother's back.
He grins at me, and I can *feel* the same things I felt then. Confused. Embarrassed.

Desperate to do something to make him look at me like that again.

A few more blocks down, teenage Ellowyn and Zander making out in the alley between Confluence Books and the former Joyful Books & More that Maeve Mather tried to use as a way of putting Lillian Wilde out of business.

It didn't work, but I don't feel the usual satisfaction at that old victory, because I see teenage me and Zander, not caring that we might get caught as long as this kiss never ends.

It all cuts deep. Because what I can feel the most in those memories is the wild hope for all those things I know now are never going to happen.

I'm so busy trying to avoid the gauntlet of our past while not letting Zander see what I'm doing that it takes me longer than it should to recognize the new danger that's coming right for us. That being Maeve Mather herself.

Maeve who is, among other things, the Joywood's Summoner. Maeve is also the closest thing to a best friend the Joywood's leader and Warrior, Carol Simon, has ever had. As far as anyone knows. Maeve is also a shocking attention whore who inserts herself into every festival the town puts on if there's a spotlight to hog, one of the most unapologetically and forthrightly mean people in town, and the kind of grown-ass woman who likes to giggle and pout and make like a little girl, which I found nauseating even when I was one myself.

As she charges toward us on the sidewalk, Maeve squints at me, clutching her panda purse to her side. I can *feel* her magic slithering over me. I'm tempted to send out a little *zap* in return to make her jump, but Zander puts his hand on my arm.

No magic needed to zap me when it comes to Zander. Just his big hand, a great, glad warmth that holds me in place like an anchor.

"Maeve," he says in a hearty sort of voice that is perhaps the fakest personality he puts on. "Imagine seeing you here without Carol. I thought you two were joined at the hip." He barks out an obnoxious, frat boy laugh at that.

It isn't him. It's an act. One that threatens to make me laugh myself, rather than contemplate shooting daggers at Maeve. Almost like he knew it would.

Maeve sniffs. "Word on the street is your little group of deviants and outcasts is having a bit of a hard time finding a sponsor."

I smile at her. Fatuously. "What streets are you working these days, Maeve?"

She glares back. "It's a shame your parents couldn't stay married. They'd be just the sort to stick up for your fool's errand. Oh, but your father…" She trails off. Purposefully. Pretending like she forgot for a moment.

She didn't. Not one member of the Joywood would ever forget my father is so resolutely *human*.

"Well," she says, with great satisfaction. "I think we can all agree that your stepmother *is* very pretty. For a human."

I can feel my temper skyrocket, and even knowing that's what she wants doesn't help me claw it back—

"Is it a shame my mother's dead and can't help us out too?" Zander asks.

That stops me and my temper mid-flare. The way he says that. The way it's clearly what she meant to say next.

Maeve gets very huffy and pinched-looking. Her horrible familiar—a blind pigeon with flightless wings that sits in her bag, wearing a diaper and poking its creepy, red-rimmed eyes out—makes a malevolent cooing sound.

"Best watch out," Zander says, sounding something like friendly when I know he would tear Maeve apart with his hands if he could. He's probably imagining something like that right now. Then he nods at the scraggly pigeon. "Storm likes snacks."

Somewhere above us, Storm lets out an affirmative screech.

Maeve clutches the purse closer to her side. "You'll never find a sponsor. Your bid for ascension will be over before it begins."

I let out a laugh at that, almost as hearty as Zander's whole act. "Surely you're not underestimating Emerson, Maeve. We all know how that ends."

"What we know is that she's *over*estimating *you*, Ms. Good." Maeve smiles. Then she begins to walk past me. She says something as she does—and it's quiet and crackling enough that I don't know if she says it aloud in a weird whisper or sends the message *into* me.

You will be their downfall.

I know she's messing with me. That's what the Joywood do. Hit where it hurts, again and again.

Turns out knowing what she's doing doesn't make it hurt any less.

"I don't trust that woman," Zander mutters, frowning after her, clearly unaware of her parting shot.

"Oh really? You aren't going to suggest we name our kid after her?"

I say that to make him laugh, but when he looks back at me, our gazes seem to tangle, and then drop to the belly I tucked away in the usual glamour before we left Wilde House—because telling my friends and mom is one thing, but the greater world where the Joywood walk and breathe is another—and neither one of us is laughing.

We move on instead, making it to the ferry parking lot—a little breathlessly—and he waves at Finn, one of the recent Guardian graduates of St. Cyprian High who voted for us at Litha. He was one of the votes that saved us from the execution the Joywood had planned, so we like him for that alone. We also like him because Finn picking up shifts on the ferry is the only thing that's kept Zander and Zack from keeling over this summer.

Zander pauses before we head onto the low, flat boat. His hand closes over his Rivers pendant—three pieces of metal hanging from the leather chain that he always wears around his neck, except when he gave it to Emerson earlier this year. For protection.

The only other time he's taken it off was when he tried to give it to me that Beltane prom. For protection then, too, but a much different kind. The *setting free* kind of protection.

It feels like stepping on another too-sharp memory.

Clearly for him too, because he says, in a low voice, "I know what happened the last time I tried to give this to you."

"You mean when you were breaking up with me like a coward?"

His mouth firms. He doesn't argue with me or come back with any sucker punch comments of his own. "It's protection, and before you get all wound up, it's about our kid, okay? Are you really going to argue about extra protection for *our kid*, Ellowyn?"

I almost have a vision of a child with his gray eyes and my—

But no. Summoners see the past, not the future.

I'll take anything from him when it comes to protecting this kid. Particularly after last night. Particularly after running into *Maeve* and getting her creepy, sandbagging magic all over me.

I let him drop the pendant over my head. As soon as he does, I feel encased (embraced) in that warm, safe magic I recognize all too well.

Zander's magic. Rivers magic. I shouldn't look at him, but I'm only human.

Well. Half.

His gaze holds mine. Our whole complicated past swirls between us like a ghost. All those old hurts I swore I'd healed throb, like new scars marking me where I stand.

How am I going to do this parenting thing with him when we're a never-healed wound?

I don't ask him that, because that feels like a wound all its own.

"They can't know about this," he says, nodding toward my belly.

I don't argue, which is some kind of record for us. This long in each other's company without arguing or getting naked. Go us.

Instead, I consider what Zander's saying. About protecting

our baby from the Joywood. I think about Maeve Mather and her nasty, twisted little cronies—who I've always known hated me—and what they might do to my kid.

My mother had to get a special dispensation to raise me as a witch instead of letting me flounder about as a human with a few questionable "talents." The Joywood allowed her to do it, but they never let it go. They still haven't.

The current prevailing theory we've discussed in a million coven meetings since Ostara is that they could have exterminated us all at birth—especially Emerson and Rebekah, who came with a prophecy—but that's not the Joywood way. They *like* playing games with the people they consider their prey. We weren't supposed to get powerful enough to actually be a threat.

They'll know about my baby at some point, of course. I don't know what kind of energy hiding a whole pregnancy will take, but my guess is more than I've got. I start to tell Zander this, but stop when an even worse thought occurs to me. "What if they already know?"

He considers this with the kind of horror it's due. His gaze never leaves mine, and all of this feels a little too much like teamwork. The kind we might have engaged in when we were still together.

"Say it," he says.

It's the real test. "The Joywood know I'm pregnant."

Truth.

He sucks in a hard breath.

I'm not done though, because the timing of last night's attack doesn't make sense. Unless we're missing something. Or… "The Joywood *care* that I'm pregnant."

"Fuck," he mutters.

"Why the hell do they care?" I demand.

He shakes his head. "I have no idea, but we'll find out. We'll figure it out and protect this baby."

He's so sure. So…determined.

"Come on," he mutters, and I follow him up onto the ferry.

I stand by the rail as Zander goes to work, but no matter how I turn it over in my head, I can't believe this is really about *me*. It has to be about Zander. I'm just the vessel for a powerful future Guardian and Summoner baby, that's all.

I try not to think about it while I ride back and forth as Zander works his shift. As he flirts with all the women. Makes dad jokes with all the men. That's not new. What is new is when he makes a random kid laugh or gasp in wonder as he points out Storm dive-bombing from above or Ruth waiting serenely in her favorite tree by the ferry terminal.

I try not to imagine him with *our* kid, but I do.

We stop over on the Illinois side of the river to let the waiting cars pull on—but there are only a few now that it's midmorning. I am more familiar with the ferry schedules than someone who isn't a Rivers should be, so I know there will be a lunch rush soon enough. I know the ebb and flow of ferry traffic like a tide.

That annoys me, so when I find my gaze drawn toward the cemetery, I let myself look. It's not unusual for a Summoner. We're all about ghosts. Spirits. The past. All of those things tend to be more potent in the midst of a cemetery, and they always call to who I am, to that witchy thing inside of me.

I see a strange, fractured vision, of a dark world with no green growth fading toward autumn, no famous color-changing redbuds Emerson built an entire festival around, no shining graves— just black and crumbled stone.

I blink it away, because it isn't the past, present, or future. It's likely my anxiety playing tricks on me, but it leaves me feeling cold.

I look around to make sure no one is paying any attention to me. Then I reach up and curl my hand around the pendant, feeling the power and the protection of a Guardian.

My Guardian.

I don't know much about the whole half-witch, three-fourths-witch baby connection, but I give it a shot, talking directly to the little life growing inside of me.

We'll protect you with all we are. The both of us. Always.

Then I whisper it out loud, so I know.

It's the truth.

8

"YOU'RE BEAT." REBEKAH MAKES THIS PRO-
nouncement when she and Jacob tag in at the ferry, Jacob to ride
with Zander and Rebekah to buddy me back to Wilde House.

The necklace around my neck heats, pulses. Protections do
that kind of thing, but I find myself glancing back at the ferry.
Zander is standing at the door of the pilothouse, watching me.
He lifts his hand in a brief wave, then turns back to his job, piloting the ferry across the wide river.

I blow out a breath. Safety buddies. Coparents. *Adults.*

It's been a big twenty-four hours for Zander and me.

If I'm going to be an adult, I might as well let that bleed into
all aspects of my life and deal with my best friend while we
walk back to Wilde House.

"I can't be sorry I didn't tell you," I say as we reach the bricks
and start down Main Street. "I didn't tell *anyone.* Not even my
mother. Because you were right this morning, I was afraid. Not
of reactions, not of…anything to do with any of you. But because if I told anyone, I'd have to deal with it. Face it. I wasn't

ready, and there was nothing I could do to change it. But I *am* sorry that keeping a secret hurt your feelings."

Rebekah studies me for a long minute. "It's not that. Well, it's some of that." She sighs, and throws her hands up for a moment. Frustration, maybe. Drama, maybe. Both. I watch the way her tattoos and rings catch the light, and her piercings too, even though I know they're all glamours these days. "I was here for the breakup aftermath. I was here, and we were going to get out. You and me, together. Then...everything happened. You didn't leave."

"I couldn't leave Emerson."

I can't read the look she gives me then. "I did."

"*You* had to. *I* did not. I couldn't." It seems like so long ago and also like yesterday. "Going with you would have put you at more risk, just as much as leaving Emerson would have made her too easy a target. We all did what we had to do."

"I understand," she says. Then her mouth curves. "Are you saying you...had to *do* Zander?"

I hate absolutes, but it certainly felt like it sometimes. It still does. I can't lie about that, so I shrug. "The point is that I did what I had to to survive, and I didn't particularly like *all* of those things. So I kept them to myself."

She nods at that and we keep walking, finding the same comfortable pace we learned as little kids. At the end of the day, we understand each other. Always have. And will again, even if things feel weird in the moment.

Even if regrets swirl around us like a dust storm just now, threatening to choke us both. *If* she hadn't left. *If* I had. *If* things had been different, but they weren't.

I am too connected to the past—events, past lives, spirits, whole worlds gone and forgotten—to wallow in regret. I might not have a lot of hope for the future, but I know the past can't do anything but sit there. It's not dangerous.

Not unless you give it the power to eat you whole.

"We can't go back," I say matter-of-factly. "You know that as well as I do. You can hate me forever if you want, Rebekah. If you need to."

She rolls her eyes at me. "Who could stay mad at such a beacon of warmth and sweetness?"

"Bite me."

She laughs, and I think…maybe we're okay. Sometimes it's not about how badly you mess up, it's about facing it when it hurts the people you love. That's a lesson I don't want to look too deeply at right now.

So I focus on the way we walk together, like our bodies are extensions of each other's. It feels like coming home. It feels like a relief so great it's almost painful, and I find myself smiling a little as we move.

Though I'd deny it if anyone saw.

Wilde House comes into view. We both study it, and I don't know what she's thinking, but I know that I, personally, never expected to view the pretty, stuffy old house as a kind of coven dorm.

Maybe she's thinking something similar, because she sighs. "Change is hard."

"Who are you telling? *You* don't have to worry about keeping a baby alive in five months."

Rebekah laughs. "You must be kidding. That baby is going to be raised by the biggest committee around. Your mom and Mina. Emerson, Jacob, Nicholas, me. Georgie. The entire Rivers clan. You'll be lucky to have five minutes alone with your sweet little potential demon."

It is an oddly comforting thought for someone who prefers, *needs* alone time. All the places my child will be welcomed, loved, cared for…that's big. These hormones will be the death of me, because I am *not* going to cry.

I hug her instead.

She hugs me back, hard. "I can't believe you're going to have a *baby*," she says into my shoulder.

"You and me both," I reply, and we both laugh.

Though maybe it's a little snuffly too. I suspect we'd both die before admitting it.

The front door opens, and we don't let go of each other, just turn our heads to look. It's Frost.

He stares at us, the disapproval *radiating* off him. Which makes me grin, because I think that's the ancient witch's version of discomfort. "You want a hug too, big guy?" Rebekah teases him.

He gives her one of his rare smiles, then goes back to dark and foreboding when he looks at me again. That's Frost for you. "We've found your ghosts to summon," he intones.

My smile dies. Summoning. Great. That always ends well. "Hope you're ready to get in there and fix what I break."

Frost looks at me for too long. It's all much too *ancient portent* and uncomfortably blue. "My advice would be not to break anything you can't fix yourself, half witch."

Weirdly enough, it doesn't bother me when he calls me that. What bothers me is that he clearly thinks that's a pep talk, when the idea of *not breaking anything* is almost as stressful as knowing I probably will. The bull in the Summoning china shop, that's me.

We walk inside. Georgie and Emerson are hip to hip over a long table they set up in the living room, piled high with old books and elaborate-looking family trees on scrolls held down in the corners to keep the parchment from rolling up.

"You're never going to guess what we found!" Emerson says as we walk in, excitement radiating off her. That usually means she thinks she's found a solution. "Back in 1844, a man named Zachariah Rivers and a woman named Elizabeth Good got married right here in St. Cyprian."

I have never once heard about the Rivers and Good families

comingling, and truth be told, don't want to. That's a little too close for comfort, thank you.

Georgie jumps in, just as excited. "He died under mysterious circumstances. She was accused of his murder but never convicted."

"You want me to summon a murderer to be our sponsor?" Because of course she killed him. Why *wouldn't* she have? It was probably toxic. Wrong. Maybe even cursed.

It's part of the historical record that the Good temper has *always* been something to be reckoned with.

"She was never convicted," Emerson says again, as if that's the same thing as being resoundingly proved innocent. "In those days, for a woman *not* to get convicted of something by the endless parade of patriarchal men in charge of literally everything, I'd say she must have really been innocent."

In my bones, I doubt it. "Do you really think the Joywood will jump on board with your conclusions there, Em?"

"It doesn't matter," Frost says, standing over by the fireplace with his arms crossed. "The rules are the rules. There's no morality clause on the sponsors. The Joywood don't have a say in this. That's why it's a town hall."

"Who were the Joywood's sponsors?"

Everyone's quiet for a moment. Georgie looks pensive, but Frost scowls. "I can't remember. And I should."

He has not taken his inability to access his own memory gaps well.

"It *should* be in the records," Georgie is saying, a note of acidity in her tone. "We know how that goes with the Joywood and all their oh-so-helpful edits of the records. Everywhere." She makes a frustrated noise, because that's been another thing we've learned this summer. We *suspected* the Joywood were altering things as they went, in complete and total violation of all witch laws. Now we know they have. Partly because of what Frost *can* remember, partly because of how good Georgie is at finding things they don't want found. "I'll do some more deep-diving in Frost's library."

It contains ancient texts, banned books, and many other things the Joywood have tried to hide or destroy, but you have to know what you're looking for and then actually *find it* for any of that to matter.

The library has its own mind, Frost told us after Litha, when Georgie and Emerson had demanded a tour. *Best of luck bending it to yours.*

"Once we can get everyone together, we'll do a full Summoning for our sponsors," Emerson tells me in her officious way that, all things considered, feels like pure comfort today. Like everything is as it should be, with Emerson telling us what to do and arranging things so the actual doing involves pizza from Redbrick and her cute little planners that she hands out like candy and updates for everyone when they *accidentally* leave them behind. It feels like home, and that feels good. "We've got less than two weeks to get this sorted out."

Though I'd rather keep what happened with Maeve to myself, I've learned enough since March that I tell everyone about running into her earlier today and what Zander and I figured out thanks to that.

"The Joywood know I'm pregnant. They *care* that I'm pregnant," I say baldly. *For some inconceivable reason*, I add privately.

I don't mention Maeve taking a swipe at me, because it isn't relevant.

So maybe I haven't learned jack shit.

Everyone takes this in. Maeve Mather and her panda bag pigeon, taking time to drip condescension at me when we haven't heard anything from the Joywood in months—but were attacked by something malignant only last night.

"Pregnant witches are powerful," Georgie says thoughtfully while Emerson frowns. Very deeply.

I think back to what my mother said. A pregnant witch is *fearsome*. Not fear*ful*.

I look uneasily at the past laid out on old parchment and leather-bound books that Emerson and Georgie are sure will give us what we need. What if it doesn't? What if I *can't* reach these two people? Even if I do, nothing is guaranteed. No one can predict how ghosts or spirits will respond.

Then I'll have to do it again for the town hall meeting. In front of not just the Joywood, but all St. Cyprian witch citizens who want a say in the ascension—and as we haven't had one of these meetings in my lifetime, I imagine that will be all of them.

Rebekah puts her arm around me. "We've got this," she says quietly.

Like she's certain. Like she's seen the outcome, the way Diviners do, and she *knows*.

What I focus on is the *we*.

Because I'm pretty sure that I, personally, don't *got this* at all.

The next few days are all about planning for the Summoning. We're running out of time, but the timing also has to be perfect. That's Spellwork 101.

For me. For all our various schedules. For the ghosts and spirits we hope to bring into the fold.

The last time I summoned, it worked, sort of, but it also caused me a lot of pain. Hurting is part of the price, but I'm hoping to avoid that. I'd like to do this without hurting myself, or the baby, or anyone else. Something I don't voice, because I don't want any of the rousing *you can do it* speeches that would cause.

Finally, the night in question comes, the moon and the planets in the ideal positions for communication with the other side.

We gather as a coven out back, where Georgie's crystals clink in the cottonwood trees, the river sings its songs as it rolls past, and I notice the evening is cool enough that I can almost feel fall and Samhain coming in. That's how it goes in Missouri.

Summer lies on us, hard, until suddenly one night you shiver and remember that the world really is turning after all.

Georgie and Frost are the ones arranging things according to her research and his memories and experiences. They first create a kind of barrier, so that anyone happening by will think there's no one out here. Just a pretty night in this space between summer and true fall, Lillian Wilde's overgrown gardens, and the little hill that one of the Wilde ancestors once walked down to drown himself one fine morning. No one knows why.

That's the story witches will think of when they pass. Humans will see the lengthening shadows and wonder what lurks there. They'll all keep walking.

Georgie tells the rest of us how to arrange ourselves in the circle she and Frost have prepared. They've already told us what we'll say tonight, so we could spend a day or two learning the specific chants and incantations.

"We've built in a lot of protections," Rebekah says, standing next to me and rubbing my back. It doesn't ease the tension in my shoulders, but it helps to hear.

They should have found someone else, but I can't say that. You can't bring an unknown into your possibly treasonous bid for ascension. I get why I have to be the Summoner in this coven—they trust me.

But I wish they'd chosen someone else for this tonight.

Because though they trust *me*, no one here trusts my *magic*, and they shouldn't.

"We're not going to form our usual circle," Georgie says when the moon rises high above us and casts a silvery light down on the rivers. We all know it's time. "Ellowyn will stand in the center. We need the future at her front and the protector at her back."

Frost is looking over everything with his usual intensity. "The familiars will form a second ring of protection."

I remind myself that in this little space we've created, the Joywood can't reach us. No one can see us or hear us.

I hope.

I stand in the center as I usually do for Summonings. My friends arrange themselves around me. Rebekah faces me. Zander is at my back. The other four form a diamond around us.

Protection.

We are a coven now, so while there is always an order to these things, they have more meaning now. We follow the ancient ways that have governed covens across the centuries. I hold opal and calcite in my hands. The family tree that links Zachariah Rivers to Elizabeth Good is displayed on a little easel in the circle with the daguerreotypes Georgie unearthed of them.

A Summoning is a connection to the past, so we start with the future.

Rebekah lights her candle first, saying the words that are only hers. She is followed by the Healer, the Guardian, and the Warrior. Distinctions made up of the present.

Only then come the Praeceptor, the Historian, and then me.

The center of it all tonight, if there's to be a Summoning.

With the curtain drawn back to let in the other side, the candles lit and our protective animals around us, I begin.

I close my eyes and rest the backs of my hands on my knees. I tilt my head back, opening up to the moon above and the spirit world around me. I know that when I truly connect, my friends won't understand what I say.

I can't explain it. It's just magic.

I open up to it. *"Mother moon. Sister Sky. Open me."*

I feel it. The way that *Summoner* inside of me unfurls itself. It's like my chest being opened, but it doesn't hurt. And I know when I'm no longer closed up tight. When I am ready to receive.

Vulnerable, something whispers. I ignore it. I remember my mother's words. *A pregnant witch isn't fragile… She is powerful. Fearsome. Not fearful.*

I hold on to that. *"By will divine, by the stars above, spirits, I ask for your welcome."*

The wind picks up around me, and I can feel the light of the moon, the stars, the way they wash over me, rush into me. *Welcome me.*

I can feel the magic spiral inside of me, then flow out. Just like it's supposed to, thank Hecate.

I hold on to it and reach—

Into the past, into the ether, into the spirit world.

Now for the complicated part. *"We call on you, blood of my blood, Elizabeth Good,"* I call out so my coven can hear, so they can push their magic into the night.

Then, because Zander is the Rivers descendant, he says the next part. *"We call on you, blood of my blood, Zachariah Rivers."*

It's working. I can feel them take shape even before they're visible, and I'm not even struggling.

I lean into the magic in me and then there they are, standing before me. Two people in period dress, a man and a woman. They look alive and animated now instead of stern, remote daguerreotypes.

I try to stick to the script instead of letting myself get too awed by how easy this all was. Or terrified that it's *too* easy and there's another shoe about to drop.

On me, if history is any guide.

I stick to the words that Georgie and Frost made me learn, so I wouldn't have to cast around into potential dangers now. I can feel both of them looking at me. I can feel them both in the magic we make, reminding me. Encouraging me. Guiding me.

"Elizabeth Good. Zachariah Rivers." I say both their names and incline my head in greeting. "We thank you for answering this call tonight. We are your descendants, and we need your help."

Rebekah conjures up the explanation I put together of what's happened, of what we need. Why it's up to them. We made it a movie that plays in the night air, clearly fascinating our two ancestors. They peer at it, blinking now and then.

But they don't look at each other or acknowledge each other, even though they're both here. I know they can see each other because I've brought them here and they're linked. I can feel it.

Still they ignore each other.

It feels deeply, uncomfortably familiar to me.

"You want us to be sponsors for an ascension," Zachariah says, and I don't miss, even in his ghostly form, how much his eyes look like Zander's eyes. Rivers genetics imprinted on their bones, I guess.

Elizabeth has my mother's violet eyes, but her hair is brown. She's shorter, rounder. It's hard to see any of myself in her. I assume all my dad's human stuff took over to make me, because of course it did.

"Yes, Zachariah," Elizabeth replies. Her voice is acidic. "That is word for word what they have shown us."

It's the first glimpse I get of *me* in her, and I am charmed.

Zachariah gives the impression of sighing heavily without actually doing it, another genetic trait that has apparently been handed down through the ages. "*I* will support you, blood of my blood. Our light in the dark."

The *I* is pointed, and Elizabeth shoots him a narrow glare before she replies too. "I will *always* stand up for what is right. I will support you, blood of my blood. Our imperative hope."

Imperative. Zelda used that word too.

"We will ask for you to stand before us in six days' time, ancestors," I say to them, getting back to the script. "You will come before the gathering and offer your sponsorship, if you so wish to honor us."

They both incline their heads. A ghostly promise.

So easy. So simple.

I begin the chant to release the spirits back to whence they came.

We'll see them again in six days' time.

They'll sponsor us.

We'll start the actual, mysterious ascension process that no one can stop once it starts. Not even a certain evil ruling coven. So say Frost's books.

I might be a little giddy. *Take that, Joywood.*

I'm pulling away from the Summoning confident, happy, even excited. I'm ready to let our ancestors go, pull in my magic, break the circle.

Then something…fractures. It's not painful like that time on Ostara back in March. It's something else. Like holding a little too tightly to spun glass so it shatters. There's nothing dark about it—but there's that shattering all the same.

Yet my coven keeps chanting like they don't feel it.

The Summoning ends. The circle is broken, the familiars called in. My friends are talking excitedly all around me, but I only hear the murmurs of it, like I've got cotton in my ears. I shake my head and try to find my grip in the here and now.

That's when Zander comes into my vision. "Ellowyn?" he says, and he's frowning. Not at me, for a change. He's focused on something behind me.

I look over my shoulder and see that he's looking directly at the ghostly image of Zachariah Rivers. Like he can see him. When it's over and Zachariah shouldn't be here any longer, and neither should the starchy-looking woman who stands off to the right of him, as if she refuses to stand directly *beside* him, which is relatable but—

"Why are they still here?" Zander asks.

"Who?" Rebekah asks, stepping right through the mist that makes up Elizabeth Good. Clearly *she* doesn't see the two ghosts we're left with.

They should have disappeared when I released them.

But they didn't.

Meaning that the Summoning did not go according to plan after all.

Shit.

9

"YOU SEE...BOTH OF THEM?" I ASK ZANDER, not sure I'm processing this.

That I messed it up somehow, I get. I just don't know *how*.

"Of course I do." He looks around at our friends. "You guys don't?"

Emerson shakes her head. "Not *now*. You see them...right now?"

Zander points to Zachariah with one hand and Elizabeth with the other. "Uh, yeah."

The ghosts themselves don't seem too concerned with this turn of events. Granted, they're very purposefully *not* looking at each other...while also very clearly sneaking little glances at each other.

It feels like a mirror I have no interest in peering into.

"I don't understand," Emerson says and turns to Frost, but he shakes his head.

"I've never heard of such a thing, and I certainly don't see any spirits." He turns his gaze from Emerson to Zander, then me. "Are you certain that's what you see?"

"Yes, I am *certain*. The spirits we summoned are right here in front of us." I tell myself that this might be *weird* and *irregular* and *confusing*, but it is definitely better than feeling like death, the way I have after other misadventures in Summoning.

"They look exactly the same as they did in the Summoning." Zander is staring at Zachariah, no doubt noting all those similarities I was picking up earlier. All that *Rivers* might, gray eyes, and power—clear even in spirit.

"Should we make the circle again? Try to send them back?" Emerson asks.

Elizabeth waves a languid, see-through hand. "We're here. We might as well stay until the meeting. Then we'll worry about going back."

I look at Zachariah. He has an unreadable look on his face, but he nods. Curtly.

"They both think they should stick around until the meeting," I inform everyone who can't see and hear them.

"I guess that makes sense. We can conserve our energy." Georgie nods as if this was the plan all along.

"You guys can really just...stay here for six days?" I've never even *heard* of such a thing, so I'm sure I sound as skeptical as I feel.

"You tell us, girl," Zachariah says gruffly. "You are the one who brought us here. Together."

Elizabeth turns her ghostly head in his direction. "You will respect my blood." Then she turns to me. "We'll find out either way," she says, and she sounds perfectly reasonable. She even smiles. Demurely, which is a red flag, us both being scandalous Goods and all. "Nothing to worry over, I should think. We'll handle whatever comes."

"What are you going to *do*?" I ask them both. I try to think of what I would do if I was a spirit hauled back to St. Cyprian long after my death. "Haunt your enemies? Or...their descendants, I guess?"

They both start to look at each other, but seem to catch themselves before it takes. Then they both say the same thing, at the same time. "I will stay with you."

Meaning, their specific descendant.

"Great. How?" Zander looks over at me, widening his eyes.

"We'll simply go where you go, of course," Elizabeth says, giving the impression of looking down at Zander though she's a pretty short ghost even while she's hovering off the ground. "It is late. I'm sure we should all retire. If an ascension is in the offing, we must all be at our best."

I cough, then repeat this for everyone else. Complete with the way Elizabeth looked at Zander while she spoke.

My friends peer around a little helplessly, as if trying to figure out where the ghosts must be standing based on where Zander and I are looking. Or not looking. Even Emerson doesn't seem to know what to say.

For roughly thirty seconds.

Then our fearless leader recollects herself. "She's right. Let's clean up. Get some sleep. Regroup tomorrow."

The ghosts float about the yard as if reacquainting themselves with the trees, the river, and even a Main Street with far more shops and buildings than would have been here in their day. The rest of us gather our things, cleanse what needs cleansing—some magical amulets like a moon bath, some implements like the power of the river, my athame that I used at the start to perform a ceremonial severing of *now* from *then* in the old way likes a chant and a few affirmations—and magic away other items to the places they belong.

Zander stays closer to me than he would normally. I pretend not to notice, but he has a kind of energy around him that I can feel in the dark. He always has. I always know where he is.

I grit my teeth and ignore it until we're a few feet from the ghosts and he leans in closer. Much closer. I hold my breath.

"So this guy is just going to…haunt me?"

I shrug, and pretend my heart isn't going a little wild in my chest. "It looks that way."

"You're the Summoner," he growls at me, though his gaze is on Zachariah. "Why don't you *know*?"

I don't think he's trying to get a dig in that there's something I *should* know but don't. I feel the slight all the same and shove it down deep where I keep all the rest of them, polished and ready to wound.

While I'm trying to come up with a suitably scathing retort, I hear our ghosts talking to one another.

"Wilde House is as pretentious as ever, don't you think?" Zachariah asks, laughing slightly, a rough sort of sound that I tell myself is in *no way* familiar. "I can't imagine why anyone would build something like this."

"Remind me," Elizabeth returns in an arch voice that is also familiar, "what was it you built with your own hands when you were alive, Zachariah?"

Zachariah does that sigh-that's-not-a-sigh thing. Elizabeth pretends not to notice, while making it clear he failed her in any number of ways I don't have to know their story to understand.

Because I already understand. Too well. And I...don't want to be like this.

With every last part of me, I don't want to be doing this same thing with Zander *into the afterlife* the way these two are.

I don't get good and scathing with Zander. I swallow it down. I catch Elizabeth's eye and indicate she should follow me as I walk inside Wilde House. She floats along with me, close enough to the floor that it almost seems like she's walking. We wind our way through the house's main floor, but she pauses at the foot of the stairs and frowns at Azrael, the dragon newel post. Hard.

"Everything okay?" I ask, frowning at the newel post myself. Elizabeth tilts her head one way, then the other, studying the dragon on the post, whose onyx eyes seem to almost…gleam at us. Then she straightens and shakes it off. Visibly.

"Carry on," she tells me, nodding toward the stairs.

I could explain Azrael to her, and what little I know about how and why there is a newel post with a name, but she only gazes back at me. I'm too tired to get into it with a ghost, so I start up the steps, letting her follow.

I lead Elizabeth into my room. I've been around ghosts, spirits, and signs from the other side my whole life. They don't… hang out. The energy required is too much, and I'm not sure what happened to make it so she's just *here*, almost like she's whole and human again. If I don't focus on what I must have done or not done to make this happen, it's fascinating. I've never heard of anyone getting to watch a ghost just *exist* in the world the way we do.

Ghosts: they're just like us.

Elizabeth drifts in, then all around, studying the wallpaper and the view out the window. She takes in every little detail of the guest room before she turns to me, puts her hands on her hips, and says, "Well. Conjure me up a bed, then."

"You're going to sleep? In a bed?"

"I may not be corporeal, but I still need a bed to sleep in, child," she says as if I should know this when *who* could know this? I've never given a single stray thought to the *sleep preferences* of ghosts. "I may have slept on the floor after I was fool enough to marry that man, but I refuse to do that again."

"You two *were* married." I'm surprised she's acknowledging the marriage at all, but I conjure her up a bed all the same. I make it nice and fancy, because it seems like something she'll get a kick out of.

"Briefly. Before he got himself killed." Elizabeth studies the bed in such a way I can't read her reaction.

"Rumor is you killed him."

She gets into the newly conjured bed, in full ghostly dress, and pulls the soft, heavy covers up over her spirit. She doesn't respond to my version of gentle prodding, so I decide to be direct. "Did you kill him, Elizabeth?"

She makes a soft noise beneath the covers that I can't quite identify, then pulls them down to reveal her face and skewers me with a look. "Be careful, child. My sponsorship can always be rescinded." She nods at my stomach then, a pleasant smile on her face but something glinting in her violet eyes. "You wear no wedding band. I assume you've followed in our scandalous ancestress Mercy's inauspicious footsteps."

"That's not quite the burn these days as it might have been in yours." It's still surprisingly effective, no matter how okay I am with being an *unwed mother*.

I kick off my shoes, magic on my pajamas, and crawl into my own bed. I have sat with ghosts, spoken to them, danced with them, and occasionally suggested they leave the mortal coil alone, but I have never had a *sleepover* quite like this. It would probably bother me more than it does, but the idea that Zander is *also* dealing with this profound weirdness when he is a Guardian better used to *river things* puts a smile on my face.

It also has me considering all those similarities I don't want to notice between them and us. I shouldn't let myself wonder. I shouldn't consider anything but how fantastic it's going to be to get some sleep. I can feel exhaustion tugging at me.

I definitely shouldn't ask.

But it's only Elizabeth and me here.

I can't come up with a good enough reason *not* to ask.

"You must have liked him at some point to have married him, right?" I don't know what I'm looking for. I pluck at the quilt on my bed, and when she doesn't answer right away, I dare to look across the room to where she lies so stiffly in hers.

"I loved him," she says at last, with a kind of devastating finality that echoes in me. In ways I do not like. "Through many a ridiculous fool's errand—his specialty. I told him not to go on that trip. I had a premonition it would not go well, but he and his precious *legacy* wouldn't listen."

I want to ask her questions so I can outline all the ways Zander and I *aren't* like Elizabeth and Zachariah, but premonitions are not the purview of Summoners.

"You weren't a Summoner?" I ask Elizabeth.

"What's this?" My ancestress sniffs, clearly offended. "I summoned, of course. My tie with the spirit world was very strong when I was living. That's why we came so readily to you tonight. Don't let Zachariah tell you it was because of his Guardian navigating abilities, because that is *ridiculous.*"

"If you had premonitions, you can't have been a Summoner. You must have been some kind of Diviner instead?"

Elizabeth sits up in her dramatic bed and frowns at me. "I do not understand you."

That makes two of us. I sit up too. "What was your witch designation?" I ask her, aware as I do that my pulse is getting a little crazy. I can feel it in my wrists, my ankles. My baby.

She frowns at me as if I'm quite dim. "Revelare."

"What?" I'm not sure I've ever heard that word in my life.

"A Revelare. Just like you."

I laugh, but mostly in confusion. "I am *barely* a Summoner and I'm definitely not...whatever that word is. Whatever it means."

She shakes her head at me, her frown deepening. "Goods are always Revelares."

"Not this one. Not my mother either. Or Granny Good, I'm sorry to tell you."

She floats up through the covers—yes, *through* them, making me wonder how she was *beneath* them to begin with—then crosses the room to me. She's kind of hovering above my bed, and I thought ghosts couldn't really creep me out, but turns out a sleepover ghost body looming above my bed does the trick.

She's studying me closely, and I can feel her magic. When I

shouldn't. It shouldn't work here, outside the circle and away from the ritual. Nothing is as it should be tonight.

"You have something special," she says after a moment.

Being half human has often led to me being called *special*, but usually with a nasty sniff or an eye roll. Elizabeth sounds proud.

I find I have no place to put that.

"Very special," she says, nodding her head. "I knew there was a reason we stayed."

"What's the reason?" I need to talk to Emerson about this. And Rebekah. Has Georgie heard of a *Revelare*? Surely Frost has.

Elizabeth shakes her head, and she smiles at me. And it's genuinely warm. "Ah, my child. There are so many."

Then she puts her spirit hand on my forehead, and I shouldn't feel it. Not so fully formed, almost like a real hand, but I do.

"Sleep, my children," she whispers. To me and to the baby inside. Like a spell she shouldn't be able to cast in ghostly form.

But that's the last thing I remember before I wake up the next morning.

10

I'M A LITTLE FUZZY WHEN I WAKE UP, LIKE I have some kind of Summoning hangover, which is not unusual.

The face in mine as I open my eyes, however, is.

I *remember* last night enough not to scream bloody murder at the ghost looking down at me, but it's all sort of...jumbled details and panic as my heart tries to jump out of my chest.

"What the hell, Elizabeth?" I manage to get out when it's clear I'm not actually having a cardiac event. I wish I could throw the covers back over my head rather than deal with *ghosts* today.

Or anything else.

"Is this...regular?" she demands, looking affronted for some reason.

I push myself up into sitting position, rubbing my hands over my eyes. "Is *what* regular?"

Elizabeth draws herself up while hovering in midair. "Sleeping all morning? Lazing about?"

I tap the phone on my nightstand, then scowl at her. "It's seven in the morning. My shop doesn't open until ten."

She presses her lips together. "Shop? What kind of shop?"

It's clear I won't be falling back asleep. "I sell tea."

"Tea," she repeats wonderingly, as if this is her first inkling of any real magic around here. "Do you make remedies?"

"Remedies. Potions. And sometimes just tea." I shrug, thinking of my holiday blends and novelty blends, like my perennial bestseller, Drink to Pretend You're Single—always a hit with the wine o'clock ladies. "Whatever sells."

She makes a noise, and I don't know her well enough to characterize it, but it's not disapproval. It's also not that sharpness that reminds me too much of myself. It's softer.

"I had dreams of a shop like that," she says. "Remedies for maladies of all types. I thought it was for me, but perhaps it was for you."

That doesn't make much sense since I'm not her direct descendant. But it warms me all the same. "You never tried to open one? There were all kinds of shops here back in the day."

I know this because I've been lectured extensively on this subject by none other than Emerson Wilde. Including the history of *my* building, which was first a blacksmith, then a haberdashery, then a millinery—which pleases me, as I like to think of those hat shop ladies reclaiming the building from all that *maleness*. I'm the first tea shop though, as far as I know.

Elizabeth fiddles with her dress and retreats until she appears as if she's perched on the side of my bed. "Oh, no. My father wouldn't hear of it. His unwed daughter in trade while he drew breath? Certainly not. Then I married Zachariah, without a penny to his name. My parents weren't about to help me finance a silly dream after I'd lowered myself so far, and against their wishes, not even after he died."

"A *Good* considered marrying a *Rivers*...lowering?"

Elizabeth gets a strange look on her face then. "Zachariah was very...odd. My parents were quite determined to turn around the Good name and reputation. Though it doesn't appear to have worked."

No, but what interests me is any member of the Rivers clan *so strange* that he was considered *beneath* the historically and currently problematic Good family. "How was he odd?"

"He had delusions of grandeur, I suppose." Elizabeth presses her lips together as if she wants to say more but is holding herself back. "He had this little group of fellows who thought they had uncovered a great mystery of epic proportions, but it was little more than a fairy tale."

Sounds a lot like us trying for ascension, I think to myself. Except the Joywood being evil is no fairy tale.

That's a reality that I don't really want to think about, but look at that, here comes all the anxiety that accompanies thoughts of the Joywood anyway. I decide I might as well get up to face the onslaught.

I wave Elizabeth away so I can get out of bed without climbing through her ghostly form—it feels rude—but as I do, I remember our conversation from last night. "What was that term you used? For your witch designation?"

She looks taken aback again, but in a way that makes me think she's more comfortable with that than those softer reminiscences. That feels a little too familiar. "Revelare." She sounds it out as if I'm dim. "Honestly, are all the witches in these times so ignorant?"

I want to say *yes*, mostly to annoy her, but if it's true that we're all ignorant, I don't want to prove it by saying so. I need to speak to Georgie. Frost. Emerson. Everyone?

But today I'm babysitting a ghost.

I do mean *babysitting*. Elizabeth follows me *everywhere*. She talks at me constantly, following me around the room, down the hall, and even into the bathroom when I decide I'm going to hide out there with my phone. There's no escaping her. If she's not asking a million questions about faucets and light switches, she's complaining about Zachariah, or casting aspersions on the waste and luxury of the modern world.

After at least an hour of this, I feel like I'm about to *implode*.

"Okay," I say briskly, cutting off a soliloquy about purchasing unnecessary items, brought to me by her floating out through the window to see the signs of the shops along Main Street— none of them the butcher or farrier or baker she recalls. "I need some privacy. I'm going upstairs, alone. You can stay here. Or you can go downstairs and haunt someone else—just so long as it's not me."

She's quiet for a moment, but then gives me a demure smile that I can see very well is fake. "If you insist on being ill-mannered, Ellowyn, I cannot stop you."

I actually feel bad—but not bad enough to take back what I said.

I go upstairs and use Georgie's bathroom to enjoy a very long shower, uninterrupted by spectral asides, thank the elements. I magic myself a selection of different outfits, because that takes even more time, and I'm thinking I'll have my tea in Georgie's room—where she is probably communing with her crystals, hopefully quietly—but as I start down the hall, I hear Elizabeth calling me from the stairway.

I look right, then left. Georgie's rooms are down in the turret end, but across from the bathroom up here is a linen closet.

No one, not even a ghost, is going to find me in the third-floor linen closet. *Please Hecate.*

I magic myself inside without even blinking—

And slam into a warm body.

"Ouch," comes Zander's low voice.

But I already knew it was him.

I would know him anywhere—even the dark depths of a linen closet I don't think a soul has used in decades. Not even the local spiders.

"What are you doing in here?" I demand in a whisper, trying to back away, but there's nowhere to go. It's not the tiniest closet in the world, but then Zander isn't the tiniest man either.

In fact, he's big everywhere, like the jock he was in high school—playing every game he could, simply because he could, and, naturally, was good at them at all. I can confirm that that particular athletic body type is not a glamour. Not on him.

Focus, I order myself.

"I'm guessing I'm doing the same thing you are," Zander whispers back, though even his whisper has that growl in it. "If Zachariah wasn't already dead, I'd kill him." I can't see Zander in the dark of the closet, but I can *feel* him. Heat and strength and Zander, everywhere. "All he talks about is hunting for crows. *Crows*, Ellowyn, since four thirty in the damn morning. On a day I foolishly believed I might actually get to sleep in a little, for a change."

"At least you don't have Elizabeth asking you questions about how every modern convenience works, like I have any idea, and then telling me how they did it better with less convenience and more good old-fashioned grit back in her day. When she's not doing that, she's…"

I trail off, because, belatedly, I realize I'm talking to him like we're friends.

"Let me guess, bitching about Zachariah the way he's bitching about her."

"Constantly."

"It's really fucking annoying."

It is. But. "I guess we should apologize to our friends for the last decade."

He laughs. "We aren't *that* bad."

He can't see me in the dark of the closet, so the way I roll my eyes is lost on him.

"We *aren't*," he insists when I say nothing.

"I'll be sure to take a poll later."

Because I think we have been *that bad*, actually, as uncomfortable as that is to accept when I'm watching another Good and Rivers couple act out their feelings and not liking what I see.

This seems like a really bad place to get into all that *us* stuff. Dark. Close.

Dangerous.

Especially when we agreed to get along with each other only yesterday.

Something we've never managed to do. Not even when we were together, if I'm being honest.

I clear my throat and cast around—maybe a little desperately— for something else to talk about. "Here's a weird thing, though. Elizabeth acted like they didn't have Summoners or Diviners in her day. She said she was a *Revelare*. That she summoned *and* had premonitions."

There's a pause, like he's thinking. When he finally says something, it's, "Huh."

"Huh, indeed." The silence draws out between us, but all I can feel is the heat of him, even though we're not touching. Because of course we're not touching. I estimate there's at least two inches between our bodies—and maybe more, given how I'm pressing myself back into the dusty shelves behind me. It's that awful, life-ruining chemistry forever arcing between us, closing the space, making me tell myself lies like *this time* it will be *just fine* if I *lean in and*— I cough again. "Well, Georgie will know. Or Frost. I need to go find them."

He sounds gruff when he speaks, so I know he feels what I do. "So go."

"You first."

My eyes haven't adjusted, but I can still practically see the way he lounges back against his own dusty shelves, like he plans to move in here for the duration. "I don't need to go find any-one. I plan to stay here until my afternoon shift at the ferry or until Zachariah finds me."

This sounds like a better plan, all things being equal, but if I stay here…here we are.

Zander and me.

In a dark closet.

With too much body heat and electricity and magic straining toward each other because that's what happens when we're alone and too close. Something inside of us is wired to make the same very, very, *very* bad decisions.

Case in point, our impending parenthood.

"It isn't Beltane," he says, low and *hot*.

It's the thing we say to each other. It's not a warning, though. Not when *he* says it.

It's an invitation to break our agreement.

I always say no. I take pleasure in saying it. In waiting until the last possible moment to say it, even.

Because I always put so much stock in our agreement. So certain it would save me, and yet here I am anyway. Pregnant with our child and decidedly *unsaved*.

What could be the harm? I ask myself when I know that even asking the question is the harm right there. Or maybe the harm is in how I didn't magic myself right back out of this closet when I found it occupied.

We'll never know because it's dark, and maybe it's so dark it doesn't even count that I'm the one who leans in and—

"There you are!" comes the voice I least want to hear, along with a shock of light, beaming in from the hall outside.

I nearly scream.

I tell myself this humiliation almost occurs because I'm startled. Not because I'm frustrated to be caught about to kiss my ex-boyfriend and current baby daddy—a term I realize I need to start using as much as possible to horrify all our friends.

First I have Elizabeth's ghostly head to contend with, poking through the door from the hall and letting the light in with her.

"What are you doing?" she demands, looking back and forth between the two of us like she already knows.

Maybe we all know.

In which case, there's no need to litigate it now.

I push open the door and leave without looking back. I figure Zander understands because he's the one who closes the door behind me—with him still inside. *He's* still hiding from his ghost.

I have no such luck, so I march down the hall. Elizabeth floats right beside me. "Can't you go occupy yourself?" I try to sound…not *caring*, exactly, but less salty than I feel.

"I can't *do* anything," she says, holding up her ghostly hands as proof, as if we don't both know that ghosts can do all kinds of things. If they want to.

"Why don't you go bother your husband?" I suggest, still going for the low-sodium version of my voice and not quite getting there. "Practice your best poltergeist? Haunt a villager?"

She floats around so she's in front of me and holds out a hand like a stop sign. "Listen to me, child. Goods and Riverses don't mix."

For once she sounds dead serious.

No pun intended.

"It's a little late for that warning," I say, waving at my belly. I stop walking, even though I know I could plow right through her if I wanted. "But thank you."

"Their honor always gets in the way," she tells me, her violet gaze seeming to glow brighter than the rest of her.

Blaming *honor* doesn't make any sense. Or it makes too much. Either way… "What's wrong with honor?"

"Nothing, until it's the sword cutting everything in half." She makes a *cutting in half* motion, and I don't know if that's some kind of memory charm, but I see that Beltane prom night ten years ago. Zander handing me not a *ring* or a *promise*, but his pendant that I'm currently wearing to protect me. Back then, it was to *go be free*.

Somewhere far away from *him*, was what he meant.

It is not a great memory. Not just because of that moment, but my reaction to it, which was almost as bad.

I walk through Elizabeth then, with prejudice.

Georgie's door is open at the turret end of the hall. I take this as an invitation and walk right in to find Georgie pretty much how I expected to find her. Sitting in the middle of her wooden floor meditating, her crystals floating all around her while the light from outside her bay windows pours in.

I want to interrupt her immediately so I can start firing questions at her and escape my own head, but I don't. I take a deep breath and try to sort myself out.

I *am* an adult.

Maybe someday I won't need to remind myself of that fact.

The crystals gleam, then hum a little as they float to the ground. I choose to take that as hope.

Georgie opens her eyes and smiles at me, then stretches as she gets to her feet. "No glamour today? *And* you look like you caught up on some sleep. You look good, Ellowyn."

I don't do well with compliments, so I make a sort of *grunting* noise to acknowledge what Georgie said. And I figure I might as well dive right in. "Ghost Elizabeth here says she wasn't a Summoner or a Diviner."

Cue an instant judgmental sigh from the spectral audience who followed me in here. "I summon. I divine. I do not understand why this is such a hardship for you to understand."

I ignore her since Georgie can't hear her anyway. "She says she had premonitions. She summoned with the best of them. She calls herself a Revelare."

"I don't *call myself* anything," Elizabeth grumbles irritably. "That's what I am."

Georgie is frowning at me, her big Historian brain clearly turning this over. "I don't think I know this word."

"*You* don't?"

She shakes her head. "Not in any kind of historical aspect. Certainly not as a designation. I'll ask Frost, of course, but… Well. I *have* seen the word once…"

She trails off. Then she shakes her head and gets that dreamy look about her that I've come to realize is her disguise. I used to think she was an airhead. Now I think she likes people to think that she is.

"I'll ask Frost," she says again.

But she's *lying*. "Where have you seen that word, Georgie?"

She reaches out and gives my arm a squeeze. "It won't help us."

"You know this for certain?"

She sighs and walks over to her bookcase. She has an entire room across the hall filled to the brim with books and scrolls and odd objects she claims are of historical significance, but this bookshelf is about her own personal history. The books she read as a kid. The books she reads now. All well-handled, with spines creased, unlike the historical tomes she treats like a stray breeze might destroy them forever.

She pulls out a ratty paperback, sized for the children's section. "It's not a text or a codex or anything. It's a cute kids' story."

I accept the slim volume. There's a very intricately drawn illustration on the cover. A dragon, a crow, and a redheaded princess with a shining sword. Ribbons of water, almost like rivers, twine around them and into the background.

I can't imagine anything Elizabeth is talking about is going to be illuminated by a kids' book about princesses. Still I turn it over in my hands a few times, almost like I can't bear *not* to. It's been worn and read and well loved, that's for sure.

"It's my favorite. When I was a child, of course." Then she flashes a bright, *real* smile, warmth radiating off her. "You know, you should take it."

"Take it?"

"Sure, you're going to have a child who'll want to hear such stories eventually. As Sage likes to point out, kids' books are meant for kids."

Sage Osburn is her boyfriend, and I want to like him. I do. I eye her. "What if I prefer tales of existential dread for my baby?"

Georgie shakes her head at me, because I said it as a question instead of a fact, and she knows my tricks too well by now. "Take it. Consider it your first baby gift."

I want to argue with that, but it feels good, if weird, to accept. I suspect it would be strange and wrong, somehow, to say no. So, I take it.

Then I take Elizabeth's witch designation down to breakfast, and to Frost.

The former immortal does not do breakfast. He stands in the kitchen because Rebekah is there, both watching and not watching her lounge around with her tea.

"It sounds familiar," he says when I ask him about the term, but he gets that dark, dangerous look about him. The one we're all beginning to associate with something he thinks he should remember but doesn't. He looks at Georgie, who pads in behind me, all bare feet and wild red hair. "We'll go through my library today."

Georgie nods. Emerson and Jacob stop conferring—both of them smiling the way they only do with each other—and she shifts to her Warrior mode to hand out safety buddy assignments. Yes, she's made specific assignments and a number of charts she's only too happy to magic about in the air of the kitchen, all without disturbing her familiar, Cassie, who is lying at her feet in a sunbeam.

It starts off a domino effect of days that go by quietly and without hiccup. We know the Joywood are planning something. They get quiet when bad, bad magic is brewing, and all we can do is wait.

Or, if you're Emerson, start making flyers and posters to encourage our fellow witches to choose us once we're officially

taking part in the ascension on Samhain. With so many promises of what she'll do you'd be hard-pressed to believe them—
unless you know Emerson.

We research and discuss around-the-clock now that we're
all staying in Wilde House, but there's precious little clarity to
be found. Georgie and Frost can't seem to find any further details on what ascension rituals will take place once we have our
sponsors. Nor do they find an explanation of why Revelare was
a witch designation in Elizabeth's time but not now, much less
how both Summoning and Divining were a part of it. We still
have no idea why shapeless dark shadows came for us.

We try to imagine what we would do if we were evil, the
better to predict what the Joywood might do, but it never seems
to work. And Emerson usually gets a little too wound up at
the *very notion* that any of *us* could do such horrible things, no
matter how many times Frost gets that intense look on his face
and tells her that power can change a person.

"Only if we let it," Emerson replies calmly.

We do our jobs. We are never by ourselves or off the bricks
if we can help it. As if all of this isn't weird enough, Zander and
I are also getting along for the first time in, well. Ever. Maybe
because the ghost relationship we see spooling out before us
night and day is a mirror.

And we don't like what we see.

We plan, we prepare, and we gather. Day after day, night
after night. With an agenda in place for the town hall meeting,
I find myself filled with the strangest sensation.

I almost don't recognize it.

But as the days pass, it settles in until even I can't deny it,
much as I'd like to.

For the first time in months, I have something that's been
sorely missing for this entire strange year.

Hope.

11

BY THE TIME THE TOWN HALL FINALLY ROLLS around, I'm looking forward to it. It's *action*, when everything about the past few days has felt like waiting.

Besides, it's an opportunity to dress to kill, as is always my preference. Black. Leather. Skin. *Hell yeah*. I wear Zander's pendant, though it's hidden. I haven't taken it off once.

Protection. For the *baby*.

I have to ask Rebekah for some help with my hide-the-bump glamour. The Joywood might know that I'm pregnant, and why they care about that I can't begin to fathom, but I can't help but feel like it's best if they don't know that we're aware of their interest. Secrets have power, so why not keep ours?

Elizabeth does not approve of my outfit, something she makes clear by *telling me* she does not approve. Repeatedly. Five days of sepia-tinted judgment has gotten old, I will admit. I've enjoyed conversations about my witchy ancestors and St. Cyprian's older days, but I'm not sure I'm going to be *entirely* sad that she'll be heading back to the spirit world tonight.

"You consider this appropriate dress?" she's asking me as I head down the stairs, as if repeating the question will change my mind. "For anything at all, but particularly for an ascension ritual?"

"Yes, Elizabeth. I do." I swear that Azrael, the dragon newel post, is smirking at me. "That's why I'm wearing it."

Then I walk through her some more as I meet up with everyone else in the foyer so we can head outside together, into a quickly falling night that gets chillier by the minute.

October is nearly upon us and fall is coming in fast, like it or not.

"I do not understand these descendants of ours," Zachariah says grumpily, though he's not looking at Elizabeth as he complains. He's just floating stiffly beside her, his umbrage perfectly visible even though I can see the lampposts along Main Street *through* him, wrapped with the apple boughs. "These garments aren't even suitable to cross the river in."

"Good thing we're not crossing any rivers, then," Zander mutters, his hands stuffed in the pockets of his jeans.

"Dungarees," Elizabeth said in amazement and horror back at the house. *"Like a sailor."*

As if that was a terrible insult.

Zander and I exchange a look and mutual rolled eyes, but that feels like dangerous ground, so I look away again as we walk past Holly Bishop's coffee shop and bakery, moving along the street toward Confluence Books and then, farther down, Tea & No Sympathy. The entire town is dressed up for Mabon in the form of the Apple Extravaganza that Emerson put on the same way she does every year, impending war be damned.

How do you have time to put on a festival *right now?* I asked her when I'd gone into the shop the other day to see the whole town transformed.

I have magic now, Ellowyn, she'd replied serenely. *I can do twelve times as much and I don't even need help. It's* awesome.

Because I guess we're always who we are.

Tonight we're all walking together. Actually walking, not magicking ourselves to and fro the way we might normally. This is also Emerson's idea.

We'll arrive together, she said last night. *A little procession of community business leaders, stalwart members of the wider witch community, and* actual *friends*.

It will make a stark contrast to the Joywood's usual dramatic appearances, Jacob added. Because the Joywood have never met an entrance they couldn't make as elaborate as possible.

It gets colder as we walk. By the time we reach the community center, I'm wishing I wasn't showing so much of my glamoured midriff, though I will die before I admit such a thing in Elizabeth's hearing.

That's how I know she really is family, I guess.

Tonight's meeting is the typical quarterly witch town hall that I would normally avoid like the plague, because we'll all hear about it whether we attend or not. The Joywood send out tedious scrolls that are charmed to report back if we don't open them, so no one can claim they missed out on any important witchdom happenings.

These witchy "town hall meetings" in St. Cyprian are the heart of the magical government that operates here, where no humans ever think to look for us. Meetings like this are enchanted so that even if humans manage to find the right room at the right time, what they hear are boring blatherings about dull subjects no one could possibly care about.

Mostly, humans don't make it here for the quarterly meetings that the Joywood preside over. I don't come either, because what's the point? No one's listened to a Good about town business since the legendary night Mercy Good stood up to the tutting pearl clutchers who wanted her bordello closed and told them all what their husbands *really* liked.

No point trying to beat the master at her own game, in my opinion.

As we walk into the overheated room, Sage comes over to greet us. He gives Georgie a little rose that she looks happy enough to receive as she tucks it behind one ear.

Clearly I'm dead inside, because I don't find this at all sweet. I should. I *should* wonder when I'll meet a guy who'll shower me in roses and ask me, gently, how my day has been. Then listen with *rapt attention*.

I try to imagine Zander doing any of these things but I can't, because Zander is too hot and knows me too well, and if he has ever *asked after my day* in our lives, it was with the express purpose of getting me naked.

Also, Zander is not wearing one of those strange three-piece suits with a bow tie that Sage likes so much, claiming his job as a high school teacher *lends itself* to this choice. The only sartorial choices Zander makes involve whether to wear a Henley or a T-shirt, both of which show off his 100 percent unglamoured and athletic abs at all times.

Not that I look. Not that I can picture, perfectly, the selkie tattoo on his *very* impressive shoulder.

I order myself to stop comparing Georgie's perfectly nice boyfriend to my toxic ex as Emerson marches us all into the front row of the meeting. We file in and sit while she moves around the room, talking to pretty much everyone who comes in. She makes it back up front with the rest of us by the time the Joywood appear on the stage at the front of the room with all the expected pomp and circumstance.

Assholes, I think, and hope they can all pick up on it.

Carol Simon, who is the most powerful witch in the world by virtue of leading the ruling coven, dresses like she invented *frump* and has the most bizarrely frizzy hair. It's not that frizzy hair doesn't come for us all—this is Missouri, where the frizz is free—but she is powerful enough to not only make herself look like Grace Kelly if she wants, but make everyone who sees her think that Grace Kelly copied *her*. That she doesn't do this, that she never has, is just one of the things about Carol and the Joywood that I spent my life pretending didn't creep me out.

Maeve takes her place on the stage and makes a point of smiling down at me benevolently. I make a point of remaining deadpan. Elizabeth and Zachariah mutter to each other about it, Zander makes a gruff sort of sound I think only I hear, and farther down the row, Rebekah sits forward from where Frost's arm is slung over the back of her chair to raise a brow my way. In solidarity.

Carol titters in that way she always does, always so creepy, and starts the meeting. There's an agenda, which she reads out as if we can't all see it hanging in the air on one of the screens someone has magicked up there. There's a robust discussion about street cleaning. There are *several* rants from the community about improper uses of gardening spells, attempts at love potions, and the odd wannabe-curse between drinking buddies and a whole book club.

The Joywood look as bored as I feel, and behind us, I can hear far too many people shifting restlessly in their uncomfortable fold-up chairs. Another Joywood rule is no magicking in of actual, comfortable chairs or that hammock my mother once claimed was orthopedic to have an excuse to get in a fight with them.

Look, I don't come from thin air.

"I see these haven't gotten any more interesting in the past century and then some," Zachariah mutters from where he floats behind Zander, practically on Bernie the cheese guy's lap—not that he knows a ghost is hovering in front of him. Probably too busy visualizing his cheese boards for next Saturday's farmers market.

"Perhaps *interest* is in the eye of the beholder," Elizabeth says pompously, but she has the same sort of glazed-over look of boredom I'm sure can be found on my face and every other face in the vicinity.

Almost like the boredom is the point, Emerson points out in our all-coven internal chat, directly into our heads.

That she's almost certainly right doesn't make me any less bored, though.

The droning goes on and on. It's interminable, and the Joywood are staring down at us, so I know I'm not the only one using magic to prop my eyelids open. Even as I want to take a nap, there's this prickly feeling along my skin, and I have to shrug on my jacket. It's too warm in here, but something is making me feel cold.

Finally—*finally*—there's that shuffle and buzz that signal the torture is about to be over, but Carol hasn't called on us yet. She hasn't even pretended to mention what should be the key part of this meeting—the presentation of our sponsors, which is our formal entrance into a bid for ascension.

There's a part of me, and not a small part, that is much happier about this than I should be.

But Emerson isn't about to let them exclude us on a bureaucratic technicality. She gets to her feet and doesn't wait for Carol to formally grant her permission to speak. "Carol, you're missing an item on the agenda."

There are whispers as Carol pretends to study the agenda that we can all see before us, absent any ascension items.

"Always *very confident*," says an older witch, sniffing to her friends.

"Does she ever think of anything except *attention*?" mutters a younger one, and he glares so hard at Emerson that we all bristle a little.

"You'd think North would keep her in line with that ring on her finger." This one is followed by a nasty round of snickering from the middle-aged group of men in the corner who do not appear to notice the dark way Jacob looks at them.

I glance around at the people talking quietly behind their hands—or not quietly and not behind their hands—while glaring at Emerson. Who pretends not to notice.

Or maybe she really doesn't notice. That's one of her charms.

With her memory or without it, she is cheerfully immune to the opinions of others.

Because none of it is true, or even really about her, so why should she care? The angry things people say behind your back and even to your face have more to do with *them* than the person you are.

Or the truth.

When I look back at Carol, she's squinting down at us, her face wreathed in that saccharine disappointment that she wears almost as often as that frizzy hair. "I don't see any *sponsors*, Ms. Wilde, which is what your little makeshift coven will need to progress toward ascension past Mabon. Was that not made clear?"

"That's incorrect, Carol," Emerson is brisk, not rude, as often accused. "We have sponsors."

"She's such a *bully*," someone whispers, sounding personally affronted. I would recognize Gus Howe's querulous voice anywhere. "Why can't she be *polite*?"

"Don't you wish someone would take her down a peg—or three?" someone else mutters as the rest of us climb to our feet to take a stand next to Emerson.

She counts, calmly, in our heads where only we can hear her. Then we turn to face the crowd, as one. The Joywood aren't the only ones here with magic and a flair for the dramatic.

And there are people here who support us too. My mother and Mina, of course, holding hands in their row—to keep Tanith from charging the stage as much as any of their usual affection, I'm sure. The entire North clan, who almost never venture to this side of the river, since Healers tend to keep to themselves. Corinne Martin, who runs the Lunch House. Keely Chung, the chef at Nora's—the finest restaurant in town. Witches who stood with us at Litha.

Even Zander's father ducks in the door—late, but here.

I can't help but notice it's very divided. And I know why. There are a lot of people who are afraid of the ruling coven's power and vindictiveness, which is fair enough, but there's a whole other group of people who aren't supporting the Joywood because they're *afraid* of that power, but because they get off on it. Who like aligning themselves with the powerful group so they can look down at people and whisper about all the ways someone else doesn't fit their definition of what *good* and *right* is.

Who do everything they can, as that woman behind me said so we could all hear it, to *take us down a peg*.

It's sickening when you think about it. When you *see* it first-hand. They can't just support the Joywood or disagree with us for any number of real reasons—like that we're all young and one of us isn't even a full witch.

They don't just want us to lose. They want us to *suffer*.

I can't deal with how gross this all feels tonight, or how little I want to see some of the things I can see on the faces of people I know will smile and say hello to me on the street tomorrow. I have to gear up for a Summoning.

In front of *everyone*.

Lucky for me, spite is a great motivator.

"By all means," Carol says with a titter, aimed toward her supporters in the crowd, who all laugh along. "Please produce these invisible sponsors of yours."

She might as well have called us kindergartners with invisible friends.

Focus, Frost tells us all, every inch of him the first, best Praeceptor who taught everyone in this room everything they know, directly or indirectly.

So that's what we do.

We don't do a full ritual. We don't pull out candles or draw runes on the ground. It's not necessary with our ghost friends already on this side of the veil. We still do everything needed to protect me and our ghosts in the center of our circle.

It's even hotter up here in front of everyone. Like the lights have been amped up or the heat is suddenly on full blast. Tricks

I would not put beneath the Joywood, so I let that feed the spitefulness inside me. I feel a trickle of sweat trail down my back, but I shrug it away while Emerson explains what we're doing to the crowd.

Despite my effort to cuddle on up to that spite and make it work for me, I can't seem to focus on her words. Because I'm starting to feel wildly nauseated.

I tell myself it's panic, but the breaths I take to calm myself down only seem to make it worse. Then *much* worse, like I'm really going to be sick right here in front of everyone.

It has to be nerves. I keep telling myself that, but it reminds me of something.

This year's Beltane prom that we were all forced to attend, as grown-ass adults. Where I felt *really* sick. Like I'd been poisoned.

I couldn't have been pregnant then, is the thing. That happened *later* that same night.

At the prom I felt as if I had acid inside me. In my blood, beneath my skin. Throbbing at the backs of my eyes.

I feel that way again now, so bad it makes me think back almost fondly to the bouts of morning sickness I had earlier in the summer that I thought were somehow related to all that. Morning sickness was a holiday on the beach next to how terrible I feel now—

Emerson looks to me, the sign for me to begin the Summoning.

Like it or not, I have to reveal Elizabeth and Zachariah to the crowd here tonight. I have to make this happen, even if it kills me.

So I ignore the cramping and nausea sweeping through me. I *focus*.

I say my words quietly. There's magic, there's power, and then there's that sickening *thing* inside of me, growing stronger. Nausea, pain, exhaustion. Like something bad is working its way through my body, and fast.

It feels black. It feels thick and oily, and it leeches into my bones.

That's almost a good thing, however awful it makes me feel, because it reminds me of that shadow outside Zander's apartment. It makes me think *black magic*, and if I know anything about the Joywood, it's that they aren't afraid of using a little black magic when it suits them.

Since they are the law, they can also hold themselves above it.

This seems so obvious to me that I almost laugh. Why wouldn't they poison me with this unfurling black that's sucking me under? I'm only surprised they haven't targeted all of us yet.

I remind myself that I've fought it once already. I lived through Beltane prom. I lived it up Beltane night—hell, I have the baby to prove it.

The baby.

They came at me once, and it was bad, but I won't let them get at my child.

I decide this, like a prophecy, at the same moment I lift my athame toward the sky and reveal Zachariah and Elizabeth to the crowd. I use my other hand to grip Zander's pendant, like a promise that the baby will be okay.

Everyone murmurs, shifting in their seats, as the ghosts begin their speech. Like whatever Emerson said beforehand, I can't concentrate on any of their words. It's taking all I have to hold my baby safe inside me and to make sure the ghosts stay visible and audible to all.

Meanwhile, that darkness rolls through me, hot and boiling and *mean*.

My strength is wilting, though I fight for more. I hear Elizabeth say something about a group of *special* young people with an *imperative* message. Was that part of their script? *Imperative* again.

I can't focus on that. I have to focus on staying upright instead. On keeping my connection to the two of them, and broadcasting them to the witches gathered here tonight. On doing what I can to protect my baby.

I'm going to beat you, you evil fuckers. I don't care if I send that thought out into the Joywood's consciousness. To the whole damn town.

I hope I do.

"Ellowyn."

Zander's voice cuts through the dark. I can feel his hand on the small of my back, like he's holding me up. Maybe he is, but I'm not done. I shake my head at him, concentrating on the connection. Keeping my athame high above me. The pendant in my other hand pulses. Nothing else matters in this moment.

I've accepted that someday, I will be my coven's downfall—but not yet.

Not tonight.

Not until I've given it everything I've got.

A few seconds later, I feel Jacob's hand on my shoulder. There's a little ribbon of respite. He's trying to help.

I concentrate on that. On the small feeling of relief. On Zander holding me up.

Then on Elizabeth, because her face is hovering in front of mine.

"You're special," I hear Elizabeth whisper at me, and she's the only thing I see at the moment, which feels like an epically bad sign. Then even she is fading. "Don't forget it. You are *special.* It is imperative you don't forget again, Ellowyn."

Imperative. That damn word again.

Then, for a moment, there's…nothing.

But I feel a kick, deep inside.

Like the baby is fighting too.

I don't let the dark claim me. I don't let it win.

I stand up straight, like I don't need Jacob's or Zander's help at all, and I smile straight up at the Joywood like I'm giving them the middle finger. I can't feel my hands, so maybe I am.

"Elizabeth Good and Zachariah Rivers have offered their sponsorship in the traditional fashion," I say, letting my voice ring out so they can whisper that I'm a *very confident bully* too, and dressed so abominably besides. "I think we can all agree that they fit the requirements. Or do you need me to bring them back?"

I sheathe the athame, and then I fold my arms across my chest like I've never been healthier or felt better, and challenge the entire ruling coven to come at me.

If they dare.

12

AFTER THAT, EVERYTHING IS A BIT OF A BLUR.
All my energy is going into staying upright. Into keeping that
easy smile on my face. No one knows what's going on inside
of me—except my coven, who maintain their presence in that
open channel in my head.

It's more comforting than I want to admit.

Zander's hand never leaves my back. Carol calls an end to
the meeting—and I hope she's furious that she didn't manage
to cut off our ascension bid at the pass. I hope Maeve Mather
and her blind pigeon are incandescent with rage, but I don't
dare look any of them in the eye when it feels like my organs
are boiling in acid.

We're being surrounded in the still-overwarm community
center room. People come to ask us questions, or maybe they're
just using that as an opportunity to give us quiet support. It's
not everyone. It's not the muttering masses. It might not even
be enough…but like Litha, when this town voted to let us live
by a scant three votes, there's enough. Just enough.

There's a group of people who want change. Who want something *right* instead of all these years of a growing *wrong* too many of us have been pretending we don't feel.

Emerson has been leading this charge since she got her memories back and refused to fade away into gratitude or whatever it is the Joywood wanted from her back then. But tonight there are people who want to compliment the job *I* did, and even if I was up to it, I wouldn't know what to say to this outpouring of support.

I can barely manage a smile and a thank-you.

My mother walks up, takes one look at me, and knows something is wrong. She and Mina exchange a look and put themselves between me and the people who want to talk to me. Jacob's mother and sister, both Healers, close in too. Soon enough, this little group of determined women is moving me toward the door. Once again I feel like I can't actually walk, but they're moving me anyway with their considerable magic. Helping me project a strong image while getting me out of this place.

Still Zander does not let me go.

I'm not reading into that. It's just a fact. Dimly I hear him attempt that laugh he loves to trot out when he's bartending.

I also know that the laugh doesn't land. I know it's wrong.

Is everything wrong?

I have a hard time concentrating on anything but making it to that door and getting out of here before I collapse, but there is something happening beyond this wash of poison inside me, and it makes the pain easier to handle.

Because the rest of my friends form a loose circle around me, and even I am forced to recognize that there's a long line of people who want to help. They don't want to help because they're the sort of people who always help others, though the North women are certainly that. They want to help *me*. Specifically.

I know this is true in the same way I know that the poison inside me was put there.

Again.

This little group of people making it seem like they're casually, happily walking out the door wants *me* to be okay. They would be doing it whether this was a normal meeting or not, whether I'd succeeded or failed tonight. These same people would be right here, helping me.

How can I keep having such a high opinion of all these people around me and such a terrible one of myself? I decide to ponder that later.

My mom relinquishes my arm to Jacob, and I can feel his magic. That deep, true Healer magic fights its way through me, into the heart of the poison, even as we walk outside and head down Main Street once more.

"I could magic us back," Jacob tells me in his low, serious way. "I have a feeling the Joywood are watching though. We're going to have to do it the long way."

I nod. Or I think I nod. My mother laughs at something Mina says. Jacob's younger sister, Evie, is talking loudly about tea and acting as if I'm engaged in this conversation with her. When it's all I can do to keep from succumbing to that dark thing inside me.

Maybe because of that, it takes me a long time to realize that they're all making it look as if I really am having that tea talk with Evie. Anyone passing by on their own way home—witch or human—will see a happy group of people, comfortably talking about nothing in particular as they walk home on a night that smells of fall, like leaves set to turn and a hint of woodsmoke on the breeze.

The walk goes on and on. I feel the pendant against my chest, a cooling force in all this heat. I feel Jacob's magic mending and fighting, pushing toward the poison and cleaning up the damage, but it's slow. As slow as the usually easy walk down Main Street feels to me tonight.

We eventually make it back to Wilde House, the sounds of

friendship and merriment hanging in the night air. The minute the front door closes behind us, the complicated glamour of it all drops.

Just like I would if Zander wasn't holding me up.

Jacob and the rest of his family start belting out orders. It's like a scene from one of those human medical shows, but we're in Wilde House, not an ER.

For once, Emerson isn't the one taking charge. Jacob is. There's something about how okay she looks with that. It worms its way into me, like I should be paying more attention to the two of them, to who they are, to how they work together—

I'm too loopy to hold on to it. Or to anything else. Because someone pulls Zander away from me, and I want to reach for him. I would if I could. If I was anything but limp.

I find myself in my room, now containing only my bed and no conjured monstrosity with a canopy and a ghost. I think, to my surprise, that I'm going to miss Elizabeth after all. That thought leaves as quickly as it comes, and what I notice then is that the lights are lowered. That it's nice and dim. My mother puts me to bed like I'm five again, then moves out of the way so the Healers can take their spots around me.

I know they've already done some work on me, but that they're settling in to do more. They'll fix me. I know this because it isn't the first time this has happened.

"Did we do okay?" I ask Jacob, because everything is fuzzy and spinning now.

"You did everything you needed to do," he assures me. "The ghosts did great. The Joywood were pissed. Emerson can brief you on the details when you're a little stronger, but everything went the way we wanted it to. Except this."

There's no arguing or getting more information. Not the way he says it. Healer declarations are what they are.

Evie is at the foot of my bed, playing the part of a bouncer, but it's no surprise to me that she doesn't see Elizabeth or Zachariah when they appear in the room, then move right through the other witches surrounding me.

Elizabeth leans in close, and I can feel her hand on me when—once again—that shouldn't be possible. "Tell them to let Zander in."

The Healer spellwork surrounds me. I can't think of a single reason I shouldn't do what this ghost is telling me. Not when Zachariah's gray gaze looks just like Zander's, like he's concerned too.

I turn to Jacob's mother, not Jacob. Because this feels like girl stuff. "If you're going to check the baby, Zander should be in here."

"He can come in eventually," Jacob's mother, Maureen, assures me in her calm, earthy sort of voice that makes my whole body feel like a sweet, cool rain is moving over me, quenching poison fires wherever it touches. "Once he calms down a bit."

"I'll take care of it," Elizabeth insists. "Just let him in."

"He'll be okay," I say, not sure why I'm listening to this ghost or taking up for Zander when what I'd like to do is lean into that blessed rain and maybe sleep for a week.

Maureen nods over at Evie, and she does something with her hand that lets the door fall open. The moment it does, Zander is *right there*. All fury and fire and *hot*.

Hot and not poisoned. So hot I shouldn't notice, not in this state, but I do.

Before he can say or do anything, Elizabeth puts a ghostly hand on him. Zachariah frowns sternly at him, as if the two of them are working together.

Hush.

He blinks once as that word seems to dance in the dim light, then says nothing. I'm not sure if it's a spell—another thing Elizabeth shouldn't be able to do—or reasonable astonishment at being told what to do by an ancient ghost.

Who isn't supposed to be here, but still is.

"Sit, my child," she tells him, and Zachariah points him to the armchair by the window. Then Elizabeth perches next to him on the arm of the chair, and Zachariah takes his place like a sentry behind them both. I can't hear what they say to Zander, but it seems to calm some of the fury radiating from him.

I can see it, and I don't ask myself how that's possible either.

"Baby is just fine," Maureen says in a voice that is filled with both Healer and mother assurances as her hands move over my bump, and I can feel that rain wash deep into me, then all over the baby too. "We've got to make sure all the poison is out, and then we can do a little projection." She must read my confusion at that, because she smiles. "Consider it a witch's ultrasound."

Ultrasound. I'll get to see my baby—

But.

She said *poison*.

"Poison." I say it out loud, though it's a raw scrape against my throat, like all that acid ate away at my insides. There's something we all need to know, and I need to say it before it slips away like everything else tonight. "The Joywood keep trying to poison me."

I attempt to sit up in my bed at the truth of the revelation, but Jacob shakes his head, and his mother holds me in place with an easy murmured word. "You're not to move yet," she tells me gently.

I want to argue, but I don't. Not while Jacob's Healer magic does all sorts of things inside of me that hurt—really *hurt*—but then feel *much* better.

I look at her, then over at Jacob. "It's like Beltane prom. Only worse."

Jacob lifts his gaze to mine, and his eyes glow with all that power and focus, but he nods. "Yes. Much worse."

"I don't understand."

He shares a look with his mother. Like *they* understand.

"What?" I demand, looking back and forth between them. Zander and my mother ask that question too, in tandem.

"We have a theory, but let's fix you up first, okay?" Jacob spares Mom and Zander a look. "Go on and sit down now."

I've never once seen my mother obey an order so quickly. The ghosts and Zander stay in their chair. Tanith sits on the small chest in the corner. At the foot of the bed, Evie starts to lay out spellwork, like she's acting as an extra magic generator for her brother and mother tonight.

Jacob and his mother put their hands on me and weave their magic together as they go back inside, deeper this time. Maureen is a soothing rain. Jacob is warm, rich earth. Slowly, slowly, they repair me.

I've been healed before, many times, but this is something so deep, so gross and so *wrong*, it takes time. Energy.

High-level magic.

After what feels like forever, and maybe it is, both Jacob and Maureen take their hands off me and slump a little as they sit there on the bed beside me. They look almost as wiped out as I feel.

"Jacob." Zander might be sitting still in that chair, but his voice is as intense as if he's spent the last few hours punching holes in walls. Or people. "You said you have a theory."

Jacob rubs a hand over his face and nods gratefully when I magic in three mugs of steaming tea, filled with a special blend I keep on hand for Healers and anyone else who has to fight off the truly dark shit. On or off the bricks.

I might not be able to lift my head from my pillow, but I can still do the one thing I *know* I'm good at.

"My family and I have been treating a number of witches over the years for a mysterious illness. You all know this." Jacob looks even more tired than his mother. Beat all the way through, but he doesn't ask for time to recover. He takes a pull of his tea and carries on.

That's Jacob.

"You think this is the same illness?" Zander looks stricken. Because he not only lost his mother to it, he made a vow to get to the bottom of what killed her. But there have been so many other things in the way of that vow, and nothing gets to me more than when Zander can't find his mad. When he can't hide there.

I have such a lump in my throat that it takes me a moment to fully understand the implication. That whatever I've been poisoned with—twice now—is the *same thing* that killed Zelda.

As well as seven other witches the day of the Litha celebration. Eight Summoners total. Like there's something in particular about us that poses a threat to the Joywood.

"Yes and no," Jacob is saying. "What happens to Ellowyn has all the same characteristics of what Zelda had. It's also a good match to what we know has been hurting a great number of Summoners for the past year or so, but it doesn't function in Ellowyn the same way. Not at Beltane prom. Not tonight."

"Let me guess," I manage to croak out through my suddenly too-tight throat. "I'm special."

I shrug as my mother glares at me, but when Jacob turns to me, I hold his patient gaze.

"You fight it off. It hurts you, yes, gets around your protections, because that's good magic," he says, nodding toward Zander's pendant, visible to everyone. "This is dark magic. Still, after some time, after some healing, something in you… eradicates it. A lot like when Emerson broke Carol's obliviscor."

That nasty spell the Joywood subjected Emerson to for ten years, taking all her memories of magic and her true witch heritage from her. But sure. Those people back in the meeting who think she needs to be *humbled* are *so* right.

This is not the time to rage about the way people talk about one of my best friends. "How?"

Jacob takes another big swig of the tea, and immediately

looks a little less gray around the edges. "Well, here comes the theory. We don't know for sure, but based on what we've seen, the people who've been affected, who've died…" He glances at his mother, who nods. "We think it's your blood, Ellowyn."

"My blood," I repeat. I look at my mother again. At Elizabeth. "Is it that troublesome Good blood making waves again? The way it has been since Salem?"

Both Mom and our ghostly ancestress make a noise at that, but Jacob shakes his head. "It's your *human* blood."

It sits there in the middle of the room like those smoke spells they teach us when we're kids, a small explosion of pink light and fragrance that takes over everything for a solid ten minutes.

This feels at least that long.

"It also explains the pregnancy," Maureen says after a moment, when no one else seems capable of speech. "Your magic is what's being targeted. They can't touch the human part of you, but they can mess with your magic and warp it enough that they can, eventually, use it against you if it takes hold. A full witch is too much magic to withstand it, but you're not a full witch. You have weapons. You fought this off on Beltane, enough to feel better. You survived, but we think your magic wasn't at full strength to act as birth control the way it normally would."

That all of this is a topic of conversation is so embarrassing that I have no choice but to pretend it is *fine*.

"You think her human blood is an asset?" Mom asks softly, her voice laced with wonder. I listen for the bitterness. I look at her face, watching for that little twitch I usually see when she thinks of my father.

I don't see it. Not the faintest trace of it.

Jacob is nodding. "It's the only thing that sets her apart from the other Summoners we've dealt with."

"You're not a Summoner, Ellowyn." Elizabeth's voice is very stern and serious.

I sigh at that, happy I can rest my head back against the pillows. "We don't have Revelares," I mutter at her. "Not a one. No one's even heard of it, not really."

"It doesn't matter," the ghost shoots back. "You are one. Your mother ought to be one too. I don't know why she isn't, but you're much, much stronger. Don't you see?"

"Why isn't my mother sick?"

"We have a theory on that too," Jacob says as if I was asking him. Because he doesn't see or hear Elizabeth. They must think I'm still loopy from what happened tonight, and I'm happy to let them think that.

"All sorts of theories I've never heard about until today," I say, but I keep my eyes closed for an extra moment or two because even my eyelids feel weighted.

"Sometimes it takes a while to put together things that are happening in real time, and then to make sense of the data," Maureen tells me. "Particularly when the Joywood are involved."

"We started a database," Evie says from the foot of the bed, then looks startled when we all look at her. But she's a North, so she sits straighter. "Of everyone who's been affected, no matter how. From worst-case scenarios to the best-case outcome, that being you. It doesn't seem to hit one nuclear family more than once."

"They're weakening the link," Elizabeth says then, looking across Zander to Zachariah. "They've changed things that should never be changed."

"It's like the crows."

Elizabeth's face gets a pinched sort of look. "Don't start with the crows, Zachariah."

I close my eyes against a new wave of exhaustion, so big and dark it's almost like pain. I can't take ghost fights right now. I can't take databases and theories. I suddenly feel that I can't take *any of it*, and I want to cry, but there are too many damn people—living and dead—in here.

And I don't let myself cry in front of anyone.

"Are you sure it's gone?" Zander asks, still sounding stricken. "Because I already know where this is going if it's not. That can't happen."

"This isn't like Zelda," Jacob says at once, and he holds Zander's gaze so intently it's like a physical touch. "Ellowyn doesn't have the symptoms. She fights it off when it tries to take root in her, and it can't get any purchase. We're certain."

Zander nods, jerkily, then looks at me with other ghosts I know in his thundercloud gaze. I feel another wave like pain go through me, though this time it's something far more complicated than exhaustion.

"The problem is the Joywood clearly aren't giving up," Maureen says gently, looking down into her tea mug. "They're escalating."

"If they keep escalating, it could kill me," I point out, though, probably, no one needs me to make this announcement. "Especially if they discover why I'm the only one who's immune to this thing."

"Yes," Jacob agrees, turning that intensity on me again.

No equivocations. Great.

"But," he says after a long while, "we know how to fight it off. We can use that for a protection spell. Not just for you. With the right ritual, your blood could help everyone who's been affected, even against dark magic."

I want to make another crack about being special, but this doesn't feel like the moment for that. Also, my throat feels too tight again.

"Would that be safe?" Zander demands. Once again in near-perfect unison with my mother. They look at each other, each wearing their version of a vaguely puzzled frown, but then focus on Jacob.

"There are risks, of course," Jacob says in his calm way, but none of us mistake the steel beneath it. "We'd do everything we could to mitigate them."

"But no fucking guarantee?" Zander demands.

"If you're going to swear, young man," Maureen retorts coolly, like we're all still eleven years old, "you'll have to leave until you can get control of yourself."

"She's not fu— She's not doing it. She's not risking that. What the hell is wrong with you?" Zander looks like he's about to get to his feet, clearly back in his anger in a big way, but Elizabeth puts a hand on his shoulder, and he stays put.

Furious, but he stays in that chair.

Jacob eyes him for a moment, then turns to me. "We'll go over the pros and cons and weigh them all, but not tonight. I'm going to go down and fill everyone in. Mom's going to show you some baby projections you'll want to see, and then you need to rest." When I start to scowl at him, he keeps going. "You're better now, and you'll keep feeling better, but your body, your magic—and that baby—need rest, Ellowyn."

He starts to get up, but I impulsively grab his hand. Healers don't expect thank-yous, and I've never been very vocally grateful about *anything*, but this isn't only about me.

I know I have to say something.

"You keep saving me."

He shakes his head. "I'm just helping the healing process along. It's you doing the saving."

I smile. "I said you keep saving me, so you must be." He frowns a little at that. I guess I'm not the only one not sure what to do with praise, so that makes it easier to give. "Thank you, Jacob."

He gently pulls his hand out of my grasp, gives a faint nod, then turns and marches from the room as if pursued. I let myself smile a little wider as his sister follows him out.

Maureen is still sitting next to me, but she's looking at the other people in the room. Well, the living ones.

"Tanith, Zander, you can both stay." She fixes an eye on Zander. "If you're calm."

My mother stands, and her smile is wobbly. I don't know what to do with that. Tanith Good *wobbly*? "No, that's all right," she says quietly. "I'll head downstairs."

"Mom—"

She shakes her head. "You'll show me and tell me everything after, but this moment? This is for you two."

She smiles at me reassuringly, even though her eyes sparkle with unshed tears. She slides Zander a glance, notably dagger-free, and then she's leaving.

Maureen nods at the space Jacob vacated, and Zander comes over to slide into it. He looks pale, and there are so many reasons he could be feeling pale tonight. I think about taking his hand, and I automatically start talking myself out of it, but I catch sight of Elizabeth out of the corner of my eye. She gives me a little nod.

I take his hand. He doesn't resist—I'd have to punch him if he did.

I forget about punching things when Maureen settles her warm hands over my stomach, because this is suddenly much more real. She closes her eyes, whispers some words, and then a picture appears above me that looks like a little blob...

With a head, and arms, and legs.

A baby.

Our baby.

"As I said, everything is perfectly healthy. There's no evidence of any poison breaching the walls that protect the baby. Mother's magic, right there, and your protection pendant. Now, beyond that, I can tell you both a lot from this picture," Maureen says. "Or it can also be a surprise. That's your choice."

"I want to know." I want to hold on to whatever's coming like a promise. Like an oath. We will fight, tooth and nail, come ascension—and I will fight even harder if I know what's on the other side. I look at Zander.

He nods.

Maureen hums a little, and I can't tell if that's spellwork or her own happiness showing through. "Your baby is measuring just as she should. She's got everything she's meant to have and is developing right on target."

"She," Zander and I both manage to get out.

Maureen smiles at us. "Yes. Your baby girl will be born in March. Likely the twentieth or twenty-first."

"That…" I swallow. "That seems longer than usual?"

"Oh. Witch babies take their time," Maureen says reassuringly. "Jacob was near to twelve months before he decided to join us. You know what they say. The longer within, the more powerful without."

I did not know that. Tanith does not sit around discussing gestation periods.

Maureen carries on. "An Ostara baby, I imagine, because that would make sense. I'll have a better idea in the next moon phase, when I'll insist you come in for another checkup. Babies conceived on a festival day are more likely to be born on one, though."

"My mother…" Zander's voice is raw. His grip on my hand tightens. "The twenty-first is…*was* her birthday."

Maureen smiles over at Zander. "That, too, makes sense. Love is powerful magic, passed down."

Love.

I can't find words. The baby growing inside of me is projected *right there*. I can't touch her—*her*—not *yet*, but I can feel her. She's already here, with us.

Growing. Measuring.

Safe.

"Here," Maureen says. The projection fades, but she holds out two pictures. One for me. One for Zander. "These will pass in human circles too, if they need to. And once the baby is born, of course, humans will only remember a typical human, nine-month pregnancy. It's a blanket spell on all witch births."

She's talking about blanket spells, but I'm looking at a picture of my baby. Our baby. Our *daughter*. I hold the picture in one hand, Zander's hand in the other.

I barely hear Maureen when she speaks next. "I'm going to give you two a few minutes of privacy, and then, as Jacob said, it's time to rest."

I don't hear her leave, unable to tear my eyes from the pictures she gave us, but somehow I know when she's gone.

Leaving us alone with a baby we can expect to meet in March. That seems far away to me tonight. Far, far away, on the other side of ascension. Far off in a future we somehow have to save.

For *her*, if nothing else.

I look over at Zander. He's staring at the picture. His hand is still in mine, and he looks as awed as I feel. The only reason I look away is I hear a shuffle.

Down at the end of my bed, Elizabeth and Zachariah are standing there. Right next to each other, but even more astonishing, Zachariah has his hands wrapped around Elizabeth's shoulders. I almost comment on how this baby really must be magic—

But I see a strangely sparkly tear slide down Elizabeth's cheek. Then she *poofs*. Not gone, I don't think. Just out of here.

"We couldn't have children," Zachariah says softly in the wake of her departure. He sounds as if these words hurt him. "A curse from her parents, as a wedding gift."

Then he, too, disappears.

Leaving Zander and me to hold on tight to each other, and the part of me that *isn't* cursed, after all.

13

ZANDER IS STILL HOLDING MY HAND. OR, I guess, I'm holding his. Clutching it tight.

"We Goods do love a curse," I mutter, frustrated with these things, these family legacies, that do little more than *hurt*. When they're meant to. When they're not.

Zander looks at me then, and I'm not sure what I see on his face. It's a little too naked. And serious. Maybe I can fight off a Joywood poison, twice, but that doesn't mean I can also manage to handle whatever this is between us any better than I ever have.

I look down at the picture in my hand instead. *Our daughter.* A Good. A Rivers. A mix of us, and all of our ancestors and histories, and the great big mess Zander and I have made of loving each other and hating each other for most of our lives.

But there are bigger issues than this endless tangle we've made.

I tell myself it's not a *relief* to focus on said bigger things, but I don't dare try to say that out loud. "They want me to die," I say instead. Because that's clear now, like it or not. I'm the one with the target on my back, and I have been since Beltane.

So it isn't solely about the baby. Or Zander.

He plays with my fingers the way he did when we held hands often, and I pretend I don't want to melt into it the way I always did then. "I think they'd be happiest if we all did, but they need to make sure they win over the public. That was the whole Litha deal, right? They need the people who support us to think we lost, fair and square. Or they can't do whatever it is they want."

I shake my head. "Immortality, Frost says."

Zander makes a noise of agreement, and I keep staring at the picture of the baby growing inside of me. The one I've got to survive ascension to meet. That means we have to understand more than we do right now. We have to fight harder than ever.

I guess I've proved twice already that I'm a lot tougher than they assume I am. "They think I'm the weak link. That's why they're targeting me."

"*Think* being the operative word. It isn't true if you were strong enough to fight their poison off. Twice."

I open my mouth to say something. Probably something stupid, like he should prepare for disappointment. But Zander steamrollers on, and even though I can tell he's pissed—it's flashing in his eyes, vibrating inside of him—he's quiet when he speaks. Calm.

Like somehow, while I wasn't looking, he went and got *mature*.

"You're stronger than my mother, Ellowyn." He's quiet, sure, but his voice is rough. "If you want to play the poor little half witch card, don't do it around me anymore."

I want to be incensed at that, but how can I be when it's about Zelda? And he isn't even wrong. I fought off that terrible poison two separate times, *because* I'm half a witch.

Not *despite* the human blood in me. *Because* of it.

Maybe this is what Elizabeth meant when she called me special.

I turn in the bed to look at Zander. "Even if there are risks, I have to do the ritual Jacob talked about. I have to do whatever I can to help all those other Summoners."

He lets out a short sound that would be a laugh if it didn't sound so unamused. "Like hell."

"I trust Jacob, and so do you. He wouldn't bring it up if it wasn't important. *Imperative*, even."

Another short laugh. "He also doesn't make shit up, which means you can't do it. If Jacob says it's dangerous? It's fucking dangerous."

"What he said was that there are risks."

"I love when you argue semantics with me like I'm stupid." He pulls his hand from mine. Agitated, I know. Thinking about the baby, not the big picture.

I don't want to use Zelda like a hammer, but we'd be having a very different conversation if she was alive. "If your mother was still here—"

"No." He pushes to his feet.

I sit all the way up, even though he turns and glares at me like I should lie back down. I'm going to be *adult* and *calm*, though, because this is important. I sit with my hands in my lap. I use his quiet voice. I look him in the eye.

I am a grown-ass woman, not a teenager. "You would have done anything to save her. You would have sacrificed anyone or anything."

"No, Ellowyn."

"You never had to—"

He turns to face me, slapping his hand to his chest. His heart. "You don't think I had to choose? Over and over and over?"

He's not angry at me, not fighting with *me*. Even I can see that, and I've never been particularly nuanced when it comes to Zander's temper. I usually let it light my own, but right now everything's…softer. Harder. We are both holding pictures of our daughter, who Zelda won't get to hold the way she should. "Zander."

"You never wanted to hear it, but I chose." He says it so quietly I barely hear the words.

Not that they make any sense. "What are you talking about?"

None of this feels like the us I know so well. Too much ache, not enough fire. Too much sadness mixed in with the typical anger. Too much vulnerability, maybe.

I have the strangest thought that this is what we've been running from all along. Because we're great at getting naked in one way, but this is something else.

I'm not sure I want it.

Zander sits back down, and gently takes my hand in his again. "Will you listen?"

If he made that a *demand*, I would say no. If he was all furious and contained like a few seconds ago, I would back off.

But there is a desperation, a *need* in that question.

I have been strong when it comes to Zander. An entire decade of one night a year and no more.

It's not like any of that was easy.

This is different. He said it a few days ago. *This changes everything.*

"Okay," I manage. He's hurting, not just angry. So maybe… Maybe I can handle the truth.

"Actually listen to me," he insists. "Don't argue. Don't tell me you don't want to hear it, the way you always have. Just sit there and let me say it all. *Finally.* Can you promise me that?"

I try to say yes, but it won't come out.

He laughs, just a little exhale of breath. "I appreciate the attempt at a lie, anyway."

"I can promise to try," I offer him. It hurts how much I want to offer him. Even if he's right and I've been avoiding this conversation for a very long time. Though I don't have any idea how it connects to Zelda.

"That's something, I guess." He takes a deep breath, and it's ragged with more of that hurt. I want to think that *this is what we do to each other*, the way I usually do, like that's some justification, but we have a daughter on the way.

The world's a little bigger tonight than what the two of us inflict on each other.

Zander looks down at our hands, still intertwined. "Do you remember back in high school when I had to do that stupid apprenticeship with Festus Proctor?"

I nod, though I can't imagine why he wants to talk about the Joywood's creepy Guardian now. "You had to go follow him around the locks and dams all over the rivers, right? Guardian it up. Except you didn't mind it."

I remember being irritated about that and picking a fight once or twice or maybe ten thousand times, that he could get along with someone who had such open contempt for me.

"No, I didn't. Back then, I didn't mind Festus at all. He made me feel important." Zander shakes his head. "Mom and Dad were always so relaxed about everything. Too relaxed. It didn't matter what I did. Good grades or bad, sports or lounging around, working or choosing not to work—everything was fine. They loved me no matter what. As long as I wasn't cruel or disrespectful, it didn't matter."

I roll my eyes. *"The horror."*

There's almost a smile on his face then. "It wasn't a horror. Obviously. But Festus acted like what I did—or didn't do—was important. Or could be. I liked that."

I can't begin to imagine where this is going, but there's a cold knot of dread in my gut. "Zander…"

"Until he started in on you. He thought I could do better. He thought I *deserved* better. He wondered why I wasn't with someone befitting my important station."

I try to pull my hand away from him. "If this is why you broke up with me—"

"Simmer down, I'm not that easy. I love…d you." The way

he stumbles over the word *love*, with a tacked-on past tense, has my heart lodging in my throat.

But he keeps telling his story. One I have refused to let him tell all these years.

Because he made his choice. Why should he get to tell stories about it?

I don't really want to hear it now either. My heart is beating much too fast, like whatever he's about to say is going to wound me, somehow. Or like it already has.

Still, I told him I would try. So I try—meaning, I literally bite my own tongue.

"I didn't like it when he talked about you," Zander says, in a very low, deliberate sort of way that makes my heart get acrobatic for...other reasons. "So he changed tactics. The thing is, I didn't see what he was doing at the time. He just...started talking a lot about staying in St. Cyprian."

"While you and I were making plans to get out of here." So many plans that it makes my throat clog to think of them now.

"A Rivers who doesn't stick around isn't upholding his legacy. His *important* legacy as a Guardian. My parents would never tell me, of course, because they're too soft—Festus's words, not mine, but I could see it. How they'd never ask anything of me, because they never did."

That's important enough to get past the tightness in my throat and all those lost plans we made. "Because they love you, Zander."

I don't stumble over the tense. He holds my gaze a little too long, like he needed to hear me say it. Like he needed to make sure it was true.

"I see that now. I even knew it then. I didn't take Festus's word for it. I brought it up to my parents. I asked—straight-out—what did they want me to do. Stay? Because I could. I would. If they wanted me to."

"They'd never tell you what to do."

It's hard for me to realize that Zack and Zelda loved Zander so much that they couldn't see what he'd needed. That even two of the best people I knew weren't perfect, not even back then when I considered them my other parents. My *intact* second family.

I don't know how to feel about the notion that even they could get something wrong. Because if they can be wrong… what hope do I have?

Zander is still talking. Still telling me things I don't necessarily want to hear—but the difference is, now I know I need to hear them anyway. "They told me it was up to me to do what I thought was right, but I could see how much it would mean to my dad if I *did* stay. Then they asked where this was coming from, when they knew you and I had plans to leave. I started to explain what Festus had been telling me, but before I could even get into his thoughts on my legacy, Mom just… crumpled. It was the first time she ever collapsed."

He takes a minute. I can tell he sees it all in his head, as vivid as if it just happened. Because it was traumatic. Because it changed everything for his family. Because he knows how it ends now.

"Mom was sick for a few days, and I didn't think about much but that. The next week, I had my regular apprenticeship meeting, and I felt dirty. Slimy." He shakes his head. "Everything Festus said felt wrong, when a week before I'd been positive he was right about everything. I couldn't talk to my parents about it, because Mom was still sick. I figured I'd talk to you. That we'd figure it out, because we were good at that. Once."

I want to laugh, but it's true. We were. *Once.*

"I was about to leave to pick you up. Mom was sitting up, reading, feeling better. Back then she used to get better in between attacks."

That hangs there between us. I can see there's a part of Zander that can't fully accept there's no poison in me, no matter what Jacob says.

"Dad was at the ferry, so it was just Mom and me. I told her

I was going to see you, and she smiled. I was walking out the door, thinking about how I'd tell you everything, and then she started choking. She couldn't breathe. I tried to get in there and *do something* with all this magic I'm supposed to have, but nothing worked."

I squeeze his hand. Harder and harder until he looks at me again and slowly blinks himself back to now.

He's not done though. "That was the pattern. She'd get better, but then, if I even had a stray thought about getting away or talking to you about what was happening, she would have another episode. A Healer could help, but they could never stop it for good." That gray gaze of his is heavy on mine. Steady, but weighted. "I thought I was cursed."

All I can do is whisper his name.

"I was afraid to do anything wrong," he tells me, sounding more resolute, somehow. "I knew I couldn't *go* anywhere. What if something happened? What if I said the wrong thing, or did the wrong thing, and she was left here hurting? You have no idea how much I wanted to explain all this to you then, Ellowyn, but I didn't know how. Not without hurting her more."

I feel as if I'm spinning, but not because I feel sick. That would be the easy way out this.

I knew Zelda got sick, but I guess I thought it was a cold here, a flu there. The normal way people got sick sometimes, if not usually witches. I don't think any of us realized...

But admitting that feels like it might be the death of me. "You could have asked me to stay." I mean that to come out like every other accusation I've ever hurled at him, but it doesn't. It's quiet. Raw.

More telling than I want to admit.

I would have said yes.

"You didn't want to stay here, and I didn't want to ask you to do something I knew you didn't want to do." He looks at me then, over our daughter's picture. Over our daughter herself, tucked up inside me. Over our hands threaded together. Over a past neither one of us can go back and change. "It wasn't bullshit, Ellowyn. I fucked it up, doing it at prom. I fucked up, period, but I wasn't *lying*. I wanted—needed—you to have what you wanted, even though I couldn't go with you."

I open my mouth to argue, even though there's no argument to make, but he just keeps *on*.

"I know everything changed that Litha," he says in the same rough, raw way. "You stayed here and you made it work, like maybe we could have. I couldn't see that beforehand. The only thing I could see was me, being the anchor that drowned you."

"We could have—"

"There are always going to be a million and one *could haves*, but I did the only thing I could. The only thing I could live with. I broke things off. I let you go. I let you hate me. I was determined to be as noble about it as I could. Until that night."

Because that night, our Beltane prom night, I refused to cry in front of him. That night, I refused to do anything he expected. In fact, the only thing I could think to do was prove I didn't need him at all.

By having someone else instead. One of his jock friends, so it would really twist the knife.

It didn't matter that I went home and threw up after. That I felt dirty and wrong and like *I* was the villain, because in that moment, in my head, I won.

When Zander flew off the handle the next day, the way I'd hoped he would, I knew I was right. That I'd won.

I was so sure that was the only thing that mattered. For all these years.

Yet now I look back on it and all I see is loss. All we ever did was lose. He couldn't tell the truth, and it was the only thing I could do, and all we *really* wanted was each other. How did that get lost along the way?

For a moment, all I want to do is cry. Right here in front of him, the way I never have.

But I won't.

I don't.

"It doesn't end there," he says, looking at our joined hands like he can sense the possibility of my tears. Or maybe he can feel the same thing I do inside me—that even though everything he's saying makes me ache, I'm getting better by the moment.

"Every time I tried to tell anyone about the things Festus said. Any time I talked to Jacob about the rivers rising and all the imbalances we could see everywhere. If I dared make a case at a town meeting about the confluence being messed up. If I did anything, Mom got worse. Then this coven shit killed her."

Suddenly I get it. All that guilt over the summer that I chalked up to him being a *man*, a Guardian, makes sense.

He thinks he did it to her. He thinks he killed her.

"Do you think her death is your fault?" I ask, though I already know the answer.

"She would have been disappointed in me if I didn't stand up for what was right, if I let you guys go alone, so I couldn't," he says gruffly. "So they won. And I get to live with the knowledge that I could have stopped it by shutting my mouth, for once. By sitting down. By standing up for her, no matter what she thought of me for doing it."

This past summer makes more sense than it ever did. The self-destruction, the drinking.

"It wasn't a curse," I tell him gently, and I know even before I form the words that they're true, but I like the validation all the same. "A curse doesn't leave you any choices. Look at me. At Elizabeth and Zachariah."

He looks like he doesn't know where to put that. "You think it's all a coincidence?"

"I don't think it's that either." It's worse than a curse, is what I really think. Because he had to choose. They put that on him.

He shakes his head like it doesn't matter. "I don't need to re-hash the past anymore. I don't need you to forgive me, because I did the only thing I knew how to do. Maybe it was wrong, maybe it sucked, but it was all I could do. I can't change the past ten years. Just like I can't bring Mom back." Once again, it's all thunderstorm gray and my heart too wild against my ribs. "I'm telling you all this so you get why you can't risk this. You can't risk getting hurt. You can't risk our baby. You can't risk *you*, Ellowyn. The risk isn't worth the loss."

There are things I could say, but I don't. That it isn't up to him. That this is the thing *I* can't refuse.

"I don't want anything to happen," I manage, very carefully, "to anyone I love."

"That's the problem," Zander returns, his gaze as serious as his voice. As the grip his hand has on mine. "You keep thinking I don't know you, but I do. You've got a self-destructive streak a mile wide, and I know it's only begging to be turned into a martyr complex. I can't have that. Ellowyn. I won't."

Every good movement needs a martyr, though. Everyone knows that.

I don't say that in his head. I know I don't, because we don't do that anymore. Still he squeezes my hand.

"You matter too much to martyr yourself, Ellowyn." His gray eyes search mine. He looks vulnerable and surly. He still looks like *mine*, but he also looks vulnerable in a way I know I never let myself. "To me, baby. You matter too much to *me*."

Before I can decide what to do with that—or lodge my his-toric objection to being called *baby*, even though I only wish I hated it when he calls me that—or if I should faint or jump him or surrender to tears after all, or *something*—

There comes a great tolling.

Far off and close all at once. Inside my body and all over my skin. The whole house shakes. The air seems to follow suit.

Calling it the tolling of a *bell* feels like an insult.

"Christ," Zander mutters, and the human invocation feels harsher than if he'd called out to Hecate like witches usually do. "What now?"

The sound rolls out again, worse this time.

Then a booming voice surrounds us, so loud I have to cover my ears, though that does nothing at all.

"Citizens of St. Cyprian. Witches of the world." The voice is everything and nothing. It emanates from the sky outside. From my own pores. From the sheets I'm lying in. From Zander's hand in mine and the arm he must have thrown around me when the *tolling* started. "The ascension ritual has begun, and the ancient trials must take place. Appear before me, or risk my eternal wrath."

And this time when everything seems to collapse in on itself, Zander is with me.

14

FOR WHAT FEELS LIKE MUCH TOO LONG, BUT is likely only a matter of moments, everything is chaos.

It takes a while for it to settle down enough that Zander and I are *us* again.

We stare at each other, and neither one of us mentions that we're now gripping each other with both our hands, fingers laced tight.

Zander swallows, hard, before helping me out of bed. I want to tell him I don't really need any help, but it's like when he calls me *baby*. The part of me that wants to fight to assert myself gets drowned out by the part of me that only and ever wants to bask in him. I decide to go with the basking. He mutters a spell to freshen us both up as we step out of the bedroom, and I let that happen too.

I move gingerly at first, astounded that I can't feel all that poison anymore. No matter that it's the second time I've gone through this, it was worse this time. And I am somehow fine. Because of the Healers who helped me—but also because of *me*.

By the time we make it to the staircase, I know I should tell Zander that I'm perfectly me again, and there's no need for any coddling...but I don't.

I tell myself that it has nothing to do with him or with me or with the daughter we kind of just met for the first time, but because when we can see the front hall of Wilde House, there's a *crowd* of people there.

Not just *our* people.

I can see Emerson and Rebekah's parents, apparently no longer in Germany, looking even more chilly and affronted than usual. If the familial resemblance is anything to go by, the rest of the crowd is a whole passel of other Wildes. They're crowding the entryway, all talking at the same time and sounding entirely too much like Desmond Wilde himself—meaning, haughty and filled with outrage of some sort or another—and that leaves Zander and me stuck on the stairs. I don't see Rebekah or Emerson. Or anyone else I know.

Behind us, the ghosts reappear, but they don't look the way they usually do. Elizabeth's hair is falling out of its tight bun. Zachariah's shirt is half-untucked.

"What happened to you two?" I'm pretty sure ghosts can't change their appearances. Much less physically fight each other, which is what their dishevelment kind of looks like.

Then again, the normal rules seem to be out the door tonight. And how.

I look down at Azrael, the newel post with its gleaming onyx eyes. I remember then that his occasional comments are a result of some old enchantment, according to Georgie. An enchantment that was probably enacted by one of the witches currently milling around the entry hall before us. Of course tonight is the sort of night that enchanted objects decide to come out to play.

Elizabeth is waving a hand. "Never mind that. The ascension bell is tolling. You must go." She makes a shooing motion at us.

"Go where?" Zander asks, scowling.

"To the Undine," Zachariah intones.

Zander turns that scowl on his ancestor. "The statue?"

He looks to me and I shrug, because I don't know what else they could mean. The only *Undine* I've ever heard of is the big statue down by the riverfront. It's a woman so intricately sculpted in marble it's hard to tell if she's wearing some kind of gown or emerging from the water. She's placed to gaze off toward the confluence, her hands raised as if calling the power of the three rivers to her.

Or possibly drunkenly dancing off a long night, as I heard a group of humans say once.

"There's so much you don't yet know," Zachariah says darkly.

"Aren't you glad we didn't abandon you?" Elizabeth adds.

Then they sail through us—the both of them—holding hands.

"Ghosts can't...?" Zander trails off.

"Can't what? Be annoying? I think they have that down."

Then it dawns on me. The shift in their demeanor, their appearance. The general *dishevelment*. A physical altercation, maybe, but not a *fight*—

"No," I say, shaking my head, because it's like thinking about my parents going at it, and no one ever needs to be *that* mature, surely. "Is that even physically possible?"

Zander's gray eyes gleam. "They're ghosts. What makes you think it has to be physical to be...physical?"

The truth is that witches don't know what goes on beyond the veil. Not really. The fact we can contact our lost ones doesn't mean we have a handle on their experiences. We only get bits and pieces. Messages from the universe. The odd haunting.

Knowing more than humans do doesn't mean we know it all. Even Summoners. Or Revelares or whatever the hell I am. Still, the idea that the sad moment upstairs led to any kind of reconciliation between these two ghosts of ours makes me feel... softer than I like.

That has to be secondary at the moment. The crowd in the

foyer begins to spill out the front door, and we follow, almost as if something is *compelling* us. I would object to that, but it doesn't feel frightening. It's definitely not any oily Joywood sort of magic.

It's very clear all the same. It gets us moving, taking us out onto Main Street with everyone else.

Because outside, there are even more people. Witches I know. Witches I've only seen pictures of. Witches I know perfectly well don't even live in St. Cyprian. Everyone is talking to someone else as we all move, together, down toward the river.

It takes a lot longer than it should to dawn on me that anyone can see I'm visibly pregnant. I'm not ready for that. I try to handle a glamour myself, but my magic is nothing more than a few sparks. Still recovering, no matter how strong I feel. I need help.

I look around for Rebekah to give me a hand, but I still can't find her in the crowd. I think I see Emerson up ahead, but she's talking animatedly to a group of older witches I don't think I've ever seen before. I can hear Georgie behind me, but she's doing that airy act of hers while surrounded by a crowd of witches I know are her relatives, though she is the only one with red hair, bright like flame in the night.

Zander hasn't left my side. His hand is on the small of my back, like he's not only guiding me through the crowd but is prepared to fight our way through if necessary.

"This is weird," he says when he feels me looking at him. "Why are all my Rivers cousins here? They have their own rivers to watch over."

I clear my throat, wishing there was another way, because asking for help from anyone makes me feel itchy. Especially when it's him.

Our baby girl is more important than anything though. Even my pride.

"Hey. Can you help me with this?" I dip my chin toward

my belly. "My magic is still recovering, and I'm not ready to make a baby announcement."

He looks down at me. I don't know if it's the whole me asking for help thing that makes him look so stricken then, but he swallows. Nods.

Then he *hesitates.*

There is no time for that. I grab his hand and press his palm to my stomach. He lets out a long, shuddering breath, looking down. As something deep inside flutters.

Not something.

Her.

She's moving. It's not that *kick* at the meeting, like she was jumping into the fight. This is something gentler. More like a settling in.

Like family, I think.

I wonder if Zander hears that, because his eyes glow with magic as he whispers the words of the glamour for me. When his gaze meets mine, everything is bright silver and potent, leaving me breathless—but not in a scary way.

There's nothing scary about this. It's just...us.

All the ways we're tangled together, and always have been, like our own messy little confluence, hums there between us.

The crowd is still moving, still compelled. I can feel the need to move inside me, like a physical need all my own when I know it's not. I know it's outside me, outside all of us. I know it comes from the same place as that great tolling from before. I don't know how I know this, but I do.

There are so many witches, flocking down the sidewalks and taking over the street, abandoned at this hour of the night. It's like a festival night, only I've never seen one so crowded.

Zander is right beside me, and he never lets me go as we leave Main Street behind and stream over the grass, down toward the river.

"The countdown will begin," that voice booms again, seeming to come from the sky above me, the ground below me, and my own bones within me too.

It's too loud. Thunder and an earthquake rolled into one, yet not as terrifying as I'd think either one of those would be. People start hurrying now as that same voice begins an actual, literal countdown. *Ten, nine, eight.*

Witches begin magicking themselves along to hurry through the crowd, until everyone is doing it—seized by the same urgency. Zander has to give me a boost so we don't fall behind, and he keeps that hand on me while he does it, bringing us straight to Emerson's elbow.

She nods as we arrive and as the rest of our coven finds each other. All around us, witches from all over the world convene on the St. Cyprian riverfront.

Emerson is focused on the former immortal brooding there behind her sister, murmuring the odd greeting in one language or another to the witches who catch sight of him.

"Frost. What do you know?" Emerson demands. "*Did* you know about this?"

Because it's a moving target, what Nicholas Frost remembers or doesn't remember.

He rubs a finger along his temple. There's pain, clearly, though he doesn't let it come out in his voice. "The ascension trials have been triggered. The Undine will lay out the rules. For all who must participate, and all of witchkind."

"The statue," Zander says, like he can't quite believe it. I can't either.

Frost slides one of his dark looks Zander's way but must be in pain because he doesn't get snide. Next to him, Rebekah has her arm around his waist and is murmuring spell words beneath her breath.

"She is only sometimes a statue," Frost says. "She is more properly a spell in stasis, an enchantment waiting to be invoked. A sentient being and yet not, not exactly. She has no feelings.

No emotions of any sort. She is the embodiment of right and wrong and is here for only one reason—to ensure that the ascension rules are followed, or woe betide us all."

"Sounds like a real party girl," Zander mutters, and I know it shouldn't make me laugh, but it does.

"You could have warned us," Emerson says, frowning.

"I had forgotten about her," he mutters, irritated. "No doubt by their hand."

Before we can discuss that further, the countdown ends on a loud, long *one*.

As it sounds, another toll rings out. Like the entire earth is the clapper in a universal bell. Shaking, vibrating, and making all of us ring along with it.

The summoned witches have gathered on the riverbank, surrounding what is usually a beautiful statue of a lovely woman. She doesn't look much different now…except she's moving.

Her eyes glow like the moon has taken up residence there. Hair once frozen in stone waves in the breeze. The folds of the dress she wears move as she breathes—or appears to breathe—there beneath the stars. The arms that are normally high over her head in a kind of reverence to the water are held wide, almost welcoming.

Except nothing about her fearsome face or glowing eyes feels particularly welcoming.

"Witchkind, behold me, for the ascension trials have been triggered, and there is no going back. You must all hear these ancient words. You will heed what I shall set before you or you will suffer the worst consequences."

"Cheery," I say, hoping to get a laugh out of Zander.

Heading straight on down that same old road when I know better. *It was one conversation*, I caution myself. *It was an explanation, not a solution.* There are bigger things to worry about—like talking statues and *worst* consequences.

Plus, he laughs.

"Joywood. Riverwood." The Undine calls out our coven names like another great bell, ringing loud. Like our own kind of church. "Come, covens, and stand before the witches you would rule."

This suddenly feels more real than anything else we've done. It's not just St. Cyprian. It's not the community center or a town meeting. It's not a high school graduation ceremony or the usual rituals we know so well. This is bigger.

This is so much *bigger.*

It's like I can feel the Undine inside me, and I'm pretty sure that's the expression I can see on all my friends' faces too. Possibly the faces of all the witches I see before me as a path opens up and the Riverwood—meaning *us*—start toward the no-longer-a-statue waiting for us on her dais. I can feel the way all these witches from far-off places look at us. Assessing us. Probing us for weaknesses. Wondering who we are to challenge the Joywood.

Or maybe I'm the one wondering that, given how likely I am to be the disappointment here. The weak link—no matter how special my blood is against poison. I find myself searching the crowd for Zachariah and Elizabeth as we move forward as a coven, but they're nowhere to be seen.

It surprises me that I feel that like a loss.

We climb onto the flat, raised platform that normally forms the base of the statue. Across from us, the Joywood assemble—and much more sleekly. For one thing, they are all wearing matching cloaks that would look absurd if they were marching around town in them on a sunny day.

Here, in the night, before all of witchkind and the heavens above, they look like nothing short of what they are. The most powerful witches alive.

The ruling coven, elevated over us all.

I look around to make sure us grubby members of the Riverwood aren't all clinging to each other like trembling fawns, and decide we're doing okay. Emerson looks like she could take on the world. Frost looks as remote and terrifying as ever. As my gaze moves over the rest of us, I'm pleasantly surprised. We all look like ourselves, but *better*. It's only when my gaze moves over Rebekah and she grins that I realize she's helping with the glow-up.

Like we're practically our own Marvel movie.

I couldn't stand idly by while they showed up in full costume, could I? she says in my head.

You heeded the call, I reply serenely.

Then the Undine is speaking in her voice that is everywhere, inside and out.

"You are called to prove yourselves before Samhain dawns," she tells us—and everyone else. As far as I can see, everyone gathered looks as confused as I feel. "To ascend to the position of ruling coven, you must demonstrate your honesty and transparency. You must indicate the contours of your brand of justice. You must make clear the depth and breadth of your beliefs, in which we will all share. These trials will be held upon demand, no warning and no preparation permitted. When you are called, you will appear before me to perform as requested with no excuses. The trials will be broadcast to all magical creatures and witches the world over. So it is said, and so it shall be."

"No practice?" Emerson is frowning. "How can they spring this on us? How can we do it right without practice? Studying? Making sure we know what's coming?"

"You won't know what's coming," Frost says quietly. "That's the point. There is no *doing it right*, there is only doing what is asked. It is the people who will decide what it means."

Emerson glares at him.

"It falls to me to preserve the sanctity of these trials," the Undine continues, her voice the swell of a tide within me. Within all of us. "So that the people might make the best choice available to them come Samhain. So it was written into stone and flesh, and made real throughout time. So too shall it be in this time, in this place, with these souls who stand before you."

A ripple goes through the crowd. Her words settle in me like a ringing in my ears, like a memory. I remember Litha, when Frost sacrificed himself for the opportunity to tell us all that the Joywood were evil. And that none of us could remember anything about ascension because they wanted it that way.

"These are the rules, as laid down in spell and sacrifice in ancient fires, as befits such proceedings," the Undine continues. "Competing covens are forbidden to cause harm to one another. They will not lift hands to one another. They will not use their magic against each other. There will be no violence, no bartering, no subterfuge. The trials are conducted with integrity. They exist to reveal truths, not to pit one witch against another. And so do I stand before you, judge and jury and occasional executioner, to see that this is so. That you stand with me, Joywood and Riverwood covens, is your agreement signed in blood and flesh, to abide by my verdicts as they come."

Something rumbles, like an earthquake inside me—

"So do I swear," I hear myself say, and only realize as the words come from my lips that all my friends are saying them too. That the Joywood, across from us, are speaking them aloud at the same time. "And so will we abide."

They can't attack us? I try not to look around at my coven too obviously, because I don't want the entirety of witchkind to see how shocked we all are. Because I can tell that we're all equally shocked. When I look across the way at the Joywood, there is a definite simmering fury under those political smiles I know too well.

They knew, Emerson says in our heads.

And they don't like it, Zander agrees.

They wanted no part of this, Frost says quietly on that same internal coven channel. *They went to great lengths to keep us from standing here tonight. For precisely this reason—we are now protected from their little games.*

The Undine is speaking to the crowd, forcing new responses from the assembled witches. Maybe from witches everywhere— I'm certain I can feel them too, living and dead alike.

We will abide. We will honor the trials. We will make our choices on Samhain as it is written, and as it ever shall be.

I think about everything that's happened since adlets tried to kill Emerson back in March. Up to and including that shadow that attacked Zander and me. *Both* times they tried to poison me. I think of Zelda, and the slow and terrible way Zander lost her. *That doesn't mean they can't hurt us in other ways.*

"Always the pessimist," Zander replies out loud, but he's still right here. Holding on.

This is not the time to let myself think about how much that means to me.

She's right though, of course. They'll try. Emerson's voice is certain and true in our heads, a wide smile on her face that isn't for show—because this is where she thrives. The more adversity, the better.

They'll see if their dark magic can breach it, Rebekah predicts, though it doesn't take a Diviner's grasp of the future to know that's exactly what they'll do. *Fish got to swim, birds got to fly, evil covens got to get their evil on one way or another.*

Yes, yes, but this is good for us, Frost says, and there's a grim kind of satisfaction in his internal voice. *In a bid for immortality, you don't want ascension triggered at all. It complicates things.*

He would know. I try to be pleased his fits-and-starts memory is choosing now to share this information.

Emerson looks around at each of us. "This is *good*," she echoes, out loud this time—but with all her determination and no grimness at all, like she's pressing that positivity into our very beings.

I find my gaze moving up to Zander, still standing right next to me, and he feels it immediately. His gray eyes meet mine. His hand on my back seems to heat up.

This all feels like more hope, here in the most unlikely of places.

I should know better, but I hold on to it. Hard.

"You may return to your lives this night," the Undine says then, and I can feel the way that dismissal rolls out through the crowd, a kind of loosening. "Know that when I call again, what is required of you is obedience. So shall it be."

That last part lands deep, and sticks. Like a new curse.

The light in her eyes go out, and just like that, she's back to what she's always been in my lifetime. A statue on a riverbank, marble in the moonlight. We're a whole lot of witches milling around when it's not even a festival night. And if you're the brand-new Riverwood, like we are, you're also the recipients of some epic death stares from the Joywood contingent.

But they can't *do* anything.

That feels like another wallop of hope inside me.

They can't do a thing. Not with these new rules in place. If I wasn't worried that they'll find a way around that to do it anyway, it might feel like victory itself.

The crowd finally starts to talk amongst themselves again. There's something like fireworks as witches fly off, or *up*. There's the murmur of so many witch voices that it almost sounds like a new spell, loud enough to rival the sound of all three rivers all around us.

Out of the press of magical people talking excitedly amongst themselves, Emerson's mother approaches the dais. She's still the cool Elspeth Wilde I recall from my entire childhood, when she looked at me like I was a curious insect. She doesn't *not* look at me that way now, but that's nothing compared to the way she looks at the Joywood.

She supports us. She'll rally for us again, as she did once already at Litha. Desmond might be nowhere to be seen, but here is an unlikely ally. It matters.

It has to matter.

Elspeth nods at Emerson, then Rebekah. Then at the rest of us. "Much of the family has chosen to spend the night at Wilde House to discuss this turn of events before returning to their homes tomorrow. I'll head back with them now." Her smile is a little tight, as if she's not used to giving it, but she looks at all of us and the smile holds. "We're very proud."

I can see the way that word shocks Emerson and Rebekah to their cores as Elspeth heads off, leading a charge of Wildes with her.

"Wilde House will be packed now," Emerson says, and if it's taking her a minute to sit with that *proud* comment, it doesn't show. "I still don't want you all going off the bricks. If the Joywood are desperate, and it seems this might be a desperation point, they'll try anything. We still need to stay close tonight. Stay in pairs at the very least." That no one argues about this immediately means we're all cognizant of the danger. It's hard to say if that's good or…not. Emerson is frowning at each of us in turn, now, clearly making flowcharts in her head. "Georgie, you should be able to stay in your room as usual, but the rest of you…"

"I think I will refrain from sleeping in a house full of Wildes," Frost intones dryly.

I can see that worries Rebekah, because Frost House is up off the bricks, so I offer the only solution I can think of. "You guys can take my apartment." I see Mom at the foot of the dais with Mina. "I'll stay with my mother."

"That leaves Jacob and Zander," Emerson says, looking up at her fiancé.

"I'll be staying at Wilde House," he says in that dark, thrilling way that reminds me of the old saying, *Beware the fury of a patient man.* Not a question. Not up for debate. He's sticking right next to Emerson.

It reminds me of earlier. Of the fact that they're always a *team*.

"Zander can come with us, of course," my mother says, smiling warmly at Zander. Not a real sort of warmth, mind you. This is a creepy warmth. A kind of *I might kill you in your sleep* warmth.

Zander's eyes widen. "Um."

But no one can stop the Tanith Tsunami when it gets going. "No arguments now. Everyone needs their rest. As Emerson said, you all are meant to stay in pairs as best you can." She jerks her chin at me the way she used to do when I was a kid, and I feel myself straighten in instant obedience. "Come on now, Ellowyn. Some of us have to get up early no matter how late we stay out tonight."

It feels weird to split up and go our separate ways, but that's what we do. Emerson and Jacob go with Georgie, following Elspeth's trail of Wildes. Rebekah and Frost, his arm wrapped around her shoulders, head in the opposite direction toward my tea shop.

Zander and I head toward my Mom's house, a few streets away from the house I grew up in and much more on the bricks than we were back then. Mina takes my mother's hand as they walk in front of us and kisses it. Then they lace their fingers together. I can only imagine the conversation they're having privately.

"Is she going to poison me?" Zander asks in a low voice, clearly also imagining what's being said—and threatened— where we can't hear it.

"She doesn't want you dead or you'd already be dead," I assure him. Though that's a bit of bravado talking, because I'm not sure how true it is until I say it. "If she was going to kill anyone, it would have been my father, and he's still walking the earth." Then I grin at him. "She might give you some *really* realistic nightmares though. Or find some worse ghosts to haunt you."

"You're an endless comfort, El."

It's much too tempting to let myself dissolve into how good it feels to just…walk down a dark street with him. Talking about nothing, really. We're not fighting. We're not maneuvering our way toward our hands on each other. He's walking beside me. We're not even touching.

I'm not sure I can remember feeling this safe or warm in years, and I know that's more than a slippery slope. That's a vertical drop encased in ice.

"Someone once told me that's my best quality." Sarcastically, of course.

I can't bring myself to put space between us, but I look around the crowd as it thins all around us like I have never been more interested in anything, ever. "Where *are* our ghosts?"

Zander scans the crowd too, though I feel certain he knows exactly what I'm doing. And why. "If earlier is anything to go by, they're clearly—" He stops himself. "You know."

"Are you afraid to say *sex* all of a sudden?"

"With your mother in earshot? I am, Ellowyn. I really am."

I laugh before I can stop myself, and it's a genuine laugh. Not one of the patented snarky ones that I've been aiming at him like missiles for a decade. Because this isn't ten years ago.

I know why he broke up with me now.

It wasn't because I wasn't good enough for him, which I may or may not have believed myself—but oh, how I hated thinking that *he* believed it.

It's not that it doesn't still hurt. It does.

Regret lingers, and I have to wonder if it always will. Because we could have made such different choices. Maybe we could have tried not to take so many chunks out of each other, over and over again.

At the same time, I know we needed those years.

This baby is a gift, and because of those years, I know it.

She brought us here. To a quiet walk in the dark, side by side, making each other laugh. A little breather between terrifying events beyond our control.

So I breathe. And I walk with the bricks beneath my feet and the only boy I ever loved—turned some time ago into the only man I can't forget—keeping perfect pace beside me.

Almost like this is meant to be.

Out of nowhere, in the way of ghosts, Elizabeth and Zachariah are walking next to us. They're not disheveled this time.

But they are holding hands.

I don't know if that's why Zander takes mine as we walk. I don't know if that's why I let him. I only know we walk the rest of the way to my mother's house hand in hand, like that's not a revolution in and of itself.

My mother looks back at us, Mina's head close to hers. She smiles at me, and there's something in her eyes I don't understand.

Because in the strange starlight of this long, long night, it looks weirdly like relief.

15

WE END UP AT MY MOTHER AND MINA'S RAM-
bling house. It was owned by humans before them and thus fell
into disrepair because the humans were convinced it was haunted
when it's simply enchanted.

Mina loves a fixer-upper. I once mentioned this to my mother
as a joke. Mina laughed. My mother did not.

Mom leads us inside, then directs Zander to his room for the
night. She offers him one of the small, cramped rooms on the
main floor. He blinks at the peeling paint, the caving ceiling,
and the window with duct tape over a spiderweb crack, but
doesn't say a word.

These are all things he can magic away easily enough. And
no doubt he will, no matter how much of a *guy* he can be when
it's his own place, but he's going to give my mother the *illusion*
that he will be uncomfortable. In turn, my mother will uphold
the *illusion* he can't solve all these issues with the snap of his
magic. Or she couldn't, as his host.

I cannot fathom why this silent interchange makes me want
to weep.

Though I don't.

"I imagine everyone needs to get to sleep after all that," Tanith says brightly. When she usually doesn't do *bright*, except to mess with someone.

I assume that someone is Zander, but Mina's hand is on my mother's arm—and I don't know *what* they're communicating to each other, but it's something that seems to smooth out Tanith's considerable edges.

"We'll have breakfast in the morning, kids," Mina says with a kind smile. "Good night." Then she gives my mother a tug, and they're headed off without showing me to the—refurbished and comfortable—room they keep for me here. They know I know the way.

What I'm focusing on is Mina calling us *kids*. I'm almost thirty, but I think I'll always feel like a *kid* here, even when I bring my own.

Our own.

I look at Zander. I'm not sure Mina was precisely giving us the go-ahead to do something stupid—the kind of stupid that got us here—but she's giving us the privacy to have a discussion. And my mother is letting that happen.

So, really, the Undine isn't the only wildly unforeseen and impossible thing that's happened tonight.

"I think I will find elsewhere to retire," Zachariah says with an injured sniff before wafting away. I'm only a little surprised when Elizabeth doesn't follow him and stays by my side instead.

"Enjoy the accommodations," I offer Zander, but I'm smirking.

He returns the favor. "She's going to send mice, isn't she?"

"Mice?" I blow out a breath. "Don't think small. Try rats. Snakes. Rabid flying monkeys?"

He glares at me, and I find myself grinning happily as I leave him to figure out how he's going to magic himself a bed big enough for his oversized frame in the tiny room.

If being a mature adult means you can't *ever* laugh at a man's misfortune, particularly when he's your ex, then I want no part of it.

I go up the beautifully renovated staircase to a hallway that looks like a war zone. I think my mother might have tried to wallpaper recently, but she very clearly gave up. I'll never understand witches who *like* to do this sort of thing without the magic we have at our disposal.

I head into my bedroom. Not a *guest room*, as they always remind me. My room is always here for me and always has been, even though the two of them bought this place when I had already moved into my apartment over the tea shop.

Elizabeth is wafting hot on my heels, so I turn to face her. Despite what I've been through tonight, I feel *great*. Better than great. My magic still isn't quite right, but the Healing or the Undine or maybe a little truth-telling with Zander has me *amped*.

It's like witch steroids. I'm sure I'll crash eventually, but until then, why not enjoy myself?

"What were you and Zachariah up to?" I demand of my ghostly shadow.

"I beg your pardon?"

"After the meeting. You disappeared, and when you reappeared, you looked a little…rumpled. So what were you doing? Banging it out?"

She frowns at me, clearing not understanding my meaning.

Or possibly she doesn't *want* to understand me, so I keep going. "Horizontal polka? Bumping uglies? Hanky-panky?"

Elizabeth looks more and more puzzled with every ridiculous term.

"Sex, Elizabeth," I say at last. "Did you and your husband have *sex*?"

I can't magic her a bed tonight, not with my powers at such a low ebb, but she doesn't ask. She settles herself on the little cushion that sits on the bay window, but she looks so stiff and prim I almost feel bad for teasing her.

Almost.

"What we did in private, Ellowyn Sabrina Good, is absolutely none of your business," she says reprovingly as she gazes out into the night.

She's right, of course, but... "You were holding hands."

It was sweet. Kind. I feel like I have to understand what it was all about.

For reasons.

Elizabeth turns her gaze to mine, cool and dismissive. "Are you not recovering from near death? Shouldn't you sleep, child?"

I sit cross-legged on my bed and study her. "I'm fine. The meeting is a little bit fuzzy, I grant you, but Emerson will have detailed reports upon reports. Jacob said it went well. You two did good."

"Because *you* did."

She does not say this with a kind smile or an attempt at comfort. She says it like it's an indisputable fact. *I did good.* I want to say it out loud to test it, but I can't bring myself to do it in front of her.

Besides, I'm seized with the need to find out what happened between the only other Good and Rivers union I've ever heard about. "Ever since you got here, you and Zachariah have sniped and argued and fought like you spent your entire marriage hating each other—before and after death. He told us what your parents did."

She plucks at her skirt. "Yes, well."

"I'm sorry—"

She pins me with a glare. "There is no need for you to be sorry. My grief is my own. It is not yours to carry. Besides, it has always been tempered with happiness, whether that's clear to you during our afterlife or not." She frowns, and I wonder if she's having a moment like I had in the linen closet at Wilde

House, finally considering how her relationship appears from the outside. If she is, she keeps that to herself and focuses on me. "I am happy for you, Ellowyn. Another Good woman in the world is always a good thing."

"Always?"

"Always," she says firmly. As if she has no doubt or ever could. I want a little of that.

What I should do is curl myself around that certainty and sleep. Let my magic heal up. Recover for what's coming, as the Undine promised. (Threatened?) I've never been good at *should*. "What happened with you and Zachariah, Elizabeth?"

She looks out the window again. She's quiet for so long I wonder if she'll just ignore me until I fade off into sleep, which I don't think will take long. I can already feel that *amped* feeling beginning to ebb away.

Eventually she sighs, still plucking at her skirt. "Sometimes a woman, even in spirit, gets tired of being angry."

That lands hard. I've held on to my anger so long. Those edges. The armor that keeps me from crumpling under the weight of it all. Because I have no idea what might happen if I let go of being mad.

Earlier this evening, what Zander told me, the way we *didn't* fall into old angry habits—I know that's a good thing.

That's about our baby girl, though, not any real desire to mend fences.

I tell myself that in my head.

"Anger doesn't serve you. Not really," Elizabeth says.

"Are you sure?" I ask on a whisper. Elizabeth feels like the only safe person to ask. Because she's got to leave sometime… doesn't she?

"Well, it took something like two hundred years to get there, but yes. I'm sure."

"I think what your parents did is probably worth being angry about," I argue. "For eternity." Because it wasn't like my cursing. It wasn't an accident. It wasn't meant to *help* in some twisted way.

"Maybe," Elizabeth agrees. "I used that anger as a crutch. Sometimes a weapon. If they hadn't cursed me, Zachariah might have listened to me and not gone on his fool's errand. He might have stayed if we'd had a child, or one on the way. He might have lived. I survived the rest of my life on that anger. At them. At him. For what?"

I blink at that. I have a million *for what*s and can usually list them all without missing a beat, but I can't seem to think of a one right now. Because at the end of any day...it isn't the anger that gets me through, love it though I do. It's my friends. My business. My mom.

Even my half sisters, if I'm getting soft about it all.

I prefer being angry. It keeps me safe, it protects me, but...

For what?

"I lived a miserable life, angry at a dead man I had once loved enough to defy everything my parents wished for me," Elizabeth tells me quietly. "Then I crossed over and stayed angry in the afterlife. As if love was a lie all along."

Something shivers down my back at that, and I remember that vision of Rebekah's from long ago. *Love is the only lie you tell, but it will claim you in the end. It already has.*

Though what's claimed me, I think then, is the love turned inside out. The anger I've made out of it and decided is my whole personality.

Ouch, Ruth says from her perch outside the windows.

Owl stew, I shoot back at her, but my heart's not in it, and she hoots because she clearly knows it.

"I'm not unique, certainly," Elizabeth is saying in that same quiet way. "Many of us can't let go of what held us back in life."

What held us back.

I don't like how that feels either. This time I ignore the owl commentary.

"It has been so long," Elizabeth says on a sigh. "What I failed to consider across all these years—because he died, I imagine—was that he lost something too. For the first time this evening, I suppose we acknowledged what we'd lost together."

It's like my conversation with Zander tonight. Acknowledging we weren't alone in old hurts, in curses real or assumed, in anger.

I lie back on the bed and look up at the ceiling. "Maybe the Good legacy is just being mad. At everything. Forever."

"Maybe," Elizabeth agrees easily. Too easily. "But legacies are choices, Ellowyn."

She floats over to me and perches herself on the edge of my bed. She has violet eyes like my mother and grandmother. She is a Good, her life marred by a curse. A particularly vicious one.

Now she's a ghost who seems to know too much about me and the things I never say out loud, inexplicably here doing things a ghost shouldn't be able to do.

Like rest her hand on my cheek and encourage me, without words, to sleep.

Which I do without meaning to, thinking about legacies, only to wake to the sun streaming on my face.

I sit up in bed, a little achy. Like I used muscles last night that I never do. I stretch a little, glamour myself presentable, then head downstairs, following the smells of breakfast. When I step into the cozy kitchen, I see my mother and Mina, hip to hip at the stove. It makes me smile.

I'm not saying I loved Mina from the start, or that my mother having a serious relationship after everything with my dad was easy for me. But I was an adult at that point and out of the house. It wasn't my life or my decision to trust again, it was hers. And these days I love Mina like part of my family, because she is, but I don't often get the chance to really *think* about the two of them as a couple. To observe them together, here in this home they're redoing together, with their own hands.

They make each other happy. I'm not saying there's no *spark* between them—I choose not to pay the slightest attention to the *possibility* of any *sparks* involving *my mother*—but what I notice is that they're partners. A team. There's an obvious, enviable *contentment* about them. The few times I've seen them fight, it's something small. A moment of frustration that they always make up quickly.

I've never heard any shouts or seen any tears. They never seem to hold on to bitterness or start in with recriminations. As far as I know, they always talk it out.

Almost like you can learn something from these small failures and thereby avoid the big, systemic ones.

That's not something I want to think about too closely.

Not now, anyway, because it's not just Mom and Mina in the kitchen this morning. My grandmother, and *her* mother, sit at the kitchen table. Great-Grandma Good has shrunk down into a tiny little thing, violet-eyed and immediately scowling at my belly, but she's still here. She's still *alive*.

The way Zelda isn't, I can't help but think. That makes me realize Great-Grandma Good has to have been born in the mid-1800s.

"Elizabeth Good," I say with no preamble. "She married Zachariah Rivers. You must have known her." As if saying her name summons her, Elizabeth is suddenly at my elbow.

Great-Grandma raises a scraggly eyebrow over a sunken purple eye. "Aunt Elizabeth? I suppose I did. Mean old biddy."

Elizabeth makes an affronted sound and glares at her niece. "I was nothing but kind to Esmerelda and the rest of her kin. Is it my fault my sister raised a bunch of ruffians?"

Before I can respond to Elizabeth, assuming there's a response to be made, Zander shuffles in. He looks rumpled and gorgeous as he comes to stand beside me just inside the kitchen doorway.

He smiles lazily. "Morning, ladies."

I imagine entering any kitchen full of women might make

a wise man pause, but Good women are next-level. There are a lot of violet glares and muttering that sounds a lot like spells.

Or curses.

"Better put the armor on," I say cheerfully to Zander, who pretends not to hear me.

The only one who returns his smile and greeting is Mina, who is not a Good and is better for it.

Granny Good launches into an anecdote about my grandfather, long-lost and unlamented by her reckoning, and the way he seemed to believe he could win over any group in every room by the power of his smile alone.

I'm sure it's a randomly chosen story, not pointed at all.

I find myself smirking. "It must be hard, not being able to win us over."

Zander turns his gray gaze on me. "I know how to win you over."

I shiver, very much against my will.

Mina starts carrying platters of pancakes and eggs over from the stove. Then we all sit down with the grandma convention, and it's not exactly awkward. Not that Mom doesn't give it her best shot, just to be ornery, but Zander manages to make even Great-Grandma laugh before I make my excuses to get to the store.

I stand up, but freeze when Zander stands with me.

"Pairs," he reminds me, with an innocent look on his face and a thunderstorm glint that's just for me. "Like Emerson said."

"That's good thinking," Granny Good says with a sage sort of nod as she takes the last of the sausages. "You never know what might happen when you back the Joywood into a corner. Known for their harsh retaliations, that lot."

"Granny. Do you remember the last ascension?"

She frowns a little, clearly thinking back. Eventually she shakes her head. "It's all fuzzy. Must have happened when I was too young to care."

It's more than that though. It's as Frost told us.

There's no one who remembers because the Joywood *want* it that way. Which means we'll have to rely on ourselves as we charter these unknown waters that only the Joywood know.

Zander and I walk down Main to Tea & No Sympathy in what feels a lot like the contentment I saw back at the stove in Mina and Mom's kitchen. I could let that settle in me like panic, like anger, but maybe I'll just have to accept that next to Zander is where I feel safest.

"I suppose Emerson will want to have a meeting tonight," Zander says conversationally as I unlock the front door of my shop.

I snort at that. "Please. She would have sent a ten-page agenda by now if she was going to call a meeting. She's probably too busy drowning in Wildes."

"Then come to the bar with me tonight."

He says this casually. Like he might have before our first Beltane prom. Like we just hang out. As friends. Or more.

I know there isn't anything casual in the offer. Or how badly I want to take him up on it. I move around my usual opening routine, giving myself that time to breathe, to think. To push myself beyond *feeling*.

Beyond *panic*.

"I can't. I have plans." I could leave it at that. I could let him think I have a date, the way I normally would. "Brynleigh's cheering at her high school's football game tonight. It's her first time, so I promised her I'd go."

Because I have a relationship with my half sisters that has nothing to do with my dad. Like it or not, and mostly I like it.

Or maybe I like that he *doesn't* like it, and sticking knives into good old Bill Wallace—the metaphoric kind because humans are so breakable—is one of my favorite parlor games.

Zander nods. "I'll go with you."

I want him to come with me, and that's a truth I don't feel like addressing. "What about the bar?"

He is watching me a little too closely. A little too intensely. "Grandma Rivers has the cousins jumping in to help since they're here. She said Dad and I are *required* to take three days off ferry and bar duty and let them handle it."

He's clearly a little irritated by this, but he shrugs. You don't argue with Grandma Rivers, this I know. She was the only reason Zander had any time off around Litha, or after Zelda's death.

"Emerson wants us in pairs," he says, so innocently. As if he's spent his entire life up to this moment doing exactly what Emerson—or anyone else—tells him. His eyes get grayer. "Besides, if you're going to tell your dad and Stephanie about the baby, I should be there."

I hadn't exactly been planning on that. For one thing, I can hide it from them easily enough. It's not like we're in each other's pockets. They live *just* far enough away, over by Lake St. Louis, that I only have to worry about the occasional weekend ambush here in the store.

From Stephanie and my sisters, not dear old Dad. *He* never sets foot in St. Cyprian if he can help it. He doesn't have to remember that his ex is a witch to know he doesn't want to run into Tanith.

As Zander stares me down, looking entirely too *patient*, it occurs to me that trying to hide the baby in the first place wasn't, maybe, my best idea. I really do love my sisters. It would hurt their precarious little teenage and preteen feelings if I didn't tell them. No matter what memory spells they'll be under later, they'll remember if they had to find out by accident.

"Fine," I say, begrudgingly. "Okay."

Zander takes his time grinning at me, and he can still light me on fire. Just like that. Just...that easily.

There's not a lot of *thinking* when he's around, and less by the second.

There's that look on his gorgeous face and that grin and all the thunderstorms we make together, one rolling into the next and the two of us all alone here in my shop on a quiet morning.

And me made of nothing but deliriously jumbled thoughts and wants and *yes*—

But Zachariah and Elizabeth pop through the walls then, as if they've been hanging around in the alley outside.

I take that as the freaking life preserver it really is, letting me break the spell that's always been my downfall where Zander is concerned. That bright, hot fire between us that I wish really *was* a spell, because spells can be broken.

This thing between Zander and me, on the other hand, is eternal.

Maybe that was why we fought about it and around it so much, back when we were kids and it about flattened us.

Whatever it is, I take the life preserver and duck back behind my long counter, happily using it as a barricade and not caring that, judging from the way Zander's mouth curves, he knows exactly what I'm doing.

"I told you she was a merchant," Elizabeth is saying to Zachariah, like she's settling a bet. Then they start arguing about what constitutes a *merchant*, but there's no animosity to it. They're smiling, and there's a little sparkle in Elizabeth's eye that I recognize all too well.

"I suppose we need to talk about sending them back," I say, because they're starting to freak me out. I think the bickering was better. Easier.

Better than *hope* that tends to crash and burn when it's just within reach.

Zander says nothing for a few moments, watching them waft about the store, arguing about which teas are better. I wait for him to jump on what I said. To say we should give it a shot right now and be done with them.

For reasons I don't choose to examine, the thought of letting the pair of them disappear into the ether of the afterlife makes me think I might...sob, maybe. Just like the notion that Zander will want to send them away, because I brought it up.

Because I am nothing if not the architect of my own despair.

He shrugs instead. "It can probably wait."

"Yeah," I say, though I have to clear my throat. "It probably can."

And when he looks back at me, he smiles.

16

THERE IS SOMETHING ABOUT GOING TO VISIT my father's side of the family that always fills me with dread. That something is dealing with Bill, obviously, but add the overly, desperately cheerful Stephanie always trying to smooth things over so we can be one big happy family, and I'd rather just stay the hell away.

Tragically, I enjoy my sisters. Who are also cursed through our father's bloodline thanks to my mother—though they, as full humans, know nothing of witches or magic or curses. Everyone calls them *forthright*. *Direct*. Stephanie despairs of their lack of *tact* no matter how she tries to teach them the polite benefit of a little white lie or two.

Only I know they *can't* lie.

I'll admit this brings me more enjoyment than it should.

Stephanie tries to convince me to meet at the house before the football game. *Dinner! Drinks!* Anything to get me into her over-perfumed but well-meaning orbit.

I tell her I'll meet them at the game. I should probably warn them I'm bringing Zander…but I don't. This might or might not have something to do with the fact that I'm in Zander's truck, like we really are sixteen all over again, fielding these texts from my stepmother.

"Don't you want to tell them before the game?" he asks in what is, for him, a neutral tone of voice.

"No. Brynleigh should have her moment. She loves the spotlight."

He spares me a glance, all gray amusement that I pretend I can't feel inside me like heat. "Coward."

I could argue. Maybe I try. But okay, I'm a coward.

Obviously that means I have no choice but to turn it around on him. "You didn't bring your letterman jacket out of storage? You and Bill could talk glory days. How many touchdowns did *you* make in a single game?"

"He doesn't still tell those stories," Zander says as he maneuvers his truck through the human high school parking lot.

I make sure I'm looking right at him as I say, "Of course he does. All the time."

Not a single lie to be found.

Zander shakes his head as he finds us a prime parking place in the overcrowded lot in what the humans would call another example of his ridiculous good luck, but we both know is a quickly muttered spell.

Truth be told, my dad *loved* Zander back in the day. *Adored* him. In fairness, that's a pretty common reaction. Zander has always been talented at being well-liked just about everywhere he goes.

You could try being nice, you know, he would tell me, back when I did my best to ignore Stephanie to her face. And Bill, but more rudely.

I can't lie, I would reply. Smugly.

They might actually have mourned harder than I did when we broke up.

Zander buys us our tickets, and we file toward the stands. I didn't do a glamour, but I'm wearing something uncharacteristically loose so no one can tell I've got a bump unless they really look. A little human-level subterfuge. Hidden, but not hidden once I drop the bomb.

I scan the crowd looking for all that *blond* that will be the Wallace clan. Well, the women anyway. Bill's gone bald, which brings my mother endless joy.

Stephanie starts waving maniacally once my gaze lands on her. It's possible if Zander wasn't there with his hand on my back to herd me along I would turn around and walk right back out. Promises be damned.

But we're moving through the crowd despite my misgivings. We climb up the uncomfortable bleachers to the little Wallace contingent. The four of my sisters who are not down on the field cheering sit in a row with Stephanie on the end. I don't see Bill.

I decide that's better.

"Hey," I offer by way of greeting.

Stephanie tries to hug me, but with the crowded bleachers and the girls between us, she settles for kind of reaching out and missing touching me entirely. I might also have leaned away, pretending to scan the field for Brynleigh, who I finally spot in the huddle of cheerleaders down at the edge of the field.

"Doesn't she look pretty?" Stephanie is always good at a pivot, making it seem like what she wanted to do in the first place was discuss Brynleigh, not attempt to have a moment with her grumpy stepdaughter. "We spent two hours getting her hair *just* right." She finally seems to realize Zander is with me and turns toward him. "Who's your... Oh! *Zander!*"

I tense, waiting to see what the reception is like. Zander, meanwhile, has never worried about his *reception* in his life. He just grins like he belongs here.

Stephanie blinks, then smiles broadly. "It's been too long! Sit. Sit." She makes shooing motions at the hard bleacher bench. "Girls, you remember Zander."

"I do not," Sadie says over her large-rimmed glasses I know for a fact she doesn't actually need. She immediately stares back down at the book in her lap, which looks like it's at least a thousand pages long. She likes to make a statement at a football game.

"You're breaking my heart, Sadie," Zander replies, squeezing in beside me as I sit down next to her.

Sadie rolls her eyes, but there's a little blush on her cheeks. On her other side, little Gigi sees it and giggles.

"Are you the high school boyfriend we all hate?" Avery asks innocently enough. Just truth, nothing overtly malicious about it.

I really do love them.

Zander laughs. "Guilty as charged."

"So why are you here?" Madyson demands, leaning around Avery. She's tossing a lacrosse ball back and forth between her hands. Bill calls her *Sonny*—claiming it's just a take on her name and not the manifestation of his deepest, most unreachable desire to have a *son*. It's clear she's his only sporty hope. Though he's all for Brynleigh cheering, because it means he can come to high school football games and pretend he's a young stud all over again.

"Where is Bill?" I ask, wishing I didn't feel the need.

"Your father is down there talking to the football coach," Stephanie says, waving down toward the field. Stephanie is always kind. Warm. Desperate. She never corrects me or asks me not to call Bill by his first name, but when I do, she *always* responds with *your father*.

I wish I didn't respect that.

The game starts, and I expect Bill to climb back up to join us, but he stays down by the field. I try to focus on Brynleigh, not his bald head shining in the bright lights of the football field. Or the game that claims Zander's attention immediately, the way any and every sporting event always does.

I cheer and whistle right along with Stephanie, because she looks so proud and Brynleigh is down there flushed with pleasure and I...am having a daughter of my own. I might hope that she won't be in the market for two-hour hairdos and *this*, but maybe it's good to practice all the ways to be happy for your kid even when it's not the way you would be happy.

Assuming you know how to be happy, says Ruth in my head. I don't turn around to look for her. I don't want to give her the satisfaction.

That's a little aggressive, I retort. *For a jumped-up chicken dish.*

I return my attention to the game, the entirety of which passes—complete with cheering and marching bands and all the rest of it—without an appearance from Bill. This is typical. Bill likes his compartments to stay compartmentalized. A *blended* family was never in his toolbox, no matter how Stephanie wishes otherwise.

We climb down the bleachers with the crowd, Zander's hand on my back again. This earns me speculative looks not just from my sisters, but from Stephanie herself. I manage not to meet a single one of their speculative looks.

We meet Brynleigh and Bill down at the bottom.

"Let's go to Fritz's!" Brynleigh shouts at us as we gather around her, doing a little cheerleading jump. "I deserve some frozen custard after that."

The last thing I want to do is go to a second location with everyone. "I don't think..."

"Oh, come along," Bill says in such an overtly affable voice that I blink in astonishment. He's not grinning at *me* though. "It's been so long since I've caught up with Zander."

Of course. And I guess telling them on a sticky patio over frozen custard is better than in a crowd of human high schoolers.

"Sounds great," Zander replies, as he and my dad do a complicated handshake, shoulder bump, *man thing*.

I try and fail to smile, and then we're walking in a big blond group. Sadie manages this without seeming to lift her eyes from her heavy tome, and I always respect total commitment to all things, but especially to being needlessly dramatic and *not like other girls*—my personal high school specialty.

In the parking lot, Zander and I get into his truck that is right on the other side of the turnstiles, with promises to meet everyone at Fritz's. It's a short drive. We wait by the side of the road in front of the school so Zander can offer a little salute to Bill as he drives by a few minutes later in his oversized SUV.

"I can do it if you want," Zander says, his eyes steady on the road. "Rip off the Band-Aid and let you handle the fallout."

The wave of relief that threatens to take me down is unexpectedly huge. I want nothing more than to let him do exactly that, but I also know I won't be able to live with myself if I'm *that much* of a coward. "No, I've got it. Look, if you want to drop me off until—"

"I'm not dropping you off, baby," he says matter-of-factly as he once again claims a prime parking spot that wasn't there for Bill, five seconds ago, in the Fritz's parking lot.

It reminds me of last night and the way Jacob said he'd be staying at Wilde House. The way Mina and my mom *hold on* to each other. It *resonates*—and I tell myself that I really need some Zander-free time tomorrow. As a mental health thing, at this point.

We get out and join the rest of my family in line to order. My stomach is threatening to revolt, something I haven't dealt with since the early stages of pregnancy. Or the last Joywood attack. I tell myself it's a resurgence of morning sickness, not nerves.

Because I don't care what Bill or Stephanie thinks. I never have. As much as I love my sisters, I'm not worried about their reactions either. They're kids.

And yet.

We shove in at an uncomfortable plastic table that's bolted into the asphalt. With the sun down, it's too chilly to be eating something frozen outside, but no one seems to care. Teenagers laugh around us. Couples huddle together.

"We have something to tell you," I say instead of taking a bite of what I ordered, a Raz-ma-Taz concrete—a name that pains me but is a delightful blend of custard, raspberries, marshmallows, and chopped nuts that I normally inhale.

Beside me, Stephanie's eyes get *huge*, and she immediately grips my left hand, inspecting my ring finger.

It never occurred to me that anyone would think *that*.

"I'm pregnant," I blurt out, lest she start planning white dresses and acres of orchids, though I might be too late.

"I thought you had to be married to have a baby," Gigi says, her eyebrows beetling together.

"Uh, well, it's best to be," Stephanie says. "I mean, it's okay if *you're* not, of course," she tells me, gripping my hand even harder. Then she turns back to Gigi. "*You* really should wait until you are."

Poor Stephanie. I'm surprised smoke doesn't start coming from her ears as she tries to make both things *okay*. The way she always tries so hard to make *everything* okay.

"We learned all about *procreation* in health," Sadie announces proudly. "I can explain it to you, Gigi."

"No, Sadie. Not now." Stephanie sounds desperate enough that Sadie keeps her mouth shut, but she grins at me. I want to laugh or return the grin, but my father is just sitting there, a blank look on his face.

Stephanie wraps her arms around his neck and squeezes. "Bill! We're going to be *grandparents!*"

My dad says nothing. He doesn't look at me. And despite how low I would tell you my expectations are for this man, I still expected...*something*. Some reaction, even if it was faked. A hug. A pat on the back.

A *smile*, for fuck's sake.

Instead he stands, awkwardly slipping his phone out of his pocket. "Congratulations. I'm so—" He trips over whatever word he tries to say, and I know that trip. I know he tried to lie.

And failed. Mom and I have no idea how he sells a thing. His face gets red. "I have a call to make."

He walks away, jabbing at his phone like it betrayed him.

A *very* uncomfortable silence follows. Eventually Stephanie interrupts it with a nervous titter. "You know how touchy he is about getting old." She shrugs like it's a cute little joke. "He'll come around."

Did I really expect something different? Genuine excitement? It's not like I don't know my own father.

Zander's hand is still on my back, but he shifts to sling his arm over my shoulders. "I hate to break this up, but I've got to get to work."

"At night?" Madyson asks, holding her lacrosse ball in the crook of her neck as she shovels in her frozen custard. "That's weird."

"I run a bar," he tells her.

I know he doesn't have to work tonight. He's just getting me out of here.

I feel a rush of sheer relief. Like we're a team again, the way I imagined we could be back between blowups when we were teenagers. Maybe that's why looking at other couples doing their *team* thing makes me feel…almost nostalgic.

"Sounds exciting," Brynleigh says, all but fluttering her lashes Zander's way.

"I'm sure your father will be right back…" This is maybe the first time I've ever seen Stephanie *this* overwrought—aside from the few times she's had to deal directly with my mother.

Zander and I stand, so she stands too. Then wraps me in an overly scented hug, squeezing tight. Holding on like she means it as she whispers, "I'm so happy for you. We're going to throw you the *best* baby shower."

Tonight, probably for the first time, I hug her back. When I whisper my *thank you* right back to her, I mean it. Even if the idea of a baby shower with her is high on my list of worst ways to spend an afternoon.

She hugs Zander too, while I go through my sisters. We're not *huggers*, but they congratulate me, suggest names, show excitement. Except Sadie, who is watching with clear understanding on her face. Because she isn't just low on tact like the rest of us, she's perceptive.

When she doesn't say anything, I give her a sisterly poke. "Don't forget to text me a birthday list. You have to give me some time to shop."

She studies me for a moment with eyes like mine. "Just take me to Confluence Books someday. Your friend has the best store."

I try to smile. "You're so easy, Sadie."

"You are literally the only one who thinks so."

Knowing she can't lie, I want to hug her then— but I don't because she'd get all stiff and ask me what's wrong with me.

A question I won't know how to answer.

I start to move for Zander's truck, but Stephanie hasn't quite given it up yet tonight. "I'm sure your father…"

This time we all turn to look at him. He's standing over by his SUV, still clenching the phone to his ear. When he sees us all watching him, he lifts a hand in a wave.

Not a greeting. A dismissal. Because in classic Bill Wallace fashion, he doesn't want to deal with it. With *me*. So he won't.

I'm surprised to find myself *sad*, like all my mad deserted me. Maybe that's Elizabeth's fault. That talk about getting tired of being angry last night. I swear I could muster it if I didn't hear her in my head. *Legacies are choices.*

We walk to the truck and I get in, feeling fragile. I tell myself it's last night's poisoning finally catching up with me. Because I won't let it be anything else.

Zander says nothing. He starts the truck and begins the drive back to St. Cyprian.

I assure myself the silence is good. Certainly not *oppressive*. The throbbing inside of me must be the aftereffects of yesterday. With a nice helping of morning sickness.

We came here to make an announcement, and the announcement is made. Everyone knows. The end.

I close my eyes on a wave of sadness, laced with a very old, very familiar pain. I can't seem to bundle it all up and shove it down the way I usually do. Every time I think it doesn't matter, that I don't care, that my life is better without old bald Bill in it—he finds a new way to shove the knife to my heart a little deeper.

Bill's not evil, but that only makes me sadder. It wouldn't occur to him that he hurt my feelings, because in his mind, he was confronted with being *old*—the thing he hates most in all the world. So he walked away from the person and conversation that made him feel that way.

It's as simple as that.

I realize as this quiet drive goes on that I expected much more from him tonight.

Not because he's been such a great dad to *me*, but because he's been a pretty decent one to my sisters. He goes to almost all their various events. He eats family dinners at home when he's not traveling for work. He seems to love Stephanie, whatever that means to a man like him.

He's *there* for them. And it's possible that deep down I thought maybe a baby…a *child*…could bring us together.

The way we haven't been since I was a little kid myself.

A tear wells up and makes it over my eyelid, but I magic it away so Zander doesn't see.

Because this is dumb. I know who Bill is. I know his limitations. He's not a cruel man. Not abusive. He just doesn't give a shit about anything that isn't the Bill Wallace show.

Never has, never will.

"I'm sorry, El," Zander says in that quiet, almost-gruff way after we've driven a while.

"I don't c—" I suck in a painful breath and try again. "It doesn't ma—"

I am not going to cry. I chant this to myself. Its own spell. Its own magic. I am *not* going to lose it sitting in the passenger seat of Zander's ancient truck. Not over Bill Wallace, of all unworthy people.

I have never let myself cry in front of Zander. I convinced myself it was because I didn't want him trying to fix it for me. I only cry over things that can't be fixed and *trying* to pretend they're fixable only makes them worse.

Case in point.

I press my forehead to the passenger window. "Just take me home, please."

He makes a low sort of noise, but I know he's agreeing, and I relax a little. He'll take me...somewhere, anyway. We don't have to do this. He won't see me cry.

"What home are you thinking?" he asks. "Your mom's? Your apartment? Or do you want to go back to Wilde House?"

The fact that there are too many options hits me. Hard and wrong.

Why don't I know where home is?

I've spent years avoiding that question, ever since my father left the house I grew up in and nothing was ever the same. That isn't to say it didn't have upsides, but it still wasn't the same.

Tonight it breaks over me, in me. Into a long, painful sob. Into tears I can't stop.

I cover my face with my hands and try to find a spell to *hide* this, but it just doesn't come. It doesn't matter how mortified I am. The sobs wrack my body.

Over and over again.

Zander must have pulled over, because a few seconds later, he's moving me into his lap. I want to fight him, but I don't. I can't.

For the first time in my life, I cry in front of another person who isn't my mom.

I cry directly into his chest. What else is there to do?

He tucks me under his chin, wrapping me in his strong arms

and holding me close. He doesn't tell me not to cry. He doesn't tell me it will all be okay.

Zander doesn't say any of that. He just holds me and calls me *baby* and kisses my hair.

I cry until I'm weak. Until I'm spent.

Until there's no pretending I don't know that his shirt is soaked with my stupid tears and almost worse, I am curled up in his lap in a truck on the side of the highway.

"Fuck," I mutter.

He laughs a little, still smoothing a big hand over my hair. Then he presses a kiss to the crown of my head. "Buck up, El. We've got one more stop to make."

I can't bring myself to look at him as I crawl back to my seat. Like an embarrassing morning after, but without any of the good stuff to reflect on in the shower.

"We need to go tell my dad," he says.

I'm surprised enough by that to look over at him as he pulls the truck back out onto the road. "You haven't told him already?"

He shakes his head. "I thought it would make him sad. And it will."

He turns to look at me then, and his eyes are a blaze of silver fury.

Not *at* me, but on my behalf.

It makes me want to melt. Maybe I do. I'm too waterlogged to tell.

"It will also make him happy, Ellowyn, like it should." His voice is hard then, the kind of hardness he never shows my dad to his face. "He's going to be sad because Mom isn't here to see it, but this is also going to be his *grandkid*. And to him? That's going to be pure joy and happiness. I promise you."

17

IT'S NOT THE FIRST TIME I'VE STOOD IN FRONT of the old Rivers house, set back from the riverbank but within walking distance of the ferry, feeling nervous and unsure of my place here. Zelda was always about warm hugs and obvious delight at the sight of me, but Zack tended toward gruff. I never quite knew what he thought of me back then.

I still don't. I'm not sure this announcement of ours is going to help. Zander seems to be pinning a lot of *hope* on it, and I wish he wouldn't. I feel like there's a high probability that I'll need to soothe away *his* tears in fifteen minutes, and nobody wants that.

I've glamoured all traces of tears off my face, and just wish that there were glamours for aching hearts too. Zander has his arm around me as we walk toward the house, and I know I should say something about that. I should point out that it's not only too familiar, too intimate, but it's definitely hurtling down a slippery slope *at the very least*, but I can't quite get my mouth to do my bidding. Maybe because he hasn't mentioned the crying.

I tell myself it's because he knows that if he did I'd *poof* myself away. Immediately.

Why didn't I think of that when the crying dam inside me broke wide-open?

Zander doesn't knock at his father's door. He walks right inside the house, calling out for his dad as he goes. He sweeps me along with him, straight back into the kitchen, so there's not much for me to do but go along with him and notice that nothing much has changed since the last time I was here, over a decade ago. Like the place has been frozen in time, or in my memories.

Maybe because that's when everything changed here and the house couldn't keep up.

Zack shuffles out from the hall and the bedroom down that way, looking rumpled. As if we woke him up, but he offers a brave sort of smile.

"Everything okay?" he asks, scratching a hand through his beard. "It's a bit late."

"It's nine, Dad."

"Oh." Zack squints over at the clock on the kitchen oven. "Well." He looks at me, and though his gaze is puzzled, and sharpens at Zander's arm around me, he doesn't comment. "Did you two need something?"

"We need to tell you something." Zander pulls me closer. So fierce and determined and sounding so *sure*, but I can feel the faint tremor of something else under it. Not nerves, exactly. Maybe the knowledge that this isn't going to be *easy*.

No one ever says joy and happiness are easy, do they? What they say is it's worth it.

"Tell me," Zack says, and I'm sure I'm not the only one who sees the way he braces himself for something terrible.

Zander stands a little taller. He holds me a little tighter. "We're going to have a baby. A girl. In March."

He lays it all out. Quick. Simple.

Exactly how I should have done it, in retrospect—especially when I realize my dad didn't even ask. Stephanie did. The girls did. *When are you due? When can we have a baby shower?* Those are the excited things they jockeyed to ask me while we were leaving.

But this is about Zander's family now. As we stand there in a kitchen that seems cold and empty with Zelda's absence, Zack's eyes fill. Just *fill right up.*

This is worse, I think in a panic. Ten million times worse than my father's nonreaction. This big, gruff man on the brink of tears.

I want to turn and run, but Zander is holding me in place.

I realize he's holding on to me not only because he's still giving me comfort, but also because he needs something to hold on to himself while we wait to see if Zack really will sob the way it looks like he might.

I had no idea that it would feel this good to be needed. To be someone else's anchor when I've always been so bound and determined to be my own.

"A girl. In March," Zack echoes. Like those might be his dying words because we've stabbed him through the heart.

Zander clears his throat. "Just like Mom."

His father nods, a bit like I might expect a soldier who just crawled out of a trench to nod. Out of place. Bleeding out. Then he exhales, like it's his very last breath.

I hold mine.

Zack clearly isn't leaving us just yet, because as I watch, his mouth curves. Upward. Until it turns into the sort of smile I can't remember seeing on him in ages. Ten years, at least.

"Isn't that something," he says, and when Zack says it, he sounds *awed.*

Like it's a *good* something.

"A baby girl," he says, out loud, with wonder. I don't know what to call this fizzy, dancing reaction inside of me. Or the way Zander holds me, still. "Won't that be something?" The tears are still there in his eyes, but he's laughing now. "Now, who would have guessed that? Besides your mother."

He doesn't sober at the mention of Zelda, though his laugh softens. "She always hoped..." He shakes his head, and claps his hands together. "Enough of that. This is good news! We need to celebrate. A toast?" He starts moving deeper into the kitchen, then stops to spin back to us. "No alcohol, of course. Not for expectant mothers." Then he lifts his hand in the air in a kind of excited *fluster* that warms me top to bottom.

I magic us all mugs of tea, even though it means Zander drops his arm from around me. And I miss it. "It's called Celebration Tea."

"Creative," Zander says, and only grins when I lift a brow at him.

Zack laughs, and it might be the most tickled I've ever seen him. "Celebration is right." He lifts the mug. "To the mother and father of *my* grandchild." He points a finger at us before clinking his mug to ours. "This girl better call me Grandpa. None of that cutesy bullshit people do nowadays. No Grampy, G-dog, *Big Z*—Grandpa."

"No, sir." Zander says, grinning at his dad over the rim of his mug. "Grandpa it is."

This is exactly how it should be. This is *right*. So much so I can't even feel sad about Bill in this moment, because we have Zack. We have my mom and our coven. We have Stephanie and my sisters. We even have Zelda too.

I know I'm not the only one who feels her now, right here with us.

We sip at our tea for a few minutes, all grinning at each other until my cheeks start to ache from such unnatural activity, and then Zack puts his mug down on the counter.

"Hold on one second," he says, before disappearing down the hallway he originally appeared from.

I mean to scowl when I look at Zander, but that grin seems stuck on my face. Maybe that's why he grins back. "Told you, baby."

I tell myself to file that away so I can be mad about it later. The *told you so* as well as yet another *baby*. I get the feeling Zander knows exactly what I'm doing and doesn't much care.

When Zack returns, he's holding something in his hand. As he comes closer, I see it's a necklace—a lot like the one I've been wearing since Zander gave me his for protection. It has the same design, though it's smaller and the chain more feminine than a band of leather.

"I know you're wearing Zander's right now for all that coven garbage," Zack says, holding it out to me. "Take this one instead. It was Zelda's."

I try to step back, to refuse, but the Rivers men have me surrounded. "I don't think I'm the right one—"

"That baby you're carrying is part Rivers, which means so are you. She'd want you to have it. You know she would." Zack sounds definitive. Without waiting for me to agree, he places the necklace over my head with his own two hands. Then he mutters a few words that magic Zander's back to his own neck.

"It has Zelda's magic in it," Zack says to me, putting his hands on my shoulders and giving me a little squeeze. "When the baby is born, it can be hers."

To my horror, I realize I'm going to cry again.

I could stop it this time. I could zap myself back to my stock room, but I don't. This feels like the kind of moment that *deserves* tears.

As if tears aren't always a sign of unbearable weakness, like they are when you're half human in a world of full witches. As if maybe, sometimes, they're no more and no less than a sign of too many things to feel at once and no words for them.

I sniffle as I look up at Zack, who is already so excited to be my baby girl's *grandpa* that it makes everything in me feel... different.

"I hope you know, I loved her too," I manage to choke out.

"Who didn't? No one worth a damn." Then he pulls me into a kind of one-armed side-hug, because he's using his other arm to pull Zander in. He squeezes us tight to him—something I don't think would have happened if Zelda was here. Or maybe she would have pulled him right in too.

"Oh, she'd be so happy," he says, his voice cracking.

I hate crying, I do, but these tears aren't so bad. "She is," I tell him, not even caring that someone is hugging me against my will. "She's delighted."

Because I feel it. Because I know.

When my gaze meets Zander's, I know we all do.

Zack holds us close a moment longer, then huffs out a breath. "Well. Enough of this." He releases us, wiping at his face. "I've got to tell everyone I know I'm going to be a grandpa. You two probably have work to do. Just promise me you'll take care of yourself—and my granddaughter—while you kick some Joy-wood ass."

I nod, but then it occurs to me what this moment needs. I close my eyes, think of what I want, and when I open them I hold out the mug Zack was using. With its new design.

#1 Grandpa

He barks out a laugh. "I'll use it every morning." He beams at me, holding that mug like it's a pile of precious jewels. Then he does that thing men do when they clear their throats of emotion. Or try to. "We're proud of you," he tells me, his voice raspy.

He and Zander share a hug. A real one, not just a manly approximation of fist bumps.

"See you soon, Dad," Zander murmurs.

Then he leads me back outside, his fingers threaded through mine.

I know as we hit the fresh air, the dark with autumn crisp on the breeze, that everything is changing. It has been for a while, I guess, but it keeps shifting on me. There's no sturdy ground.

Except Zander's hand in mine. Except the way he keeps to my side, matching his athletic stride to mine. This thing between us like steel girders, the architecture beneath everything else, no matter what I usually tell myself three hundred sixty-four days of each year.

I should freak out about that. I'm sure I will—but maybe tonight is not the night. Maybe tonight I can just…hold on.

He stops at the passenger side of his truck. "Now that we've gone through the fucking emotional gauntlet, what other wounds should we poke at?"

He's joking, I think, but I suddenly see clearly exactly what we have to do. Not only because it's what I want to do.

Something inside of me *insists* upon it. "Let's take a walk down by the confluence."

I feel him stiffen, because that's what his mother used to do. "El—"

I ignore his resistance, squeeze his hand, and begin to walk. Down the hill the big house on stilts is settled on, along the pathway Zelda took every morning before she got sick.

Zander isn't happy about it. He's grumbling as we go, but I know this is right.

We walk, closer and closer to the confluence, and then I see her. Just where she should be. Standing, looking out toward the confluence. "Don't you see her?"

"Who?" he mutters irritably.

I grab his hand and squeeze it tight as we walk toward her. I don't think, don't plan. I pour some of my magic into him so he can *see* as she turns, as she begins to walk toward us.

I feel his whole body go rigid. Instantly.

Then the breath goes out of him on an exhale that forms the word "Mom."

He stops walking, and I can't pull him along. He's too big.

But it doesn't matter because Zelda is floating across the ground to meet us.

Her smile is wide. Her eyes glisten. She's not like Elizabeth and Zachariah—not as fully formed as they are, but she moves for Zander and wraps her ghostly arms around him. I can tell he feels it. That the touch of her spirit shudders through him almost as if she's really here. Body and soul, instead of soul alone.

"You don't know the work it takes to make this spirit body thing," she says to him, pulling back and placing a hand on his cheek. She struggles to do all this, I can see it in her face, though it's easier here, close to the confluence and its magic.

"They say I'll get better at it. Stronger. And I will." She looks from Zander to me and then back again. "You know I'm right here. Whether you see me or not. You know."

There's a kind of arrested look on his face, like he's shocked to see her. Hear her.

Then Zelda turns her silver gaze to me. "She'll know me too." She reaches out, that ghostly hand moving against my stomach. I feel it like a breeze, not an actual touch, but it's enough. It's more than enough.

Then she lifts her fading hand up to the necklace that was once hers around my neck, and she smiles at me. "As it should be."

She's getting quieter, disappearing right in front of us. I grip Zander's hand, knowing he'll feel it like another loss no matter how much he believes she's here, just out of sight.

"You did the imperative," she whispers into the wind. "Take care of each other."

Then she's gone, but I realize in her wake that her insistence I tell Zander wasn't only about wanting her son to know. It was about *all* this. He had to know, my coven had to know, for us to make the choices that have brought us, slowly and carefully, here.

Where we might win. It's *imperative* that we do.

Zander sits down, heavily, on a bench that looks over the confluence, St. Cyprian, and where we won our Litha head-to-head with the Joywood on the other side. His whole body is shaking, so I magic us a blanket and wrap it around him. Around the both of us, because I'm still here, holding on to him the way he held on to me.

"Ellowyn."

He doesn't say anything else. Just my name, ragged and pained.

"She's trying so hard," I assure him. "She'll get there."

"I know. I could tell. I just…why?"

"So you'd know. Really know. No doubts." I understand why he might have had doubts about Zelda visiting him. He was worried she would blame him. Worried that he'd been wrong.

Even though he doesn't cry, it's my turn to stroke his hair. To press a kiss to his temple. To comfort him. While the stars and moon shine above us, like they're watching out for us too.

I can hear the sound of birds roosting, likely an eagle and an owl. Maybe even a raven. When I lift my head, I see the glowing eyes of a huge buck I can *feel* is Jacob's familiar, Murphy.

Everyone's keeping track. Taking care of us even on this side of the river, far off the bricks.

"Emerson's going to be pissed if we stay much longer," Zander finally says.

"Yeah," I agree.

Neither of us moves.

He looks down at me.

I turn in to him.

I think maybe we're both going to speak, but our eyes meet, and no words come out. Not because I want to lie, for once, but because I *don't*.

I don't know how to speak past all this longing. All this dangerous, revolutionary *pining* for something good. Something safe and hot and *mine*.

Something that feels the way joy should, too close to tears and brighter than the sun inside me.

He lowers his mouth to mine. Slow, when I'm not sure we've ever been *slow* about anything unless we were trying to torture each other.

This isn't that. It's not hesitation either. Zander seems absolutely sure.

It's like he's giving me a choice.

A choice I should turn away from and don't, but this isn't a surprise. *Choices* aren't my strong suit.

But I make one, don't I? I lean into him.

His mouth touches mine. A *touch*. I wouldn't even call it a kiss.

The brush of lips.

Our breath mingles for a second before he pulls me closer.

He hasn't kissed me like this in over ten years. I wouldn't have let him if he'd tried. I shouldn't let him now. There's too much up in the air. Too much I'm almost certain to mess up to let myself be kissed with *tenderness*.

Still, I don't pull away. I don't put a stop to it or turn it wilder, like I could. Like I would have even a few hours ago.

I sink into the soft, into the gentle.

Into him.

Into all that love we won't admit but can't leave behind.

18

SOMEWHERE, DEEP DOWN, THERE'S AN ALARM
bell ringing inside me. It's so faint under the warmth of this
blanket, the heat of his arms around me, the familiar sweet fire
of Zander's lips on mine.

It's gentle. Like a question instead of the usual Beltane ex-
clamations. Like we have eternity to sit by the river and kiss
each other like we're new. Maybe we do. I could be on board
with that. Because all the places I've cracked apart today have
been filled in—by joy, by love, by this kiss.

"We can head back to Wilde House," Zander says against
my mouth.

He's giving me an out—well, sort of. His hand sliding up
my spine to curve around the back of my neck doesn't give me
much space for *outs*. His mouth traveling down my neck has me
forgetting, momentarily, that he's said anything at all.

Wilde House. People. Our ghosts.

All the relatives have probably cleared out by now. We can
reset. Go back to how things were before the Undine started
issuing orders.

I know I should take that option. I'm sure the wise move is to step back from this, because it's too much. The past twenty-four hours have been *too much*.

Maybe it's because I know I *should* that I don't. Can't. Won't. "We could go to my apartment instead."

Zander's thunderstorm gaze goes dark and thrilling. He stands, pulling me with him, and then we're flying. I think that we can worry later. That we can deal with anything and everything else…later.

When we land, it's not in my bed as I expect, because that's how we usually do things. We break the seal, we go a little crazy, we rip each other into pieces in as many ways as possible—

Tonight we land on the stairwell that leads up to my apartment door.

Maybe we're both being a little more careful with each other tonight. Because it's not Beltane. Because things are different in ways I really don't want to analyze right now. I unlock my door with a quick, muttered spell since my not-so-magical keys are back in Zander's truck at the Rivers house.

The truck. The night. This. "Isn't your dad going to wonder why your truck is sitting outside his house all night?"

I push the door open and head into my apartment while Zander mutters a few words to magic his truck outside my shop. "Problem solved," he says, following me inside.

He carefully locks the door behind him. He shrugs out of his jacket. His gaze never leaves mine, but he doesn't reach out for me either. Like we would if this was a normal night between us. Meaning if this was Beltane—not that I ever let our Beltane thing happen in *my* space.

This changes everything. He said that to me what feels like forever ago, even though it's barely been two weeks. Two weeks can't change *everything*, is what I want to argue, though he hasn't said it again now.

I think of Zelda dying. Her last breath would have been a moment, nothing more. It changed everything.

I think of this baby inside of me. The making of her only took a very long night and a single moment where my magic was too tired to work.

Little moments with such big consequences.

Sometimes everything changes so gradually that it's impossible to notice. Like growing up. Like accepting what other people have chosen for themselves that you might not have chosen for them. Like having friends who shift into a coven that's trying to save the world.

Then, other times, change happens so fast you don't really notice until it's done. Until you're sorting out the repercussions and glamouring away your pregnancy.

I'd rather have his hands on me than decide what this is tonight, but he's standing at the door, and I'm standing a few feet away. I'm not sure I know who I am right now because I feel *nervous*.

Like this is our first time, when I've seen this man naked so many times I can't begin to count. When he's been inside me every way there is to be inside a person, *repeatedly*.

Maybe it takes an eternity or two to stand there, watching each other like this, in the quiet of a fall night that isn't lit with Beltane fires.

Then, slowly and deliberately, Zander makes his way across the room to me.

I am rooted to the spot. My heart is going haywire. Nothing is settling in me the way it should. My control, my walls, the reassuring presence of my comfort and my boundaries—they aren't all *weak* tonight, they're missing.

Like they never existed at all.

Especially when he reaches out and holds my face with his hands. His thumbs sweep across my cheekbones. His gray gaze isn't filled with thunderstorms, not this time. It's something softer, quieter. A gentle rain, maybe.

I tell myself I hate that, but I don't. It feels like it's filling me up. Like I've been thirsty, so thirsty, for far too long.

We could magic our clothes off each other. We could rush. We could insult each other a little to get the edge back into this. We could do all the things we usually do.

But we don't.

He lifts the oversized top I'm wearing up and over my head. I unbutton his flannel with less-than-graceful fingers. We're wearing matching Rivers pendants, and his hands smooth over my bare skin as I slide mine up his impressive back.

Our mouths fuse. Our hearts beat out some rhythm all their own, but together.

Together.

He backs me into my bedroom with lazy strides and deeper kisses. No rush, just doing our level best to rid each other of clothes without our mouths parting. A game we lose and win together as he takes me to my bed.

Then there's nothing but his calloused hands against my skin, my fingers in his hair. Then the perfect, smooth slide of Zander on top of me, around me, and finally inside me. Everywhere.

Puzzle pieces that have always fit too well to bear.

I could stay here, right here, wrapped up in Zander and never think or worry again. Just this. Just us.

But, "Let me in, El," he whispers at my ear.

"Pretty sure you're in." I settle myself, gripping him with my thighs to accentuate the point and bring him deeper. So deep it makes me shiver.

He smiles, his fingers tangling in my hair. "You know what I mean," he says before pressing his mouth between my breasts. Where my heart thuds hard.

Because I do know.

He wants me to open that internal channel I blocked a long

time ago. He wants me to let him into my head as well as my body, the ultimate intimacy that witches have. That humans can't imagine. I don't have to open it up for the sex to be world-shattering, if the past ten years are anything to go by, and usually this sort of thing is a no-brainer.

I refuse whatever he asks. Then we take it out on each other in every inventive way we can.

Things are different tonight.

We're going to be parents to a baby girl. I cried in front of him, when I pride myself on never crying, and certainly not with *witnesses*. What Elizabeth said to me last night seems to echo in my head. *Sometimes a woman gets tired of being angry.*

Anger has protected me for a long, long time, but tonight I find I'm tired. Tired of wanting what I can't have. Tired of fighting anything and everything. Tired of too much truth and nowhere to hide.

I let out a shuddering breath. His gaze is hot on mine, his body on *top* of me, the way I like it best. The way I have always liked him, too much.

He could break through the blocks I put up. I'm sure we're both very aware that he could have from the start, but didn't. Part of me wonders, suddenly, if I blocked him in the first place so he *would* break through...

Tonight he wants me to let him in of my own volition.

"It'll be okay, I promise," he tells me, echoing the kind of vows we made each other long ago. "I'll always protect you, Ellowyn. Always have. Always will."

I tell myself to be careful of promises, that they too often turn out to be curses.

Tonight I don't care.

Or I care too much about other things.

Either way, I let them go. The protections I've held tight around me for years. The walls I built to keep him out of the one place he could always hurt me. Because I knew perfectly well that keeping him out like that, treating him like a human, hurt him too.

And when the walls crumble all around us, I can *feel* his sigh inside of me.

There we are.

I want to cry. Again.

Because his voice inside me, with no one else in this link between us, is the scratch to an itch I've been pretending I don't feel for a decade. For every moment of my adult life.

The tears don't fall though, because we move together. Slow and hot and infinitely, gloriously *patient*.

The past ten years, on every Beltane night, it has been rushed and hot and needy. Edgy, angry, desperate. So much so it's become habit. I tell myself it's unhealthy and mean. *Toxic.* That's the only thing I let myself remember when an inevitable thought about sex with Zander slips through the barricades.

I tell myself that's how it's always been.

I don't say it out loud, because I know better.

Because there used to be *this*.

My body. His. This careening feeling in my chest that used to feel like drowning is more grounded, but I still spin until I fly. This time I'm not so lost, so desperate to find an anchor to drown me and sure it's going to be him.

I'm not that girl any longer. He's not that boy.

We can anchor each other, and we do.

We fly, but we stay connected.

Inside and out.

I find that even when I think I want to hurry it all up, chase all this sensation, something spools out into a kind of sweet, heavy light, slow and hot. It doesn't stop the unraveling—the pulsing, gasping cliff fall of release.

Zander's low laughter *inside* me drives me up all over again.

I tell him what I want. *More.*

He responds in ways he shouldn't, in ways I shouldn't let him. *Always.*

On and on we go, light and hot and *forever,* until there's nothing left but the both of us, shuddering our way through a meteor storm.

Out there in the cosmos, upending everything.

Open your eyes, baby.

It's only then I realize I closed them a while ago, as if I'm trying to fight back the sea change that I can feel inside me, sweeping us both away. Maybe I don't want to see where we've ended up.

I would love to claim I can't be ordered around, but I open my eyes on command. I let my gaze meet his, and there are no words for this. There are no words for *us.*

I feel something inside me tremble as Zander presses a kiss to my mouth. Then again as he smiles while he's there, then rolls over and tucks me next to him, as if it isn't momentous that he thinks we're actually going to *sleep* together when that, obviously, has been outlawed between us forever.

In fact, now that I think of it, I'm not sure we've ever slept a whole night together. We were teenagers with parents who wanted to know where we were—because they knew what we were likely to get up to.

It's okay if you want to stay here, I tell him, piously, *because we're* safety buddies. *We have to stay in pairs. That's the only reason it's okay.*

Say it out loud, El, comes his sleepy, amused voice inside me. Daring me. *Go ahead.*

I don't. Because I can't.

Instead, Zander reintroduces me to the cosmos, and I don't care that I cry all over him when he turns me into starshine and comet tails. Then holds me as we float back down to earth.

This time I don't talk shit when he holds me against him in the dark of my bedroom. I settle in, breathe him deep, and sleep.

When I wake up some hours later, I can see the sunlight outside my windows. Morning has come to Main Street. I can hear the odd car bumping over the cobblestone bricks and the voices of pedestrians—at this time of day, likely kids walking to school.

What I really notice is that I'm the only one in my bed.

I rub at my eyes. I smooth my hands over my bump, saying *good morning* to the baby. Then I sit up and *listen* like my life depends on it. I don't hear any water running. No shower. Nothing in the main living area. The apartment is still and quiet.

A whole lot like Zander up and left without a word.

It's good he left, I tell myself. It's *great*. Otherwise, we might have to discuss what happened, and why would I want that? It was…well, it wasn't a *mistake*, exactly.

Let's call it a *misstep*. The reality is, we can't make those. Not as grown-ass adults who are going to become parents.

This wasn't a beginning as I might have imagined at certain moments last night. This was an ending, and I congratulate myself on how maturely I accept that as I twist my hair back and tie it in a knot on the top of my head. I take pride in how *calmly* I then get up and put on my fluffy robe, in how not at all angrily I shove my feet into my owl slippers.

Though, speaking of owls… *Aren't you supposed to warn me?* I demand of my familiar, whose tail feathers I can see out my window, indicating she's on her favorite perch. *When I'm about to backslide?*

Ruth is resolutely silent.

Dick move, I tell her.

If I was *angry* instead of *mature*, I would make some owl stew commentary, but I'm not. So I don't. What I am is *starving*—apparently a new stage of pregnancy, I tell myself, having nothing at all to do with any caloric outputs last night—and I walk with tremendous dignity and calm out of my room, ready to eat everything in sight.

Then come to a stop that is very nearly a stumble, because he's here.

Right here.

Sitting at my kitchen table like it's his. A mug in his hand—*my* mug, filled with what I can smell is one of my tea blends when I know he prefers coffee. A book is in his other hand. *My* book. Well, the book Georgie gave me that I put with the small amount of baby things I've accumulated so far.

Zander looks up at me and smiles, happy and friendly enough to make my heart hurt. "Morning. Didn't know you were into fairy tales."

I can't seem to find my normal…anything. I can't seem to find *me*. I stand there and *gape* at him.

Until he drops the book on the table and raises his eyebrows. "Everything okay?"

"Fine," I manage to say then, belting my robe tighter. Because it's that or start saying inadvisable things like, *you're here*.

Or allowing myself to feel a swell of relief so big it threatens to take my knees out.

I tell myself that what I need is alone time. And food.

As if he can read my mind in addition to taking up space in it, Zander murmurs a few words, and a big plate of breakfast appears at the empty seat at the small, cozy table. He nods toward it. "I tried to wait, but I already ate."

I drift toward the table as if pulled by some invisible force that I'm afraid is all me. Then, before I can sit down on the empty chair, he pulls me into his lap. He presses his face into my neck, and I melt against him and—

No, no, no. We've got to set some boundaries. Boundaries kept us going for ten years. Now we need some that will keep us going for a lifetime. Because ascension and the Riverwood and this baby girl mean there's a lifetime of us, so we need to plan for it.

For her sake, I tell myself.

I force myself to get up because a world without those boundaries ends the way it did ten years ago, and I already did that.

I don't need to be crushed like that again.

And for the first time in a long, long time, I let myself think that, actually, I don't like hurting him either.

I take too much time retying the belt of my robe, and I give it way too much attention too. "We need to make some ground rules here."

Zander says nothing. He doesn't nod or shake his head. He sits there, kicked back in *my* chair at *my* table, watching me. Just watching me, which is weird enough.

What's weirder is that I can't read his expression at all.

I choose to keep right on talking, the classic response to weirdness of any kind. "You know, there's the whole coparenting thing. The whole we really ought to get along thing, so we don't screw her up." I point at my stomach in case he's confused by what *her* I mean. "Don't you think us without ground rules is a disaster waiting to happen?"

"Why don't you eat something," he suggests. With a smile.

What he does not do is react to the statement I dressed up like a question so we wouldn't have to analyze if there's any truth in it.

This, too, is weird.

But he doesn't look like he's planning to do anything but sit there and wait. And I *am* hungry. So I sit in my own chair this time. I start to eat, and my entire body rejoices at the first bite. As I shovel in more, I try to order my thoughts. "A lot has transpired in a short period of time. Don't you think we need to slow it down and think it through?"

I stop eating the pancakes only to stab at the eggs. When I look at him, his expression is still unreadable. I can't think of anything less Zander.

I'll admit I expected a hint of temper on his face, even if he tries to hide it. An actual argument—our happy place—but there's nothing.

Just this ridiculously gorgeous man sitting across from me like this is the domestic bliss we gave up on years ago, and I don't like the shuddering thing that seems to start inside me and fan out everywhere. I restrain it—I hope.

I try not to scowl at him. "Last night was great, but it can hardly be a…usual thing, right? We know where that leads."

"Do we?" he murmurs. Not antagonistic. Not edgy.

If I didn't know him as well as I do, I'd say he sounds almost innocent.

It's too much, and we know how badly we handle too much, I tell him in his head, so there's no escaping what I'm saying. Or maybe so I don't have to worry if I'm speaking the truth. *I want to be able to be friends with you, Zander. To raise our daughter without wanting to curse you. I think that requires a certain level of… emotional distance.*

I happen to think I sound very reasonable and adult.

So I'm not sure why I suddenly feel depressed as fuck.

Zander's eyes gleam. *Say that out loud*, he suggests.

I sigh. "Last night was a reasonable response to a lot of emotional upheaval," I continue around a bite of bacon. "Nothing wrong with that. But we could be putting ourselves in a risky position, going forward. One that doesn't put our child first. I just wonder if we need to take a very careful step back."

He doesn't interrupt. He doesn't say anything else in my head, not to argue or agree. When I'm done, I sit there. Waiting.

But it's like he plans to sit in silence and stare at me forever.

"Well?" I demand.

"Well what?"

"Don't you have anything to say?"

"Not really."

He gets up and rinses out his mug in the sink. I find this performative, given that we are witches and he could have done that with magic. "So you agree with me?"

Zander lets out a laugh at that. He turns to look at me, lounging back against the sink. *My* sink. Where I will now always picture him like this. "No."

"No?" It's lowering how squeaky my voice sounds. Or how hard my heart is beating.

He shrugs. "No."

"It's not fair to just say *no*."

"Who said I had to be fair? Eat the toast, El."

I look down at my plate and at the toast liberally slathered in peanut butter. I'm still starving so, fine, I eat it. Not because he told me to.

Then the next thing I know, he kneels next to me and takes one of my hands in his. Everything in me freezes. Or bursts into flame. Maybe both at once.

There's no smile on his face. Everything he says is delivered very gently, but it lands like bullets all the same. "Life isn't safe, Ellowyn. You can't live your life setting up rules to keep yourself from getting hurt. Stepping back to keep the potentially bad things at a distance. You can put on all the armor in the world, but it doesn't stop the hurt either. You know this."

I want to argue, but all I can hear is Elizabeth saying, *Anger doesn't serve you.*

Zander keeps talking. "They tell us life is long for witches. They tell us we have time. My mom didn't have time. Zachariah didn't have long either. Elizabeth did, but I bet her years felt a hell of a lot longer being so *mad* about everything." He keeps *looking* at me in that way that seems to get inside me, beneath my skin. "I don't want to be mad anymore, El."

I do, I think to myself. I want to hold on to it so I don't crumple.

We're not going to do this again, I tell him, and okay. Maybe I'm a little panicked. *Ever.*

I say it so resolutely that it's not until his eyes fill with amusement that I realize I didn't say that out loud.

"Tell me that with your mouth, baby," he says.

I want to. Or I want to be able to, anyway. Yet all I can do is stare back at him.

Caught there in all that gray.

Then he laughs at me as he gets to his feet. *Laughs*. At me. And doesn't do a thing to hide it. I surge to my feet as he starts walking for the door, my cheeks hot and red.

I tell myself this is the anger I've been missing, though it feels more complicated than that.

You don't call the shots, Zander, I throw at him, hot on his heels.

He turns then, and I don't know what to *do* with this version of him that isn't easy to rile up.

I open my mouth to say *something* that will *show him*, but he drops his mouth to mine before I can decide what it should be. Then he bends and does the same to the little swell of baby. He presses a kiss there and gives her an affectionate pat.

And ruins me, that easily.

He rises. "Frost and Rebekah are downstairs. He's coming to the ferry with me this morning, and Rebekah's staying with you. Emerson sent a schedule." He nods behind me. "It's on the fridge. I'll see you tonight for dinner at Wilde House."

Like...we're a couple.

An *adult* couple who sleep in the same bed and share tea and...and...a *life*?

"I don't—" I throw at his back. "I can't—"

It's not clear if it's the curse stopping me, or just me stopping me. But I have to revert to that inner channel where I can say whatever I like, regardless.

I don't want this, I tell him, and I mean it.

He turns and grins at me. *Grins*. "You sure about that, baby?"

I magic a vase at his head, because I am only so adult. He catches it, and I don't even think he uses magic. He's always been naturally athletic in all the most annoying ways. He calmly places the vase on the end table by the door.

"Don't miss me too much," he says cheerfully, then exits.

I might even hear the sound of *cheery whistling*, like salt in the wound.

My fists are clenched. I'm sure my blood pressure is through the roof. The only thing that keeps me from *screaming* is the likelihood Zander would hear it and *laugh* again. The happy laugh that warms me from the inside out.

Or would if I didn't want to murder him.

Rebekah sails through the still-open door, takes one look at me and smiles.

"Well," she says. "It looks like we have some things to talk about."

19

I DON'T KNOW HOW TO DEAL WITH REBEKAH, or anyone, in this moment when I feel like what I'd really like to do is cry. For a year. "Did you know," I say, "that male babies can get erections in the womb?"

As if taking a page out of Zander's book—as if they're all *colluding*—she doesn't answer. She just closes the door behind her and walks into my kitchen as if I'm not standing right here, scowling at her.

"Emerson is losing her mind," Rebekah tells me. "Trying to be *totally fine* with the fact we haven't had a meeting since the Undine showed up. I'll admit that it's fun to watch. Much more fun than dodging the extended Wilde family. Though as of this morning, every last one of them has morphed back into the primordial ooze. Obviously, my parents practically beat them all out the door, desperate to get back to Germany."

I relax a little. She's letting it go. We can talk about other things.

"How was it?" she asks me, looking concerned.

For a minute, I think she means last night with Zander.

I get it as she looks down at my belly. She's asking about telling my dad that I'm pregnant. "It was what it was."

"That bad?"

I shrug and return to my seat at the table. I didn't touch my tea, and I'm still hungry. I decide a pregnant lady deserves a cupcake for breakfast dessert and have some appear on the table before us, along with a mug of tea for Rebekah.

"It doesn't matter." I take a delicious bite of frosting, relishing the fact that *today* I can say that out loud. Because Bill's reaction really doesn't matter. It doesn't change my life, one way or another. Now that I've grieved whatever I thought it *could* be or *should* be, I can move on to dealing with what *is*.

"It does," Rebekah says quietly. "I wish he got that."

I shrug at that, so she sips her tea and picks up the book from Georgie. She flips through it. "Cute," she offers. "Em and I were never encouraged to love a fairy tale, though personally, I rebelled."

"It's the only thing Georgie knew of that mentioned Revelares."

She hands it to me, and I can't seem to help myself. I open the book and flip through the pages, like Zander was doing this morning. I've read through it already, but it's just a fanciful story set in some made-up land. The Revelare isn't even the main character.

We don't need to discuss how she's bound to a Guardian though.

"This Revelare can see the past and the future," Rebekah says, pointing to a page in the book. "You said Elizabeth mentioned the same thing. Maybe it's more than a story."

"It looks like the kind of thing Mom might have read to me as a child with all her many caveats of *not* being saved by princes, *not* determining my worth by any *chosen one nonsense*, and love not being a magic cure-all if you aren't willing to work at it. In other words, just a story."

Rebekah makes a considering sound. "So." She waits until I look up at her, then smirks at me as only she can. "Are you willing to work at it yet?"

I laugh, despite myself. "I don't want to talk about that."

"*You* might not. *I* decidedly *do*." She reaches over, takes my hand, and holds it hard so I can't pull away. "Ellowyn. You love him. You always have. Remember? *Love is the only lie you tell, but it will claim you in the end*."

As if I could forget that vision of hers.

But I shake off her hand. "I'm going to shower and get ready to open the shop."

Rebekah sighs as if I'm being ridiculous or dramatic, and I decide then and there that *someone* is going to listen to me.

"We have an ascension to deal with. I have a shop to run. There are statues coming to life and ghosts running around and…" I shake my head, looking into the bedroom that I can see from here is filled with my rumpled bed and too many images of Zander to count. I rub my hand over my chest where something *hurts*. "It has to be too much."

"I'll note you said *it has to be*, not that *it is*. Because one's a truth and one's a lie."

"I don't want it to be like last time." That's honest. I don't know if that's the source of *all* the panic whirling around inside of me, but it's enough of the source.

"Who says it has to be?" Rebekah asks me gently.

I think about his misplaced honor, which Elizabeth called a sword that cuts things in half. Isn't that what led him to break up with me in the first place? I think about my uncontrollable temper, which led me to someone else that very night. A full-blooded witch with a legacy of helping and protecting. A half witch with a legacy of curses and unhappiness.

People can grow up, sure, but can they change? Can anyone really change?

I refuse to answer her. Instead I march away and lock myself in my bathroom, then take my time getting ready. When I head back out to the kitchen, Rebekah is still sitting there, reading that fairy tale and eating a cupcake.

"I have to open the shop."

She gets to her feet languidly and brings the cupcake and book with her when she finally deigns to *amble* toward the door, her tea mug floating along behind her.

Also, she's talking. "A Revelare who's blocked from seeing the past by forces she doesn't understand. A dragon and a princess fighting for truth. A Guardian watching over them all." She waves the book at me. "It's part witch designations, sure, but part very *human* stories."

She gives me a look of *great significance* in the exact same way she used to do when we were seven.

"I don't recall you paying this much attention in English class. I know I didn't. Maybe I should call up Sadie and see if she can explain the symbolism to me."

Rebekah smirks, her piercings glinting in the morning light streaming in through the windows. "Will you listen if a twelve-year-old says it?"

"I can see the past just fine, and the only dragon I know is a newel post," I retort, waving her out the apartment door and slamming it behind us, so I can lock it with a spell. "And this is Missouri. We're fresh out of princesses."

I don't mention my Guardian.

Because he's not mine, I remind myself, and this is when Ruth chooses to respond. With a derisive hoot.

"She goes to a sorceress to unblock her past. But look." Rebekah stands on the landing and taps the illustration on the page, always the artist. I see a shelf of jars behind the sorceress. "This is all Healer stuff. Maybe you need a Healer to unblock you."

I roll my eyes and head down the stairs and into my shop, Rebekah clomping down behind me in what look a lot like my combat boots. "I'm not blocked. I'm not a Revelare. I've never really seen any future stuff. Not the way you've dabbled in the past. Maybe *you're* the Revelare here."

"I am pure chaos and you know it," Rebekah says with a grin, because we all discovered that she isn't just any old Diviner— a rare enough designation in witchdom—but a *Chaos* Diviner. This makes sense, because Emerson is a Confluence Warrior, not just a regular Warrior like, say, Carol Simon. They're special sisters, bound by prophecy and powerful witch blood on all sides. It would be weird if they *weren't* somehow extra special.

You are special. I hear Elizabeth's voice in my head. I remember how she told me that, and so fiercely. *She* believes it. And look, maybe the whole half-human thing worked out in my favor for once, because here I am, alive and well. I even get why Zander doesn't want me going around thinking I'm weak when his mother couldn't fight off the very same poison I've survived twice now.

It's still just a kind of luck. Nothing to do with *me.*

I think better of saying this out loud, and not because I suspect I can't. I'm sure I can.

I'm even more sure that Rebekah won't like it.

In the tea shop, Rebekah sweeps over to a little corner table with her mug and book, the cupcake polished off and all remnants magicked into the trash can. I unlock my front door and do some accounting while waiting for the first customers to come in.

Because *this* is my life. My real life. I'm a business owner. I'll be a mother in a few months. I'm the link that makes a blended family, with my sisters on one side and Tanith on the other, and they all need different kinds of attention from me. Maybe, if Emerson pulls off one of her patented miracles, I'll even be the weak link in the most powerful coven in the world. That's a full existence right there. I don't need my past with Zander messing that up.

I swallow at the weird lump in my throat, because I can't help thinking… If we're really and truly adults—despite the vase I threw at his head today—and if there are important things we have to face and deal with, and we managed to do that, could we do the same with each other?

Could we really be different this time around?

That kind of thought has fangs, and I should know better.

Before I can face the fact that I'm offering my throat to the worst vampire of them all, *hope*, that horrible *toll* rings out. Inside me. Outside. *Everywhere*.

I slap my hands over my ears. Rebekah does the same as the store, the building, maybe the whole world, seem to shake around us.

"Come before me, Joywood and Riverwood," commands the Undine. "The first trial commences."

20

I CHECK MY HIDE-THE-BABY GLAMOUR AS RE-
bekah and I hurry to get down to the riverfront, rather than
feel that strange *pulling* sensation the Undine sent out last time.

"I hope this Undine is planning on paying me for time lost,"
I mutter, locking my shop up as we step out onto the sidewalk.

"I didn't expect middle of the day trials, that's for sure," Rebekah agrees as we start down Main at a good pace. "Aren't we
supposed to be witches? Whatever happened to blood rituals in
dark forests beneath a sullen night sky? Or bubbling cauldrons
and children getting eaten in gingerbread houses?"

"Disney," I say.

We look at each other and laugh like we're fifteen again.

Just for a breath or two.

After a few moments, we see Emerson and Jacob are walking
down the street toward us, holding hands as Emerson inspects the
Apple Extravaganza boughs on the streetlamps, no doubt already
planning the upcoming switch over to Samhain/Halloween
cornstalks. Georgie wanders along behind them as if distracted

by voices in her head, shiny lights, or the book she's clutching to her chest like a security blanket. The ghosts are with them.

Emerson's smile is broad and bright, but that *Confluence Warrior* deep inside is a little on edge, I'd say. Maybe that's why she's allowing Jacob the uncharacteristic PDA when usually, she's about as private as you can get without locking yourself away.

"Long time no see," I murmur in Elizabeth's direction when she wafts up next to me.

"You seemed *occupied* last night, child."

I choose not to answer her, and if I'm not mistaken, her ghostly mouth curves.

By the time we make it to the grassy riverbank, no one is saying much of anything. Frost and Zander make their way up from the ferry dock, and I'm sure I'm not the only one who sees the way the crowd parts for them, muttering following along as they walk.

The crowd isn't as big as it was the other night, but the Undine did say something about a *broadcast*. I guess no one needs to be here in person unless they're us…or have a burning desire to watch the Joywood crush us in real time.

I assume that's the reason most of the people I recognize are standing here near the statue today. It's like a witch cage match.

Emerson marches right up to the dais, so we all follow. Zander falls into place beside me so easily, it almost feels choreographed.

Or just right.

Long time no see, he says in my head, as he slides his arm around my waist. He speaks where only I can hear him, and *feel* him, everywhere. He uses the same words I said to Elizabeth, but that feels less like *synchronicity* and more like weird ghost echoes.

What I should be focusing on is that everyone can *see* the affectionate way he holds me next to him. I shouldn't allow it.

Just like I shouldn't let him in my head. It's too intimate. It feels like much more than it is. I need to block that up again, no matter what he said about life and the rest of it earlier. I promise myself I will. Soon.

Right now I have to dance attendance on a living statue in the middle of the day. I look around and see some humans taking a walk along the river, though St. Cyprian is too enchanted for them to see anything of import. They'll think it's just community theater. Eccentrics putting on a show.

Some of them might even come over to watch, never realizing the "play" they think they're watching is real life, with real consequences.

We haven't had any time to prepare, Emerson complains in all our heads, where no one, not even a stray human passerby, might hear that the youngest chamber of commerce president in the town's history isn't 100 percent ready for whatever might be happening.

That means they haven't had any time either, Jacob points out.

Trust that regardless of the Undine or any attendant protections, the Joywood are prepared. Frost this time, in his role as the voice of doom.

Rebekah aims a tight smile and a rolled eye at me as if to say, *that's my man.*

Then, proving Frost's point, the Joywood appear out of nowhere—risky in full daylight when humans are about—and *process* toward the Undine. Like they've practiced this very thing all their lives. They don't climb up on the dais so much as *smooth themselves* there, and then arrange themselves in a pattern that gives the impression of a rune without actually being anything but a bunch of people standing about. They look out, regally, to our witchy spectators and incline their heads here, there.

All that's missing are the scepters, I say on our coven channel.

And the odd guillotine, Georgie adds darkly.

"The first trial shall begin," the Undine says in her booming voice, her moonlit eyes making it feel like the sullen woods and dark night Rebekah and I were just bemoaning.

You'd think a town full of witches would turn away from the word trial, *given the chance*, I offer to the group.

Zander laughs, his arm still casually around my waist. Which is the trial I should be concerned with as we stand in front of a group of judgy St. Cyprian onlookers.

My mother chief among them.

Chairs begin to appear, and we are magically nudged to sit in them, so I don't have the chance to push him off. He's pushed off for me. I pretend I'm grateful.

"The first trial demands that each coven demonstrate honesty and transparency to the people it wishes to lead," the Undine intones in her voice of stone and centuries. "Therefore, each coven will be compelled to tell the truth to those who challenge you. The rules are thus. The opposing coven will ask three questions. One representative from the receiving coven will answer. These answers *must* be the truth. Lies will be broadcast across the world and called what they are."

How? Georgie wonders in our coven channel.

Magic, Georgie, Rebekah replies dryly.

The statue is still *intoning* into the early October sunshine. "Whatever representative answers will ask the next question of the opposing coven. Be warned that there will be limited time to react and talk amongst yourselves. As the ruling coven, the Joywood may ask the first question. The trial has thus begun." The Undine's eyes dim as if that's a sign she's handed over the metaphorical microphone.

"You must be careful, Ellowyn," Elizabeth warns me. "The truth is important, but the Joywood and their ilk will twist it. You must all be clever."

Carol stands up immediately, clearly already prepared for this.

She knew what was coming, Emerson says, outraged, to the rest of us.

What I think is that Elizabeth is correct. And that means I really do need to be careful here. We all do.

Before I can pass that on, Carol speaks, her voice carrying out over the small crowd without her seeming to try. This is one of her party tricks. What astonishes me is how good she is at all of them.

"Your so-called *Warrior,*" and Carol imbues this word with enough inflection, and a knowing eye roll with her coven to make it clear that she does not approve of Emerson's designation, "and self-proclaimed leader draws a lot of…" She trails off, pretending to search for a word, with that tittering laugh of hers I have always hated. "*Mixed* reactions from the public she claims to want to serve. She can be *abrasive.* I think that's a kind word for it." She turns that stone-cold glare, chilly enough to rival the Undine herself, on Emerson. "Emerson Wilde, self-styled *Confluence Warrior,* how do you justify wanting to lead people who clearly don't even like you?"

Because everyone is such a fan of Carol's? Rebekah's voice is dark and irritated.

The difference is, no one is afraid *of Emerson,* Georgie retorts hotly.

I'm not afraid to get up there and list all the reasons we should lead, Emerson says at once.

Elizabeth floats in front of her as if to stop her, though Emerson can't see the ghost, but Zander can. He grabs his cousin's wrist. *Wait, Em.*

"The rules are that your coven gets to choose who answers," Elizabeth tells me. "Just because Carol directed her question at Emerson doesn't mean she is required to answer. It should be *you,* who *cannot* lie. *That* sends a message."

I blink once, taken aback. Then, without thinking it through, my gaze darts to Zander. He's still holding on to Emerson. He looks at me and nods. A nonverbal *go ahead.*

But…

I should answer it. I can't believe I actually put that out there to my coven. Public speaking isn't my thing for a *lot* of reasons, but Emerson certainly can't get up there and defend herself. It can't be her sister or her cousin or her best friend. It can't be her fiancé. All of those relationships that in my mind undercut any accusations anyone might throw at her are what the Joywood will use to make her look suspicious.

Elizabeth is right. It should be me.

I should answer, I say more firmly this time. *Everyone in this audience knows I can't lie. Besides, Carol wants Emerson to answer, and I think we can all agree that we don't want to give Carol what she wants.*

Everyone looks at one another. Then slowly, every single member of my coven gives me a nod.

So I have no choice but to stand and watch the Joywood's expressions harden when I do. Ever so slightly, but they all do it. You'd have to know where to look, maybe—at Maeve's pinched lips, or Carol's clenched fist, or the deep line across Felicia Ipswitch's forehead.

Point one for me and Elizabeth.

I face the crowd, because that's who these answers are for. The people who are going to choose who leads come Samhain, not the ruling coven who have hated me since before my birth. My hands threaten to shake, but like every time I was forced to give a speech in high school, I find my mother in the crowd. Her gaze meets mine.

I can never disappoint my mother, no matter what I do. Her violet gaze is all love, and I know this is what has gotten me this far. Knowing she loves me, and *she* will think I'm amazing no matter what I do.

I vow then and there to be that for my daughter.

In order to do that, I need to survive. That means I have to play this game.

"I've heard what some of you like to say about Emerson," I begin, and my voice is strong. Because this is about what's right, and there's nothing hard about speaking *this* truth. "In whispers and behind hidden hands. Loudly and proudly when she's in earshot, but not to her face, right? You fancy yourselves so polite, almost friendly, keeping it behind her back."

There are some uncomfortable shifts in chairs in the audience. I don't smirk, though I want to.

"Emerson Wilde has been a champion for all of you," I continue. "All of you sitting here—including the Joywood, who stripped her of her magical memories improperly ten years ago—have watched Emerson dedicate her entire life to this town and the people in it, magic or no. Maybe the world doesn't know that, but St. Cyprian does. Maybe you don't like the fact that she's confident, that she isn't afraid to call people out, that she has a plan and sees it through." I'm warming to this now. I let my voice ring out like its own bell. "Maybe that's a little confronting for those of you who'd rather hide behind your hands and tear down things rather than build them up. Maybe it's a bit confusing for those of you who have been taught that in order for a woman to be powerful, she has to be demure and accommodating. That a woman can't be *too much*, heaven forbid. Maybe it's not your fault. Maybe you were taught that confidence in a woman is *all wrong*, and you never thought to ask who that benefits. I'll tell you—not women."

I don't dare glance back at Emerson. This is way more honest than I want to be with anyone *alone*, much less in front of a crowd. But the truth is the truth.

Emerson doesn't deserve the hate she gets around here. She never did.

"Emerson Wilde loves this town, and she will fight harder than anyone for who and what she loves," I continue, letting my gaze drift from one familiar face to another in the crowd, noting who looks away and who doesn't. "She proved it every day she tried to improve this town *without* the magic that was her right and her due. She proved it when she dove into the confluence and beat back a flood with the magic she was told she didn't have."

I let that settle, then go in for the kill. "No one will ever like their leader one hundred percent of the time. A leader's function isn't to be *liked*. It's to be honest, and honorable, and true. Dedicated to the best possible outcome for all of us, and that is Emerson Wilde in a nutshell. So, Carol, *that* is how we justify being part of Emerson's coven, and thanks to her, this bid for ascension." I look at the Undine. "Thank you."

Her eyes glow back at me, terrifying to behold. I can't look away. "The next question is yours." I try to move back to my seat, but I'm held in place. "You must ask the next question. Now."

Now? Like there's some kind of time limit? What should I ask?

There are too many competing voices in my head, drowned out by the Undine's loud countdown. *Five, four, three—*

"Have any of you engaged in black magic?" I blurt out. Because we know they do. Why not ask them here, where they have to tell us?

Felix Sewell, the Joywood's Healer, stands immediately. His voice booms out, almost shaking with sincerity. But my mother has always sniffed dismissively when his name is mentioned and made sure we saw other Healers for our witchy needs.

"I can honestly and with conviction say, I have never in all my life partaken of any magic I knew to be anything but good and pure, not black." He nearly sputters, such is the force of his indignation. "The temerity of these upstarts to accuse us of such a thing is *despicable*."

He said I. *So he just means* him, Rebekah says.

Jacob sounds pissed, a new sound from our calm, steady Healer. *They're evading the question.*

Should we point that out? Emerson asks.

"No," Elizabeth says. Like she can hear our coven's inner workings, although that shouldn't be possible. When I give her a quizzical look, she shrugs. "Blood is a funny thing."

Elizabeth says no, I tell them.

I don't share that she heard them. We don't have time for that.

The Joywood must ask their next question. Felix specifically, and he's more than ready. The moment the Undine's eyes take on that glow, he jumps on it, glaring at us from across the dais.

"How do you expect the people of St. Cyprian, the citizens of the entire witch world, to trust an *immortal* when we all know that only evil things can be done for immortality?" he demands.

"Former immortal," I mutter. This is a mistake. Apparently, muttering means choosing to answer the question. The Undine keeps me in place, and it seems no one else can speak for us now that I've started. *Shit.*

I glance at Frost. His expression is unreadable, but the fact of the matter is, they're right. A long time ago, he must have done something bad to be immortal for so long. We all know that's how it goes. Despite that, a short time ago, he sacrificed it all.

For love.

He even admitted his sins while he did it, but naturally everyone's acting like that part didn't happen.

"We've all made mistakes," I say carefully. "I, for one, can't claim perfection, and I've only been on this planet for twenty-eight years. Can you imagine the kind of mistakes you'd make if you'd been around for two thousand? Yes, Frost once did something terrible, a long time ago. He also did something just a few months ago. He risked his very long, very powerful life to protect us. And I don't just mean the Riverwood. I mean all of us. Frost knows what the Joywood are capable of, and if you think the way he got his immortality is shady, then you should remind yourselves what he said at Litha."

I don't need a reminder, because I can pull up his words from a few months ago without even trying.

"Maybe some of you missed it. He told us the Joywood discovered how they could make that power too big, too vast, to be challenged. In order to wield that power, they need immortality."

I hear the murmurs from the crowd. I see the fury in the

gazes of the Joywood across from me and wonder if part of the summer's quiet was erasing people's memories of this.

So I keep going. "He told us, 'Nothing can change what the Joywood have done or will do if you do not stop them.' Right before the very blood oaths he took struck him down for breaking them, in service to St. Cyprian instead of to himself, he told us very clearly, 'If they succeed, they will be immortal. And you will all be slaves. You are already halfway there.'" I laugh as I gaze out at the crowd, at the world. "I know which is more likely to keep *me* up at night."

Frost's expression betrays nothing, as expected, but Rebekah's eyes are full. She's sitting next to him, her thigh pressed to his, and she smiles at me in a way that makes my own eyes feel prickly. All he does is incline his head, maybe a centimeter. A very grudging *thanks*.

I think he means it.

I let out a shaky breath. I think we're doing okay. The Joywood haven't messed up either, but they're not blowing us out of the water. I haven't failed in this.

Now I have to ask another question. Quickly. Something damning. I look at Elizabeth, but she and Zachariah are having an argument about *crows*, of all things. I glance at Zander.

And I know.

"You guys speak of trust, but the flood that overtook the confluence and nearly drowned the whole town had to be stopped by *us*. Meanwhile, Summoners are dying early. Far too early. Yet there have been no attempts by you, our leading coven, to address or solve these very pertinent issues. Why?"

Maeve steps forward this time, all smirking delight, and I know this means my question didn't hit the mark. My heart sinks.

"There are lots of things going on behind closed doors. In an effort to maintain *safety*, Ellowyn, we can't broadcast everything we do."

"Sounds like a lack of transparency to me," Frost says idly.

"Questions only, covens," the Undine warns. "Only from the designated questioner."

Maeve's smirk deepens. She meets my gaze across the dais as she gears up to ask her question. Or drop her bomb, more like.

"I hate to bring this up." She clasps her hands together and sends a sorrowful look out to the crowd. The *tutting* is implied. "But the leadership of St. Cyprian is about protecting witches against humankind. This Riverwood coven, such as it is, has a human amongst them." Maeve shakes her head at me as if I sadden her. I accept that I probably do, but she's still going. "Ellowyn, do you really think you're witch enough to *lead*? Shouldn't that be left to the full-blooded, truly magical among us?"

Zander shoots to his feet. I shake my head at him, because I know the thing he's best at is blazing temper, and other, more private things, and this is not the place for either—

He doesn't wait for anyone's permission. He dives right in.

"As the Guardian of the Riverwood, and a member of a family who have protected St. Cyprian since its inception, I have a unique understanding of the threats we face from the outside world. I know that across this realm and the next, there are plenty of witches who have human blood." He pauses, and I remember him on high school football fields, playing to the crowd. I know that's what he's doing now—making sure that every witch out there with any drop of human blood will choose him. Us. He turns that thunderstorm gaze of his on our opponents. "As the ruling coven, the Joywood have always impressed upon us the importance of the pubertatum as the evidence of our *power*, not the purity of our blood. It seems a little disingenuous to be worried about it now."

Carol opens her mouth—we all see it—but something happens. I don't know if it's from the Undine or her own coven, but she cannot respond.

Like she tried to lie and couldn't.

I know the signs.

Carol looks absolutely incandescent with rage, but she isn't the one who speaks. Surprise, surprise, it's Maeve again.

"You don't expect people to trust the man who's *impregnated* a human," she asks, pretending to mutter beneath her breath, but each word carries. Enough that a shocked murmur goes through the crowd.

Just in case people weren't staring at me before.

"Enough." The Undine's scolding tones ring out so loud even the Joywood wince. Maeve's wretched pigeon ducks back into her panda purse. "You have asked your three questions, Joywood coven. You may not ask another. Riverwood, your last question."

It has to be Zander. His gaze cuts to mine. He looks fierce and beautiful, and I feel the force of his fury even though I know he's not directing it at me. I want to reach out to him, but something holds me perfectly still on my seat.

Zander's gaze turns to the Joywood. "You speak of safety and concern. You belittle us. Question us. You tear us down. You try to change the course of our lives, and you end others. What have you *built*? For St. Cyprian? For the witching world? What have you *done* for us?"

There's a whole lot of huffing and puffing from the Joywood contingent. It's Festus who rises to speak in response, glaring at his fellow Guardian as if Zander took a swing at him. "*We* have kept the witching world on the right course by making sure we are *safe* from the likes of immortals and half witches and weakling—"

He's cut off, and I get the sense it's from Carol, who's frowning deeply and disapprovingly. Because Festus's outburst looks a little desperate. It almost, *almost* proves Zander's point.

Is it enough?

"The questions have been asked," the Undine tolls. "The answers have been given. All who wish to may know what was said here, truths only, and let it inform their decision come Samhain. You are released, witches. Until the next trial."

Once again, she is nothing but a statue. In the back of the crowd, the bewildered-looking tourists clap.

The witches in the crowd begin to drift off. Mom makes a production of standing, then marching over to us along with a few other people we already know support us. A handful of people trudge over to the Joywood too.

It looks like the same lines we drew at Litha.

Still, I notice Susan Martingale, famous for confronting Emerson about the state of the flower boxes along Main Street every spring, look over at us with a question in her eyes. It makes me wonder if we might have started to turn the tide.

Emerson's wide grin tells me *she* thinks so.

Mom squeezes my arm as I climb down off the dais. Then she does the same to Zander. We both look at her like she's lost her mind.

"Good job, kids," she whispers.

I look back at the Undine. The light's still out. She's nothing but stone as the clouds roll in above us. I want to feel a sense of victory, but I can't.

Emerson, on the other hand, sees this as a win. She claps her hands together as she jumps down to stand with us. "You guys. You did *so* good."

"I think you're supposed to hate us and be mad you didn't get the spotlight to yourself, evil narcissist that you are," Zander returns lazily.

Emerson laughs and pulls us into a swaying hug before quickly releasing us. "*That* was amazing. Now, back to work, Riverwood. We'll celebrate over dinner."

Then she's marching off toward town and the bookstore and the last day of her Apple Extravaganza. Jacob trails after her. Georgie, I see, has found that boyfriend of hers I keep forgetting about.

"Do we think that Sage is good enough—" I begin in an undertone.

"No," Tanith replies at once, before I finish the question.

Then, before I can sidestep it, think to stop it, do literally *anything*, Zander drops a kiss to my mouth. Quick and casual. In front of *everyone*.

"See you later," he says as if that's the most normal thing in the world.

Then he walks off toward the ferry again, Frost with him, while Coronis, Nicholas's ancient raven familiar, and Storm fly in lazy circles above.

I stand, frozen in what I would love to tell you is pure fury, all-consuming rage, call it what you want. But it's none of those things.

Not even when he looks over his shoulder and smirks at me, which he *knows* I hate.

Rebekah doesn't even try to hide her laugh. My mother's face is conspicuously blank. I want to scowl, but I can't seem to manage it as I mutter a goodbye to Mom and let Rebekah pull me back up the riverbank to Main Street.

I glance back and catch Maeve's eye. The look she sends me is pure evil. Hatred amped up about as far as it can go. I brace myself against the nasty slap of magic I see coming when her lips move, but nothing lands.

That's when I remember that we're protected by the Undine. By the ascension rules.

I want to believe that will keep us safe and well through Samhain. I glance at Elizabeth beside me, and her gaze is on Maeve as well. She looks concerned. Deeply concerned.

Until she catches me looking at her. Then she smiles.

Bright enough to remind me that hope is a dangerous thing, with treacherous fangs.

And winning battles hardly means winning the war.

21

"CAROL'S *FACE*! I SWEAR IT TURNED PURPLE."
Rebekah is all but cackling, curled up on a small sofa in the
Wilde House living room with Frost. Who *almost* looks like
he's enjoying himself—or her, anyway. Jacob and Emerson sit
hip to hip on the hearth in front of a crackling fire. Georgie
and her familiar, Octavius the big orange cat, are lounging in
the oversized armchair.

I tell myself that I would be having a grand old time if Zander wasn't invading my space. If he didn't throw himself on
this couch like I wasn't already sitting here and throw his arm
around me too. Like it belongs here. Like *he* belongs here.

I intend to set him right. Any second now.

We're enjoying some posttrial downtime. The ghosts took off
early on, and I am deliberately not imagining what they might
be up to. Instead, I'm about the food. And a whole lot of dessert.
Maybe it's the sugar, but Emerson's fist pumps make me far happier than I like to admit. We might be enjoying a premature victory here, but I like having some space to relax with my friends.

Even though I know I need to get out of here before Zander's arm becomes more, before my friends start oh-so-casually poking into what we were doing last night as I can see they want to, and definitely before Emerson stops celebrating and starts drawing up battle plans for the next trial we can't predict.

Any second now, right? Ruth asks in my head. Slyly.

I can't allow a future bowl of stew to challenge me like that, so I decide *any second* is *right now.*

That's really showing me, my unimpressed familiar responds.

I ignore her, but as I get up, something falls behind me as if it dropped from the ceiling. When I look around at the sound, I see that book again. Gleaming at me from right where I was sitting.

Zander picks it up, studying the bright illustrated cover. "You're carrying this around with you now?"

I frown at him. And the book. Mostly at him. "I didn't bring it over here."

I'm trying to remember if Rebekah brought it with her to the trial when I know she didn't. I distinctly remember her leaving it in the tea shop.

Zander starts flipping through it again. "It's weird, you know," he says, not to me but to the group. "This sweet little children's book is the only known reference to Revelares. It has some eerie coincidences in there too."

Emerson turns the full force of her attention his way. "What kind of eerie?"

"There's a Guardian," Zander says. "A princess who's drawn to look a lot like Georgie. A Revelare who has one of her sights blocked."

"It's a fairy tale," I return, a weird wave of panic sweeping up inside of me. *I'm not a Revelare,* I want to yell. But I don't, because that would be alarming.

And wouldn't prove anything one way or another.

"It was my favorite book when I was little," Georgie says, stroking Octavius's fur. "Possibly *because* the princess has red hair."

"Sometimes fairy tales have their beginnings in fact," Jacob offers. "Humans have tales of witches and familiars and all kinds of magic. To them it's all a fairy tale."

"Many facts become fairy tales," Frost agrees. "Given enough time."

"Let's read it," Emerson says. "Maybe it can tell us something that will help."

"Like what?" I ask. Possibly too aggressively, given the way Zander's eyes gleam at me. I clear my throat. "I know for a fact it doesn't have the Undine's secrets or a list of the trials in there."

Emerson waves this away. "A book told me I was a Confluence Warrior. A book explained that Rebekah was a Chaos Diviner. Now this book has the only known mention of what a ghost that only you and Zander can see says *you* are."

"Those were big, ancient texts, not *fairy tales*." I feel like I'm having a panic attack, and I can't allow that. I make myself laugh. "I'm a Summoner."

Not a very good one either.

I don't say that out loud, but Emerson isn't the only one who shoots me a sharp look. "After everything we've been through over the past year, you can't honestly think any of us are just one thing, can you?"

Emerson can't understand because there's a prophecy about her. Because she *is* special.

I look over at Georgie. She's ridiculously smart, has been dedicated to her role and her job from the start, and is a full witch, but she's the closest to my situation in that there isn't anything extraordinary about her family or her place in this community.

She shrugs at me. "I think Em's right."

"Let's sit down and listen." Emerson, clearly no longer in discussion mode, says a spell that has the book floating above us. A disembodied voice begins to read, like we're a kindergarten class being read to by a teacher.

One who's invisible and doesn't actually exist.

"Sit down, El," Zander says in a low voice, and he doesn't wait for me to ignore him. He wraps his fingers around my wrist and tugs me down to the sofa. Right back into the heat and strength of his arm around me and all of *him* beside me.

A fate worse than death, Ruth comments dramatically.

I ignore her.

But that means I have nothing to do but concentrate on this story I've already read. More than once.

A princess and a dragon are trying to save a community of fairies from a dark curse. A Revelare is trying to unblock her hidden past with the help of a Guardian she keeps trying to escape. In the end, the Revelare finds a sorceress to unblock her and is saved by the Guardian, who then takes her to the princess and dragon so they can all save the fairy world together.

I can feel our baby fluttering around inside me. Zander places his hand over my stomach, like he can feel it too. Like we're a *unit*.

As if I need something else to really amp up my panic.

The story concludes, and we're all silent for a few minutes. As if *brooding* over what we've just heard.

It's ridiculous. Are there similarities? Sure, but then, all stories have *some* similarities. Are there odd coincidences? Yes, again—but it's not what's *actually* happening here in St. Cyprian. There's no Emerson and Rebekah and their prophecy in the story. There's no grumpy immortal. There's an army of crows on each side—one fighting for the fairies, led by a crow who could *maybe* be construed as Emerson-like. Meanwhile another group fights for the dark magic curse.

"She *does* look like Georgie," Emerson says, pointing at the picture of the princess on the cover that is now blown up on a screen hovering midair.

"I'm hoping to avoid getting eaten and spit out by a dragon," Georgie replies, a bit primly.

I can't help but think that would be interesting, at least. Especially since once the princess is spit out by said dragon, they work together to save the fairies. That has to be more exciting than whatever *Sage* does for fun around here. In his three-piece suits and bow ties.

I order myself to stop being mean. It's not like *I* have to date the guy.

"I don't understand the good crow leader character," Emerson says, clearly frustrated that the story doesn't line up perfectly with us or what we're doing.

Zander smirks. "Maybe it's Frost."

I snort out a laugh, and so does Rebekah. Frost sighs, but I'm beginning to wonder if that's his version of laughter.

"We must be exhausted if we're prepared to start reaching like this," I tell everyone when they all continue to stare at the book like if they do it long enough, it will mean something. Because this is a pointless exercise.

"I don't know. This Revelare character is a lot like you, El," Zander says, and he hasn't drawn his hand back from my belly, like he can't keep his hands to himself.

I refuse to acknowledge the warmth inside of me at that thought.

I roll my eyes at him instead. "She doesn't appear to have human blood, a curse, or a pregnancy. So."

"She's kind of cursed though," Rebekah argues, which feels like betrayal. She shrugs when I glare at her. "Her past is blocked, and the dark magic did that. Plus, she's got herself a Guardian, whether she wants one or not—usually not. I have to say, that sounds a little on point."

"Her past is blocked. That's not the same as me." I don't know why I'm so insistent. Or why I suddenly wish Elizabeth was here to back me up, when she'd likely be as contrary as anyone.

I'm *not* a Revelare.

My unique characteristics that have helped us out are all because of Bill. There's no way I also have some mystical designation no one's ever heard of. Besides, wouldn't I *feel* it if I had access to the future that way? I have enough trouble envisioning the future I can already feel as a solid, growing weight inside my belly.

"Maybe your future is blocked." Emerson considers. "Elizabeth thinks you should see the future as well as the past, and she seems right about most things."

"It could be that the story's not so much a direct representation but a reflection," Georgie offers. "A little symbolism."

"Well, when Jacob and his family are doing the ritual with my blood to help the Summoners, he can dig around in there and unblock me. Problem solved." I get up again, because I don't know what to do with this. Any of this. Zander's arm. *Revelares.* It's too much. I look over at Jacob. "When's that going to be?"

I don't get the outburst from Zander I'm hoping for, and Jacob takes his time answering, with that deep patience of his that makes me want to scream.

"The best and safest time would be as close to Samhain as we can get," he says in his measured way. "Problem is we'll have the actual ascension to work around. We're still trying to determine how to manage that, but it will be very close to Samhain before we can do it safely."

"Great. Okay. Well. I'm tired, so—"

"Something like what the sorceress does in this story, however, could be done at any time," he continues. Somewhat pointedly. "At the next full moon, for example."

It never occurred to me that anyone would take a children's book *this* seriously.

I'm not a Revelare. If they still existed, there would be more of them, but there aren't. And if there *were*, they wouldn't be half human.

Still, I can understand why my friends want this. They're desperate to believe that another one of us is something special the way Rebekah and Emerson are because that might give us an edge in this ascension.

Maybe I should push for this ritual too. Because if Jacob tries to unblock me, they're all going to finally get it through their heads: I am not special.

Elizabeth is not right about that.

"I'm going to bed," I tell my fairy tale–addled coven. Then I pop myself upstairs to my room because I'm done. A pregnant woman deserves a good night's sleep. I *definitely* need—

My door opens. No knock. There's just Zander.

I try to slam the door on him with my magic.

This, of course, doesn't work.

"Why are you so edgy?" he asks, but not in any sort of accusatory way.

Though I could certainly twist myself into believing he was accusing me of something. If I tried.

"I'm n—" I narrowly resist kicking the wall. "I'm almost *always* edgy."

"Almost," he agrees, with that *gleaming* thing in his gray eyes.

As much as I should put a stop to this, sex would be better than dealing with why I feel so churned up about a silly book.

When he crosses to me, he doesn't take off his shirt, or mine. He doesn't pull me into his arms or get his mouth on my lips, my neck.

Instead he says words I don't want to hear.

"Baby, I know you're afraid." I want to swing at him, but he smooths his hand over my hair in a way I do not find soothing. I do *not*. "You have it in your head that you crumble under pressure, but look at what you did today. You were amazing."

"With Elizabeth's help," I say.

"So what if you had help? That was still all you today, standing up in front of the Joywood and the town and the whole world, saying those words and asking those questions." He tips my head back so I have no choice but to look at him. He stopped caring if I look mutinous long before we turned sixteen. "If you're so big on giving Elizabeth credit, *she* thinks you're a Revelare. Why not listen to her on that too?"

Because I already know, I want to tell him, and for the same reasons as always. The whispers that have always followed me around.

I don't want these friends who have always been so sure that I was special, like they are, to finally have indisputable proof they're wrong.

The only thing I want right now is the man in front of me, but not like this.

I don't want him trying to comfort me, or getting through to me, or whatever complicated thing he's doing tonight. I don't want his *belief in me* or his *concern for me*.

I just want him.

That simple. That direct.

Even that is covered in warped thorns, though, because to give in to this, to him, is to believe it all might be okay.

That I might be okay and worthy and…good. *Special*, even.

I can't do it.

So instead, I fall back on the tried-and-true method I've used in the past. I pretend it's Beltane. I jerk him to me, devouring his mouth with teeth and anger and frustration.

Maybe last night was different, deep and meaningful. Maybe I let him inside me in all those ways I shouldn't have, but that doesn't mean it has to *change* things. It doesn't have to shift the way we usually are with each other—the way we have always been with each other.

He kisses me back with all that old heat, and I feel a surge of desperation that I decide to call elation—

Then something…gentles.

I pull back at the same time he does. I don't want *gentle*. I don't want last night. I want something familiar, something rooted in a world I understand. The versions of him and me and reality that I already know.

And control, Ruth says from somewhere outside. I don't have time to say something pithy in return.

Zander's thunderstorm eyes look into mine. "We can go down that road again. It's a good road. We both like where it ends."

His hand smooths down my spine as if he's proving it. *But I'm still going to be right here in the morning. You're not building those walls back up on me, El.*

"Because you get to decide?" An accusation that probably doesn't have quite the force I want it to when my fingers are curled in his hair and my mouth is on his.

He lifts me, easy as you please, and I shouldn't wrap my legs around him, shouldn't sink into the wild universe of his kiss. Because he doesn't answer. Because he's not letting me pick a fight.

When I'm positive a fight is exactly what I need.

Zander— I start.

Let me talk for a minute, he replies.

He doesn't mean with words. He means with this. All of this sensation and pleasure, heat and wild need.

Instead of the fight I want, the anger I know, I'm drowning. In him. In light.

In love and hope and his body over mine, inside mine.

Drowning.

I know what happens when I let myself drown. When I allow myself to believe. When I give in to hope.

But I keep doing it.

Pleasure arrows straight down, and I find I don't care about anything right now but him.

But this.

But *us*.

I dive right in and stay there, as long as I can.

Because the real truth is, I like it. This new version of us. It burns bright inside me like happiness, the kind of light even I can't dim.

So maybe, I think then, wrapped around him and as lost in him as I've ever been, I'll just give in.

Because if I know one thing about Zander and me, it's that we're as doomed as everything else.

22

IT'S WEIRD HOW DOOM IS EASIER TO BEAR WITH regular sex, my life settling back down to something almost like normal, and waking up every day to a man who *refuses* to be needled.

No matter how I try.

And I try a lot.

To call this *unsettling* is an understatement, because antagonism is what we do, but it's not such a bad *unsettling*. Not compared to the fact that we all expect the next trial to begin in a few days, at most, and have no idea what it will ask of us. Every day we brace ourselves and wait for the Undine's call.

It doesn't come.

Meanwhile, Jacob keeps telling me that if I'd give him five minutes, he could poke around inside of me and see if there are any of those blocks we all read about in a children's book.

I don't believe I'm blocked. I'm all for risking myself and donating my blood to save the other Summoners out there, but wasting everyone's time on a *fairy tale* is going to give me hives.

So I throw myself into work, into herbal alchemy and accounting, and yes, into Zander.

At first we expect the next trial to commence the following
week, but ten days pass and nothing happens. Except we all
get wound tighter and tighter. Even the ghosts seem on edge.

I try to make myself relax by spending a late afternoon taking Sadie around St. Cyprian for her thirteenth birthday. Sadie
and I take a tour of October as interpreted by St. Cyprian. A
delightfully autumnal mess of pumpkins and hay bales, scare-
crows, and a preponderance of crow figurines. Face paints,
apple cider, and dancing humans dressed in witch costumes.

We end up wandering lazily through Confluence Books for
ages. Just me and her, like the fellow family introverts we are.

When I drop her off, Rebekah in tow for our safety-in-pairs
deal, I dodge Stephanie's twenty questions on pregnancy and
Zander-related things as best I can. Then Rebekah and I drive
out of their neighborhood, debating whether or not we should
go out to Forest Park and take in the art museum, maybe get a
snack—

Obviously, that's when we get the next call from the Undine.

Joywood. Riverwood. Your second trial is imminent.

I glance at Rebekah as the summons *booms* through us both.
She shrugs, then handles the transportation spell herself since
I'm driving the car. She pops us—car and all—into the parking lot along the river. We climb out as Jacob and Zander are
walking over from the ferry. Once the four of us hit the grass,
we see that everyone else is already on the dais, waiting for us.

The Joywood are dressed in new, bright red cloaks that I
think are a misfire. *A little* Handmaid's Tale, *no?* I ask on our
coven channel.

Under His eye, Georgie replies dryly.

Too creepy, Emerson says. *The Joywood would like that a little
too much.*

Blessed be the fruit, Rebekah replies, earning the glare she was clearly after from her older sister.

Then we all settle in.

"Today you will indicate the contours of your brand of justice," the Undine intones once there's the appropriate silence.

The sun is setting, a riot of colors over the confluence. It's chilly at last, and the smell of October bonfires lingers in the air. The leaves in the trees are starting to turn. The grass is no longer the bright green of spring or the deeper green of summer. The gathered crowd whispers and murmurs, no one daring to speak at a normal decibel level with the Undine's eyes glowing.

I tell myself what I feel is *excitement*, not dread and anxiety.

"Both covens will discuss Skip Simon," she pronounces at last.

A rustling goes through the crowd. It turns into a murmur. The Joywood *almost* look flummoxed. I'd feel smug about that if I knew what the hell this was. I don't really remember what happened to Carol's son after high school. Why would someone I barely remember have anything to do with an ascension trial?

In our heads, I hear Frost's voice: *Reveal to thee what you must see.*

The spell sweeps through me, into my head. I blow out a breath. Then, on the next inhale, it all comes back to me.

"In the spring, the witch known as Skip Simon bartered his blood for dark magic with the express intent of causing harm," the Undine pronounces, as my memories flood back. "Each coven contended with this witch. One ignored his offenses. One fought him. Which approach will witchdom favor?"

She's speaking to the crowd, but then her sharp, soulless gaze turns to us. "Riverwood. Explain to those you wish to rule why you believe your brand of justice was correct."

For a moment, we all stare at each other. Explain our *brand of justice*? What justice was there? I can remember it now. Skip came at us. We fought him off. I don't remember all the details, but I remember that.

Vividly now.

We don't need to discuss this one to know that Emerson is the one to address the crowd. He attacked her first. She called to us, and we helped her fight him off.

Rebekah hadn't been back in town then. It seems like a lifetime ago now—but as I think that, I remember something else. Skip's black magic felt a lot like the shadow that came after Zander and me a few weeks back.

Emerson looks out over the crowd, and I wonder if this is hard for her. It's not really discussing a justice *we* chose. It's discussing what we did in response to someone going against all we stand for—and striking out against us.

But she manages to look unruffled, and she begins. "Starting last Ostara, Skip Simon used dark magic to try and hurt me. He lured me off the bricks and across the river so that adlets could attack me." A shocked sound runs through the crowd at that, because adlets are old monsters that shouldn't exist. "He branded me, without my consent, when he thought I was spell dim. He tried to get physically rough with me one night." She looks at Carol when she says that, for a beat or two. Then she squares her shoulders and faces the crowd. "When all else failed, he attacked me himself. Out in the open, on the hill in front of Frost House."

There's a little tittering sound. A sound everyone in St. Cyprian knows all too well. It sends the usual prickle of apprehension down my spine, and we all look toward the source.

Carol Simon sits back in her chair with her red cloak flowing and her messy hair dancing in the evening breeze. "This is all very convenient, isn't it? You claim my son attacked you. Alone. No one can vouch for this, but we're meant to believe you had no choice but to kill him?" Carol looks meaningfully at the crowd. "This is justice?"

The crowd is muttering again, but Frost laughs. Not nicely.

"The black-magic-tainted witch did not die that day, woman. What kind of mother does not know her child yet lives?"

"Give them proof of what happened, Ellowyn," Elizabeth says in my ear. She's clutching my shoulder, almost as if she's hiding behind me, and I get it. Everything about these trials and the Undine feels terrifying.

"How?" I ask her, under my breath, because people *can* hear me.

"Revelare, you can show the crowd the past," my ancestor tuts at me. "Just as you showed them Zachariah and me at the meeting where we declared ourselves your sponsors." She grips me harder. "Do not tarry."

I personally try not to think of that night, because it was extraordinarily painful. The Joywood tried to kill me—again. I remind myself that I'm protected now. Thanks to the Undine.

Still, while I know I can *see* the past, connect spirits to the living, create a historical retrospective for ghost sponsors, and so many other things, I've never tried to project an *event* to a group of people. I was there for part of Skip's attack, but not for the whole thing, and I'm not sure I can show things I didn't see. Things that don't connect to me.

I showed Zander his mother by holding his hand. Maybe, if I hold Emerson's hand now and connect into her, I can show the crowd what happened to her before the rest of us heard her cry for help.

We can show them, I say, not just to Emerson but to our whole coven. *We can show them what happened. Just like last June when they showed everyone Rebekah's past.*

Best night ever, my best friend says darkly.

You can do that? Emerson asks me. Not in disbelief, exactly—more like I've been holding out on her.

I can, I say, as if I know this for a fact.

I step up and take Emerson's hand in mine. I listen to Elizabeth's whispered instructions on how to cast the spell. Then I address the crowd, because apparently that's something I just *do* now.

"Earlier this year, the Joywood showed you Rebekah's adolescent transgressions." Most of them saw the show even if they weren't in the high school gym with us, forced to relive our teen years because the Joywood wanted to embarrass us. "They added their own twist, of course, but I have no twists. I can't project a lie. I can only show you what actually happened." I realize I'm not 100 percent sure about that until I say it, but I nod as if I knew I could all along. "This, then, is the truth."

"As I said," Emerson says, glaring at Carol. "Skip Simon attacked me. Alone. While I flew."

I hold on hard to Emerson's hand. I take a deep breath, center on the magic inside of me, and say the spell words Elizabeth feeds me.

"The sphere of time, tangled and mine, show the memory, for all to see." I may or may not lift a theatrical arm on the other side, like a witch you'd see dancing up on Main Street.

Above us, like some human drive-in movie, the entire crowd can see Emerson being slapped out of the air by Skip's slimy magic.

I suck in a breath, hard, but Emerson is calm and collected beside me. Even if her hand trembles slightly in mine.

"He attacked me," she says again. Her words are measured, her gaze steady. Every inch of her the leader, even as we see Skip and all that nasty, obviously black magic go at that earlier version of her. "When I realized I couldn't hold him off alone, not when his magic was so dark and *wrong*, I called my friends for help."

A murmur snakes through the crowd. I can't be the only one who thinks it makes her seem even more powerful that she could ask for help. That she did. That she wasn't hampered by that ego everyone likes to say she has.

I shouldn't be surprised that the Joywood feel it too.

"A whole coven arrayed around one misguided witch?" Felicia asks, sounding startled.

"Seems a bit like bullying to me," Maeve agrees, and she should know, as one of the biggest bullies who's ever lived.

"Not a whole coven," Emerson says, in that way she has, as if she feels compelled to correct errors when she encounters them because, surely, everyone wants to *correct errors*. "We were just friends. And a not-so-friendly immortal witch who helped us for his own reasons. My sister was still in exile. Still, we fought. All of us in the light against one in the dark." She looks over at Carol. "We knew he'd bartered his blood, Carol. But we had no idea what kind of power that would give him. How could we? But look."

In the image, where Emerson stands holding a sword of light given to her by Jacob, a Healer, Skip pulls together a sword of his own from the swirling, oily mess of vile black that surrounds him. It's obscene. It's horrifying. It makes my gorge rise to look at it, and I already know how this ends—

Before I can show everyone what else happened that day, a terrible pain shoots through me. It flares up along one side of my body. My leg gives out. I nearly tip over, but Emerson's beside me, holding me up. Then Zander's arm is wrapping around me from the other side, though I don't see him move.

It doesn't help. I can't maintain the spell, and the images fade. I'm upset about that, but I can barely stand up. I thought they couldn't do this again.

I realize I cry that out to the rest of our coven.

Jacob surges to his feet and crosses to me, and I can tell it's not exactly the same as before, because I'm so much more aware of what's happening. This is no blessing. Jacob puts his hands on my back, and I feel his magic wind its way into me, trying to heal me.

"They're doing something to her," he says, but in a ringing voice so everyone watching this can hear.

"Again," Zander growls.

I breathe through the waves of agony, but I can feel Jacob's magic. It's cool, almost sweet, and it works. The bright, hot *hurt* begins to recede into a fading kind of ache. After a moment or two, I can take a full breath.

It isn't like the poison from before, but that doesn't make me feel better. Maybe this is the one that will kill me. I slide my hands over my stomach, concentrating all the magic I've got into protecting this baby.

"If I recall correctly, the Undine said we cannot harm one another." Carol smirks while she says this.

She's lying. I don't know how, but the way she phrases that makes it clear enough to me. Somehow they got around the Undine.

I think, *this is it*. I am going to die. Right here on a dais next to a sentient stone, even as my friends—my coven—surround me and the ghosts float above us, all of them chanting and trying to help.

I can't imagine what the audience thinks, but it's amazing what clarity your own fast-approaching death can give you. I realize in that moment that I don't care what the audience thinks. I don't care about St. Cyprian because of a bunch of judgy witches. I care about the people surrounding me, holding me. I care about my family. I care about Zander and our baby and the future I suddenly want more than I can remember admitting to wanting anything, ever.

I never should have cared what all these random people thought of me. Another wave of pain sweeps through me, and I can't recall why I ever did.

"Joywood," intones the Undine as if my death at her stone feet is as meaningless to her as anything else, "it is your turn to explain your take on justice."

"This is quite the story and performance," Carol says, her voice smooth and calm, rippling out over everyone on the dais and off.

A spell in and of itself.

"My son made poor choices," she says, in what seems to me—even through the haze of pain—to be a direct response to Emerson's show of approachable leadership. She sighs. "Skip was dealt with, as you saw. He can no longer hurt us. He can't even tell us what drew him to the dark."

She's way too good at that, Rebekah says internally. Loudly. *Making it somehow sound like it's Emerson's fault her creepy son* bartered his blood *and tried to* kill you all *with black magic.*

I remember this is her first time seeing this.

He became the weasel he always was, witchling, Frost says.

"Rather than dwell on these unfortunate events and let those who would strike out at the heart of our government make up stories to win petty points, I decided to use a memory spell. This choice is within my rights, under witch law and as your leader. I cannot deny what he did, without my knowledge or approval. It shames me to this day. But Skip was punished by their hand, was he not? So, I thought it best we forget. I still do."

She stands there, looking *brave*. No one says anything, and yet I know that everyone watching her is tutting a bit internally, thinking we did something *unseemly*, if not outright *rude*, by saying true things out loud.

It's only a curse because no one wants to hear the truth, I think through another wave. Not because there's anything wrong with the truth itself.

Not because there's anything wrong with saying it.

"She's a liar," I grit out, because that's another truth, and I just proved it—but I'm in so much damn pain, and whatever Jacob is doing isn't quite as helpful as it usually is.

I need to get her somewhere else, Jacob tells us in our heads, and I suspect it says something about my state that he tells me too. Or doesn't take the time to *not* tell me, more like.

"Riverwood," comes the Undine's impossible voice. "Do you have a rebuttal?"

I know Emerson has a million things she wants to say, but she shakes her head, her eyes flashing gold. "My only rebuttal is this. Justice is taking care of people who are hurting. Not hurting people more."

The glowing eyes turn to the other side of the dais. "Joywood, what say you?"

They all look at each other, a ripple of bright bloodred. And I know. They're going to drag it out. I'm on fire from the inside out, but they know that already, and they want this to hurt.

Before I can come up with any strategies to protect my child no matter *what* they throw at me, I hear my mother's unmistakable voice, shouting in the crowd. "You end this, Carol. Maeve. I'm not going to stand here and let you hurt my daughter again."

"Tanith, sit down," Carol orders her, sounding bored.

"Mina," Maeve adds, with her particular brand of sniveling malevolence, "maybe you could try controlling your partner. For her own good."

The sound of Mina's incredulous laughter is almost as good as Jacob's Healer magic as it tangles with the wash of pain inside me.

"The covens have spoken," the Undine belts out in her dispassionate way. "This is how they see justice. Consider this as you make your decision come Samhain."

"We aren't finished," Carol retorts, outraged.

When even I know you can't argue with a stone statue.

"When you addressed the audience, you ended your time." Then, with no further explanation and allowing no other hint of argument, the Undine goes dark.

This time, instead of fake-walking back to Wilde House, my coven flies me there, my mother at our heels.

"I'm getting really fucking tired of being everybody's voodoo doll," I grit out while they lay me out on my bed. Again. Jacob is still working on me, but this time, everyone else has shoved their way into the room. It's not big enough, but someone has the presence of mind to utter a spell that makes it bigger.

Everyone breathes. Another wave hits me, I writhe, and it takes a moment to breathe my way back.

"Can you tell me what happened? Or what it felt like?" Jacob asks, his magic probing around inside of me.

"It was like half my body..." I trail off as it dawns on me what Jacob might already know. "The human half." It all clicks into place, horrible though it is. It even makes a certain, poetic sort of sense, if you're evil. Human blood helped me once, but it's also its own kind of target. "I got around the poison by having human blood, but the Joywood can get around the Undine by attacking the nonwitch part of me. The Undine doesn't care about humans."

"That's bullshit. This is *bullshit*." Zander shoves his hands through his hair, a whole Midwest summer of storms in his gaze. "There has to be some kind of recourse."

"The recourse is the people." Emerson sounds like she's thinking aloud. "They get to choose what to believe. Who they agree with. The point isn't right or wrong, or even truth versus lies, it's that there's a *choice*. Once we win—"

"I don't care about choice or winning or anything else if they're going to attack her," Zander roars. Maybe acting so unbothered and *unneedled* the past few days hasn't been *quite* so easy for him. I want to live long enough to revel in that. "This can't keep happening. We have to stop it."

"We need to be careful," Emerson agrees. "What's the alternative, Zander?"

"I don't know, maybe one where the pregnant woman carrying our daughter isn't fending off every single fucking attack?"

"So we should...what? Quit? Let them win?" Rebekah demands. "Do you think that's what Ellowyn wants?"

He glares at her. "It's too big a risk."

"I'm not weak," I manage to get out. "Or dead yet either, by the way."

My mother and Jacob murmur words over a mug. My herbs,

my mother's words, and a Healer's touch. I'll have to drink it to heal me, because that's what a human would need.

And hey, that's half me.

"I didn't say you were weak," Zander bites out, but he doesn't bite my head off.

There's something about the way he doesn't that begins to unravel something inside of me. Protections, I think. *Armor.* We all *have to* be our adult versions here.

Maybe that's what a coven really is.

So it's my turn to step up. Zander and I have a ticking clock leading us straight to parenthood. There's no time left for *maybes.*

When I think that, despite the pain inside me and all the many years I've beat myself up for all manner of weaknesses large and small, I know the real truth. The one that's been waiting for me all along.

The one that has never had anything to do with a *curse.*

"You don't understand, Zander," I say. Gently, so gently, when I've probably only spoken to him this gently once before, right after his mother died. "It's something my mom told me." I smile over at her, fierce and proud Tanith, who has always demonstrated exactly what kind of grown-ass woman I'd like to be. Not without flaws, but made of love and wit and flames, all the way through. "'A pregnant witch isn't fragile, she is powerful. Fearsome. Not fearful.' That means even though they can hurt me—they have—it doesn't work. Not long-term."

Jacob hands me the mug and doesn't have to tell me what to do. I tip back my head and drink the elixir that will heal me, every last acrid drop.

It cools the fire, eases the pain. It snakes through me, fighting back whatever the Joywood sent into the human parts of me, flooding me with relief.

But I have more than relief. I have that truth, at last.

I've always thought I was the weak link. *Known* it. I should feel it even more now. I should be wracked with insecurity that

I'm the reason the Joywood could get around the Undine's protections.

I think they've overplayed their hand. Every time I turn around, I'm sick. I'm poisoned. I'm the one attacked. Why me?

I don't mean that in a self-pitying way. Not any longer.

I look at Elizabeth, my favorite ghost. She's been right here, urging me toward something all along. She's told me I'm special. She's guided me toward almost every choice I've made since this whole ascension stuff was triggered.

Almost like she knew where we were headed, because she can see the past *and* the future.

"They don't want me hurt, dead, whatever," I say, while Elizabeth's violet eyes gleam bright at me. Urging me to take that thought all the way to its conclusion. "Just because they're the evilest evil to ever evil. They *need* it."

Elizabeth clasps her hands before her and beams at me. I sit up in my bed and look around at my friends, my family. My coven.

My man.

"They need it for whatever they're planning." I'm not asking. I *know*. "Immortality, or more. They didn't want Emerson to remember. They didn't want Rebekah to come back. If they'd managed those things, we wouldn't be here, in the middle of an ascension trial. These have been steps they needed to take to get where they wanted to go."

Frost nods from the wall, where he stands with his arms crossed.

I look at Emerson. Our leader. Our linchpin. But without *us*, she would have died in that dark confluence. I look at Rebekah, my best friend since we were tiny, and I know she would never have come back here if Emerson had died. Or if she had, if the Joywood had missed Emerson and that flood, she would have fled this place in shame after they unveiled her darkest secrets to the world.

We're all meant to be right here.

Together.

Each and every one of us belongs right where we are.

"These have all been steps that we've kept them from taking. Because we—" for the first time in my life, I count myself in that *we*, and I mean it with every part of me "—are more powerful than they could ever be."

And I said it, so it must be true.

Something happens then. A kind of...*opening* inside of me.

I see a past stretched out, stitched together out of near misses. Sneaky magic slapping at me, and me always more than ready to slap right back. Because I might have had some issues, but I'm always up for a fight to defend myself.

I see all their barbs, all their disgust, specifically designed to make me weak. To make me doubt myself. To make me brood about all the ways I'm *less than*.

It did, inside, but it never fully took root. Because I'm not alone. I have these people. I have *this*.

Love.

Support.

The man who's loved me no matter how many times we've broken each other's hearts.

Tonight, I finally understand what that means.

I am a power in my own right, and it's no accident I'm in this coven. I'm as big of a threat to the Joywood as the Wilde sisters and their prophecy. I'm the witch they can't quite kill. I'm the human they can't erase.

Every single thing I am is a threat. To *them*.

I am the power, I think, like an incantation.

When I do, something bright appears in front of me, so bright it's blinding. I have to close my eyes against it.

It's not a new agony that fills me up this time. It's uncomfortable, but it's bearable, and I lean in.

Like it's just another part of this power I've had all along.

There it is, Elizabeth whispers inside my head. Where I didn't think she could speak. *I knew you'd find it. Breathe, my child. Breathe, and when you open your eyes, say what you are.*

I breathe in. I blow it out.

I open my eyes, and Zander sucks in a breath.

My mother gasps. "Violet eyes," she whispers. "Like mine."

"But ringed in sapphire," Rebekah says in awe. "Like Ellowyn times ten."

I know who I am, who I have always been. I see my past. I sense my future, paths stretching out, tangling, and starting anew thanks to the choices we make.

I don't need a mirror to know myself. That comes from within. *I know who I am.*

So I say it, at last. "Revelare. The last of my kind." But I hold my baby, and I feel her kick. "For now."

23

MY VOICE ECHOES THROUGH THE BEDROOM that's still bigger than usual, but I like the way it sounds. I sit up, taking in the way everyone I love is looking back at me. It's Rebekah who conjures a mirror in the air so I can see what they all see—me, but with witchy eyes at last. A deep violet like all the Good women, but ringed with a bright, bold blue.

I like it more than I should, as a woman who has made dressing in black throughout my life my personality.

"You've got to take it easy." Jacob sounds very serious. All Healer. "Your magic is making you feel great right now, but your human side still needs rest to heal."

I nod and, shockingly, do as I'm told. I can be reasonable.

Because I didn't *become* a Revelare today. I've always been one. The future is right here, in me and in my grasp. The best part is that I have enough practice controlling the way the past spools out before me that the future doesn't come roaring for me at once the way we all know it can.

Maybe this is what balance feels like.

"Jacob is right. You need rest. Come on, everyone," Mom

says, and then she starts herding everyone out of the room while I sit there, watching the room shrink as everyone files out. With my *gemstone eyes*, thank you.

Tanith doesn't try to herd Zander anywhere, because he's brooding over by the window, his own brewing storm. And she can't see Elizabeth and Zachariah, sitting beside each other halfway up the far wall, *just* letting their fingertips touch.

Mom comes over to the bed and brushes a hand over my forehead. "Rest, you brave and glorious thing. I'm glad even you see it now."

She glances over at Zander, a considering look on her face. She takes a breath. Then looks down at me again, but this time she gives the bump a gentle pat. The baby does a soft flutter, just for her, and my mother smiles. Then she leaves the room to me and this little family of mine.

Zander and me. Our ghosts. The baby girl inside me who's still moving around like she's the one making room for all of us.

Elizabeth comes over and sits on the bed with me. There's an expression on her face that reminds me of the night I was poisoned. The night she cried over the curse that kept her from the motherhood she wanted. But this feels more…bittersweet. A gladness with threads of sorrow woven through it.

Maybe because she's been leading me here all along, to this understanding of who I am and what I can do.

"You were right," I tell Elizabeth, and we both smile, because I said it. Out loud. "You know I don't admit that lightly."

She has her hands folded in her skirt, and she looks down at them. "I was right, this is true, but you had to believe it yourself. It was easier in my time, I suppose, when Revelares were common enough. It was a natural part of growing up to have one sight stronger than the other. The opposing sight came later. With work, with acceptance, with belief."

That makes sense. I *feel* it in a way that seems new and solid, like a foundation I've been standing on all this time but never knew was there.

Yet I can't let go of that children's book. Over near the window, Zachariah is reading the book himself now, using ghost energy to turn the pages.

"What about the story?" I ask.

Elizabeth lifts a shoulder. "We're familiar with the story, but it was no more than a fairy tale in my time too. The meaning I would take from the similarities here is that we should always heed the messages that come to us, no matter how it is they arrive. It is the message that matters."

I'm not so sure I believe that. But I glance over at my Guardian, so like the one in that odd little book. He's still standing there with his elbow propped against the wall as he stares hard out the window, even though it's now dark outside.

So the things he's glaring at must be internal.

In the past—maybe even yesterday—I would have decided I knew the reason he was brooding like this. I would have centered it on myself. *He thinks I'm weak, so he's going to make some grand proclamation about protection*, I would have thought. *He's changing his mind about messing around with a targeted half witch*, I would have seethed. I would have made sure to work up my temper so whatever he might say couldn't hurt me.

Because I liked to hurt me first.

Then whatever he said hurt me anyway.

Maybe the brand-new gemstone eyes are helping me see what a waste of time this has always been.

"Good night, child," Elizabeth says to me.

There's something about the way she calls me *child* that once felt dismissive but now feels…important. Maybe it's because I can see that bittersweetness in her gaze. Threads of joy and sorrow, light and dark.

"I am *your* child, Elizabeth," I tell her. "You led me here. You've *been* here, every step. You're part of this. Part of me."

She strokes a ghostly hand over my face, much like a mother would. Much like my own mother did before she left tonight. I know I shouldn't be able to reach out and touch her, because she's a spirit. She isn't *here* as a physical body, but there's so much she's done that ought to be impossible, so I think...why not try?

I reach out and curl my fingers around the appearance of her wrist. I don't feel anything except a kind of cold air pocket, but I know that's her. I guide it toward me until her hand rests on my bump. "And part of her."

Her visage kind of...throbs then, or flickers. A sort of ghostly emotion, I think.

Because it's amazing the lengths a person can go to, to convince themselves that all this *love* is fleeting. That there's a scarcity of love in the first place. I've been supported from so many angles for so much of my life, but it was always the people who were mean to me or the people who pulled away that I focused on. I rested my self-worth on whether or not they loved me when I knew they didn't.

I think of the Joywood, these men and women that we're all supposed to look up to. These witches who are meant to protect us and keep us first in their thoughts, so they can do right by all of witchdom. When instead they focused on the threat of *us* to their power—instead of what we could offer our community, our world. When instead of *helping* us, they spent years trying to crush us.

But won't, I think now. Without the faintest hint of anything bittersweet.

Because I'm done worrying about the love I don't have. There's too much love right here. Too much support. With my baby, too much to fight for.

Life hurts. Love hurts.

Maybe hurting is how you know it's working, like every Healer's cure I've ever taken. The ache is how you heal. The pain is the whole point.

This is how a person is *alive*, not numbed into nothingness.

Not hiding and ignoring and twisting all that hurt into anger. Anger is heavy, and sometimes, it doesn't serve. Just as Elizabeth once said herself.

I don't intend to forget that again.

"Thank you, Mama Elizabeth," I say, feeling a lump in my throat. It's not that I'd be horrified to cry in front of her, because I'm not that person any longer. It's more that I think we're both trying to be strong. Strong Good women.

One strong family line, stretching backward and forward forever, ornery and *us* to the end.

Elizabeth smiles at me, her ghostly eyes overbright with the same tears I don't shed.

"And thank *you*," she whispers. She doesn't elaborate, but I don't need her to. I'm not worried any longer that other people might see—or not see—things in me I don't.

She pulls her hand away. Then she smiles at Zachariah and gestures toward the door. He smiles back, and they leave together in what looks like a comfortable, companionable silence.

I think—I know: *this is what forgiveness looks like.*

I glance over at Zander, still facing the dark over at the window. If I push aside all the insecurities that ruled me for so long, I understand that what's going on inside of him right now might be about what happened to me tonight, but it's not about *me.* It's about the whole mess of a year, and that long, slow loss of his mother, and no doubt a great many other things.

Some things are the kind of darkness we keep to ourselves, not because we're hiding or hoarding it, but because it's only looking at those dark spaces that teaches us how to walk instead in the light.

Tonight I don't want to laugh this away, avoid it, or run. Tonight I have no fights to pick. I don't want to do any of the things I usually do, and not only when it comes to Zander.

I want to be the kind of person who comforts other people instead of bludgeoning them with my own awkwardness and insecurity. I want that in a sweeping, general sense that feels more like coming of age than that terrible Litha ceremony ten years ago ever did.

Tonight I want the simplicity of being exactly who I am. What I am. I want to lean in, with joy and optimism, to what I *could* be. If I start like this. If I start right now.

I get up out of bed and silently move over to Zander. I wrap my arms around him and press my cheek to his stiff back. That's all. It's such a strange, beautiful, *new* sensation. To initiate comfort like this. To let my heart open wide without running away.

"Tell me what's eating you up," I whisper.

I've never been any good at this, but I have friends who are. A family who is. Maybe not always in the same ways, but with the same goal. To take care of each other.

The way they've always taken care of me.

Because they have, I know what to say.

"You're supposed to rest," he says gruffly, but some of the tension I can feel in his body eases. From me not launching into a new fight the way I usually do. From me holding on and not letting go.

"Then come to bed."

He grunts. "Hardly restful, El."

"It wasn't a sexual proposition," I say. Then smile, my mouth against his back. "Yet." I manage to get the tiniest laugh out of him, but then it turns into a whole-body sigh. "Come on, baby. Let's sleep."

He turns around, keeping me in his arms, and pulls me with him as he heads for the bed.

A million versions of an old me exist—the one who would let him, the one who would pick a fight instead, the one who would needle answers out of him.

But now there are also a million versions of different future mes that stretch out before me.

Lessons, if I'm willing to take them.

I am. I hold on to his other hand to stop his forward movement toward the bed. "Talk to me, Zander."

He looks at me then. His mouth curves. I think he's trying to smile, but it doesn't quite get there. "You can't understand, and that's okay. I don't need you to. Let's just go to bed."

I don't let go. I don't move. "Explain it to me."

He sighs like he's frustrated, and that sound usually infuriates me. It usually spikes me straight into something boiling hot, shouting or sex, whatever works.

It's not that I don't feel the urge to swan dive straight into the familiar. I do.

That's why it matters that I don't let go of his hands. That I don't give up.

He must sense this in some way because his shoulders slump. "I'm a Guardian," he says gruffly.

"Wow. I guess you think you've really dropped a bombshell on me." Because I might be changing, evolving, *maturing*—but I'm still *me*.

Zander scowls. "You don't understand. Just like I can't fully grasp everything that comes with being a Summoner, or a Revelare, or hell, a mother carrying a baby. There are some things that are too hard to explain."

I know that feeling. The *comfortable*, *safe* feeling that you're alone in your misery. I have certainly hoarded my misery like it was something precious, but my mother never let me hoard it forever. She'd always say the same thing when it was time to, if not let it go, find a way to live with it.

I say those words to Zander now. "Maybe I can't understand, but I can listen."

He starts to shake his head, but I place my palm over his heart. "Zander."

I meet his gaze, and I don't hide. I don't pull the punch. If I thought facing the Joywood was terrifying, this ranks right up there. "I need you to explain it to me, okay?"

He studies me, and I guess he gets it. How hard that was for me to say. How hard it is to stand here like this, telling him I *need* something and waiting to see if he'll give it to me.

But he does. "My family is literally here, on the rivers, to watch over the confluence. We failed. We should have been able to protect my mother. We failed. I should have protected you from too many things to count. I failed at that, every time. There is no *guardianing* happening. There's no actual protection. There's nothing but one failure after another."

I hear what he doesn't say then as clearly as if he had. I know that he's still holding on to the idea that he's cursed. That what he sees as failures are proof of that.

"You helped Emerson beat back that flood and save the rivers. You just didn't do it alone," I remind him. "You can't protect people from illness or from a deliberate poison that killed other people too. All the Healers in St. Cyprian couldn't manage it. Your mom died, and that will always be unfair. There's no arguing otherwise, but that's not *your* failure. I am here right now in part because of all the people who stepped in to hold me up while the Joywood got their kicks in. You're one of those people."

He looks down at me, brow furrowed. "Don't be positive, Ellowyn. It's fucking creepy."

That gets a laugh out of me. "What, you don't think I should turn into sunshine and unicorns? Rainbows and shit?"

He reaches out, brushes a thumb under one of my new gemstone eyes. Violet ringed in sapphire. Something wholly different. Something all me.

Revelare. That word is a whisper inside me. Of what could be. Out of what has been.

"This makes you an even bigger target," Zander says in that gruff, serious way. "They're not going to give up on hurting you."

"Then I guess it's a good thing I've got a kick-ass coven and a hot Guardian at my disposal."

This time when his mouth curves, it really is almost like a smile. "At your disposal, huh?"

I shrug, grinning. "I said it, so it must be true."

He doesn't smile, not really. He stares down at me, at my bright new eyes that I can almost see reflected in his. In all those storm clouds I've loved for so long.

His face looks naked, open. A lump forms in my throat, because if I'm not mistaken, the way he's looking at me right now has more to do with pride than any lingering worry or sadness.

Just call it what it is, Ruth interjects. *He's proud of you. Obviously.*

It's a sign of my emotional maturity that I ignore her, without a single threat involving stew.

It's a knee-jerk reaction to want to crack a joke, or fling out an insult, or maybe just press my body and mouth to his and forget everything else.

I breathe through that reaction, holding his gaze the whole way.

Who do I want to be now? Now that I've finally realized who I am. The old me who couldn't handle all this *emotion* that somehow feels, at the same time, like my lungs are being squeezed from the inside *and* that I'm light and bright enough to float away?

Or a brave new Revelare—not afraid of the past or the future because I know how to wield both?

"A while back, you told me everything changed," I say quietly. Because it has.

Then again, it hasn't. Maybe it took access to the past and future to finally fully see it, realize it, accept it.

Zander's gaze tracks over my face, a kind of measuring I didn't realize he's been doing for a while now. "I guess I sort of lied when I said *everything*."

It's not that he's hesitant, because that's not who he is, but he's feeling it out. Feeling *me* out, more like, and probably waiting for me to blow up at him the way I usually do. So he can calm me down the way we like.

I play up the explosion, and he plays up the cool response.

The unflappable Zander who he performs for the world is a lot of who he is, out there. Here, between us, it's also part of a mask.

One he's been wearing for a long time while he waited for me to catch up.

He's still not sure I have, but I am. "Tell me what hasn't changed," I encourage him.

"You sure you want to hear it?"

I nod. Even though something shimmers through me. Nervous energy. Fear. A million things, and yet I know I want this. I *know* it.

Maybe it's always scary—no matter how much you believe in yourself—to be vulnerable enough for this.

Maybe that's the whole point.

He smooths his hands over my hair, like this hurts. Or like he expects *me* to hurt *him*. "I've always loved you, El. That never changed. You know that."

I probably should have, and maybe sometimes I did know it. But mostly...

I shake my head. "I did everything in my power to make sure you wouldn't. That you *couldn't*. I can't imagine you were feeling loving toward me the morning after our Beltane prom."

The old Zander would have punched a wall at me bringing that up. This one laughs, if not exactly happily. "I don't really want to go down that memory lane again, thanks. But yes, even then. Always, Ellowyn. Isn't that why it hurt?"

"I felt awful," I confess. I haven't before. "During. After." I sigh. "Still."

"Good," he throws back emphatically.

I never thought I'd laugh about that mess, but something escapes me then that's close enough to count. "You weren't a monk."

"Hell no, I wasn't. But why do you think every woman after you was a human? A relationship with a human couldn't go anywhere. I would never tell them what I was." He shrugs like that was inevitable, not a choice. "It always felt like if I actually got involved with another witch, that would mean..."

"Mean what?"

"That there was no chance," he says, his voice a scrape of sound in this room that now feels too small. "Ever. For us."

He was out there preserving our last chance, and I was doing everything to destroy it. Sounds like us, but I've changed. He's changed. So much around us has changed.

There's one thing no version of me has ever done.

I curl the fingers sitting over his heart into his shirt, pulling him closer. Because I know my voice isn't going to come out strong, no matter how strongly I feel this. The emotion is clogging my throat so much that I'm not sure I'll be able to speak at all.

But I have to. Because I mean it with every last cell of my body. It's the stark and simple truth and always has been. "I love you too, Zander."

His mouth curves, his hand cupping my face. His eyes gleam, thunder and certainty, and I feel the rumble deep inside. "I know."

This time when he kisses me it's soft, slow.

Perfect.

A new promise amidst all sorts of old broken ones. We'll lay it down between us tonight and build a future on all we've learned.

I wrap my arms around his neck and deepen the kiss.

Because this is the secret to why the sex was always amazing—no matter how angry we were with each other. *Love.*

It's been love all along.

Zander pulls his mouth from mine and even tries to put some distance between us. "Baby, you've got to get some sleep. Those were the Healer's orders."

"No, Jacob said *rest*," I correct him. "I happen to find sex very restorative. Don't worry, I'll *try* to be gentle."

He laughs as I pull his mouth to mine. As he lifts me up, then puts me down again, but comes with me this time.

Until we're wrapped up with each other, deep inside and out, lit up with the ways we love each other and always have.

Because we're exactly where we belong.

24

IF WE THOUGHT WAITING FOR THE SECOND trial was long, the wait for the third and final trial feels like an eternity. No amount of meetings filled with Emerson's endless optimism and pep talks, no amount of living our normal lives and running our businesses, no amount of nights with Zander that end, always, in the simple *I love you*s that still feel like gifts can ease the slow, anxious tick of time.

All we do is wait. Then wait some more.

Any time Jacob is free, we go over the plans for the ritual that will take my blood—carefully and with good, clean magic—to be used in a cure that will keep the rest of the Summoners in the world from dying the way Zelda and too many others already did.

Any time Rebekah and I are together, we work at trying to magic our way into the future, or back into the past, looking for a *hint* at when the Undine will strike next. We congratulate ourselves on having two members of the same coven with these gifts, as no other coven can. That makes us powerful because it's safer this way, with both of us to find our way along these sometimes murky pathways forward and back.

Like it should have always been like this.

But no amount of searching gives us those answers. Because the options are *infinite*. So many paths, twisting this way and that way and back again, that we can't sort through them all.

Even if we could, I'm beginning to realize it wouldn't matter.

The choice must be ours. In the moment.

More, *of* the moment.

I find that frustrating, but this time around, the frustration makes me want to dig in and keep trying.

Now it's only a few short days before Samhain. I'm part of the group headed to Frost House to search the immortal library for books on old ascensions, dragons, crows, princesses, blood magic wards, or whatever else we think might help.

Or that's what Georgie and Frost are doing. Rebekah and I are along for the ride to try reaching into the past for lessons from old ascensions. We decide to walk because it's a crisp, pretty day, and maybe we all also want the opportunity to get outside and breathe the air.

With Samhain nearly upon us, it's a simple pleasure none of us can take for granted.

Even beneath a deceptively warm late-October sun, St. Cyprian looks suitably ready for Samhain. The Halloween madness spills out everywhere. Cornstalks are tied to lampposts, and jack-o'-lanterns, gourds, and decorations of witches, zombies, and vampires fill just about every storefront. There are crowds all over the sidewalks. Tea & No Sympathy boasts an impressive display of spiderwebs and—special for this year—ghost decorations everywhere. Some creepy old dolls and daguerreotype photos that I told Elizabeth reminded me of her.

She was unamused.

I should get excited for Samhain the way I usually do *any*

second now, but as we walk toward Frost House, the coming holiday only looms like a shadow.

A threat.

Rebekah and I spent hours perfecting the glamour for my new eyes, because there's no need to advertise that sort of thing to the Joywood. I stopped bothering with the pregnancy glamour. Everyone already knows *that*.

The four of us walk to the end of Main Street toward the hill that rises up at the end, cresting to a high bluff over the river. The stairs carved into the hillside lead directly to the towering mansion Frost keeps glamoured to look like a dilapidated old house. With enough charms to keep even thrill-seeking humans far away.

The stairs are long and steep, and I'm almost six months pregnant. Or anyway, I tell myself my pregnancy is the reason I'm out of breath, and not the fact I've done nothing but eat too much Redbrick pizza and have entirely too much mind-blowing sex most of this month.

At the top, we all slow down to look out at the gleaming rivers. We let the breeze play over our faces, and listen to the song it carries, made of magic and power from the heart of the confluence in the distance. I feel a pang of sorrow for humans, who see two rivers and don't feel the power of things the way we do. Who see the charming bustle of St. Cyprian down below, but have no idea what it means. What this particular river town stands for, from brick to belfry and back again.

As if a mutual decision was made, we all turn to the house at the same time, but Frost stops, turning immediately and obviously wary.

It says something that I wasn't aware that his usual aloofness is…him relaxed.

"Something is wrong," he says quietly. Coronis caws his agreement from above the old Victorian.

"What is it?" Rebekah asks, her hand finding Frost's automatically.

"I don't quite know," he says in that same quiet way, ripe with menace. He scans the house, and it's clear he's not just *looking*. He's using his magic too. "Every ward and protection is as it should be and yet..." He frowns. "Something isn't right."

"Then maybe we shouldn't—"

Before Georgie can even finish the sentence, Frost and Rebekah are gone. No doubt they've magicked themselves inside, and it's not like they can't take care of themselves. But four is still better than two when there are potentially lethal shenanigans afoot, or so I tell myself. I shrug at Georgie and she sighs, taking my hand so we can follow them in.

We land in the library. Frost stands next to a little cage that I don't think I've ever seen before. Even as I think that, something about it tugs at me, and I can't help thinking it *should* mean something to me.

"Did any of you touch the weasel?" Frost asks.

"Is that a euphemism?" I ask Rebekah, loud enough to make Georgie laugh.

Frost only gazes back at me with the excessive mildness that reminds me he really was the first, best Praeceptor in witch history. He has that vibe. That, *yes sir, thank you, I'll just sit down and be quiet* thing.

"Skip," he says, and it jogs something in my brain. It sweeps out the cobwebs that I didn't realize were gathered around that name. Skip.

Skip Simon, Carol's nasty creep of a black magic–loving son, who she makes sure we all keep forgetting.

"Oh," I say. "*That* weasel." I can suddenly recall broadcasting that weasel's antics to all and sundry at the last trial. Carol's memory magic at work. I scowl.

"The weasel is gone."

Frost's expression goes dark then, and this is not a teacher thing. This is the kind of dark that makes me understand why witch armies followed him into battle thousands of years ago.

"Maybe he chewed through his cage or something," Georgie offers, with more hope than certainty.

Frost shakes his head. "The Joywood are the only ones who could skirt the protections I keep on this house, not to mention the wards in this library, without alerting me." He looks around in that same dark manner. "This bodes ill."

I swallow at my suddenly dry throat. Frost doesn't come out and say what *ill* he means, but I think we can all draw our own conclusions here. Skip bartered in black magic. With blood. He broke every last good witching rule.

If the Joywood have taken him, they must have a reason, and we know it's not because Carol suddenly cares about the son she made everyone forget last spring. I can't be the only one who thinks this is the Joywood getting their black magic on.

None of us say it out loud.

"Let's fly back to Wilde House," Rebekah suggests after a moment. "Warn Emerson and everyone."

Frost nods. "Georgie, collect the books we were to use today. The three of you fly back, and I will—"

"No one goes it alone. Not even you." Rebekah says this briskly. "Ellowyn and Georgie will take the books back. I'll stay with you and cleanse the house. Add protections."

He looks as if he might argue, but he doesn't. He holds Rebekah's gaze for a long moment, then turns and sweeps off into the bowels of his library, leaving the impression of a witch's cloak and the like when I know perfectly well the man is wearing jeans and a Henley.

It might not seem like it, Rebekah says in my head. *But this is a violation. I think he needs a few minutes alone.*

I nod, turning to Georgie, who's already whispering spells to send a stack of books back to Wilde House.

"Be safe," we all murmur at each other with a little more urgency than the standard witch farewell usually contains.

Georgie and I link hands again, whisper a protection spell for both of us as we travel, then fly.

A beautiful Missouri fall stretches out below us. A riot of colors, bright and happy, as if they don't represent the coming winter, the year's inevitable death reaching up from the ground to the sky. I shiver a little, fighting off a feeling of foreboding as we land in the living room of Wilde House.

It's just us for now. Zander is with Emerson at the bookstore, and Jacob is with his family, deep in preparations for the Summoner blood ritual. With the Undine supposedly protecting us, we all figured it would be okay for Jacob to handle his Healer duties without a partner in tow, but now I wonder.

But Jacob's familiar is with him, I reason. His family is made of strong Healers, like him. He'll be okay.

I try to *believe* it.

Georgie immediately sinks into the books she's magicked over, flipping them open on the table where they landed in tidy stacks. "Sage has been helping with research," she says somewhat absently as she turns a few pages in one book, then another, with a spell. "He found an interesting translated bit about a crow army, like your ghost and the fairy tale mentioned. It's a line we're tugging on."

I know I shouldn't say anything about Georgie's boyfriend. She hasn't asked. I've never enjoyed having people comment on my romantic life unsolicited. I bite my tongue and sink into a chair at the table, cracking open a book myself.

I regret it immediately when I realize it's not in any language I know. "What if you're the princess in the book?"

Georgie laughs. "Then I'd be carousing with dragons, apparently. Not reading books about it."

I eye her. "The thing about being pregnant is that I have to pee in the middle of the night. Like, a lot. Sometimes, when that's handled, I start thinking that what would be *really* nice is a snack, and maybe I don't feel like sharing. Which I'd have to do if I just magicked myself some food that Zander would wake up and eat."

Georgie makes an encouraging yet distracted sound. "I support your secret snacks, Ellowyn."

"Last night, for example, I got up around two and popped down to the kitchen to eat some ice cream," I say in the same offhanded way, but I'm watching her closely. "When I was done with my extreme chocolate and peanut butter moment, I decided to virtuously walk back up the stairs."

She's not distracted any longer. Georgie looks up at me, gaze intense.

"How long have you been sleepwalking?" I ask her softly. Her throat works, but she doesn't say anything. "Or in this case, sleep-sitting, I guess? Is that what you call it when a person is curled up on the stairs, talking to a newel post?"

Georgie looks at me for a little too long, a little too intently, before she laughs. "That's so embarrassing. Why didn't you wake me up?" Before I can answer that, she's flipping pages again. "I used to sleepwalk all the time when I was little. It must be the stress of all this ascension stuff that has me regressing. I'm going to have to charm my bedroom at night again so I don't end up out in the street, easy pickings for the Joywood."

I want to chase that down a little more, and maybe work my way around to why her research-happy boyfriend isn't here, making sure she doesn't wander off into traffic or worse in the middle of all this—but I can't. Because Frost and Rebekah appear, quickly followed by Emerson and Zander, and the moment is lost.

"Jacob will be here soon," Emerson says, a little tightly. Worry in her eyes.

Zander puts a reassuring hand on her shoulder. "I sent Storm over to fly back with him."

She nods in appreciation and looks around the room, literally vibrating. "I'll go make us some snacks while we wait."

I can see Zander is about to follow her when she charges off, but I hold up a hand and point to myself. Wound-up Emerson seems like a job for me.

She's back in the kitchen, magicking a ridiculous amount of food together. I know she doesn't realize the way worry radiates off her, or she'd hide it.

"It's okay to not be okay, Em," I say when I come to stand beside her in the kitchen where her grandmother used to teach us silly little spells. How to clean up all the crayons. How to make the wind chimes sing without a breeze. How to really talk to plants.

I can hear Grandma Wilde's voice as clearly as if she's right here with us.

Beside me, Emerson sucks in a deep breath. "Sometimes, even when you're worried or scared, you're still okay." Then she smiles. Exuding Warrior confidence. "I can feel it all, all at the same time."

So I make the small drooping plant on the windowsill dance a little, the way her grandma would have, until she smiles.

It's not until Jacob appears, right here in the kitchen, that relief washes over her enough that her shoulders actually slump. "Hi," she offers.

"Hi," Jacob says, his voice deeper. Maybe darker. He heads for her with an intent look on his face that has me immediately vacating the premises.

Jacob and Emerson take a few minutes to follow. Both carrying trays of the food Emerson put together. They set the trays down on the coffee table in front of the hearth, where Zander has lit a fire. When they straighten, Emerson is all leader again. No hint of that overwhelmed woman I glimpsed briefly.

Old Ellowyn would have seen that as a sign that *love* is weakness, but I see it now for what it really is. The strength to feel it all, all at the same time.

Emerson fixes Frost with a look. "Let's hear it."

Emerson's expression darkens as Frost recounts the story of the missing Skipweasel. There's that Warrior glint in her eye, but it's not quite as gleeful as it has been at some other points.

"We knew they were going to do something," she says after we all sit in the things we're not saying for a bit.

Georgie strokes Octavius on one side of her in her favorite chair and Rebekah's Smudge on the other. "I'm not sure how they got around Frost's protections—"

"Nor am I," he bites out glacially.

"They covered their tracks. We can't accuse them of anything. We can't bring this to the Undine." Emerson crosses her arms. "It feels like they've been working on this a long time."

"It would explain their quiet times," Georgie agrees. "Storing up energy, working on spells. With all of us here, it likely gave them time to weaken the protections there."

Frost's gaze is frigid as he inclines his head.

Emerson meets his gaze. "I'm sorry, Nicholas," she says, using the first name that generally only Rebekah uses.

Maybe that melts something in him. "It is better we protect ourselves and each other than a house." His mouth even curves. "I have had quite a few of them in my time."

Emerson nods. "We know what they've got, but not what they'll do. Which means all we can do is focus on what *we* can do. What are the updates on the Summoner ritual, Jacob?"

"We've decided to hold the blood ritual the night before Samhain," Jacob says, "assuming the ascension trial doesn't create a conflict."

"If it does?" Emerson fires back, clearly his leader, not his fiancée, just then.

But Jacob wouldn't be the man for her if things like that bothered him. They don't. We can all see it in the way he nods. "Good question. We have to hope it won't, and if it does, plan to move directly into the ritual when the trial is done. We have to do this at the safest time, but everyone agrees that the ritual needs to be completed before Samhain."

Before the Joywood secure their power and kill us all for our temerity in challenging them, he means.

Beside me, I feel Zander tense. Emerson, usually the soul of optimism, frowns—but doesn't argue, which is probably the scariest part yet.

"We know the bricks are the most protected, but it's safest if we do this ritual somewhere with more room," Jacob continues in the same steady way, and I let his steadiness soothe me. "We've decided on the cemetery. With Summoners' connection to the spirit world, it seems the safest place."

Everyone makes affirmative noises, as if they can't think of a safer place themselves, even Frost.

Well.

Almost everyone.

"Why isn't anyone saying what we're all thinking?" Zander demands. Tense and stormy. "They've got the weasel—who bartered in dark magic with his *blood*. Maybe that was his true, useless form, but if the Joywood went through all the trouble of stealing him, it's *for* something. That something is to hurt us, but first and foremost to hurt Ellowyn."

"We're all in danger," I say carefully.

And I *say* it, so.

He glares at me. "Name one person who's been attacked the way you have."

"Other Summoners, Zander. They need protecting too." I keep holding his gaze. "You know this."

Better than most.

I can see the way the loss of Zelda ravages him all over again, or still, right here in this taut little moment.

"No one will be more protected during the ritual than Ellowyn," Jacob says, calmly. "We've talked to Tanith about participating, along with your father, Zander. It isn't only us against the dark now. It's a community of light." He pauses, then sounds almost reluctant as he finishes his list of participants. "Elspeth will be joining us as well."

I don't know if everyone can hear the way Zander growls at that, but I can *feel* it. "Oh, my aunt who refused to talk to my mother because she *married down* is going to help? Awesome."

"She's powerful, Zander," Emerson says. "You know that too."

He shoves his hands through his hair, but he doesn't explode. "Knowing it and liking it are two different things."

"I don't think any of us has to like this," I say. Not just to Zander, but to the whole group. Because maybe Emerson can Warrior herself through this, but the simple fact is we're all a little shaken by the weasel being taken.

It means something. Something bad.

"We always knew there was going to be a fight. One where maybe we fail or even die." I send Emerson a sharp look so she doesn't take my saying this as a call for fist pumps. "The Joywood can still win, but so can we. Jacob is right. This isn't just us against them anymore. We have a whole community. The slightly more than half of St. Cyprian who have supported us since Litha, and who knows how many more since then? If we depend on them—the way the Joywood would *never* depend on people they see as beneath them—we already have a leg up. Plus we're bright and good instead of wrong and dark. That matters."

I look around the room, suddenly all too aware everyone is staring at me. Including our two ghosts, appearing from wherever they've been hiding, their eyes shining.

I clear my throat and sit down, now that I realize I'm standing.

"A pep talk from Ellowyn Good," Rebekah says in a voice of sheer wonder, her mouth curved and her eyes sparkling with emotion. "That has to mean *anything* can happen."

25

THE DAY BEFORE SAMHAIN DAWNS WITH THE
sweet rarity of Zander still in bed with me when I finally decide
to wake up. Usually he's already off at the ferry, taking those
early shifts with Jacob or Frost accompanying him.

Today he's here. The morning outside is gray and drizzly,
and he pulls me into him. Warm and steady. We don't say anything. We just hold on to each other for a little bit.

When my stomach demands we get up, we head downstairs
into the kitchen. It's clear Emerson and Georgie have already
been down here, magicking breakfast feasts and leaving them
on magical warmers for those of us who prefer to stay in our
beds until a more reasonable hour.

Before Zander and I can even settle ourselves at the table,
Elspeth Wilde walks in. She doesn't seem surprised to see us
here, the way we certainly are to see her. Sure, Jacob mentioned she'd be at the ritual, but I'm not emotionally prepared
for awkward breakfasts with this woman who's never liked me.

Something she's made all too clear over the years.

I brace myself as she stands there, looking at us both with that cool gaze of hers. Then I notice that her hands are clasped tight...an odd sign of something that on anyone else I would call nerves.

Maybe I'm still asleep and dreaming.

"Good morning, Zander. Ellowyn."

She says this without her trademark sniff of disdain. I look up at Zander, expecting to see a similar befuddlement. His expression is blank.

That's not good.

Elspeth clears her throat like she knows it. "It seems congratulations are in order," she says, and though she sounds stiff, the way she nods toward my rounded stomach seems surprisingly genuine. She even attempts a smile. "A child is a great blessing."

I think not that long ago I would have found something really scathing to say to that, but my hand is in Zander's, and I can feel his tension. I'm not sure being my usual snarky self would help this situation.

"I...brought a gift," Elspeth continues, letting the shocks keep coming. She holds out her hands, palms up, and a small box appears. She makes as if to hand it to Zander.

He doesn't take it.

There's a beat where I can't tell if Elspeth is hurt or angry, or if I might want to jump in and *do something* to make this moment less awful, but then she simply lifts the lid off the box herself. "When we were girls, Zelda and I used to make each other things. Flower crowns, bracelets, rings. Your mother was always better at it than I was, Zander."

She tilts the box so I can see a delicate crown of violet blooms. All braided together by the stems. Clearly enchanted, so the flowers remain living all these years later.

Zelda's work, I think, even as Elspeth confirms it. "She made this for me many years ago, and it was one of the few things I kept all these years, even though we didn't…" She breaks off. "I'd like the child to have this."

I glance at Zander. His gaze isn't exactly friendly, but he doesn't turn away or look too thunderous. So I take the box from her.

"Thank you," I offer. I don't know what else to say. It's very kind and sentimental—two things I would have told you Elspeth isn't.

The fact our daughter will have something made by Zelda's own hands, back when she was a girl herself, threatens to make me so emotional my eyes might fill up again.

Elspeth doesn't leave the way I expect her to, now that she's bestowed her gift. She keeps her gaze on Zander. "I suppose I haven't been a very good aunt to you, Zander."

"You *suppose*?" he returns, his brow raised.

Elspeth's mouth firms, but she doesn't back away. She also doesn't let loose with one of her lectures. It's like she's possessed.

"I will endeavor to take my role as great-aunt more seriously." She really, truly smiles at us both then. It's a tight, frigid kind of smile, sure, but it's real. "Tonight, I'm not standing only for my daughters and their coven, or my nephew, or my grandniece, or even my community. Tonight, at the ritual, I'm standing for my sister in a way I should have when she was alive."

I'm struck absolutely silent. Almost more than when Elspeth stood up for us at Litha. If you'd asked me ten years ago what adults would be only too eager to sign our death warrants, I'd have put Elspeth pretty high up on that list.

Zander still says nothing. Elspeth gives a little nod, then turns to go. She's almost out of the kitchen before Zander finally speaks again.

When I thought he wouldn't.

"She'd forgive you, you know." His voice is raw. "I don't know if I can, but I bet she already has."

Elspeth turns back. Her eyes are bright, but she doesn't cry.

"Thank you," she says, a lifetime of emotion there in her voice. Then she does leave the kitchen, her back straight, and I blink back as many tears as I can.

"Don't cry," Zander mutters gruffly as he pulls me in close, resting his chin on the top of my head.

I clear my throat. "Who, me?"

He kisses my temple. I lean into it, to him, to *us*, and then we both make a concentrated effort to have a normal breakfast. We talk about eccentric customers and the gloomy weather outside. We talk about people we knew in high school who buy love potions and sensual aids from the tea shop like I don't know them. We talk about things people tell each other or say into their phones out on the low, flat ferry platforms that they think no one can hear.

The things we don't talk about are so loud we have to lean in close, breathing each other in, to keep ignoring them.

When Frost enters, ready to head to the ferry with Zander, I give Zander a kiss and my best attempt at a smile.

We don't say the word *goodbye*. We don't talk about what will happen next.

Because the Joywood aren't the only ones who can plan. We have Emerson for that. Tonight we'll have so many versions of ourselves running around St. Cyprian that the Joywood won't be able to figure out who's us and who's a projection until the ritual is over.

We hope.

Rebekah and I walk over to Tea & No Sympathy. I recount the flower crown story on the way, and she's as blown away as I was. Once we're in the shop, she settles into her usual seat with her tablet while I wait on the steady stream of customers. I play music loud enough to fill the store and spill out into the street every time the door opens. I enjoy the feel of the way my baby girl moves inside of me like she's dancing, her movements a little more pronounced every day.

I even enjoy refereeing a fight between Zachariah and Elizabeth about those damn crows. Again.

"They're important," Zachariah insists.

"Maybe they are," I say, trying to sound soothing. "But not today."

He lets out an affronted sort of sound, but by the time I'm closing up shop, the ghost couple is back to hand-holding and warm gazes. But then, I know better than most that a tempestuous thread through a relationship isn't the end of the world.

Rebekah and I head down Main Street in that inky fall dark that comes so early, ghosts trailing behind us, the town full to the brim with people ready and eager to start the celebrations a night early. The humans are hyped for the Halloween trick-or-treating in all the shops. There are little kids in their costumes, lining up outside stores. Tomorrow there will be a gathering of humans dressed in witch costumes, and a costumed parade.

Meanwhile, witches from all over the world come to St. Cyprian for Samhain even when it isn't an ascension year, because the veil is so thin and magic is heightened this close to the powerful merging of the three rivers.

You can feel all this in the air, thick and complicated.

You can see it in the shadows down every alley, all a little too deep, too dark.

We walk down to Confluence Books, where Emerson is locking the door while Georgie waits patiently on the sidewalk with her face in another book. Emerson links arms with me, so I grab onto Rebekah, who takes Georgie's book from her and magics it away. After a brief moment for Georgie to frown about it, we walk toward the ferry, arm in arm.

The ferry isn't our destination though. Before we make it to the dock, we veer off onto the path that ambles along the riverside before delivering us to Nix, the bar that's been in Zander's family almost as long as the ferries have. The bar itself is a long, low, unprepossessing affair that seems eternally *this close* to toppling straight into the Mississippi, but the sparkling lights that are threaded all over everything make it seem magical, even to unmagical eyes. The patio closes for the season on November 1, but tonight it's merry with Halloween revelers and Samhain celebrants alike.

When we enter the bar, it's also packed, but my gaze finds Zander immediately. Like there's a light that shines down on him that only I can see, and I like that idea so much that it takes me a moment to see what he's doing. Just now he's smiling at a human couple while making their drink. Midway through, he looks over at a human dressed as Catwoman who's leaning very provocatively over the bar, trying to get his attention with more than her gaze.

I wait for this to bother me, to send me into a rage as it might have before, but nothing really sparks.

I realize two things at once.

Something I never realized before—and probably couldn't when I was young and full of doubts and fears and insecurities wrapped up in armor and edges and fear—is that the flirty smile for all and sundry is different than the smile he gives me.

Only and ever me.

Because the other thing I realize, which maybe I've always known deep down, is that Zander is loyal. He's a Guardian through and through. A Rivers. He might have been with more than his share of human women, but he never juggled multiple ones at the same time. Not to mention, he was dabbling in *only* humans because of me. Because of the *hope* of me.

The point being: he's not Bill.

We're not my parents.

I understand something else from there. The way a man chooses to betray a woman is *never* about the woman. That shit is theirs and theirs alone. I should have known that all along. My mother said it enough.

Maybe it takes a love of your own to heal that last, secret fear inside of you.

As if he can hear me think this, Zander looks up, and his eyes gleam, thunder and need, and all for me.

It's better than a love letter.

Emerson tugs my arm, and I let her pull us toward Jacob and Frost, who are standing down at the end of the bar. We all nod our hellos, but it isn't really a small talk kind of moment. Zander finishes behind the bar, saying something to his cousin who's come to fill in for the night.

No one says, *or after tonight too, if necessary.*

Zander winds his way toward us. He greets me with a kiss, then lifts a hand toward his cousin. "Thanks for the help, Zeb."

Zeb nods from behind the bar. "Good luck, Riverwood. We're rooting for you."

We all pause for a moment, taking that in. We look at each other. Then Emerson grins and offers what I hope is only the first fist pump of the evening.

As her younger sister, Rebekah is duty bound to roll her eyes. Georgie laughs. Then the Riverwood coven is out in the October cold again.

We walk away from the bar, letting the dark swallow us whole. We pause for a moment, there where the trees seem like mere suggestions and the river rushes past, singing its songs of power and portent. The stars and moon are hidden behind clouds, but that suits us for right now because we're doing a spell to create as many different versions of us as we can.

We gather into our circle, and I sense our familiars drawing near to lend their power to ours. Ruth hoots in the trees I can barely see, it's so dark.

We don't have to see to start the spell though. Together in unison.

"Confluence, strong and ours. Moon, bright and mighty. Hide us in plain sight. Protect our purpose this important night."

The magic spills out from the center of us, creating versions of ourselves. The Riverwood at Wilde House. The Riverwood back at Nix. The Riverwood up at Frost House again. Decoys of us meant to distract and confuse the Joywood so they can't track us or figure out what we're really up to.

Once that's taken care of, we walk over to the ferry. Zack and Finn are there, but Zack is ready to leave the ferry in Finn's hands tonight and come with us this time.

Finn guides us over the river like the newly minted Guardian he is, and I stand with my coven, my friends, watching the confluence with all its gold, good magic sparkling through. Even in the dark.

Because of *us*.

When we get to the other side, we walk up the trail from the river to the cemetery on the hill, where Jacob's family have already set up for the ritual. Not far from the grove of redbud trees that figured so prominently in bringing Emerson back to herself last spring.

To me, this feels like coming full circle. She fought off adlets here so she could live and do all the miraculous things she's done so far. Now I will sacrifice what part of me I can, so that even more witches will live, and who knows what they'll do?

Elspeth and my mother are already there, standing next to each other in what no one with eyes would call a friendly sort of silence. It's Maureen and Evie and a few of Jacob's other relatives who are carrying the conversation and acting like they don't notice the strain between Tanith and the current Wilde matriarch.

But it doesn't matter what ancient feuds they're still prepared to fight. What matters is that we're not on our own anymore.

It means more than I ever thought it could.

We've all gone over (and over and over) the order of what's going to happen. What I need to say and do. That doesn't mean I'm not nervous. Not that I might fail, but that it might not go the way we want. That any number of irritating spell things might happen, because spells are tricky, and rituals like to make you work for them.

And there's always the possibility that the Undine might call us in the middle of it.

Yet I know there's nothing more to be done. No amount of thinking changes what will be—good or bad. I try to think only about what needs to be done and when.

Here, Jacob is in charge again. When everything is set and the time is right, he leads me to the center of the cemetery. Everyone else takes their places, as planned and exhaustively rehearsed. Our familiars and Jacob's family in a wide circle around us. Our parents in four points within the circle.

Me, in the middle, with my coven lined up in front of me.

The ghosts that still only Zander and I can see take their places too. Elizabeth on my right. Zachariah on my left.

Jacob begins by lighting a candle, murmuring words of incantation and invitation alike. Then everyone in the circle and our compass points light theirs, echoing him.

Until we are all dots of flickering light against the dark night. With me at the center. I blow out a slow breath.

"We are here tonight to counteract the dark, the poison, and those that would hurt the Summoners among us," Jacob intones, calling in the spirits and the spells, all powers and portents alike.

I feel as if a new wind kicks up, but only I seem to feel it. Rushing through me, wrapping around me.

"It is a Healer's spell," Jacob continues. "A Healer's ritual." His gaze meets mine, gold and bright. "But you are the center, Ellowyn. The blood. The choice. The cure."

I pull in a breath. I don't look at Zander.

I try to remain strong and centered as it all begins at last.

First up, the protections from my coven.

Jacob holds out his hands, and a crown of flowers, much like the one Elspeth gave us this morning, appears. "For your bravery, a crown of borage."

The plant has been woven into a ring and infused with Healer whispers of protection and healing. The pretty purple blooms resemble stars. Jacob carefully places it over my head, his smile warm and kind, before he gives way to the next in line.

Emerson approaches. Her eyes are shiny with pride. "For your strength and determination." She slides a ring of iron on my finger.

Frost and Rebekah follow, together.

"Hold out your hands, Revelare," Frost intones, in that Praeceptor's voice of his.

I do as I'm told. It doesn't even occur to me to offer one of my usual snarky remarks. The moment is too big, the meaning of this too important.

They each slide a bracelet over one of my wrists. On the right, Frost's offering is a tangled brown and gray—tumbled petrified wood. "To strengthen your connection to the past. All that was, all that you came from," he says.

Rebekah's bracelet is made of rose quartz. "For your inner voice, your connection to all that can be, may it be clear and good." Then she gives me a hug and whispers, "You've got this."

Georgie approaches, her head burnished red in the candlelight. She looks more like that princess from the fairy tale than ever. She hands me a tiny book, no bigger than my palm. "To protect what you know, in your heart, in your mind."

Then it's Zander's turn. I am already emotional and far too close to tears, but the silver of his eyes makes my whole being shake.

He holds Zelda's necklace, which I've only taken off before this ritual, for this ritual.

"From your Guardian," he says, strong and true. That scent of his magic, woodsmoke and the power of the rivers, wraps around us.

Mine, I mouth, hoping to make him smile.

Not quite, but close. I'll take it.

He puts the necklace over my head. "So the rivers and the mighty power of the confluence protect you from all that would wish you harm."

He leans down and presses his mouth to mine. I know he wants to linger, hold me tight, do *more*, but he steps back. Because love and protection and duty are difficult concepts to balance. His honor, that deep-seated need to be noble, struggles to overwhelm what needs to be done, risked.

We're working on it.

Together.

Before he releases me, though, Elizabeth is whispering at us.

"If you let me in, accept me, I can be another layer of protection. For you, for the child. You only have to accept me."

"And you," Zachariah says to Zander. "Accept me."

Zander and I look at each other. It's weird request, but they haven't led us astray yet. Who would turn down extra protection in this moment?

"Say it," Elizabeth says, a little more urgently than feels comfortable. "In your heads, as one."

I breathe out, lock eyes with Elizabeth, and hear Zander utter the same words I do, like we're an internal chorus.

I accept you.

I feel something cool and fizzy, almost. Like drinking carbonation, but with far more energy. Warmth follows, and then something curls around inside me. Like another layer protecting the baby from the outer world.

I know Elizabeth will protect her in whatever ways she can. I look at Zander. His silver eyes are slightly different, like I can see Zachariah's shadow in there. Looking out for us both.

Zander nods at me, then steps back, but only a little. While the rest of the coven forms an inner circle around us, Zander takes each of my hands. It reminds me of months ago, when we did a ritual in Confluence Books and I sat knee to knee with Emerson while she tried to find answers.

I try not to think of how, thanks to Skip's mark on Emerson, it didn't go as planned. Because it still turned out okay, and everyone was all right.

Eventually.

I swallow and focus on Zander. On the feel of Elizabeth protecting my child. Zachariah protecting Zander.

We kneel, as we are meant to. Me on one side of Zelda's grave, Zander on the other, our hands linked over the stone.

More protection.

Then Jacob begins in earnest.

"By Earth. By Air. By Fire. By River's Confluence here. With the power of birth, of death, of life, give unto us the magic to heal, to protect."

His eyes glow, deep and powerful. His gaze meets mine, magic in the air, in our hearts. "Ellowyn Sabrina Good, do you consent?"

Part of the danger of this ritual is that I have to go under a kind of anesthesia spell so they can carefully and correctly collect my blood. It requires giving myself over fully, and since I'm still *me*, that isn't easy.

But it's right. "I consent," I say, loud and clear.

"With the Revelare's consent, take care of soul, while we collect from the body the blood of life, of power, of protection, of good and right and hope."

I let the words lull me, then float away, separating soul body from physical body. Not in a scary or wrong way, because this is what needs to happen. A separation of sorts. My body below—me above.

So that Jacob can take the blood he needs in that good, clean way only Healers can do. With consent. With good intentions.

I'm not separated from my body fully, and my soul is its own body. Both parts of me are tethered together by the ritual, by Zander's hold on me, by all of these protections I wear and carry inside me. All the same, my soul, my essence is in a kind of magical waiting room. Not fully aware of what's happening around me.

Until something *cold* slithers up my spine, causing me to shiver. I try to open my eyes before I remember I'm not supposed to do that. So I squeeze them back shut.

Elizabeth?

Don't let go, she says, there in my head. But I'm not letting go. Am I?

Then I hear Zander's voice. Booming, tinged with worry.

Ellowyn. Where are you?

Here. I'm right here, I say at once.

I don't feel my physical body. I don't feel him.

And he clearly can't feel me.

26

DON'T PANIC.

I respond to the voice before I fully realize it's Elizabeth's. I feel a sudden sense of calm and well-being that I'm not sure matches the moment, but all I can think about just now is that I'm grateful that I can still hear her at all.

Because I can't hear Zander anymore, and maybe he's not talking...but I kind of doubt that.

The cold is spreading. Elizabeth's *don't panic* wears off pretty quickly as I'm floating around in some weird black space.

This wasn't supposed to happen.

We've been untethered, she tells me in that same sedate way, though this time it doesn't have that ghostly Valium effect. *We must stay calm.*

How the hell am I supposed to be *calm* when I'm floating about some magical space void, *untethered*?

How did this happen? I ask.

Elizabeth sighs audibly, there inside me. *Look to your protections, child.*

I look at my hands. The bracelets and the ring are all intact.

I reach for my head to find the crown still sits there. Georgie's little book is in my pocket. I can feel Zelda's necklace around my neck, but when I lift my hand to touch it, to wrap my fingers around the metal the way I sometimes do to reassure myself everything is okay, it burns.

I look down, and it's covered in an oozy kind of black. Deep and dark and *wrong*.

In the distance, in the dark, I hear what sounds like a scream. The kind a weasel might make.

Black magic, I think. Worse, blood magic. It's burning there against my skin.

My first instinct is to pull it off, but something in me tells me that's all wrong. Like intuition, but louder. And far more certain.

I try instead to wipe away the oily black. It burns when I pull at the gooey substance, but it also moves. So I ignore the burn and claw the black off the necklace. It keeps growing back, but I don't give up. It seems like the only thing I can do.

It hurts, it all hurts, but it's centered here like they can't get to me any other way, and that gives me some relief.

I manage to clear a spot off the metal.

Ellowyn. Baby. I can't find you, comes Zander's voice at once, and it nearly makes me weep. I hear him, and that means there is hope.

I want to give that back to him. *You can*, I tell him, there in that channel that's only ours. *You can find us, Zander. All of us.*

I don't just say it, I believe it. I trust it.

I trust *him*.

Something makes the back of my neck prickle, and it reminds me of that night that feels forever ago. Stepping out of Zander's apartment on stilts and that black shadow swooping at me. Zander saving me in the nick of time.

I don't see a threat here in this void, but I throw up the protective bubble anyway. Just like he did then.

I'm just in time, because the entire black world around me explodes in flame. I nearly lose the shield around me, it's so shocking.

I am surrounded by fire. The flames are huge, raging. Angry and *hot*.

They are everywhere.

They are licking at me, at the protective barrier, and I can feel them too well.

I feel Elizabeth lend her strength to mine. That means we can hold off this fire for a while—

But it won't last forever.

Sooner or later we'll burn our power out, and then what?

Maybe, I think in a dark sort of way that reminds me of the Ellowyn I used to be—and in that moment, also tells me how much I've changed since I accepted the Revelare in me—that's the whole point of this. Whatever this is.

Don't panic—but this time it isn't Elizabeth telling me that, it's *me* telling me that.

Because I'm not that girl I used to be, with a human-sized chip on my shoulder, convinced I was a target and the butt of every joke. I'm not the teenager who decided I might as well dress the part of the town's black cloud, and act like it too, since truth might be a curse, but it can also be a weapon.

She's part of me, that girl I was, but I am so much more than she could imagine I'd become.

I swallow and try to think, though the roar and hiss of the flames makes that difficult. I know that I was able to hear Zander when I cleared off the necklace, so I look down at it again. I hold my breath as I wipe away the black ooze, waiting for the pain to hit me, but it doesn't burn.

Instead, it turns into a crackly kind of ash and falls away.

Just like that, I know. The Joywood's black magic is working to make this fire. To make it rage and potentially consume me.

They can't do both. They can't keep the fire going like this *and* maintain the dark, grimy block on my protection at the same time.

They don't *want* to. They want to make the fire last longer than I can last, trapped here, protecting myself.

I have to force myself to breathe. Not to hyperventilate.

I can't panic.

I have to *fight*.

Because I won't let them take this away from me. This new life I've found in the last year—in these last few months. My baby girl. The love of my life. My coven's very good chance at kicking the Joywood's ass in the ascension, through the voice of the people they claim to protect but have only controlled.

I won't let anyone take this away.

I heard Zander before, so I try to reach out. *Zander. Baby, where are you?*

I know he can't hear me, because that man would tear down heaven and earth to hear me call him an endearment of any kind. I have to accept that our connection is blocked.

No doubt by more dark magic. The necklace was only the beginning of the ways they've cut me off from my coven.

I understand that this is supposed to wreck me and leave me sobbing in a ball on the metaphoric floor as the fire sweeps in and gets rid of me once and for all. They couldn't harm my physical body, but they can get my soul out here.

Only if I let them.

I have more weapons than the Joywood ever gave me credit for, then and now. *Elizabeth, I can't reach Zander, but they don't know about you. You can reach Zachariah. Tell him we're in the fire. They'll find us then.*

I won't be able to help you with the protection.

I look around me, at the way the bubble has shrunk down. The way I can already feel my strength start to flag, but if we don't do *anything*, I'm literal toast anyway.

Reach out to him. Connect to him. Lead them to us, Elizabeth.

I can feel her inside me. Her fear, her worry, and her determination. Then a kind of sigh. *All right, Ellowyn.*

Because she knows, as I do, that this is our only shot.

I try not to shake at the enormity of that.

All it means is that failure is not an option.

Be strong, child, Elizabeth whispers to me, and then she slowly begins to ease her magic away from the protective bubble. I don't hear her call out to Zachariah. Maybe I'm too focused on keeping the fire back, but it doesn't matter. I have to trust her too.

I tell myself she'll only be a moment, but the moment seems to stretch out into an eternity.

My muscles are shaking from exertion. Sweat trickles down my temples, my back. I'm not sure how much of this I can sustain.

But I have to, I think with a resoluteness that feels more like me than anything else ever has, though I've never encountered it before. *So I will.*

And I do.

Moment after moment after one more terrible moment, I do.

Then I see something. Something out there in all those writhing flames. At first, I think that it's just a mirage. Me making up what I want to see most—a little spot in all that fire that means someone is reaching through.

That someone is coming to help me.

I can't let myself believe it.

I hold on. I shake and sweat and cry, but I hold on—

Then I see a finger. I feel the wetness on my cheeks. I want to scream with relief, fall apart and sob, but I have to hold the protective shield around me. Around *us*.

Slowly, interminably slowly, so many moments I barely survive, the finger becomes two, and then half a hand.

After a few more forevers, I feel Elizabeth pour her magic back into our bubble, but her voice in my head isn't relief or celebration. It's all warning.

You have to wait, Ellowyn. Wait until you see his forearm. When you do, you'll need to grab his hand and drop the protection all at the same time. If you don't do it at exactly *the right time, we're all lost.*

Maybe that would have felt like an unbearable amount of pressure—if I wasn't already under too much pressure to handle. Yet I am handling it, because there's no other choice. Maybe, too, because her magic is helping.

I nod.

I watch the hand press forward through the fire, knowing without having to be told that it's Zander. I would recognize one of his hands anywhere, and besides, I know nothing will keep him from me.

Not even a wall of flame.

No matter how much it hurts, and…you don't just *stick a hand* through a fire. Even as a witch with protections, it must be agonizing. He's reaching toward me, but his skin is darkening.

He's burning right in front of me, and *this* is the thing I can't stand.

I might let the fire burn me, but not *him*—

I nearly reach for him right then, but Elizabeth's voice holds me back.

You can't, she warns me. *Not yet.*

I can't stand this. *He's hurting.*

Sometimes love means letting those we love hurt a little, she replies, and there's a kind of sorrow in her voice I don't want to recognize, that speaks of old wounds I don't want to look for in myself, *to save them from suffering far worse.*

Nothing in my life has ever been this hard, and I pray to all the gods and deities, seen and unseen, that I'll never have to endure this again.

Watching Zander hurt himself. For me.

When what we were always best at was hurting each other so much it almost felt good, in the end.

I don't want that either, but I want this less.

I don't dare blink, silently urging the rest of his arm to push in just a little more. To give me something to hold on to. I won't let him suffer a second longer than he has to.

The moments I have to wait for this, watching burns deepen on his skin, are eternities. Each and every one of them, but then at last I see he's almost there, carving his way through the flame *just enough*—

I take a deep breath and hold it. I make myself wait longer than I want to, so he pushes his way in just that much more through that wall of terrible fire. I let it out in a rush.

At the same time, I wrap my hands around his wrist and let the protection go.

Then, finally, everything speeds up.

He yanks me through the fire, his strength unwavering even though, when he catches me on the other side, I can feel him shaking.

Suffering.

The fact we're falling through space when we shouldn't be feels beside the point next to that.

I'm so weak now. I have so little power sparking in me, but I can feel Zander as well as I can feel me, and I know he has *none* left.

I try to slow our fall. At least attempt to ease into some kind of landing, but I can't quite see below us. I don't know where we are, I don't know where we're falling *from* or *to*, and it's taking all of my strength just to wrap myself around him and hold on tight.

Everything is burned, fading, barely bleeding. All of this hurts. "I swear to Hecate, if I lose you, I will find a way to kill you all over again," I promise him, my mouth against his shoulder.

He hears me. I feel him move a little and a small sound escaping his mouth.

I want to believe it's a laugh.

The other things it could be, like a death rattle, are unacceptable.

Without warning, we're suddenly crashing into a high tree branch. I grunt, then try to brace us for more impact—

Instead we're jerked sideways.

Leave the tree landings to me. Ruth. An echoing eagle's screech from Storm.

Then, finally, I hear the chanting of our coven as they slowly lower us to the ground. My soul body and physical body merge as I land as if the earth is a cushion, thanks to everyone who loves us. It takes me a deep, half-panicked beat to realize that we're back at the cemetery.

Whole. Breathing.

But barely.

There's an immediate commotion as we land. People surround us, pulling Zander and me apart and blocking us from each other. That's okay, because I feel Healer hands on me and I assume they're taking care of Zander too.

My eyes fall shut, and I can't seem to open them. Even though all I see is Zander, fighting his way through that fire despite the cost to him, his skin, his poor hand—

Still, I'm whole again. I'm me. And there were other things that happened tonight, or should have.

"Did it work?" I ask Jacob, but when I open my eyes, he's not there. It's Maureen sitting next to me, working on the burns I didn't let myself feel while they were happening, as long as they didn't get the baby.

I don't need her to tell me the baby's fine. I know she is.

Maureen smiles at me, and I see my mother beside her. "We got exactly what we needed to make the cure and protection. Rest now."

There's something in her eyes though, and the fact that it's her and my mother next to me and not Jacob. Not my coven.

Not Zander.

"Ellowyn," my mother says, but I ignore her, twisting around and looking for him. I see Jacob hip to hip with his sister, kneeling over a form on the ground, broken—

No.

I stumble over on a half crawl. Over my mother's objections.

"I'm okay," Zander rasps when I get to him. His eyes are closed, but he must feel me, or he heard my gasp, felt my horror. I don't know.

What he's not is *okay*. Not even a little.

Still, he spoke. Even though he's burned all over. So much worse than what I saw on his hand, or the small pink marks that show where the fire licked at me.

It's only then that I see the flickering form of Zachariah next to him. The ghost doesn't look burned, but something isn't right. He's him and not him. Almost as if the light is going out of him.

I get it then. "You saved us."

I didn't think ghosts could get *hurt*—they're already dead and all—but his energy is fading. Even though Zander is in a bad way, it's clear Zachariah used just about everything he had to keep it from being a whole lot worse.

Elizabeth emerges from me then, still buzzing the way she did while she was protecting me and my baby. Her light is dimmer too, but not like Zachariah. Not still like him and almost gone.

She makes a pained sound and falls to her knees next to him. She doesn't say anything at first, just stares at him. "If he disappears here..." she whispers, then coughs, like she inhaled smoke even though she doesn't breathe. Not really.

That's magic for you. An asshole to the grave and beyond.

Elizabeth coughs again, clearly in shock. She doesn't finish her thought. She doesn't move from Zachariah's side. She murmurs something, pressing her hand to his head—or trying, because even her ghostly hand goes through him.

I know what's happening. I see it clearly, as if I've seen it many times before. His soul will be lost if he doesn't get some of his energy back.

Even in death, no one is fully safe. He needs to recharge, or he'll go dark for good. There will be no raising him again, no talking to him in visions, nothing. It reminds me of Zelda, working so hard to find enough energy to be herself on this side of the afterlife.

He needs to go to *his* side. Now.

"You have to get him back," I say to Elizabeth.

She looks from Zachariah's nearly disappeared form, sparkling tears falling down her face, but she doesn't argue. "You still need me," she whispers back.

Except that's not true, not the way she means it. I will always need her, the way I need Zelda, the way Rebekah and Emerson need their grandmother. But life isn't about getting everything you need when you need it.

It's about love.

Sometimes love is losing the people you need the most, and then honoring them by living on without them. Because love never really goes anywhere. It's inside us. It's the sunrise on a still morning. It's the stars in the sky. It's the scent of lavender on the breeze when no lavender is growing. It's the way a bright blue bird appears on a windowsill in a cold winter, reminding you.

Love is everywhere, but inside us most of all. "You've given me everything, Elizabeth," I tell her fiercely. "*Everything.* Take him back. Before you lose him. Before *we* lose him. Take him back and make him well, and when you're right again, you'll *both* come back. You'll meet our daughter."

Her tears flow, and her voice trembles when she speaks. "I fear we're stuck here. Or surely we would have faded long since."

I won't allow this. Not for these ghosts who have helped us, loved us, and sacrificed for us.

Not for family.

Because that's who Elizabeth and Zachariah are to me. To us. To Zander and our baby and our whole coven too.

I look down at myself. I have these protections all over my body, and this power that I can draw on no matter the state of my own tonight. And I have more than that.

I reach into the past, to the Goods who were Revelares before Elizabeth, stretching through generations of witches who led to Elizabeth.

My head tips back, and thanks to the centuries that worked to make me, I find the words.

"Spirits below, energy around. Time and space, work as one. Protect as they have protected. Save as they have saved. Souls beyond the thinning veil, bring your brother and sister home."

Something bright and hot glows around them, holding them. Elizabeth reaches out and clasps the faded hand of the man she loved and lost once already. She's openly sobbing now.

So am I. I can hear the chanting of spirits, voices I recognize and voices I don't.

"Goodbye, my children," Elizabeth says through her tears. "Be well."

A crow caws somewhere in the distance, and then they're gone in another bright flash. Almost in the same way they came.

I sit there in the aftermath of that, feeling hollowed out.

It's not forever, I try to tell myself, so maybe I can stop weeping like I've just endured a funeral. They'll regain their strength. They'll visit. They'll send us signs from beyond. Happy signs.

Birds on sills. Rainbows. A butterfly landing on my arm. Clocks that read things like 11:11 or 4:44 every time you look at them.

I have to believe that.

"I'm sorry," Zander rasps out into the dark of the cemetery.

"You don't need to apologize for a thing," I reply, a tear dripping down my chin and splashing onto his face. I wipe it away. "You walked through fire, Zander. They'll be back. No one we love is ever fully gone. *Never.*"

He won't be gone either, because they saved him. I hold on to his undamaged hand while the Healers work on him. Burns turning to blisters. So much energy. So much pain.

Pain is the price, I told Emerson once.

It's a price worth paying if I get him. If I get us. All of this life, all of this love. This is worth paying for.

There's more cost to come though, because that great toll rings out across the witching world once again.

"Joywood. Riverwood." She seems louder tonight. Deeper, somehow, as if she's made her way into my bones. "Come before the Undine for your final trial."

We all look around at each other, in the shadow of the redbud trees and the gravestones of our ancestors. Everyone looks as exhausted as I feel. Hurt and injured. So much energy used for the ritual, for finding me, saving us.

Of course she calls us in now.

I'm surprised she didn't call while I was stuck in a fire. If she had, maybe that pull would have saved me so I didn't have to lose my ghosts.

I won't let myself believe they're lost. I sent them back. They'll recover. They'll be back, and maybe it won't ever be like it's been. Maybe it shouldn't be, because Zander and I have to be just us, surely. We have the baby on the way.

Five is definitely a crowd. Like back in that linen closet, a thousand lifetimes and not that many weeks ago.

But Elizabeth and Zachariah changed the course of my life. *Our lives.*

I won't forget that. Ever.

"We'll handle finishing and distributing the cure," Maureen says. She puts her hand on Jacob and gives him a squeeze that has a little of the color seeping back into his complexion. "We'll be there soon. Be well, Riverwood coven. Be strong."

I help Zander to his feet. Emerson doesn't help Jacob rise so much as hug him, hard, when he does. Frost and Rebekah stand with Georgie, and we are us again. The Riverwood, and this might be our last stand, but we'll do it together.

So we let the Undine tug us across the river to face the evil bastards who tried to kill us once tonight already.

27

THE JOYWOOD, NATURALLY, LOOK RESPLEN-
dent.

Again, like they knew. Certainly not like they've been engaging in trying to kill me by fire. Though Happy Ambrose
Ford, their crusty Historian, seems to be missing. I wonder if
he was the one wielding Skip, the dark blood magic demon
weasel, to attempt to kill me.

And I have no doubt it was the Skipweasel whose dark, ugly
magic was all over me before the fire took hold. At least I can
remember him—for the moment.

Rebekah tries to glamour us up a bit, but the ritual took a lot
out of her too, so really, what we have going for us is that our
clothes are now clean and Zander doesn't look quite like he's been
recently burnt to a crisp. Only a little singed around the edges.

I can tell he's still hurting, and yet I have to put that away
and focus on this trial. Meanwhile I hurt too, and miss Elizabeth and Zachariah like phantom limbs.

They are back on the other side where they belong, I remind myself. Fiercely.

Because this last trial, only an hour before the clock turns over to Samhain, is ours and ours alone.

It has to be.

We can handle it. We've come this far already. No number of assassination attempts from the Joywood has taken us out yet. I chant this to myself again and again as the local crowd takes their seats on the grass in the dark.

The Joywood don't *look* surprised to see me, whole and here, but I hope that faint twitch in Carol's right eye has something to do with the fact that I just won't go away.

Ever, I think, staring right at her.

The Undine's eyes shine brighter than ever as she stands before us, but before she begins to the lay out the trial the way she has in the past, Carol strides forward.

"Before we can engage in the trial, we must address a horrible tragedy that has occurred at the hands of the Riverwood." She really says that. With her whole chest and her mouth set in that *brave* way she uses when she's being the most evil.

We all stare at each other, because…*what*? We just fought them off. There was fire and oily black magic and *they're* accusing *us* of something?

Emerson looks as if she wants to argue, but even she can't seem to find the words.

The Undine's eyes glow more fiercely.

Carol clearly takes that as encouragement. She sucks in a breath and faces the crowd, her chin trembling, her eyes wet, and her Medusa frizz more disheveled than usual.

Something cold and foreboding slithers down the length of my spine.

"As we prepared for the Undine's call, taking what comfort we could in the notion that soon this display of overconfidence and youthful arrogance would soon be over, we could not get ahold of…"

Carol trails off, makes a *snuffling* sound as if the pain is *too great*, then dabs at her eyes.

"Happy Ambrose has been murdered!" Maeve shrieks out, as if she can't contain herself a moment more.

Murdered. The word echoes through the night, a symphony of confusion in all of us and the crowd alike.

"Perhaps he has finally seen the error of his ways and has taken himself off—" Frost begins, seeming the least upset at the very notion of *murder.*

Before he can finish the sentence, a body thumps down on the dais between the Joywood and us. It's clearly good old Happy Ambrose—or, I correct myself, because I don't trust the Joywood on any level, some approximation of him.

The crowd is less skeptical. Some of the gathered witches in the crowd scream and jump back. The muttering is practically a shout.

The Undine says nothing.

"This is…shocking," Emerson says, peering down at Happy. "And terribly sad." The *if it's true* rings through all of us. Emerson takes a deep breath. "You can't honestly blame us for this, Carol. For a wide variety of reasons, but the bottom line is that the ascension rules *should* prevent us from hurting each other."

She says this pointedly, since obviously the Joywood managed to hurt us just fine tonight. I have to restrain myself from holding up Zander's burned hand and forearm as proof. Meanwhile, I'm trying to work out what their game is here. Did they fake the death of one of their own to cover up what they did to us? Or worse…

Could they have actually done it? Just so they could blame us?

"We're not accusing *you*," Carol returns with a sniff and another dab at her eyes. "We caught the perpetrator in the act. It wasn't a witch, but then, you know that, don't you? It was a human under your control, clearly, because *this* is what happens when bloodlines are polluted."

Everything in me goes cold. I'm the one "polluted," and—
That's when my sister appears.

Poor little Sadie, thunked down on this raised dais, much too close to what's left of Happy Ambrose. They've tied her hands behind her back and her feet together, and while there's nothing covering her mouth, I can tell she's been hexed mute.

I want to kill them all. Every last standing member of the Joywood, all of them smirking at us now, when not pretending to be *deeply disturbed* for the crowd. I want to call down the gods and rain fire all over them—

But I don't.

Only partially because I'm sure they'd love that.

Another part has everything to do with the way Zander laces his fingers with mine. Not to hold me back, but a simple, non-verbal, *I'm here for whatever we do next.*

If I had time to sink into that, I think it would make me break.

Instead, all I can focus on is my sister. "Sadie."

She's clearly been crying. Her eyes meet mine in terror and confusion.

"What the hell is wrong with you?" I demand of the Joywood—our audience and the Undine be damned. I try to reach out for Sadie and pull her to me magically, but they've put some kind of shield around her. "She's a *child*. She's a human child who has no idea she's related to a witch. She shouldn't be here."

I bang at the shield a little with bursts of my magic, though I know it's no use. Panic will only make things worse. I remember Elizabeth urging me to be calm earlier, but haven't I used all the calm in my arsenal at this point?

"She is a murderer," Carol says flatly.

I can see the gleam of triumph in her eyes.

"This is beyond ridiculous," I say, and reminding myself to be calm has also let me remember to broadcast my voice. The voice that wouldn't work if I was a liar like Carol. "Sadie *couldn't* kill a witch if she tried. We all know this. Failing to take me out tonight during our ritual must have messed with your heads. No one out there is going to believe a thirteen-year-old human killed one of the Joywood."

"You supplied her with the tools! You!" Maeve shouts, and I'll give her one thing. She sure *seems* panicked. I just can't believe it's because of Happy Ambrose's decidedly unhappy fate. "You were parading her around Emerson's bookstore a few weeks ago. We know you all gave her the tools!"

Her sickly pigeon coos in agreement.

"We did not," I say, and I make it ring out a little. Then I look at the crowd. "If I'm saying it, it must be the truth."

Maybe I should have expected them to be ready for that by now.

Carol scoffs. "A tired old excuse, when we all know that curse was lifted during that little ritual you all went off and did this evening." She looks at us, her hair getting bigger, her mouth even curving enough that the spectators can see it. So obviously satisfied with herself that she can't be bothered to hide it any longer under her fake grief. "That's why there were so many of you running around, isn't it? Trying to hide your dirty deeds across the river?"

That isn't what we were doing at all, which is when I realize that they don't know.

They don't know what ritual we did, I tell everyone else.

Good, Jacob says, sounding as darkly furious as I've ever heard him.

They know we did a ritual. They know I was at the center of it, but they can't figure out what it was for.

Jacob is already there. *They must not know that we've found a way to circumvent their poison.*

I'd like to force-feed it to them and see how they like it, Zander chimes in, sounding almost conversational. Meaning he's lit up with fury and loss.

I'm pretty sure the rest of my coven jumps in then too, but all I can see is Sadie. Staring back at me, horror and anguish all over that face of hers that ought to be stuck in a book.

They even broke her glasses. For some reason, that's the thing that feels like the straw snapping the spine of any camel who cares to look at her. She's a clueless human *kid*, and they terrorized her *and* broke her *glasses*? Who cares that she doesn't need them to see. It's the *principle*.

For some reason, this moment is when the Undine decides to wade in. "Joywood, you accuse the Riverwood of inciting a human to murder your Historian?"

"Yes," they echo emphatically, so the word seems to bounce off the river and roll back over us all.

"Riverwood," the Undine continues, "you deny this accusation?"

"Yes," we all say, and we do it too, that long, loud, confident roll of our voices, our authority, our innocence. It seems to fill up the night.

"Very well." The Undine looks almost pleased, I think, if an animated stone can look like anything. "Joywood. Riverwood. Debate your positions on this matter before your community, making clear the depth and breadth of your beliefs. You have until the clock turns over to Samhain, and then the final casting of choices will begin. Whoever the people choose to ascend to position of ruling coven will make the final decision on the human's culpability in the murder of the Historian, and any repercussions thereof."

The worst must be true if the Undine is acknowledging it. *Someone* did kill Happy.

"Joywood, as accusers and defending ruling coven, please make your case first."

Carol's face takes on that beatific look that makes me think this was somehow her plan all along. Like she's been in cahoots with the Undine this whole time, or maybe she knew that she could use the statue's neutrality to wield a sword against us.

What I know is, after everything that's happened since they attacked Emerson after our Litha ceremony senior year, and especially since they unleashed adlets on her this past spring, we can't put anything past them.

They are rotten straight through.

That doesn't mean the rest of St. Cyprian will see that. Evil so often hides in plain sight, under endless speeches and bureaucratic red tape most people don't have the energy to wade through. Especially in small towns like ours.

Thank the universes for Emerson Wilde and her tireless dedication to just that. Or we'd all be lost under this tide of evil, and never really know it.

Carol steps forward, and the moon chooses that moment to appear, bathing her in light. I suspect a little stagecraft, but that's not against the rules. It's annoying, that's all.

She sounds quiet when she speaks, but it's an authoritative quiet that seems to hum in my bones. More theatrics. She's good at it.

"Citizens of the witching world, we have found one of our own murdered in cold blood," she says, and she sounds as if she's both deeply saddened by this as well as *determined* to *do what's right* and address it like this. "All because of the desperate thirst for power these young upstarts can't seem to hide. They couldn't win these trials, they knew this, and so they had to strike out in some other way."

She stops as if overcome. I watch—we all watch—as Felicia bustles forth to stand beside her, as if Carol needs the support.

Carol gives her a brave smile. Then she addresses the crowd once more. "Humans have been used as tools against us for eternity, and the Riverwood have a half human among them who knew exactly how to wield this human child to hurt us. What a sickening, despicable act."

She waits for the muttering that comes from the crowd, then seems to grow taller as she stands there. Bolstered by the people. By her own *determination to do what's right*.

It's scary how good she is at this. "We will not be cowed. We will not be intimidated into stepping away from our great duty. Which is, as it has always been, to keep witches all across the world *safe*."

We can't speak. We can't argue. I know, because I try. Just as I keep trying everything in my power to get through that shield around Sadie.

My little sister, who's crying again, looking at me with wide, wild eyes that scream *save me*.

I look out at the crowd. Surely other people have to find this horrible. Tying up a child. Parading her in front of a crowd of witches, all more powerful than she is, weak and human and helpless.

I see mouths moving out there on the grass. Bernie the cheese guy looks redder in the face that he usually does. Baker and coffee shop owner Holly Bishop, in particular, has her hands cupped around her mouth like she's trying to project her voice, but no sound comes out.

It takes me a moment to understand.

There's a murmur in the crowd, so there are clearly some people who can speak, but as I scan who's silently moving their mouths and who's able to talk, I realize that the Joywood have muted anyone who supports us. The dread inside of me curls tighter.

I look back toward Emerson. Her mouth is firm, and her eyes are on Holly too.

"This human," Carol continues, pointing at Sadie, "was caught red-handed. Enacting her half sister's evil plan. We cannot let such a heinous crime go unpunished."

"Carol, she's a child."

This statement, shockingly, comes from Susan Martingale,

who's always been a staunch Joywood supporter. Presumably that's why she wasn't muted.

Carol's expression goes pinched. "I wasn't suggesting we take this out on her."

Though it was obvious she was doing exactly that.

Carol flicks a hand. Now even her supporters have been muted. No dissent. No questions.

"She didn't do it on her own, of course," Carol says as if there's been no interruption. "She did it at Ellowyn Good's behest. She will remain a danger to witchkind as long as her half-witch sister walks the earth. Because Ellowyn has always been an enemy of witchdom and a threat. We must punish them both accordingly."

"The death penalty for Ellowyn Good!" someone shouts from the crowd.

Except we're all muted. It's the Joywood projecting a voice to make it sound like it's from the crowd.

Parlor games, Frost says derisively in our heads. *The province of the desperate.*

As long as they don't work, Georgie retorts.

Death penalty, my ass, I say instead.

Are you even a member of this coven if the Joywood haven't tried to kill you? Rebekah asks dryly.

I look out at the crowd and notice that even some of the Joywood faithful seem uncertain about the turn this has taken. It occurs to me to put my hands on my bump and really emphasize it, in case *that's* the source of the discomfort for some of them. Because it should be.

They're all about taking me out, but this life I'm growing inside of me is innocent, and I'm not above playing that up. I meet the gaze of anyone who looks at me. I challenge them to *really* think about what the Joywood are trying to accomplish here.

The Undine perks up again then. "Joywood, you have outlined your accusations. Riverwood, how do you respond?"

Before Emerson can say anything, I step forward. "Let Sadie

go. You can tie me up in her place while we argue this out, but let her go."

"Ellowyn." My entire coven mutters my name, clearly not thrilled with my choice, but I can't let Sadie suffer through this a moment longer—even if this is exactly what the Joywood want, me making a spectacle of myself over a human.

Baby, this is that martyrdom I was talking about.

No. At first the denial is knee-jerk, but it settles within me. Just another truth. *Sometimes you have to let people make sacrifices for you,* I tell him pointedly, because why else is his arm all charred up? *And sometimes you have to be the one making the sacrifices.*

I can see he doesn't *like* that, but he doesn't argue with me. He is holding on to Emerson and Rebekah like he's preventing them from moving forward to physically stop me.

"Do you hear me?" I demand, ignoring my coven. I feel bad about it, but I can't think beyond getting Sadie out of here. Nothing else matters. "Switch us out. Mute me. I don't care. I won't let you hurt my sister."

"Such dedication to a *human*," Maeve murmurs slyly.

Making sure that said sly murmur echoes in all of our heads.

"My sister, you monster." I look out at the crowd. "Just remember, they're all monsters. I can call them that without a problem."

That sends a kind of electricity through the audience.

Carol rolls her eyes and sighs deeply. "Honestly, Ellowyn, it's painful that you're so determined to continue with that self-serving fiction of yours."

They're trying to take away your ability to tell the truth, Emerson says.

I know. But it doesn't matter. They're already undermining it, and likely have convinced some of the audience we were off lifting a curse I've suffered under the weight of since I was fourteen—like it'd be that easy.

As long as it gets Sadie out of here, I don't care what they say about me. What truths they take away. Besides, if I'm muted—what does it matter if I can tell the truth or not?

I look at Zander. His eyes glow silver, and *pain* radiates off him, easy to see for anyone who knows how and where to look. He doesn't tell me not to do what I'm doing. He doesn't shake his head.

He's with me, whatever I choose.

"If you insist," Carol continues merrily, because this is what she wanted. Me in the proverbial stocks. I feel their terrible magic slither over me, and just like that, Sadie is gone—*gone* and I don't know where—and I'm in her place.

My ankles and wrists are bound, and I can feel the muting hex, deep and tight within me, constricting even the thought of words. Sadie is gone, and I can't have that. I look out at the crowd until I find my mother, who looks predictably furious. I know she would storm the stage for me. I know she would run straight at Carol without a second thought.

But that's not what I need.

I can't speak to her, not even in our heads with the hex in place.

Yet Tanith nods at me. She knows. She disappears, off to make sure Sadie's okay, home and safe.

Because Sadie means something to me, and I mean everything to Tanith.

I collect all these things, trussed up and rendered silent on this stage. These lessons.

My mother's love for me, even though dealing with my father's other family is the last thing she wants to do, ever. The way Ruth flies after my mother, an added protection to my family. The way Zachariah saved Zander, at great cost to himself, likely not knowing that we *could* send him back to recover. Elizabeth protecting my baby, tucked up around her inside of me.

Zelda's necklace, Zack's quiet presence.

Friendship and love, sacrifice and hope.

The Joywood have none of these things.

They have only their intimidation and hexes and black blood magic. There's no love—Carol herself used her son as some sort of minion, and was happy enough to make us all forget him when she thought he was dead. They are selfish and self-absorbed, cruel and demeaning to all, no matter how they wrap it up and pretend otherwise. They have always been power-hungry, though tonight I think they seem desperate too.

I look out at the crowd. Some eyes are hot with anger and blame. Some people hate me, clearly. As they always have, but some other people's expressions are full of concern. Of worry. I see my coven's familiars, eyes glowing out beyond the crowd, waiting to help. To give what they can.

I have to take comfort in the fact that it's Emerson's turn now. I don't let myself doubt. As I told Maeve not all that long ago, underestimating Emerson Wilde never ends well for anyone.

"The Joywood have taken away one of our voices. It's what they do best, isn't it?" Emerson is vibrant with rage, and does not hide it well, but maybe that's a good thing. We're not cal-cified into our cruelty, like they are. We care. For better or worse, we still *care*. "They've taken away most of your voices too. I have to ask myself, what are they so afraid of that they don't want to let us speak?"

Almost immediately, a murmur goes through the crowd. Like Carol lifted the muting—but again, just for some. Because mouths move and no sounds come out, which makes people more agitated.

Until Gus Howe, an antiques dealer, obnoxious Praeceptor, and *biggest* Joywood supporter, gets a sentence out. "She's right, Carol. This isn't a good look. Let the girl talk. She might be half human, but she's just a girl."

If I could talk, I'd tell Gus to fuck right off, but Carol's withering look his way does it for me. Because that's the thing about Carol. She's a powerful woman herself. The leader of the entire witching world—but she'll say and do whatever she has to if it keeps a certain kind of man on her side.

The men who think any and all women are *just girls*.

Before she can respond to him, Felicia whispers something. Carol seethes, visibly, her gaze cutting to mine.

I feel the mute spell let go of me.

"You're right, of course, Gus," she says through clenched teeth. Always ready to play it up for the menfolk.

I know that's not what changed her mind. She's good at redirecting too. That means it has to be whatever Felicia said to her that got me my voice back.

Felicia is a shitty Diviner, but she's still a Diviner, Rebekah says with great satisfaction to the rest of us. *She must have told Carol that none of the potential outcomes of this were good for them if they kept everyone muted.*

That doesn't fill me with great confidence for the things I might say with my newly returned voice, but I'm not who they think I am. They think I'm that weak, scared Summoner I was for years.

I'm not.

I'm a Revelare. I can also see the future. I can reach into the possibilities. I know what *can* happen.

I can see it all clearly, down one path and another.

The Joywood can win, sure. There are a lot of possibilities that they might, unfurling out in front of me.

I know what scares them are all the other possibilities.

So many more possibilities, crowding up my vision and likely Felicia's too, and all of them point to the same thing:

That we're the ones who win instead.

28

THE JOYWOOD SEEM A LITTLE OFF THEIR GAME, and I don't think it's because I want them to be and have seen that they might be, in certain futures.

I feel it. Even bound at their feet.

Maybe it's their inability to kill me the way I know they want to. Maybe it's poor Happy Ambrose's still, stiff body there before us. Maybe it's the fact that no matter how hard they try, no matter how many digs they make and little skirmishes they win, they can't understand us. They can't stop us.

We keep defying expectations.

Emerson senses this too, because she tamps down her rage. I can feel it all along our internal coven channel. She's calm now. In control. She even smiles over at Carol.

"While I appreciate you releasing Ellowyn's voice, if not the bindings on the *rest of her*," Emerson says in that cool, calm leader's voice of hers, "you're going to have to let the people who support us talk as well, Carol. All this muting keeps us from truly diving into a discussion of our beliefs, as the Undine has stated is our goal here. The ascension ritual is about explaining who *we* are, not silencing everyone who might disagree."

Carol sniffs, her eyes as narrow as her hair is big. "We have made it very clear what *our* beliefs are."

"Yes, you have," Emerson returns with that enviable calm, as if this is a tea party and she is the one pouring. "I'd like to talk to our citizens. About *their* beliefs. *Their* concerns. What they'd like to see us build." She turns to the audience gathered and everyone watching from afar. "Because the Riverwood is about *building* a community and serving that community. Not wielding fear, questionable 'protection,' and desperate accusations like a hammer."

There's a beat where it almost seems like the Joywood can't believe Emerson said that. When they should have known she would. She spent ten years saying all kinds of things, a lot like that, directly to their faces when she was the only one at the town council meetings who didn't know she was a witch—and so was everyone else.

The thing about Emerson is that she's consistent. True blue, straight down into her soul.

People always seem to find that confronting.

"This is supposed to be about your coven conspiring to kill one of our own!" Maeve shouts into the silence. She's spluttering, red-faced, her blind pigeon making low sounds like he's pissed too.

I get it. She can't understand why Emerson isn't jumping at the bait. A dead body. A young human accused. Her very own friend and her coven's Summoner—because I don't think they know my true designation—tied up and accused of masterminding it all.

We're all supposed to be so focused on this little curveball that we forget what else is at stake here.

That's not how Emerson Wilde rolls. It never has been. She

waves this away. Her eyes glow gold, and I think she looks exactly like a leader should. Not expensive and otherworldly in a theatrical cloak, not condescending and terrifying with a sickly sweet smile and Medusa hair, but like *one of us*.

Like she'll fight with *us*. For *us*.

She's not following the Joywood's plan at all.

I would *hug* her if my arms were free.

"We are supposed to be making clear the depth and breadth of our beliefs," Emerson says, and she isn't looking at or fighting with the Joywood. She's addressing the assembled witches. The people who are going to decide.

Even the Joywood can't change that.

"Our belief on this particular matter is simple. That poor, scared little girl didn't kill anyone—certainly not a powerful Joywood witch. That would be unlikely even if Ellowyn helped her, which is not only forbidden by the rules of the Undine, but impossible. There's no point debating it. Our covens' differing beliefs on what the witching world and community should look like and be…now, *that's* complicated. And it's exactly what we need to discuss in order for witchkind to make an informed decision."

Carol tries to speak, but nothing comes out. She must have been stopped by the Undine—the only being around who *could* stop her. Because the Riverwood has the floor now, so the Joywood get a little taste of their own muted medicine.

I can tell by their bulging eyes and red faces that they are not fans.

"We might have engaged in this ascension ritual for a chance to lead," Emerson continues calmly, as if she's noticed none of this. "But not to wield our power over you. That's not leadership, as we understand it. Or as we have practiced it, together and separately, in all the years we have run businesses and farms here. You already know us. You know that to us, leadership is working together to form the best community we can, one that reaches and supports as many witches as possible. Not because we want to force our beliefs *on* witchkind, but because we want to work alongside you to flourish. Safely, honorably, and hopefully. Together."

If my hands weren't tied up, I think I'd applaud. I hear a smattering of clapping out in the crowd, but Emerson doesn't stand there like she's waiting to be adored. She nods, her statement delivered, and steps back into line with the rest of our coven.

The Undine turns to the other side of the dais. "Joywood, do you have a response?"

They do. Of course they do.

Carol looks like she's sucking hard on a lemon, and I'm close enough to see the sheer fury in her gaze. "Emerson can speak of pie-in-the-sky honor all she wants, but everyone knows there is no honor in this group. They can't protect themselves, and they won't protect you. Emerson is an evil narcissist who's never spent a second caring about anyone but her precious self. Her sister is a rootless, shiftless danger to all of our lives. Frost is a criminal—no matter how much they claim he's reformed now that he's not immortal. Round it out with a half-human Summoner with murderous tendencies, a subpar Healer who let too many witches die young, a brainless Guardian who let the confluence nearly kill us all, and a Historian so clueless she doesn't even see the truth of her own past. They destroyed my son and killed our Historian. What more evidence do we need to conclude what some of us knew when they were all disappointing students? They are violent and dangerous."

"Wait. I'm confused." I look to my own coven to get around the Undine's rules on who can speak and when. "Are we violent, dangerous, and a threat? Or brainless, clueless, and subpar?"

Half a life spent getting around truth curses has left me with a few tricks up my sleeve.

The debate goes back and forth like this. The Joywood issue

accusations and go hard at each and every one of us. Emerson does not respond in kind. Instead, she builds worlds of what could be when we work together. She talks about hope and happiness, not personal failings and vague threats. Real joy, not the Joywood's sick version of it.

Eventually the crowd gets restless. Maybe even confused. At a certain point, it's all just talk, even with Happy Ambrose's body on the ground.

Even when Emerson points out that no one liked it when there was a human girl trussed up before the crowd—so why do the Joywood want their supposed friend and coven mate to just...lie there like that? Forever?

Meanwhile, the clock is ticking down to midnight, to Samhain, to the decision that will be handed down once witchkind casts their choices. I know the Joywood have certainly backed themselves into an uncomfortable corner with some people— threats against children and pregnant women, insults against anyone with human blood, snide mentions of Zelda and the confluence that everyone knows almost drowned the town, when the Joywood helped with that *not at all*. All these things have undermined the power they've wielded for so long.

I know too well there is also a contingent here that doesn't care what the Joywood do as long as it means nothing will change. For them. Just so long as the people who've promised them personal prosperity are in power, they're good.

That means, though, that there's a middle ground person we have to reach tonight. Emerson has been painting a picture of a future worth fighting for rather than a threat worth hiding from—but sometimes, people need specifics. The Joywood have made promises that we can't, but that doesn't mean we can't offer some options. When the Undine turns to us again, I speak in my coven's heads.

My turn on this one, okay?

I can feel a little surprise from them, but Emerson nods.

I can't move forward, what with still being tied up and all, so I have to send out my voice loudly. First, I drop the glamour that's kept the truth from them.

There's not just my tied-up pregnant belly to deal with, which I'm glad they've been able to see this whole time. Now I show them my eyes. Violet and sapphire.

A sign of a great power, whether they understand what it means or not—and a gasp goes through the crowd.

"The Joywood have tried to erase our pasts," I tell them matter-of-factly. "They've poisoned Summoners, killed Zelda Rivers, and tried to kill part of the high school graduating class at Litha only a few months ago. Emerson, Warrior that she is, *leader* that she is, wants to focus on the positive, on what we can accomplish, rather than childish name-calling and middle school clique bullying. She's right to do that, but I don't mind telling a few hard truths."

I let that settle in those who know I can't lie and those who believe that we did a ritual to break that curse tonight, because either way, my eyes tell a story that's far more compelling than my word against the Joywood's.

I can feel those Revelare eyes shining as I continue. "This is what I know. They've tried to erase my kind—not just Goods, not just half witches or Summoners, but the ancient witch designation that came before Summoners and Diviners were separated. When we were one, wielding both the past and future. A Revelare."

Something thunders in the distance, and I can *swear* I hear a distant crow sound. Like a sign from Elizabeth and Zachariah. That's what I choose to believe it is.

I don't let that sense of loss overwhelm me.

"I am a Revelare," I tell the crowd. The world. "One with the past and one with the future. Not bound to look forward or backward, but able to do both."

Another great murmur erupts through the crowd, but I'm

watching the Joywood. Because while they look shaken, I don't see shock.

They knew this could happen. I can see it clearly. All their talk of weak half humans my whole life, but they knew Goods were Revelares way back when.

This is why, once they decided that the Riverwood could be a threat to them, they came for me. This is why I was such a target.

Why we've all been targets. They knew what we *could* be and so they've tried to take us out, one by one, for our whole lives. Belittle us, scare us, demonize us. Memory-wipe us, exile us, target us.

We're still here.

I look back out to the crowd. It's habit to look for my mother, and this time, when I find Mina in the audience, Mom appears beside her and gives me a nod.

Your sister is safe, she tells me. *Ruth is watching over her.*

This is not the time to tear up about the fact she was the one who made sure Sadie made it home—a home and family Bill made with Stephanie when he was still married to my mother—when that had to be one of the last things Tanith wanted to deal with. This is not the time to reflect on the things my mother taught me my whole life—like it's okay to be petty to those who deserve it, it's okay to lose control—as long as you apologize and do your best to fix what you broke—and when it matters, when it's *right*, you step up. Even if you don't want to.

I nod back.

Then I spot Jacob's mother and sisters. They look pale and exhausted after doing hard work out there while we've been playing games with the Joywood. Maureen's smile is bright, and she lifts her hand as if to say *we did it*.

I know I'm not the only one who feels relief wash through me. The Summoners are safe. My blood has given them strength against the Joywood's poison.

I take a deep breath. Emerson has stated the Riverwood's

case, but I want to *show* it, and I only have five minutes till Samhain.

"Ask me anything about what a future looks like with them running it versus us running it," I invite the crowd. "Ask me anything you like, with the time we have left. I'll show you what could be."

"You can lie!" someone—one of those conveniently un-muted Joywood supporters—shouts from the crowd. "Maybe that's a glamour!"

"I can't lie," I say. I don't know how to prove it to them. Any attempt to lie and my inability to get it out could be seen as act-ing. But isn't that true with everything? Isn't that kind of the point of all of this?

The Joywood lie *constantly.* Some people believe them. Some people are too scared not to. Some, I have to assume, don't care either way.

It's up to each individual to decide what the lie is, and then decide what they can live with.

"You don't have to believe that I can't lie. You get to choose whatever reality you want." I look at Carol and Maeve, and I know it's my eyes that put fear in their expressions, because *they* know it's no glamour. Good. "*That's* what ascension is supposed to be about."

The Undine turns to look at me then, her eyes glowing al-most bright enough to beat mine. "Time runs short, and the trials must end so the ascension choice can commence. There is time for *one* question," she intones.

She does not say *choose your question carefully*, but I feel like that's implied. When I look out at the audience, no one moves. I don't know if it's because they *can't*, or they don't believe me, or it's just that no one has a decent question to ask.

"Ellowyn." It's Elspeth Wilde who steps forward. I brace myself. She's been a supporter, she showed a moment of kind-ness to Zander and our child, and still I can't fully believe she's going to *keep* doing those things after nearly thirty years of her doing and being the opposite.

"I want you to show us the confluence in the future," Elspeth says firmly. "Since it nearly flooded the town and killed us all this year, it's important to know. What will it look like under the Joywood and the Riverwood?"

I nod, but before I can sink into my magic, Zander speaks.

"You have to untie her," he orders the Joywood.

It's not a request. His voice is little more than a rasp, and I feel it like my own pain.

I shake my head. "No, they don't. The Joywood can hold me back in all the ways they've been doing most of my life. They've tried belittling me, poisoning me, you name it, but they can't seem to stick the landing. Let them keep me tied up. It doesn't change what I can do."

Or who I am. They've never been able to change that, even when I gave them the power to make me doubt myself.

Never again.

I breathe deep and tilt my head back to soak in that moonlight Carol so helpfully trotted out for us. I speak the words that come to me from deep inside, as if they've been there all along:

"Ancestors in the past. Descendants in the future. Revelare power deep inside, be with me, guide me, show them."

Then I let what comes to me, come.

An image appears, and I project it out to every witch in St. Cyprian and beyond. A knowledge that must have been buried in me, passed down generation to generation, until the Revelares rose again. Until *me*.

The first image is dark. Oily. It's the confluence, but it takes me a minute to figure that out because the river isn't high this time like it was earlier this year. It's nearly dry. Scraggly river birds poke at the bones of fish long dead. I can practically smell the decay. The confluence is a ribbon of black, no sparkles of gold.

But there *is* gold. Magic sparks up above the confluence,

where a huge castle sits on the bluff. It's the least Midwest thing I've ever seen, and it's a stark contrast to the death and desertion below.

The image moves in close, and the Joywood are clearly visible through the window—sans Happy Ambrose—eating a giant feast beneath tapestries that show all manner of witch scenes and magical creatures.

"This," Frost says coldly, though all I see is the spell, "is what immortality looks like."

I can feel the heat in my eyes, and I can hear it in my voice when I speak. "The Joywood's rule brings nothing but darkness to St. Cyprian."

I know the Joywood are shouting and arguing then, but I'm in the spell. It's like being rolled up in cotton. If I focus on the Joywood, I'll lose what's next: the Riverwood's future, which is what I want to see anyway.

So I stay in the spell, and the picture begins to fade, morph. Then it shows the same scene, but it's bright. A sunny day with the ferries running back and forth on a full river. I see Zander and Zack piloting, and a little girl on the ferry deck.

My heart nearly stops, and I find myself zooming in on her. This little girl with my eyes and Zander's dark hair. But there's more—Elizabeth's nose, Zachariah's ears.

Zelda's necklace and my mother's smile.

Our daughter.

For a moment, I'm so struck by the image that I don't know what to do. It's like I want to live right here, stuck between the moment we're in and the moment I'm witnessing, forever—

Then Zander's hand is on my back. His voice is in my head.

Breathe, baby, he says.

I can hear it in his voice. He sees her too. He knows her too, as well as I do.

I suck in that breath. I want to revel in *her*, but we have to get there first. All of us. This isn't about *me*, it's about St. Cyprian.

It's about the confluence—that's the question Elspeth asked, and it's a clever one.

St. Cyprian exists because of the three rivers that flow together here and give this place its power. The health of the confluence is the health of witchkind.

I pull back, zooming the image back as best I can so we can look down the river to the place where all three meet. I feel the sigh of the crowd, or maybe it's just in me, that low sound of deep approval. Because the confluence is gold and bright, and the magic it makes is like a song, singing into the three great rivers and out into the world.

There's nothing *special* about the scene except in contrast to the dark Joywood one. This could be any average day in St. Cyprian. Isn't that what we all want?

Not castles. Not power.

Our lives, as happy as we can make them.

I know Elspeth didn't ask, but I zoom out farther. So that the people can see a bustling Main Street. Emerson meeting with business leaders on the stage on the green. Humans and witches alike buzzing in and out of stores.

I can still feel the heat in me when I speak, but this time, I want to bask in it. "The Riverwood's rule is community. Family. Love. Light."

"She lies! Isn't it obvious she lies?" It's Maeve losing her shit over there, which kind of makes me smile.

Because it doesn't matter what Maeve thinks. It doesn't even matter what I think.

It matters that I know who we are. I know what we'll do. Even if the Joywood win this, we'll find a way to keep fighting.

No fate is set in stone.

"Look into your hearts, witchkind," I say, not even pretending to give Maeve the time of day. "What do you believe to be true?"

Somewhere far away, or maybe right here from within the Undine, something begins to chime.

Twelve times, loud and long.

It's midnight.

The trials are over. Now it's time for choices to be cast.

The Undine's eyes are so bright I can't even look her way. She seems to grow, become huge there before us.

"Samhain is upon us," she booms out, so that her voice seems to spill out of all of us. Then into us again, fusing us together and yet tearing us apart. "The ritual comes to an end. The choice is between the Joywood or the Riverwood, according to all the old laws. Make your choice. Make it now."

It is not a request. It's as if we are all gripped in her stone fists. I feel my feet leave the ground as she holds on, lifting me up, as if she intends to squeeze the answer out of me—and it's clear that she is doing the same thing to every witch in my vicinity.

Every witch in the world, then, as magic hangs heavy in the Samhain air around us. The veil is thin, and spirits begin to whisper. I listen hard, hoping for a glimpse of Elizabeth or Zachariah, but I don't hear them. I can't move, but I can feel my coven all around me. I know where everyone I love is, like points of light I can see with my heart. I can feel Zander and my child wiggle there inside me.

I saw a glimpse of my daughter born, who she could be. Dark-haired and violet-eyed. Happy in a world we helped make safe for her.

I think then that I will do anything to make sure she gets that future. Anything at all.

I don't care what happens to me.

The grip on me from the outside demands a choice. *Riverwood.* I make it, with everything I am. *This is my choice. My future.*

Once I choose, that stone grip releases me. My feet hit the dais, and Zander is already there, his arm around me, muttering the words that release my bonds at last. The ropes fall away, and I turn in to him.

Around us, the rest of our coven have chosen too, and we link our arms together. We connect. We hope. We look out at our community, and we see so many faces smiling at us, believing in us.

All around us, feet hit the earth, and it's as if I can feel an earthquake wrapping all around, witches everywhere forced to choose and then choosing in a great, fast wave—

Then the Undine—huge and bright and loud—holds out her marble arms.

"The choices have been cast. Your future has been decided." She turns away from us. Toward the Joywood. We all hold our breaths. "Joywood, kneel before me."

29

FIRST THERE'S THE TRULY GLORIOUS SPECTA-
cle of the Joywood kneeling to the Undine.

Which looks a lot like them kneeling to *us*, and I don't have
any plans to become a power-hungry witch bitch like any of
them, but I'll admit that there's a part of me that likes the view.

Even if it's only a temporary thing, before they rise up again
and smite us all down the way I know they're itching to do.

Though the look on Maeve's face is...odd, I think.

I frown, gripping Zander a little harder.

"The rule of the Joywood has ended," the Undine booms out.
"The Riverwood will ascend to ruling coven. The transition
of power has begun and will last until Yule. In the interim, the
Riverwood will have the final say in everything, starting now."

She turns to us, all blazing eyes and intimidating size. "Riverwood, you have ascended. You now lead witchdom."

I hear her, but I think I'm in shock.

Maybe we're all in shock, because none of us move. None of
us react.

"May we use our power wisely," Frost says darkly, and I suppose it's not surprising that he shakes off the shock first. After all, I'm pretty sure he's done this before.

Even Emerson seems stunned. Until she blinks, and then smiles, like she was born for this.

I stop tracking what we're doing, because the Joywood are losing their proverbial shit. A bunch of children who lost their toy and now want to break it, leaping up from their knees like they intend to *rush us*.

"This is impossible!" Carol screams, her hair looking electrocuted, her eyes bright and furious. Her veneer is gone. She's practically foaming at the mouth with rage. "I won't allow it!"

Then, without warning, Carol shoots something at us. A bolt of dark, oily magic, no Skipweasel required.

There's the sound of screaming from the audience, but we can't look to see if they're reacting to Carol or fending off their own attacks, because we have to throw up a protective shield to fend off all that nasty black magic—

Emerson is the one who leaps out in front of the rest of us, like she wants to take the hit herself—because we've *all* got a little martyr in us when it comes to the people we love.

The Undine cries out, another booming sound, and the bolt of oily black turns to stone, then explodes, showering down on the dais between us like an ugly hailstorm.

For a moment it's like we're all frozen. Staring at the black rocks, everywhere, that prove, once and for all, the Joywood are agents of evil. Black magic and power trips, no matter what they try to pretend.

If they were ever good, they turned away from it a long time ago.

I scan the crowd, relieved to see that no one looks attacked. That must mean the screaming was in shock at the Joywood's attack, or, knowing my mother, a little battle cry of her own.

"Joywood," the Undine booms, so loud we all cover our ears.

Some people in the crowd even cower. Every single Joywood member freezes. "You have disgraced yourselves."

They do not look as if that bothers them much. Maeve is glaring directly at me, and if I didn't know her sickly pigeon familiar was blind, I'd think he was too.

"The laws of old are clear in this," the Undine intones. "You must accept the choices of your fellow witches or forfeit everything you have achieved, everything you are. Should you persist, you will be judged—not by your peers, but by *me*."

I'm sure I'm not the only one who believes her. Completely.

Across from us, black stones scattered before them and all around Happy Ambrose's body, the Joywood—no longer the ruling coven—seethe. Gil Redd and Felix Sewell are muttering to each other. Festus Proctor and Felicia Ipswitch are huddled together, looking hollow-eyed.

It's Maeve and Carol who look unhinged, but they do not try to take us out again.

Not here. Not now.

Not in front of witnesses both on the green and watching from afar.

I wouldn't say Carol remembers herself, but it's as if she suddenly remembers that she has an audience. Even her staunchest supporters can't seem look her in the eye after such a childish tantrum. After such a loss.

Or maybe everyone is as stunned as we are that everything in St. Cyprian has changed.

Just like that.

This, I think, is why ascensions used to be more commonplace. So it didn't feel like the world turned upside down—and on Samhain, of all nights, when the veil is so thin we can feel the ghosts of every witch who ever was crowding in to bear witness.

"Very well," Carol says after a moment, so regally, as if we didn't all just see her basically stamp her foot like a child. A murderous, black magic-y child, that is. She turns to the audience,

and I blink, because she changes as I look at her. Everything…
smooths out. She looks taller. Almost elegant. She inclines her
head. "Witchkind, you have made the wrong decision, and I am
terribly afraid you will live to regret it." She sounds so caring.
So *concerned*—but I take this as what it is: Carol signaling that
she might be down, but never out. "When these children with
delusions of grandeur have run witchkind into the ground and
subjected us to trials far worse than Salem, letting humans run
roughshod over all of our lives, you will rue this night. And
you will cry out for a deliverance that will not come."

"That sounds a lot like a curse," I say, as the reigning expert
in curses.

But it's drowned out in the loud *bang* that sounds when the
whole of the Joywood disappear. I'm surprised an actual puff of
evil smoke doesn't follow in their wake, but it doesn't. There's
just moonlight on black stones, down on the green near the river.

The Joywood are gone.

Maybe not forever—I can't quite believe that—but *for now*
feels pretty good.

Because we *won*. We've ascended. *We're* the ruling coven.

This little band of misfits has done the unthinkable and the
impossible.

We had our families and each other and Emerson's unwavering faith to lead us here, but I know I still had my doubts.

Everyone looks as dazed as I feel as we turn to each other,
pulling together in a kind of huddle. Even Frost, usually too
prickly for such things, looks…as mortal as the rest of us are.

We don't say anything, not even Emerson. No speeches. No
fist pumps.

This is enough. *We* are enough.

Each of us maybe a little banged up but whole, here, *alive*.

Tonight, that's what matters.

"Do you really think that will be the end of it?" Georgie

asks, chewing on her bottom lip as she stares down at the black rocks still scattered everywhere.

I glance at Rebekah, because she too can reach into the future. She can weigh all the options, see down all the paths. But sometimes…it isn't worth it. Bad things happen. Threats exist everywhere, not just in this one small river town.

You can lose your way under the weight of the possibilities.

Rebekah and I look at each other, the whole of our long friendship there between us, and the futures we see winding together like a confluence all their own.

"All we can do is focus on the present," she says quietly.

"That's how we make our future," I agree.

And tonight, the rest of our coven lets that go.

Emerson takes a deep breath, and then she grins. "And in the present, we have a *ton* of work to do before Yule," she says, making us groan.

But the group huddle turns into a hug, and we're grinning when we pull away again.

Then there's St. Cyprian to deal with, and all of witchdom—and it seems like the green is three times as full of witches as the last time I looked.

Like people came from everywhere to see this momentous thing, our scrubby little coven overturning the Joywood after so long that no one can remember who came before them.

Emerson steps off the dais and immediately starts shaking hands and hugging people who've always supported us. She even hugs her mother.

Zander and I climb down together, and my mother finds me immediately, pulling me away from him and squeezing me so tight I can hardly breathe. But I don't mind.

I hug her back, hard.

When she finally releases me, I spot Zander behind Mina, being awkwardly hugged by his father, no doubt worried about the damage that's still visible on Zander's body.

I don't want to think about that near miss he's still not fully recovered from. If I never think about that terrible fire again, that weasel scream, it will be too soon.

We all field lots of positive congratulations, and even some grudging ones. It seems as if a lot of people go out of their way to say a few words to all of us before they begin to filter away, off to celebrate Samhain in the old ways.

I look back toward the Undine, feeling a little strange that she looks like nothing but a statue now. Now that I know she's watching, waiting, even when it seems that she's nothing but insensate stone. Still, I like knowing she'll be judging the Joywood.

Just like I like knowing that we'll continue to protect each other the way we have our whole lives, no matter what comes next.

By the time the first hints of dawn show up on the horizon, the crowd *just* begins to thin out. I have the sense that we should all go home and sleep—rituals and trials and unexpected wins take a lot out of a person—and yet none of us suggest it.

Because Samhain has dawned, chilly but right. We have businesses to run, parades to watch, community events to participate in.

And we are the ruling coven now.

I magic us all one of my favorite concoctions, and we sit on the edge of the dais as the sun comes up, sipping a proper witch's brew and greeting our first day in the whole new world we made, together.

In the late afternoon, I close my shop a little early and make an impromptu trip out to the Bill Wallace house to check on Sadie. Tanith assured me that she cast a little memory spell to make her think anything she *might* recall is nothing but a Halloween dream, but I want to make sure she's okay.

Zander insists on coming with me. Not because we're worried about danger this time, but because I don't think we're quite ready to be apart for very long just yet.

And I think he wants to see for himself that Sadie really is okay.

We arrive to much Halloween fanfare. Bill is, no surprise, away on a business trip, doing whatever it is he does out there. But Stephanie is so excited to see us that she nearly shackles us to chairs so we stay for dinner before we even get our coats off.

Inside, all the girls are dressed up and vibrating with excitement at the dining room table. Brynleigh is dressed like an angel, but it's kind of a slutty angel. Madyson is in the same costume she's worn the past ten years—an Albert Pujols baseball jersey—the only other detail some baseball eye black under her eyes. Sadie is wearing a little pair of antennae and a T-shirt that reads, *bookworm*. Avery is dressed up like some Disney princess I've forgotten the name of, and Gigi is a cute little scarecrow.

So cute that I think I might melt, until she looks right at me and says, deadpan, "I have a knife in my bag."

I want to laugh, but I remember that my sisters are as cursed to tell the truth as I am.

"That's terrifying," Zander mutters as Stephanie serves up big bowls of chili and slides them in front of us.

Sadie keeps staring at me from across the table. I stare back, trying not to be worried. "Everything okay?"

She frowns. "I think I must have had a funny dream about you, but I can't remember it."

"Then how do you know you had it?" Brynleigh asks like a smart-ass.

The girls start sniping at each other, good-naturedly enough, and I reassure myself that she's okay. Maybe she remembers more than I'd like her to about the ordeal she went through, no matter if it's just a feeling and a dream, but she seems okay.

Especially when she lights into her older sister.

While the two of them poke at each other, Madyson rolls her eyes and swipes up more corn bread from the platter in the middle of the table. "They always do this. It's so annoying."

I have to accept that everything is good here, and I find that harder to take than another round of bad stuff. Like I'm primed and ready to fight another wave of Joywood nonsense—but the possibility that we not only won, but everyone I love is okay?

That's almost too much.

"Love is the only lie you tell, but it will claim you in the end," Rebekah told me a long time ago, and I get it now. And I have to allow it to claim me, in all its forms, or it was nothing but a lie all along.

I can hear Elizabeth's voice, almost as if she's standing there beside me the way she used to. *Legacies are choices, Ellowyn.*

Maybe the thing about really, truly being okay is choosing to be. And the doing it.

Maybe it's that simple, and that complicated.

I decide, then and there, that it is.

"What happened to your arm?" Gigi asks, poking at Zander and the jagged pink burn scar running down the length of his forearm. A parting gift from the Joywood.

"Just a little bar accident," he lies easily.

Brynleigh's eyes widen in a mix of horror and delight. Her angel halo vibrates with her excitement at something so ghoulish, and the rest of the sisters follow suit, until we're having a frank and fairly gross conversation about scars and wounds for the rest of dinner.

Perfect for Halloween.

We finish dinner, and even though Stephanie begs us to stay and enjoy trick-or-treating, we can't. We have our coven to get back to.

But what I say to Stephanie is, "Thank you. For everything."

When she hugs me, I hug her back. Hard.

Then Zander I climb in his truck and head for St. Cyprian. Because Emerson decided we should all meet at Nix and celebrate. Even though I'm not sure how any of us are standing, no one objected.

I've been magicking everyone herbal pick-me-ups all day,

and I do it again now, so Zander and I have something to sip on for the drive.

The Missouri highways spread out before us, strings of light against the October night. Zander has his hand on my leg and the music playing loud, and it could easily be any night from back in high school. Ruth's flight ahead of us is occasionally illuminated by the headlights or the moonlight. She stayed with my sister until I had a chance to see her myself.

You're welcome, Ruth offers.

And instead of joking, I answer in our heads emphatically. *Thank you.*

Uncharacteristic vocalized gratitude aside, this has been a very normal day. After all the melodrama of last night, today has just been…like any other Samhain.

It's a relief. Another indication that choices are what create a legacy, not dramatic intervals with black magic covens and all the rest.

Life can just go on, filled with family and friends and the jobs we do, the businesses we run, the world we know.

Some things will change. Our responsibilities will grow, and there will be demands on us I'm sure I can't predict, but the best gift is that we get to keep being us.

We didn't have to transform ourselves to win.

All we had to do was tell the truth.

I look over at Zander as he drives, and I carefully rub my palm down his arm, avoiding his scar. I know it must still pain him, even with the Healing and the teas I've pushed on him today.

"How are you holding up?" I ask.

"All right. Dad forced me to take a nap while you were at the tea shop. No work allowed for the next three days again— Grandma's orders." He rolls his eyes, but I can see he's not fully himself yet.

I trace outside the jagged scar. I imagine that while it might fade, it will never fully go away. We've all been marked by what happened this year. Maybe it's a good reminder.

As for me, I don't have scars. But I have new eyes and a baby on the way.

I don't think I'll be forgetting any of this anytime soon.

Zander parks in the ferry lot and we walk along the river, letting the water lead us and whisper to us as we go. Songs and secrets. St. Cyprian's soul, rushing into the bright gold confluence in the distance.

Nix is buzzing. There are many costumes, much merriment, and humans wearing witch hats and those funny wart noses while standing next to actual witches dressed in regular street clothes. Our coven is already here, and we wind our way through the crowd to join them at the same booth we sat in when Rebekah first came home.

Except this time, instead of making a dramatic entrance, Frost is one of us.

We're the *ruling* coven, I keep having to remind myself, especially when I see the avid attention we get. The sidelong looks and whispered conversations from all the witches packed in here.

Zander signals his cousin for some drinks, and once Zeb brings them over, Emerson lifts her glass. "I'm going to give a toast."

"You're going to give a *speech*, you mean," Rebekah returns, grinning.

"I can be brief," Emerson says loftily. Then she laughs. "But why should I be? For over seven months now, we've been fighting for our lives. And for a lot longer than that, in our different ways, we've been fighting to just...be us. Think of all the ways they tried to take us down, take us out. And in the end, it wasn't a battle that won this war, it was *us*. Just *us*. It was our community believing in right and good and *light*. Hard work and building instead of belittling and *believing*—"

"Emerson," Rebekah groans, but her eyes look a little too bright.

"And a ton of other things that we represent," Emerson continues, bumping her shoulder against her sister's. "It's not about power for us. It's about doing what's right. That's what we'll keep doing. Every one of us has sacrificed something, learned something, grown up some, and now we're here. It's not the ending point. It's only the beginning."

"But let's celebrate like it's an end to threats against our lives," I offer, lifting my glass of sparkling water.

"Hear, hear," Zander says, tapping his glass to the table.

An effective cutting-off point before Emerson continues on, before she inevitably starts listing our individual positive points until we all need to run away and hide.

Instead, we spend the next few hours talking. Not about the past twenty-four hours, weirdly enough. Someday, I think, we'll want to rehash it. Minute by minute. But it's almost too *real* just now. We came too close to losing everything, time and time again.

We set it aside for now. *Until we're ready*, I think.

Before midnight, we're all drooping. And tonight, we don't have to go back to Wilde House and hunker down together. We're safe.

That takes a moment to really hit all of us. We're *safe*.

We split off into our usual pairs. Jacob and Emerson to the North farm, Rebekah and Frost to Frost House. Georgie finds Sage—and I don't let myself wonder if they'll go to Wilde House together or like…go research in a library.

I try to be happy that Georgie has made a choice she claims she wants. I brush aside the odd look I saw on her face when Emerson mentioned *sacrifices*.

Tonight, I let Zander take me to his place, because he's still healing and the Guardian in him needs that proximity to the confluence, but I pick a half-hearted argument about where we'll live, for old times' sake. His place is too run-down. My place is too small—both things magic could easily fix—but there's something about the fake argument that feels like home.

I can tell by the way he grins while he argues that he agrees.

Outside, the rickety house on stilts looks the same, but as he ushers me inside, I come to a dead stop. Everything is different. Bigger, cleaner. The furniture is new, the kitchen is huge—with plenty of room and supplies for me to brew my teas.

I turn back to him, to find him looking all smug. And hot.

"When did you do all this?" I ask, because he's barely got the energy to *fly*, let alone magic himself a brand-new home.

He skims his hand down my back. "A few days ago. You can change anything you don't like, but I figured I'd get it started." Then he drops his head to kiss me on my forehead, which is somehow sweet and hot and beautiful, all at once. "But we can do the baby's room together."

We can do the baby's room together. My poor heart. And I'm not *magically* cured of the resistance to crying in front of him just because I've done it a few times now, so I blink back the tears as he keeps talking.

"If you need to keep the apartment above the tea shop, that's fine. We can—"

But I don't. I really don't.

Not when there's this *whole home* he created for the both of us *and* the baby.

I hear Ruth hooting outside and Storm's approving call.

And I shut Zander up by pressing my mouth to his.

It feels like too much joy to bear. But then again, we've suffered to get here. There's been so much pain and sacrifice, trauma and loss. Some of it what the Joywood did to us. Some of it what we did to each other.

Some of it just the price of being alive.

Maybe, I think tentatively as he pulls me into his arms, this is actually what we deserve.

Because leading witchdom won't be easy. Having a *child* won't be easy. There will always be natural losses ahead, that's the inescapable problem with life, so maybe there's no such thing as *too much* joy. Even witches get old eventually, no dark magic required.

Maybe the best thing to do is soak in the good stuff for as long as we can.

Maybe that's the best choice I can make, a legacy with every breath I take, the swiftest path to the best and brightest future.

Tonight, I believe it.

Before he can carry me into the bedroom—something he's still not well enough to do no matter what he thinks, and I know he thinks he's invincible, despite the scar on his arm that suggests otherwise—I pull him with me. But I stop at the threshold.

"Men," I say in despair. "Such a dedication to the color *brown.*"

"What's wrong with brown?" Zander demands with a laugh as I magic some color and much-needed style into the room.

Once I'm satisfied, for now, I turn to face him. I wrap my arms around his neck, the bump that is our daughter pressed tight between us.

It's too much to think about everything it took to get here. Too much to think of all that lies ahead. So I just focus on this. Here. Now.

Him.

Us.

"I love you, El," Zander says, lowering his mouth to mine. "Always."

I sigh into that always, and then into him.

Always, I reply in his head.

I might be able to see the past, reach into the future, and see the different ways a thing might be, but I don't need any of that to know *always* is our promise to each other. Regardless of what comes, what hurts, what changes.

Our path is always clear.

Because we have each other, and we have this love, the way we always have and we always will.

Always.

30

THE DREAM STARTS SIMPLE ENOUGH.

Me in a forest. Alone. But I'm too…aware. I can feel the cold earth beneath my feet. I can smell the rich, wet dirt and the wood of fallen trees. There's the threat of snow in the air, and my skin almost hurts, exposed as it is.

Like this isn't just a dream.

I keep my breathing even and look around. In the distance, Georgie rides a dragon, red hair flowing out behind her. She has a sword.

This can't be a premonition, I tell myself. It's too much like that silly fairy-tale book that we've already given entirely too much attention.

Still, I walk over the soft ground and toward the opening in the trees where I saw her ride past.

But then whispers behind me start.

I stop.

I don't want to—I *really* don't want to—but I look behind me.

A mist has begun to form, rolling through the winter trees, obscuring everything. I see what look like statues, just visible in the mist, with glowing eyes—but if they are fully formed into one thing or another, I can't make sense of them.

I just know, in the way you do in dreams, that they want something from me.

That they're watching me.

I want to call out for Princess Georgie and her dragon, but I don't quite dare.

"Don't let your guard down until the crows are free," something whispers at me. A familiar voice, but I can't quite put my finger on its identity in the mists of the dream.

Because the mist is dark and thick—dangerous, I realize. Ominous.

I'm alone in the middle of it, cold and vulnerable, and that mist keeps coming and coming—

Lightning slams to the ground in front of me, splitting open a bare tree, and in the dream I scream.

Suddenly wide-awake, I realize I simply jolted myself out of the dream. Because that's what it was. I'm in my bed, not the woods. I'm right where I belong.

My jolt isn't enough to fully wake Zander, but he mumbles something and pulls me close, snuggling in. I'm breathing a little heavy, but I feel a rush of something like relief, because that was all just a dream.

Not some new Revelare thing, no matter how vivid it was. *Clearly*.

I wait for my heartbeat to settle. Then I curl into the warmth and strength of Zander and the future that stretches out before us.

I'm just about to fall back into sleep, my head on his chest and the dream mostly forgotten, when I hear a loud *caw*.

I open my eyes in surprise. Something makes me sit up.

And there, sitting outside the window in the earliest hours of All Souls' Day, the moon a dramatic spotlight, is a crow. Not Ruth or Storm or Frost's Coronis, but a *crow*. Which wouldn't be alarming or remind me of the dream, even with the view of the winding river and confluence beyond it.

Except its eyes are violet.

And it's staring straight at me.

Like it knows exactly who I am.

★ ★ ★ ★ ★